Never Had I Been Appraised in Such a Clearly Male Fashion

In self-defense, I feigned a cool air and returned a long look of my own.

His shoulders, unnecessarily broad, exuded a physical power that made my heart flutter, and those sprawling legs, clad in fitted breeches, emphasized his blatant masculinity.

The effect of his gaze was more than disquieting. To my dismay, I felt incapable of making the slightest movement, like some frightened animal caught in the sights of a gun, waiting for the death that must surely follow.

And yet there was something exquisite in the fear, as though we had become one—hunter and hunted, stalker and prey—and every particle of me yearned for the denouement.

MASTER OF BLACKWOOD

Penelope Thomas

HarperPaperbacks
A Division of HarperCollins*Publishers*

HarperPaperbacks *A Division of* HarperCollins*Publishers*
10 East 53rd Street, New York, N.Y. 10022

Copyright © 1991 by P. J. Thomas
All rights reserved. No part of this book may be used or reproduced in any manner whatsoever without written permission of the publisher, except in the case of brief quotations embodied in critical articles and reviews. For information address HarperCollins*Publishers,*
10 East 53rd Street, New York, N.Y. 10022.

Cover illustration by Aleta Jenks

First printing: October 1991

Printed in the United States of America

HarperPaperbacks and colophon are trademarks of HarperCollins*Publishers*

10 9 8 7 6 5 4 3 2 1

Chapter One

Lord Blackwood was not a handsome man. A good two inches more than six foot, he was unfashionably tall and broad shouldered—excessively so, my aunt would have said—although he had a trim waist and long, muscular legs. But I could not imagine him sitting in the polite drawing rooms of his peers, his large frame supported by their fragile gilt chairs, those long legs cramped beneath him. Even among the more countrified Cornish gentry he would have been decidedly out of place; I cannot imagine what they must have made of him in London.

My own impressions of his uncivilized nature may have been provoked by the rude awakening I suffered due to his unheralded appearance. The clatter of his horse's hooves against the flagging in my uncle's stables had jarred me from the drowsy reverie into which I had been lulled by the late summer heat, the sweet scent of fresh hay, and the soft murmur of the pigeons in the dovecote. Deserting the shaft of sunlight which fell through the open loft doors, I peered over the bales of hay to see who had ridden into Briarslea.

The face that I beheld was unremittingly dark. Unruly black hair fell in tangled curls about his face, stopping short above the emphatic line of his heavy brows. His jaw was shadowed by a dark stubble that appeared to have but recently and successfully waged a war with his razor; and a nasty scar outlined the cheekbone on the right side of his face, running from the outer edge of his eye, then twisting sharply downwards, and finishing a hair's-breadth short of the corner of his mouth. His lips were drawn in a tight, sardonic line, and he held his square shoulders stiffly, as though braced for unpleasantness, thereby making his demeanor as dark as his coloring. In all, his manner made him seem a good deal older than his eight and twenty years.

His eyes held the only touch of brightness in his face, being a clear green and all the more startlingly vivid for their grim setting. They reminded me of a dagger my father had bought in a marketplace in Calcutta and placed among his collection. It had an ebony handle set with emeralds, and while it was by no means the most expensive he had owned, it had always been my favorite. I had often cajoled him into bringing it out of the locked cabinet so that I might wrap my small hand around that smooth, cold surface and admire the light that flashed from the stones. Light that burned like a cold green fire—the same green fire that now blazed from the eyes of Lord Blackwood.

He stood with his legs apart, one hand gripping his horse's reins as he glared into the depths of the stables, doubtlessly searching for our groom; his crop smacked impatiently against his leg as though marking the time he wasted while he remained there.

Had he chanced to look up, he could not have avoided seeing me—my gaze fixed upon his face in childish fascination. But perhaps it did not occur to him that anyone would have the audacity to lie in silence and study him rather than rush to attend to his needs.

At thirteen, it amused me to speculate about my elders, especially when those speculations could be performed in secrecy, saving me from the indignity of having to suffer their scrutiny in return. On those occasions, I was invariably found lacking in beauty, grace, and good manners, observations which were promptly voiced while I fidgeted uncomfortably and feigned an indifference I did not feel.

Certainly, good manners demanded that I reveal myself and provide a suitable welcome to the man who poised impatiently beneath my hiding place. Beside him, his horse stamped and blew with the ferociousness of an unbroken stallion, echoing his master's temper, and I felt drawn by the force of their demand to leave the safety of my niche.

Only my odd dress and dishevelled appearance forestalled me. I had no doubt that my cheeks and chin were smeared with the same grime that coated my hands, since mud and dirt seemed drawn to me as foxes to a hen house.

And as was my habit when visiting the stables, I was wearing a pair of my youngest cousin's breeches which were two sizes too large and cinched at the waist with a strip of leather that had once been the reins of an old pony bridle. Over this, I had pulled a smock that had been torn and patched at the elbows, and my thick chestnut hair was caught up and hidden by a stableboy's cap.

While my aunt despaired of my shocking attire, even she had had to admit that my dresses could not bear the abuse to which I subjected them. But having given me permission to wear my cousin's castoff garments when I visited the stables, she had also extracted my promise that I would not present myself to company while dressed in this "wretched fashion."

His lordship had no notion of the problem which confronted me; he gave out a loud cry to summon our groom. It resounded through the stables and stirred a clamor of nervous snorts and nickers. He followed this with a string of oaths that added generously to my vocabulary.

Not wanting to see Henry's absence brought to my uncle's attention, and unwilling to cause my aunt grievous embarrassment by presenting myself as her niece,

I could think of but one solution. Pulling the brim of my cap low on my forehead, I sprang out from behind the bales and quickly clambered down the rickety ladder, garnering several splinters in my fingers for my troubles.

"Sorry to keep 'ee waiting, milord," I mumbled, raising my eyes no higher than his highly polished Hessian boots. "Can I take yer horse?"

"Where have you been, boy?" he demanded, and I could feel the heat of his temper without raising my eyes. "Sleeping, I daresay. Be glad that I do not give you a good cuff for your laziness." He handed me the reins. "See that he is rubbed down and fed a ration of oats. If I come back and find him poorly tended, you will answer to me, not the squire."

" 'Es, milord," I said in a cowed voice, although it amused me to think of his reaction should he discover he had promised to cuff the squire's elder niece. Had it not been for Henry's sake, I would have been tempted to provoke him.

Emboldened by this surge of mischief, I chanced a quick glance upwards. The cloth and cut of his lordship's garments were finer than any my uncle possessed, and I guessed his cravat had been made of silk and edged with French lace. But it was his face which drew my gaze.

For all his solemnity and air of brooding, there was a presence to the man that made his ugliness less important than it might have been in someone less formidable. Having heard the servants whispering tales of his disreputable behavior and innumerous conquests, I suspected I was not alone in thinking his appearance secondary to the power and authority he emanated.

"What is wrong with you, boy?" he demanded as I delayed, and his puzzled frown told me he found something amiss in my behavior, although his sharp eyes had not managed to penetrate my disguise.

"Nothin', milord," I said, hastily stepping backward and jerking on the reins as I retreated.

The gelding, a dappled-gray with a small head and delicate legs, reared in protest of my careless handling, and the reins slipped from my grasp. Only Lord Blackwood's hasty grab for his bridle prevented the animal from doing damage either to himself or to us.

After he had quieted him, his lordship turned on me angrily. "What ails you? Have you no more sense than to frighten a too finely bred creature?"

"Beg pardon, milord," I stammered, sincerely apologetic. "Must 'ave lost me footing."

"More likely it is your senses that have been lost," he retorted sharply. The muscles in his face twitched as he struggled to control his anger. When he had mastered his emotions, he said more calmly, "If you cannot manage him, you had only to tell me."

" 'Twas mischance. Shan't happen again."

"See that it does not."

Given a second chance, I took care to hold the bridle with a firm hand as I led his mount to an empty stall. But having had his confidence in my abilities shaken, his lordship did not trust me to do his bidding unsupervised. Instead of departing, he strode down the row of stalls, following so closely upon my heels I could feel the heat of his gaze upon my back and hear the even intake and exhalation of his breath. Had it not been an affront to the squire's hospitality, I suspected he would have gladly seen to the needs of his mount himself.

As I worked, Lord Blackwood leaned against a post, his green eyes narrowed in contemplation. His intense scrutiny made my heart pound erratically, and I forced myself to concentrate on the tasks he had set for me. But when I thought he could not observe me, I snuck glances at my companion, trying to fit his somber image into the scandalous tales I had heard whispered in the kitchen at Briarslea.

His lordship had inherited his father's title at the

youthful age of twenty-two, his father having suc-
cumbed to the madness that haunted the Blackwood
line, attacked his valet in a murderous rage, and threw
him down the stairs. The hapless man suffered a broken leg and several cracked ribs, but his master was
struck down by an apoplectic fit due, no doubt, to the
exertion of lifting a man almost twice his own weight.

The story had always impressed me, despite my
aunt's insistence that it was nothing but servants' gossip and not to be believed. But the tale persisted, and
I could not help but regret that I had not been on hand
to see the valet's face or his master's spectacular assault.

It made me think fondly of his heir and wonder hopefully if we might expect some similar performance during his stay. There were many who claimed he suffered
from the same affliction as his father and others before
him.

Lord Blackwood seemed to sense the thoughts which
absorbed me and said abruptly, "Tell me, boy. Have
you lived at Briarslea long?"

"Squire took me in nine years gone, after me folks
passed away," I said truthfully.

"What kind of a man is he?"

His question shocked me with its impropriety: One
simply did not gossip with servants about their masters. Nor should those servants respond if such questions were put to them. Aunt Emily would have been
scandalized. Then I pictured his discomfiture had he
been aware of my true identity, and the hilarity of the
situation took hold of me.

"Well, what say you, boy?" he demanded, his impatience born, I suspected, of his own embarrassment for
having asked such a question.

"Squire, milord? Why, the best," I said as though no
other answer could have occurred to any who worked
for him.

"Even-tempered, would you say?"

I nodded vigorously. "Why, in all the years I been here, 'im 'asn't cuffed me but once."

"Laudable." He ran his fingers across the stubble on his jaw. "And his family? Are they cut of the same cloth?"

I paused in my work. "Me a . . . mistress," I corrected myself, "be 'ard-working an' soft-spoken. An' the lads . . ." That demanded more thought. I had never looked upon my three cousins objectively, having simply accepted them without bothering to view them as a stranger might. The question intrigued me, and I did not pause to wonder why Lord Blackwood would want such information.

Physically, my three cousins were much like their father, although their temperaments differed greatly: They were as wild as he was sober. But their hearts were good, and James, the eldest, had grown horribly dignified since he had turned the great age of fifteen. I suspected—not without regret—that his two brothers would soon follow his example. " 'Es," I said after long consideration. " 'Twould be fair t' say they does their folks proud."

Lord Blackwood seemed pleased by my answer. "I had heard as much, but I am not sorry to hear it from a member of their household." Then he surprised me by asking, "Are you acquainted with the squire's nieces?"

" 'Es, milord." Realizing my answer might be seen as inappropriate, I quickly added, "They ride out daily and 'tis me what tends their mounts."

"What have you to say of them?" His dark face glowed with interest.

I was beginning to warm to my role of confidant and took some pains with my answer. "Charlotte, the littl'un, is proper 'ansum, and good wiv 'er needle, they say." I did not pause long enough for him to ask who would give me—a lowly stableboy—such information.

" 'Er 'as a good 'and on the keys, an' sings like a bird. An' she be a grand help to me a . . . mistress."

"And *her* temperament?"

I scratched my hair beneath my cap as though searching for lice and chewed my lower lip for good measure. "She be young, even fer 'er twelve years. An' summat nervous-like," I added with a touch of scorn, remembering her aversion to the frogs and grass snakes I would catch and bring to the bedroom we shared. "But 'er be good-tempered, just the same," I admitted.

He frowned and I wondered what it was about my answer that displeased him. "And the elder girl?" he asked, his eyes betraying their first glimmer of anxiety.

"What, Redigan? Of the two, I be liking 'er the best," I said with unabashed bias. "She ain't 'ansum—nor so plain as some might say," I added with complete disregard for everything I had ever been told about myself. "An', if it ain't forward to say so, to my way of thinkin', 'er be best of the lot."

"And what makes you say such a thing?" he asked, his curiosity stirred, no doubt, by my vehemence.

"Well," I stammered, searching for a response that seemed reasonable and grabbing at the first answer which came to mind. " 'Tis 'ow she treats 'er pony, milord. 'Tis a dull beast but she dussn't lose 'er temper and whip the creature as some might. An' . . . an' when I be making mistakes—which I does sometimes, though they be slight and the fault dussn't allus lie wiv me— she dussn't go making a fuss."

"She is not nervous like her sister?"

"Oh, no, milord. She be steady as Parson and twice as sensible." I proclaimed this with such fervor he must have thought me suffering from the pangs of a youthful passion, and I could barely contain my laughter.

But being unaware of my true identity, Lord Blackwood was most solemn when he thanked me. "You have been more help to me than you can know," he said with such sincere gratitude I could not meet his eyes, and my deception no longer gave me such enjoyment. I was not sorry when he decided to trust me to curry his horse without further incident and go about whatever business had brought him hither.

He strode away, whistling an off-key tune that struck me as pleasant nonetheless, and left me to ponder his reasons for showing such great curiosity about our family. There seemed to be little about us to warrant his interest, while he could have fascinated the dullest of creatures.

Indeed, if behavior was any gauge of sanity, he might truly be mad, for he was unlike any gentleman I had ever met. Even his sudden appearance in the stables was unusual. Visitors stopped at the front door where they were greeted by my aunt or uncle, and their mounts were left standing until Henry could be fetched. I wondered what kind of man gave more thought to his horse's comfort than his own, although I cannot say that his conduct displeased me.

His gelding was clearly a thoroughbred—sleek, with good lines and intelligent eyes—and I longed to replace his saddle and bridle, and ride out into the lane where I could give him his head. Bessie, the pony I usually rode, had grown fat and sluggish, and while I had begged my uncle to let me ride my eldest cousin's mare while he was at school, he thought the animal too headstrong for me to handle.

James did not share his misapprehension, for when he was at home, if there was no one around to relate our activities to his father, he often dismounted and let me take his place in the saddle. Then I would gallop wildly along the cliffs, allowing my waist-length hair to stream back from my head, and feeling the wind sting my cheeks with a salty spray that had been swept from the surf below.

But even when James was at school and his mare forbidden to me, I came daily to the stables. There, I tormented Henry with my incessant questions about the days he served my father as his majordomo when we lived in India. After my parents died of cholera, it was he who had brought Charlotte and me to Cornwall to be raised by my father's eldest brother.

Had it not been for us, Henry would have remained in Calcutta and taken a post with another British officer. Being only a groom to a Cornish squire was a great fall in both status and wages, but he had been deeply fond of both my parents, and it was a matter of honor that he stay close to their daughters where he could keep a watchful eye on their progress.

I had barely finished currying Lord Blackwood's mount when Henry returned. His wrinkled face was creased into a permanent smile, and the scent of tobacco clung to his gray hair. As he often did, he had slipped off to fill his pipe with tobacco and satisfy the craving that regularly overcame him.

It was a habit my uncle despised, and he threatened to discharge him if he caught him smoking in the stables, leaving poor Henry no choice but to desert his post for short periods throughout the day. Usually, his absence went unnoticed, since he chose those moments when my uncle was unlikely to appear, but his lordship's visit had not been expected.

Who be this'n, then?" he asked with a nod toward the stables' newest occupant. "Have 'ee goaded yer uncle into getting that horse 'ee been wanting?" He winked, knowing as well as I that had he been willing, my uncle could not have afforded this magnificent animal.

I tossed the currying brush at him, and he dodged nimbly to one side. "He belongs to Lord Blackwood. Who, I might add, was none too pleased to stand and wait upon a certain groom. Be glad I was here to see to his needs. Uncle Arthur has already spoken to you twice this month about your mysterious disappearances."

"Ah, 'ee be a fine maid. Best there be. Take after yer father." He scooped up the brush and absentmindedly pulled the long hairs from the bristles. "Did I tell 'ee how him saved me life when us'n were hunting tigers?"

He had, but neither of us concerned ourselves with that detail. Knowing that Lord Blackwood would be ensconced in the small drawing room at Briarslea, I was happy to remain in Henry's company for the rest of the afternoon. I settled back onto a bale of hay and suggested he abandon his duties and join me. Henry hesitated, frowning at me as though I was pestering him, when we both knew he enjoyed our conversations as much, if not more, than I did.

Before he could complete his show of unwilling capitulation, my cousin Peter ran into the stables. His leather soles clapped across the flagstones and his breath came and went in loud pants. A mop of blond hair fell into his eyes, and his plump cheeks were flushed a deep pink from the exertion of having run from the manor to the stables. Like both of his brothers he was stout and, being less than average height, appeared boxlike in shape, an unfortunate condition my aunt assured him he would outgrow.

Peter was six months my junior and the only one of my cousins who remained at Briarslea. Like James, Michael had been sent away to school shortly after his fourteenth birthday, leaving only the two of us—since Charlotte rarely enjoyed our games—to entertain each other with harmless pranks or egg each other into daring stunts that were promptly forbidden by my aunt the second our activities reached her ears.

"Ha! Just as I thought," Peter said, his hazel eyes lighting up with glee. "When Lord Blackwood said he had given his mount to our stableboy I knew he meant you. Luckily, Mother assumed he had mistaken Henry for a boy, though with all his wrinkles I cannot imagine how she reached such an extraordinary conclusion."

"Perhaps, she prefers her misconception to the

truth," I retorted. "Either that or she suspected her miscreant son of playing tricks upon her guests."

"Not likely. I was up to my ears in Latin textbooks and ink while Mr. Etterley looked on in profound disapproval."

"It is a pity he did not keep you longer. Goodness knows, you need the instruction."

"Had mother not interrupted us and insisted that I be introduced to his lordship, I might never have escaped. I believe my tutor intended to keep me at my desk until Latin verbs seeped from my weary ears. Be glad you are only a girl and not forced to suffer the torments of gaining an education."

I reached out and gave his nose a hard tweak, and he lunged at me. Henry quickly stepped between us. He was a small man, but his body was sparse and trim, and every inch was hard muscle. He emerged the victor of many a scrap when his opponents foolishly misjudged the strength hidden within that compact frame. Now, he separated us with ease, forestalling an all-out brawl.

"What 'ave I told 'ee about scrapping in the stables?" His wrinkles deepened with irritation. "I'll not have 'ee upsetting the horses with yer goings on."

We apologized, both of us having the greatest respect for him and aspiring to gain his praise before that of any other. But our contrition was not enough to escape the rebuke Henry felt bound to give us.

" 'Twould do 'ee better to put them high spirits to yer riding lessons," he told Peter, who was a diffident rider at best, then turned to me and said, "an' I cain't think what yer dear mother would say if she knew 'ee be spending yer days fighting. Shames me t' see 'ow I be letting 'er down."

My lower lip jutted out, but I knew better than to justify my actions to Henry, even though Peter's condescending manner had been to blame—as it usually was. I hated to be treated like a girl, or be reminded of the opportunities that were deprived me because of my sex. But my attention could not remain on the unfairness of any situation for long.

"Tell me about my mother," I wheedled, and Henry's face softened as I knew it would.

But before he could open his mouth, Peter said, "There is no time for that. Lord Blackwood has expressed an interest in meeting you."

"Meeting *me?*" I gaped at him. "Whatever for?"

"Be assured, he did not explain himself to me. And had he done so, I should have told him not to waste a second upon you, for you are neither pretty enough to draw the eye nor charming enough to please the ear." He stepped backwards before I could tweak his nose a second time and grinned impudently.

"Off with the two of 'ee, then," Henry said, giving me no choice but to obey. "I be glad t' be shot of 'ee."

I followed Peter across the sun-washed courtyard, my feet dragging over the cobblestones, for I suspected that my little charade had been discovered and would garner me a tongue-lashing from both my uncle and my aunt. Rarely did they join forces in such fashion; my uncle preferred to leave all discipline in my aunt's capable hands. But on those occasions when my behavior warranted stronger measures, I sorely regretted drawing down their wrath. The knowledge that Lord Blackwood would be a keen observer in the procedures did not improve my mood.

"Do hurry, Redigan," Peter insisted. "Lord Blackwood will not like to be kept waiting." He tugged at my arm to pull me along, and I dolefully increased my pace.

"Was he upset when he asked for me?" I questioned, wondering the extent of his anger.

Peter swept a lock of blond hair from his eyes and looked at me curiously. "Not that I could tell. But given his great ugliness, I would be hard put to judge the state of his temper. Still, he spoke to me politely when I addressed him and smiled at Charlotte—if you can call that fearsome grimace a smile."

"Did he ask to meet her, too?"

"Mother called her away from practicing at the pianoforte and extolled her virtues for several minutes while Lord Blackwood sipped a glass of brandy and sought for a comfortable position in which to place his legs. But his expression was more polite than interested, I should have said, and as soon as she paused to take a breath, he insisted upon meeting you as well. Father harrumphed and squirmed as he always does when faced with an awkward situation, and Mother pretended you were shy and disliked being brought before guests. But he would have none of their excuses."

I frowned. Did he plan to denounce me in front of my entire family, or had our conversation in the stables provoked an interest in me that would otherwise have not existed? If so, my game had gone awry, and I had only myself to blame for what might happen. That knowledge did not lessen my dread of the confrontation which was to come. I resolved to change into my dress slowly in the hope that he would become impatient and take his leave.

I smiled and Peter looked at me shrewdly. Knowing him as well as he knew me, I thought it likely that he had guessed my intentions. If so, he seemed willing enough to let me get away with my tricks. But since he took as much delight in making trouble for me as he did in sharing my crimes, his lack of remark was unusual. Had my own schemes concerned me less, I would have known to be suspicious.

The shadow cast by Briarslea fell upon my shoulders as we neared the elm-shaded manor that had been my home for almost as long as I could remember. It was a rambling, two-story building. Swallows nested below the eaves of the slate roof, and woke us in the morning with their twittering; rose briars clambered about the mullioned windows and enlivened the stone walls with their jade-green leaves. A few pink blooms, their petals drooping sadly, still clung to the vines, but one stiff breeze would sweep them away until summer came again.

Charlotte and I shared a bedroom upstairs which could only be reached by the front stairs. These led off a central hallway that stretched the length of the manor. Since the drawing room lay off this same hallway, reaching the stairs meant passing by the small gathering who were awaiting my presence.

My throat tightened when I saw the door had been left ajar, making it doubly hard for me to slip by without being noticed. I said a silent prayer that Lord Blackwood had been given my uncle's sturdy saddle-check chair—the high-backed chair which faced the windows—for neither my aunt nor uncle would call out for me to join them if they saw me clad in my stable garb.

Placing a finger on my lips to warn my cousin not to speak, I tiptoed down the hallway; the rug muffled the steady rise and fall of my boots. Peter followed close behind me, making a valiant effort to ease his solid bulk forward noiselessly. It pleased me to realize that our muted footfalls and hushed breathing could barely be caught by my own ears.

Snatches of conversation punctuated our progress. My uncle's deep laugh mingled with Charlotte's high-pitched giggle, and I fancied I heard a soft chuckle from his lordship. A whiff of my aunt's eau de Cologne wafted from the six-inch opening, and the faint smell of smoke drifted towards us from the fireplace.

Then, through the crack, I saw the back of Lord Blackwood's head; his dark curls gleamed above the leather upholstery. I turned triumphantly to Peter. His eyes glowed with mischief. Before I could guess his intentions, he grabbed my arm and shoved me into the drawing room.

"Here she is," he announced gaily, and whipped the cap from my head.

My hair tumbled about my shoulders, destroying any hope there might have been of keeping my first meeting with his lordship a secret. My aunt half rose from the settee where she sat with my sister, then she fell back, weakly gasping for air. Charlotte's softly rounded cheeks colored a deep scarlet, and I supposed it humiliated her to have it known that we were related. With a sob, she buried her face in my aunt's full bosom.

Uncle Arthur grasped the mantelpiece for support. His eyes bulged and he made a strangled noise in his throat, putting me in mind of a frog which had been held too tightly around the middle. Lord Blackwood swivelled around in his chair and stared with open amazement at the sight that met his eyes.

Peter burst into laughter, and I turned on him in fury, boxing his ears and making him yelp with pain. Without hesitation he threw himself at me and wrestled me to the floor, where we kicked and pummeled each other, oblivious to anything but our own anger.

My leg collided with a table, and a vase toppled with a crash and shattered. Then a strong hand gripped my shoulder and hauled me to my feet. Lord Blackwood held me at arm's length; his hard gaze stilled my thrashing fists.

Peter scrambled to an upright position and ruefully rubbed a spot on his cheek where my fist had landed. Except for his labored breathing and muffled sobs from Charlotte, the room was horribly quiet.

Lord Blackwood's green eyes were dark with annoyance. My cheeks burned but I lifted my chin and met his gaze boldly, daring him to do his worst. With my chestnut hair falling across my face in knotted strands, and rage burning, I must have looked as mad as any of his ancestors.

He shook his head, and a look of pity crossed his face. It was the same look I saw in the faces of my relatives when they compared me to Charlotte—always unfavorably. In the stables, I had claimed to be neither plain nor bad-tempered, a vain boast prompted by the many slights I had borne in the past. Having my deepest anguish revealed to a total stranger was humiliating. For him to pity me was more than I could bear.

I struggled to free myself so that I might run from the room and escape those penetrating eyes, but he held my shoulder fast. In frustration, I twisted my head and bit down hard on his hand. His head jerked back in surprise but, despite the pain I must have caused him, he did not slacken his grip.

The marks of my teeth stood out against his wrist in a broken red line. I hung my head, mortified by what I had done. Of all my past misdeeds, none had caused me greater shame or brought me to a quicker realization of the scandalous nature of my behavior.

Lord Blackwood let his hand fall, and he turned to my aunt and uncle. "I apologize for any embarrassment my demands have caused you," he said evenly. "It was unwise of me to disdain your judgment. Charlotte is undoubtedly more suitable."

Chapter Two

CHARLOTTE AND I looked at each other. Her thickly lashed eyes widened with the fear she always displayed when faced with an unknown, and possibly difficult, situation. I imagine mine reflected the resentment aroused in me by the growing certainty that she had somehow benefited through my rash actions.

Not that I cared. I flounced onto the window seat and stared sullenly out of the mullioned windows, determined to ignore both his lordship and his provocative announcement. But my insatiable curiosity clamored for an explanation and, although I had too much pride to speak them aloud, the questions swarmed into my mind.

Lord Blackwood did not have—so far as I was aware—any children, and therefore had no need for a governess. Besides, both Charlotte and I were over-young for such a post. We were also too young to be considered as companions for his wife—had he been married. That, to my knowledge, was again not so. And while neither of us were of a sufficiently high station to be considered suitable marriage prospects for his lordship, our station was well above that of any persons he might employ as servants.

The problem intrigued me; it did not seem to me that either Charlotte or I were suitable for any of his needs. My traitorous gaze wandered back to the dark figure who dominated the drawing room, searching for some clue that might explain away his presence at Briarslea.

But Lord Blackwood had concluded his business. He had risen from his chair, and his empty brandy glass sat on the nearby tea table. After bowing stiffly to my aunt, causing her to flutter nervously with embarrassment, he suggested amiably that he and my uncle should work out the details of their agreement in the privacy of his study.

As the squire followed agreeably, his lordship cast an irritated glance at me over his shoulder—one that should have crushed me on the spot, but failed since my temper had not lessened one whit. I stared back coolly, choosing to think of his improper behavior in the stables rather than my own. If he was aware of my thoughts, he did not have the grace to look discomfited, but I had the consolation of regaining some of my pride before he departed.

After they had gone, my aunt fingered the folds of calico that enveloped her ample form, and her hands patted her neatly braided hair as she confirmed that the strands had not escaped her pins. Then she gave an indescribable sigh. The strains of pleasure and regret in that exhalation made me wonder what unlikely romantic notions she was entertaining.

Socially, my aunt was nearly his lordship's equal, much more so than the simple country squire who had succeeded in winning her hand in marriage. But even the kindest and least critical of judges would have called her plain. That, and a complete lack of dowry, had almost guaranteed her a future as a spinster. Still, at the unlikely age of twenty-eight, she had eloped with Arthur Grenfel rather than live out her years as a governess. Her family had been horrified but, to me, the marriage had always seemed a success. Now, I wondered if she had harbored dreams of marrying someone whose rank in society equalled or bested her own.

Aunt Emily did not let us into her thoughts, but

turned instead to stare at her three charges: Charlotte, her cherubic face pale with anxiety, poised on the edge of the settee and desperately seeking some way to escape; Peter, crouched by the hearth, nursing his wounds with more theatrics than genuine pain; and me, curled up on the window seat and glaring at my filthy nails as if they, not I, had been responsible for my outburst. All of us waited for the tongue-lashing we felt certain would come.

It took my aunt a full minute before she regained her composure and the use of her tongue, a lengthy period of time for that usually verbose woman. Then, with an unexpectedly mild look, she said, "Well, for once your antics have done us no harm, and Charlotte some good—though one can only wonder why his lordship did not depart this house forthwith after your wicked display. Still"—at this, she leveled her sternest gaze upon me—"you have convinced him with your deeds what our advice failed to convey. You are entirely unsuitable for the high position he seemed inclined to bestow upon you."

"What position?" I demanded, shooting an irritated look at Peter, whom I held wholly responsible for whatever loss I had suffered.

Aunt Emily refused to elaborate. "It will do you good to learn patience," she rebuked me. "When your uncle returns he will tell you himself."

"*I* know why his lordship came." Peter grinned with a patronizing air which he would not have dared to use had his mother's stolid body not been planted firmly between us. "He wants to buy Pendene's Wood. He has plagued father for years to sell him the property. What other reason has he to come to Briarslea?"

Pendene's Wood covered a wedge-shaped valley that cut through his lordship's estates and divided them into two sections, save at the southern end where a rectangular stretch of shoreline linked them together. Originally, the entire section had belonged to the Blackwoods, but the wood had been gambled and lost to the Grenfels almost a century ago.

Both the present Lord Blackwood and his father before him had pleaded with my uncle to let them buy back the property. But land was hard to come by in Cornwall, and the squire stubbornly refused to give up so much as an acre.

"Nor will I," he had vowed to us. "Not so long as I can put food on this table."

But since it was the only portion of my uncle's land that was not adjoined to Briarslea, in a moment of expansiveness, he had promised it to Charlotte as a dowry. His gift, along with her remarkable beauty, gave him every reason to hope she would make an excellent marriage. And faithful to his word, my uncle refused all offers to buy the wood; for as we all knew, sooner or later his expenses always forced him to delve into any capital he had set aside.

Now, I wondered idly if my uncle had given in to his pressing financial needs and accepted Lord Blackwood's offer.

"But that is to be my dowry," Charlotte protested, for once, her thoughts taking much the same turn as my own, and her pretty face darkened with concern.

"Hush, child. It is impolite to question your uncle's decisions." Aunt Emily's admonition was delivered with a gentle smile, but if the rebuke she received was mild, the thought of losing her dowry—and her only hope for a good marriage—was too dreadful for Charlotte to bear. She promptly flung herself into the satin pillows that adorned the settee and burst into tears.

Aunt Emily rushed to console her. "There, there," she said, gently stroking my sister's blonde ringlets. "You must not be upset. You will have your dowry, and a better marriage than you could possibly have hoped for."

Her announcement could have only one meaning. I stared at my aunt incredulously, while Charlotte promptly sat up. With one last hiccough, she quelled her sobs, and her blue eyes were round with surprise. "You cannot mean—"

My aunt nodded. "Lord Blackwood has offered for you."

I gasped. So that was where my charade had nearly dropped me. Into the hands of Lord Blackwood. The thought of being titled and wealthy—and in the position to own a horse as magnificent as his gelding— paled beside the prospect of being the wife of that horrid man.

I enjoyed few romantic notions. Those that did slip past my daydreams of thoroughbreds and wild races (in which I always emerged the victor) involved slim, fair-haired gods, with blue eyes and dimpled cheeks and natures as pleasing as their countenances. Lord Blackwood was as unlike a youthful blond god as I was unlike their fair counterparts.

Charlotte was completely overcome by the prospect of being his lordship's betrothed. Her eyes had glazed over and her features were immobile. But my aunt's pleased smile told me she was ignorant of the meaning of the vacant look that her announcement had evoked.

Having placed spiders beneath Charlotte's sheets and waved frogs in her face, it was an expression I found familiar. At any moment, my sister was likely to succumb to a fit of hysteria.

But my aunt, having never tested her in this fashion, did not recognize the warning. "Pendene's Wood will return to his family," she continued happily. "And this arrangement will provide him with a wife who is not as high-strung as the daughters of his peers. He feels that too much gentle breeding within his family has led to an unfortunate strain of"—she hesitated, and her forehead wrinkled—"nervousness, which he hopes to correct with his own marriage."

"But I do not want to marry him," Charlotte cried, unable to contain her fears a moment longer. "He is too big and too ugly and—" She glanced fearfully at the closed door to make certain her voice could not be overheard by our illustrious guest. "He *murdered* his first wife!"

"Nonsense, child," Aunt Emily said tartly, and two bright dots of pink colored her cheeks. "She died in childbirth. How many times must I tell you not to listen to gossip?"

"Then it is untrue?" Her lower lip trembled, and her young face filled with misgiving as she looked at Peter and me.

Aunt Emily glared at us both, knowing full well who had filled her head with such wild tales. "I would sooner have ten children than be burdened with the two of you," she said crossly. "You will be the death of me."

Peter and I grinned at each other. We had listened to that same warning at frequent intervals throughout our childhood. Since my aunt's full face glowed with good health, and her prophecies were often followed with a vigorous belting, neither of us worried over-much about her well-being.

"If I were not so pleased at the outcome of Lord Blackwood's visit I would take a strap to both of you," she added, confirming my feelings that her health was not failing. "You, Redigan"—she rounded on me—"do not deserve the good luck that has befallen you."

"Befallen *me?*" I asked. While I did not envy my sister her ugly bridegroom, it surprised me that my aunt also viewed my unbetrothed state as fortunate. "Do you mean," I asked with unintended malice, "that while Lord Blackwood is an eligible match, he is unlikely to make a pleasant husband?"

Aunt Emily's face reddened, and she looked as though she was choking on words she could not speak. This time it was she who glanced hastily at the door to be certain no word of our conversation could escape the room.

"I mean no such thing, you awful child," she said

when she had assured herself that the door was still tightly closed. "Charlotte has been blessed with good fortune, while you have lost—and most deservedly so—a position that would be beyond your capabilities and temperament to assume. But since the property is quite valuable, Lord Blackwood generously offered to provide a small dowry for whichever of you he chose not to wed, as well as give her a season in London. Being an honest man, he will not rescind his promise, though little good a dowry will do you if you do not mend your ways."

So I, too, was to have a husband. I chewed my lower lip thoughtfully as I absorbed this piece of news and tried to decide if I was, or was not, fortunate. Peter, who seemed to be growing bored with this talk of dowries and husbands, snorted in derision at the notion, and contorted his face into the passable likeness of a pig.

His foolishness promptly brought me to the conclusion that both marriages and husbands were overrated. With a lift of my chin, I announced grandly, "I would rather have a horse."

Lord Blackwood took his leave without being advised of my preference. And having assured himself of both the property he desired and a suitably sedate wife to bear his children, he did not deign to cross our threshold again for almost five years.

One would almost have thought he had forgotten the bargain he had struck with the squire. Certainly, if our aunt had not dedicated herself to giving us the kind of education necessary for young ladies who would be expected to appear in society, Charlotte and I would have questioned whether or not the entire afternoon had taken place in our childish imaginations.

It seemed that Aunt Emily's efforts were to be wasted, for my eighteenth birthday came and went with nary a word from his lordship. Then, on a foggy day in late winter, he rode into Briarslea again, arriving, as before, unannounced and unattended.

It was Sunday afternoon, a time when one might have expected to find the squire and his family at home. In fact, we had returned from church a few hours earlier, but my uncle had been dragged from his study and the French brandy he cherished to intervene in a violent dispute between two of his tenants.

Since my three cousins were all at school and my aunt was not expecting guests, she had insisted that Charlotte and I change into our everyday dresses of striped calico. Then we had settled down to enjoy a quiet afternoon in the spacious back parlor, where the furnishings lent themselves more to comfort than fashion, and the large fireplace threw off enough heat to repel the dampness and the musty odor that had pervaded the manor that dreary winter.

The clip-clop of hooves against the cobblestones sent us rushing to the windows where we stared across the empty yard into the somber bank of fog that whirled and twisted at the farthest reaches of the manor. Lord Blackwood galloped out of that gloomy twilight as though breaking through some diaphanous veil that stretched between past and present, and his funereal black cloak and black top hat did nothing to dispel the illusion. My aunt gasped with dismay as we watched him dismount and summon Henry with a brief wave that was all the more imperial for its succinct nature.

An hour ago, the skies, which had been pouty since dawn, had released the inevitable drizzle of rain; and Lord Blackwood made haste to cross the courtyard, ignoring the spray of water he kicked up as he strode through the tiny puddles and rivulets that had gathered between the stones.

"Good gracious!" exclaimed Aunt Emily. An impatient glance at her reflection in the windowpanes brought a dissatisfied grimace to her face, then she shooed both of us upstairs to change back into our best dresses and brush our hair.

"And do wash your face, Redigan," she implored. "I believe it is impossible for you to walk from the carriage to the front door without streaking grime across your forehead."

We hurried to the bedroom we shared, her words close on our heels. Charlotte banged the door shut behind us and flung herself on the damask counterpane that covered our four-poster bed. The delicate pink flush that usually stained her cheeks had faded, making her skin as white as my own.

"I dread seeing him," she cried to me. "He frightens me. I cannot bear the thought of being his wife."

"Perhaps, if you were to bite him, he might look elsewhere," I said unhelpfully as I struggled with the fastenings on my dress.

"I wish I had," she said, and her eyes brimmed with tears. "Do you think he is mad?"

"If he were, it is unlikely Uncle Arthur would consider him a suitable bridegroom—not even for me—no matter how great his wealth or desirable his title."

But she was not reassured. She curled up on the bed and listlessly sucked on her fingertip, for once, not anxious to comply with our aunt's dictates.

I finished with my struggles to disrobe and rolled my clothes into a bundle which I promptly flung at her. She brushed them aside without protest and collapsed against the pillows with a plaintive sigh.

In spite of her despair, she made an attractive picture: Flaxen ringlets drooped becomingly around her oval face; her wide-set blue eyes were made more brilliant by her tears; the desolate pout served to emphasize her full lips; and the pallor that had settled upon her gave her skin the translucence of porcelain. Faced with this vision of beauty, I was hard put to feel any sympathy for her.

Unlike Charlotte, I was tall, slim, and my eyes were

a peculiar light-brown shade that my aunt kindly referred to as amber—*amber* sounding a great deal more attractive than muddy brown. My nose, while straight, did not tilt delicately at the tip as I would have wished. My nostrils did not flare with passion; nor did my eyebrows arch provocatively and Aunt Emily unreasonably refused to let me pluck them.

If I possessed any physical attribute that could be called pleasing, it was my chestnut hair. When unpinned, it fell below my waist in thick waves, and frequent brushing had given it a healthy sheen. But instead of improving my appearance, the luxuriance merely emphasized my overall plainness. I would not have minded so much if my sister had also been drab, but it was a daily trial for me to look from my mousy image in the looking glass to her perfect features.

Not that it was her fault. Although she was a trifle vain, Charlotte was never one to point out how much prettier she was than I. Though had she been, I would have pushed her face down in the pig trough whenever she mistakenly stepped beyond my aunt's protection. Still, it was more than fear that made her hold her tongue. Since the death of our parents, she had depended on me to protect her, and she bore my teasing in silence rather than lose my sympathy by lording her beauty over me.

With a sigh that echoed hers, I picked up the black woolen dress I had flung across the armchair a short time before. The skirts were rumpled and creased and the hem was soiled, but my attire was of no more concern to me at eighteen than it had ever been.

Which, I thought, was just as well. Concern would have done me little good and caused me great disappointment. Black was not a good color for me. It made my pale skin sallow, my slim figure look painfully thin, and drained the luster from my hair.

So what is the point of bothering with the brush? I

asked myself, and announced to Charlotte that I was ready to confront Lord Blackwood.

"Really, you ought to be ashamed of yourself," she chided. "If you would only make an effort, you could look quite nice."

"I do not want to look nice," I retorted untruthfully. But if I could not be beautiful—and clearly, I could not—then I did not care to make a fool of myself trying to attain what was beyond my grasp. "Besides," I said. "It is not me his lordship has come to see. You are his betrothed."

"Do not remind me," she pleaded. "I dread the prospect of being his wife. That fearsome scar makes me feel quite faint. If I have to kiss him, I will swoon. Do you think he will expect it of me after we are married?"

"Husbands do kiss their wives," I said dryly, thinking to myself that rather more than kissing was involved, although I did not want to aggravate her fears by adding my own conjecture. And thanks to my aunt's vigilance, my knowledge of the relations between husband and wife was vague at best.

"I will not kiss him," she announced. "I cannot even bear the thought."

"James said that the ladies in London find Lord Blackwood quite attractive."

"Nonsense! Any woman who finds *him* attractive cannot possibly be a lady."

Since this fell in line with my own way of thinking, I was hard put to persuade her otherwise. Not wanting to argue the point, I warned, "If you do not hurry, I shall go downstairs without you."

"Please, do!" she pleaded. "And tell his lordship that I am unwell."

"A fine wife you will make him."

She cast a despairing glance at me. "I will have hysterics if you do not do something. I know I will."

"You really are a little ninny. If you would make an effort to stay in his company for but a few hours, you would become accustomed to his appearance and cease to find him fearsome."

"Never will I become accustomed to that scarred face or those awful green eyes of his," she vowed. "But I imagine I will not have to endure a lengthy marriage. Doubtless, I shall go to my grave at a young age."

"If you do it will be because I have throttled you," I replied cuttingly. "He will not be given the opportunity."

"You are horrid, really." She sat up, and her face blazed with more life than she had shown for some while. "You have always been jealous of me, and it amuses you to see me suffer."

With an exasperated groan, I gave in—perhaps because there was more than a grain of truth in her accusation. "If you insist, I will tell him you are indisposed," I said at last.

"You are a dear." She jumped up with a toss of her long ringlets and rummaged through her dresser drawer until she found a white linen scarf that she had been given for Christmas. "Here. Wrap this around you. It will soften the neckline and throw some light into your face." She eagerly knotted the scarf about my neck, then stepped back to admire her efforts.

"Are you quite finished?"

"You are being peevish." She grabbed up the brush and brushed back the strands of hair that had escaped my braids. "There. You look quite nice."

"If you are hoping his lordship will turn to me to console him for your absence, I fear there is little chance of that," I said acidly.

"It *was* you he wanted until you bit him."

I did not stay to explain how his lordship had nearly come to that decision. Leaving her looking satisfied with her plotting, I hurried downstairs to the drawing room.

Lord Blackwood was enjoying a glass of the same French brandy that my uncle had sadly set aside when he was called away, and he occupied the squire's chair with more aplomb than my uncle ever had. The cape and hat had been removed, and his long legs were stretched casually before him as he warmed himself by the fire.

As I entered, he rose and bowed, then waited until I had joined my aunt on the settee before taking his seat once again. Aunt Emily glared at me when she saw I was alone, undoubtedly suspecting me of locking Charlotte in the wardrobe. "Where is your sister?" she demanded.

"Charlotte is not feeling well," I said, smiling sweetly at Lord Blackwood. "She asked me to beg his lordship's pardon."

"There was nothing wrong with her twenty minutes ago," Aunt Emily retorted sharply.

I looked back with offended innocence, irritating her further, and she barely managed to erase her scowl before turning to Lord Blackwood. "If you will excuse me for a moment, milord, I will go and make certain my niece is all right."

He nodded politely, his face impassive as though he had not observed the exchange between us. My aunt hurried out, after shooting me a severe look over her shoulder to let me know that I would not escape punishment if she discovered I had been up to my usual devilment.

I merely smiled and, giving over my attentions to our guest, said, "It is a pleasure to make your acquaintance again, milord. We had begun to think you had forgotten us."

Lord Blackwood did not immediately respond. His sharp gaze fastened on me and swept me from head to toe. Not an inch of me escaped his notice. His assessment was made deliberately, with such brutal and obvious attention paid to my meager physical charms that I felt like a horse he planned to sell at market. Never had I been measured in such a clearly male fashion, and I became acutely conscious of all my failings.

In self-defense, I returned a long look of my own. My gaze traveled from his unmanageable hair, slid hastily past his green eyes which seemed more exotic and more dangerous than I remembered, and across his scarred cheek to his shadowed jaw. His countenance is no more pleasing than my own, I thought with satisfaction, but something warned me not to pause overlong on those firm lips, and I suppressed the shiver that coursed through me.

Feeling myself again under control, I feigned a cool air and tried to appraise his overly large form with open disparagement. But his shoulders which—when I was thirteen—had seemed unnecessarily broad, exuded a physical power which made my heart flutter; and those sprawling legs, elegantly clad in fitted breeches that clung to his muscled thighs, emphasized his blatant masculinity in a manner that I felt sure was ungentlemanly.

Rather than relieving me of my embarrassment, my scrutiny made me doubly conscious of his personage, and now, the effect of his gaze was more than disquieting. My strength deserted me. To my dismay, I felt incapable of making the slightest movement, like some frightened animal caught in the sights of a gun, waiting for the death that must surely follow.

And yet there was something exquisite in the fear, as though in that second we had become one—hunter and hunted, stalker and prey—two separate beings molded into one entity for all eternity. Every particle of me yearned for the denouement.

Then the heat from those mysterious eyes seemed to extend to me, and I was suffused with an unnatural warmth. It rose from those private areas of my body which I did not display, even to my own eyes. I agonized as the burning wave surged up my throat and prickled across my cheeks.

Seeing the effect his unkind perusal had had on me, he spoke at last. "You must forgive my lengthy contemplation. I am hard put to see in you the child I remember."

It was as though he had slapped me hard across the face. His churlish mention of that humiliating day rallied my senses, and I replied coldly, "But surely you are already aware of the improvement in me."

"And why would that be?"

"Did you not consult our groom before you left the stables?"

His eyes glittered and I immediately regretted the imprudent remark. But instead of the harsh rebuke I expected, he murmured, "Touché," and leaned his head back against his chair. There, in comfort, he renewed his inspection.

Unable to bear any further indignity, I said crossly, "It is impolite to stare."

"Forgive me. But I am quite struck by the change in you."

"Must you continually refer to that silly episode? If I did your wrist any permanent damage, please accept my sincere apologies. But I cannot say that I regret biting you. If I had not, you would have offered for me instead of Charlotte, and I am glad it is she who must marry you."

"Are you, indeed?"

"I am. For you are neither pleasant nor handsome, and a good husband is both."

He chuckled loudly, and had I not been the reason for his amusement, I might have enjoyed the sound and the way his face lightened when he laughed. "You must tell me," he said when he had quelled his mirth. "What other attributes should a good husband possess?"

"His manner needs be both respectful and kind to those with whom he has dealings. His demeanor should be such that his presence enlivens and cheers those who keep company with him. And he should be of moderate height so that one can exchange pleasantries while dancing." With that, I concluded. And if my answer rudely pointed out his own shortcomings, I cannot say that I minded.

But his lordship smiled as if the insults were beneath his notice, and said indulgently, "Perhaps, when you come to know men better, your tastes will change."

"Possibly. But I doubt that I could ever be persuaded to consider you well-favored."

"I can only hope that Charlotte finds me more appealing."

"I suppose it matters very little if she does," I said realistically. "Tell me, how did you come by the scar on your cheek?"

The question was too forward and deserved a rebuke, but Lord Blackwood fingered the white line that dipped down his cheek. "It happened when I was a boy. My brother Stephen slashed me when we were fencing. We had had a disagreement and, when my back was turned, he slipped the button off his foil. It was a cowardly act, for I was not prepared to defend myself. Later, he claimed it had fallen off accidentally and so escaped the punishment he deserved."

"You must have been most upset."

He nodded. "Had our instructor not stopped me, I believe I would have killed him."

"How shameful of him," I said. "You would never be handsome, but you would not look quite so ug . . . unattractive if not for that. It is unfortunate to be unattractive," I added thoughtfully. "Though perhaps more for a woman than a man." I sighed more deeply than I had intended.

The corners of his mouth twitched. "You should not worry overmuch about your appearance."

"Do you think vanity a sin?" I asked, but before he could answer, Aunt Emily appeared, tugging a red-eyed but neatly groomed Charlotte behind her.

"Do forgive us for keeping you waiting, your lord-ship," she said, hustling her charge to the settee as he rose to greet them. "A slight case of indigestion, noth-ing more."

"I hope I have not inconvenienced you, Lord Black-wood," Charlotte mumbled, her eyes cast downwards. She curtsied—somewhat less gracefully than she was able, but managed to look charming nonetheless—then offered a pale hand for him to kiss. I could only marvel at the manner in which she hid her misgivings.

Lord Blackwood accepted her hand and gently brushed his lips across her fingers. "The reward of see-ing you is well worth the wait," he assured her, bringing faint dimples to her cheeks. "Indeed, I consider myself the most fortunate of men to be allowed to wait on you. Your beauty would bring London to its knees."

Charlotte's dimples deepened, and she dared to raise her eyes. They flickered nervously across his scarred cheek, but she succeeded in saying lightly, "You are most gracious, milord."

"Not at all. I speak only the plain truth. Had I not the good sense to offer for you when you were a child, I would find myself forced to fight through crowds of ad-mirers to win your attentions."

Unused to such gallant remarks, Charlotte giggled with delight, and she took her hand back as reluctantly as she had given it. Aunt Emily was so relieved to see the change in her niece's attitude, her broad smile en-veloped us all.

I looked back at her sulkily. It was plain that Charlotte had completely forgotten her plot to give me to his lordship in her stead. Well may she have him, I thought sourly. He was not, nor ever could be, the man for me.

Chapter Three

My UNCLE did not return for more than an hour, and in that time Lord Blackwood struggled to win his betrothed's devotion. He paid her compliment after compliment, laying on his flattery with such skill and generosity that I suspected he had realized the reason for her sudden attack of "indigestion" and wisely bent his energies to making himself more palatable.

Charlotte glowed beneath his admiration. Her cheeks regained their pink blush; and the sparkle in her eyes was due to excitement, and not the tears that had brightened them earlier. Each bob of her head set her ringlets dancing over her slim shoulders. And while her face had always seemed to be lit by a soft radiance, now it shone with a brilliance that rivalled the glittering brightness of the morning sun that had risen over Calcutta.

I removed myself to the window seat, feeling more drab with each toss of those enviable blonde locks. There I sat, watching her transformation with growing resentment, while I hunched in the shadows of the heavy draperies. Droplets of rain rapped insistently against the windowpanes, echoing my need for attention. Thank goodness, I thought, that I dislike his lordship. For had I felt otherwise, I believe I could have hated my sister.

If escape had been possible, I would have slipped

away to the hayloft—still my favorite retreat—where I would not be forced to witness their flirtation. As I looked longingly out of the window, I heard, "—but it is Redigan I came to see." I turned to find Lord Blackwood looking at me expectantly.

"Me?" I faltered.

He smiled. "I have made arrangements with my sister Elizabeth. She has a house in London and has agreed to bring you out. I gave my word to the squire that both of his nieces would benefit from our arrangement. It is time I kept my promise and found you a husband."

"Much luck you will have," I muttered under my breath.

He gave me a sharp look, and I had the discomfiting notion that he had caught the remark. Fortunately, Charlotte distracted him. She rose from the settee and, seating herself on the arm of his chair and placing her hand upon his sleeve, said with the sweetest little pout, "But it is so unfair. Redigan dislikes parties and balls. Nor does she care for pretty dresses, while nothing pleases me more. But she is to have a season in London, and I must remain in Cornwall. Might I not also be allowed to go?"

My aunt gasped at her audacity. "Hush, child! You have no call to ask for such an indulgence," she admonished, and her gaze flew to Lord Blackwood in a silent apology.

Charlotte's face fell and Lord Blackwood laughed. Gently lifting her chin with his forefinger, he said, "Not for a minute would I rob you of the success that is certain to be yours. Of course, you shall go, too."

Charlotte gave out an excited squeal and flung her arms about his neck. When she realized where her impulsiveness had led her, she hastily disentangled herself. The color in her cheeks deepened, and she could not raise her eyes to meet his.

Lord Blackwood pretended not to notice her embarrassment, and calmly said, "And your aunt shall come also, as your chaperone. If the squire will give his permission."

"Eh? Permission for what?" Uncle Arthur asked as he walked into the drawing room, wiping the raindrops off his bald head with a large handkerchief. Seeing that our visitor was his lordship, he hastily stuffed the damp cloth back into his waistcoat pocket, and bowed as well as his protruding stomach allowed.

As Lord Blackwood rose to greet him, Charlotte skipped across the room and threw herself into his arms. "We are to go to London. And Aunt Emily, too, if you will agree. Please say yes," she wheedled, "for it will be such fun."

"Ha! Doubt that I'll have much to say, one way or t'other," he teased. "Your aunt'll have my head, should I gainsay her."

"Then the matter is settled," Lord Blackwood finished.

The squire nodded and gave his apologies for having been absent from Briarslea.

"No matter," his lordship assured him. "Your wife and nieces have given me ample welcome, which is better than I deserve, having given you no reason to expect me. But I had recently completed some business in Truro, and since I rode near Briarslea on my return, it occurred to me that a great deal of time had passed since my last visit. I thought it advisable to discuss with you again the future of your nieces. I fear I have been remiss in not keeping myself abreast of their progress."

"Eh? No, no. Not at all. Mustn't worry thy head on that score. Thee couldn't have timed thy arrival better if thee had planned it so," the squire replied, too awed by his guest to even suggest that by not so much as writing us a note in four and a half years, his lordship might be guilty of shameful neglect.

I did not share my uncle's awe. Clearly, all we were

to Lord Blackwood was an afterthought that struck him
when he happened to pass our gates. His highhandedness offended me, and what was I to him but a responsibility he had incurred when he contracted for my
sister. For Charlotte, I was incensed; I even found it in
my heart to pity her. I would have loved to speak my
mind.

But my uncle had decided we had no part in this discussion. With a quick glance in our direction, he said,
"Off with thee, children. Ted'n a matter for thy ears."

Dutifully, Charlotte and I left the room, although
heated resentment bristled within me. Why must I be
made to leave while they made arrangements for *my*
future? At least, they might have permitted me to stay
and listen.

It seemed grossly unfair. But neither had they consulted Charlotte—upon whom both my aunt and uncle
doted. And I didn't doubt that Lord Blackwood believed his own judgment infallible and felt no need to
seek anyone's approval. My woolen dress bunched beneath my clenched fingers, and I dearly wished that instead of the pliant fabric, my hands had encircled his
lordship's neck.

But if I was upset, my sister was not. The moment
the drawing-room door closed behind us, she danced
around me, skirts flying, and her feet could not be
stilled. "I am to go to London," she sang gaily. "To London. To London."

"You sound as though you have not yet left the nur-
sery," I said shortly but, for once, even my bad temper
could not upset her. She stuck out her tongue and then
ran off to the kitchen to announce her victory to the
housekeeper and cook and anyone else who might be
there to listen.

Sullenly, I watched her go. While I did not begrudge
Charlotte her chance to enjoy the round of balls and
parties, I could not help but reflect that once again, I
would be subjected to the same comparisons that had

haunted me throughout my childhood. And, once again, I would come away the worse for having been so compared. If I had been inclined to tears, I should have sat down on the spot and given furious vent to my frustration.

Instead, I sought to escape my turbulent thoughts. Having been freed from the duties of entertaining his lordship, I stole into the library to fetch a book that I had been reading, one which my aunt deemed unsuitable for Charlotte and myself—although she had read the tale avidly. It was kept in a locked cabinet, along with several other volumes which she thought too ribald for our innocent eyes.

Unbeknownst to her, I regularly stole the small key from the large ring that hung in the kitchen and removed the slim volume, sliding its fellows together so that its absence would go unnoticed. Now—with my aunt and uncle devoting their attentions to Lord Blackwood—was an opportune time to read further.

I removed myself from the library, since my aunt often sought me there, and crossed instead to my uncle's quiet study. It was a dark room with tall, narrow windows draped in forest-green velvet; they admitted little light, even in the middle of a summer afternoon when the sun shone its brightest. A kneehole desk made of carved mahogany dominated the center of the room, and directly behind stood a brocade wing chair. Two more wing chairs had been angled to face the desk. That was all the furniture the small room could hold, save for an unobtrusive deception table in which my uncle kept his decanters of brandy and Madeira.

Since we were forbidden to use his study, I had no reason to expect that anyone would look for me here, and to escape notice should someone chance to walk by, I crouched on the floor behind the farthest chair. It sat near the wall beside the windows, and the draperies could be pulled around my hunched form to conceal my presence from the casual observer.

It did not occur to me that my uncle would want to have "a private word" with Lord Blackwood until he announced his intentions in the corridor outside the study. A moment later, I heard his heavy tread at the door. It swung open and the two men entered.

"Will thee take another glass of brandy, milord?" my uncle asked in an eager-to-please, doglike fashion that scraped on my nerves.

"Gladly. I see your stocks have not depleted, despite Napoleon and his annoying war."

"They'll not last much longer. Damned inconvenience. But thee won't find me buying contraband. I disapprove," he avowed.

"There are many who would," Lord Blackwood said. "I applaud your patriotism."

The decanter tinkled against the crystal brandy glasses that sat on the table. After a short pause, the springs of the wing chair which hid me gave out a creaking complaint as my uncle sat down; the wooden legs pressed against the draperies, forcing me against the wall and making it difficult to breathe. The slightest motion would have betrayed my presence.

It put me in the most uncomfortable position—morally as well as physically. For if I emerged now, forbidden book in hand, I would surely be punished. Once, for having disobeyed my aunt, and again, for having embarrassed my uncle. But if I said nothing, and they discovered I had been eavesdropping—albeit unintentionally—on their private affairs, I might be confined to my room until I was well beyond a marriageable age.

While I was considering the cost to my pride, and weighing that against my chances of escaping detection, my uncle said, "There's a matter I wish t' discuss with thee."

Lord Blackwood said nothing, and my uncle cleared his throat as though to make it seem his slowness to speak his thoughts had a physical excuse. The metal springs creaked as he shifted his sizeable bulk, and I knew that any issue that set my uncle to coughing and squirming could not possibly be small.

Now, I was burdened by curiosity, as well as my inclination to avoid punishment. My conscience wrestled with my wayward nature, but having lost this battle countless times before, it seemed unlikely to prevail. Then my uncle found the courage to continue his discourse, and the decision was made for me.

"I dislike to bother thee with my problems," he said, his voice unnaturally hoarse, "but what must be said, must be said. Seems I find myself in an embarrassing position—financially speaking." He cleared his throat again. "Thee'll never know how sorely I regret my folly, but I made several investments against the advice of my banker. At the time . . . well, that's neither here nor there. Thing is, two of them have been disappointments. T'other may, or may not, be a success, but 'twill be some time afore it shows a profit. Until then. . . ." His voice dwindled away. Then he said sharply, "Damme! When a man an't able to provide for his own family, 'tis a poor do. I'm hard put to keep my three sons at Oxford and run my household. If 'tweren't for our understanding, I'd be coming to thee, cap in hand, hoping to sell thee the wood. Now. . . ."

The springs creaked again.

"Perhaps a small loan?" his lordship said easily. "To tide you over until your fortunes change."

The squire sighed heavily. "I hate to ask. Never borrowed a penny afore t'day. But I don't know where else t' turn. Thee do see my position?"

My heart ached for my uncle. Being basically self-absorbed, I had had no real idea of the state of his finances, save that he had never been in a position to buy me the horse that I wanted. Part of me wished that I had been able to remain in sublime ignorance of his situation: I could not contribute a penny towards my upkeep; nor could I admit to a knowledge of his difficulties and offer my sympathies, since the news had not been intended for my ears. Yet another part of me railed against my thoughtlessness and resolved to go without the small luxuries which I had accepted without question.

But I had barely made this resolution before Lord Blackwood asked, "Would five thousand pounds sustain you?"

My uncle's spluttered cough covered the gasp that escaped me. Five thousand pounds could have kept us in comfort for ten years, possibly longer if the funds were well managed. " 'Twould be plenty and then some, t' be sure," he said when he regained his tongue.

"Then let us say no more of the matter. I will arrange to have the monies forwarded to you."

"I insist on paying thee interest, with the balance due in—would five years suit thee?"

"Were you to pay me interest, you would offend me. As for the sum itself, I shall not consider the amount due until the day you find yourself able to repay me."

"Bless thee," the squire exclaimed, echoing my own thoughts. "Thee's a true gentleman, and that's something that can't be said of every man who boasts a title. I don't mind telling thee how grateful we are that Charlotte's going t' thee. She's as dear t' me as any daughter of my own could ever be."

"She is a delightful young lady. I consider myself fortunate."

"I wish we might do half as well for Redigan," he said. "But there's no likelihood of that. 'Tis a shame she has neither her sister's beauty nor her sweet temper—though she's got a quick mind. But that'll do her no good unless she learns to hold her tongue. I fear thee'll be hard pressed to find a man willing to offer for her, dowry or not."

I burned with shame and a feeling of betrayal. For even if my uncle's words were true, I did not care to hear him admit as much to this man, of all people.

"She has her faults," Lord Blackwood replied with a

smug arrogance that infuriated me. "Of that I am keenly aware. I will apply a firm hand should it become necessary."

Just as I grimly vowed to bite him again, should he try, the squire said glumly, " 'Twould be better had she been born a boy."

Would that I were, I thought. For then I would not be treated like baggage to be handed from one caretaker to another, made to feel inferior for possessing an agile mind, denied the right to express my own opinions, and forced to live a life that had been chosen for me.

Fortunately, the urge to storm from my hiding place and confront the two men with that very opinion was thwarted. For at that moment, they rose and left the study, leaving me with my ears burning, my vanity deflated, and my feet and legs numb from having been cramped too long in the same position.

With a groan, I squeezed out from behind the chair, and I sat on the rug, setting my book beside me so that I might massage the blood back into my toes. All in all, I thought ruefully, I had not come off well that day. But before I could pull myself to my feet, I heard Lord Blackwood say, "I believe I have lost one of my shirt studs." His footsteps retraced their path down the hall, and I hastily dove back into the shelter of the draperies. They swayed around me as though blown by a vigorous wind, and I felt certain their motion would betray me.

Then the door swung open, and his lordship strode across the room. His steps paused as he reached the middle of the rug, the very spot where I had been sitting a few seconds before. I remembered with sudden horror that in my haste, I had not thought to pick up my book. Surely, he would notice. I held my breath, praying that somehow it would escape those sharp eyes.

Seemingly, my prayers were answered, for he

crossed to the chair at which he had been seated—I presumed to look for his missing shirt stud. It took him but a moment; then he walked back to the door.

There, he paused again. "I would not make a habit of crouching behind draperies, if I were you. It cannot be good for either your posture or your self-esteem."

With that, he went, leaving me thoroughly humiliated.

His lordship did not stay for dinner. Had he done so, I should have found myself suffering from the same indigestion which had troubled Charlotte. But even though he himself returned to Blackwood Hall, his presence remained behind to irk me.

Charlotte could talk of nothing else but the upcoming season. And when Aunt Emily informed us that his lordship had insisted we send for a seamstress who could make up the necessary outfits at his expense, Charlotte's enthusiasm spilled from her in an unending stream.

"It seems that you are no longer dreading your wedding day," I said acidly. "Has his lordship's appearance improved, then?"

"He is still ugly," Charlotte said with a sigh. "But at least he is a gentleman. I do not think he would insist that I kiss him if I felt unable."

"Ha! A lot you know of marriage," I retorted, and enjoyed seeing the flash of doubt my remark inspired. Then I felt guilty for my cruelty and said miserably, "Perhaps, you are right." But remembering the look he had given me in the drawing room, I doubted that Lord Blackwood would be stopped from taking his kisses if he determined to have them.

The blood rose in my cheeks afresh as I recalled the moment, but Charlotte failed to notice. She had already forgotten his lordship and was thinking of the dresses that would be hers.

My aunt sent for the seamstress who she always employed to make up our clothing. Miss Frederickson was a tall woman, with a head too small for her large-boned frame. With her hooked nose and her small black eyes, she put me in mind of a scavenging bird who perched above your head, watching until you mistakenly discarded something which could be used to its benefit.

Her previous trips to Briarslea had taught her that the squire could afford only the simplest styles and most inexpensive fabrics, and her scorn for us was ill concealed. Nor did she fail to point out, whenever she fitted me, that her efforts could scarce be expected to compensate for nature's oversights.

But hearing that our account was to be paid by Lord Blackwood, she arrived with her carriage filled with bolts of lawn, percale, and an array of colorful velvets. She also carried with her sketches of the most fanciful dresses I had ever seen—all of which, she assured us, were the latest London styles.

Lord Blackwood had advised our aunt to restrict us to those outfits which she thought absolutely necessary for the journey; anything else could be purchased upon our arrival in London. Agreeably, Aunt Emily told us we might choose a carriage dress for travelling and a single day dress. Charlotte pleaded for more, saying that his lordship had not meant us to be so forbearing. But she insisted that our woolen dresses, outmoded though they may have been, would supplement our wardrobe nicely.

Charlotte was disappointed to have her desires thwarted, but when it came to style and fabric, Aunt Emily let us make our own choices. It was Charlotte's first experience with unlimited wealth, and she adapted with more agility than she had shown in all of her seventeen years. Even I displayed an interest that I had not hitherto possessed.

But the results, when they arrived, were less wonderful than I had imagined. I looked passably attractive in the carriage dress, which was simply cut and decorated only by mancherons stitched along the shoulder seams. The garnet velvet I had chosen gave my eyes a golden hue which could, indeed, be called amber; and my coloring lost its sallow shade and turned creamy white. I hovered in front of the floor mirror, not daring to take my eyes off my reflection, lest I look back and find the improvement in my appearance was due to a trick of the light. Even my aunt was forced to look twice at me, and her eyes showed a glimmer of surprise.

But when I changed into the day dress, my hopes for a successful season were dashed. The white ruffs and the delicate pink chemise with its long train made me look like a wooden doll that someone had foolishly dressed in frills. My aunt shook her head sadly, as though once again reality had surfaced to destroy her hopes for me.

Charlotte, naturally, looked adorable in both of Miss Frederickson's creations. The ruff suited her oval face, and she had chosen a blue percale which flattered her eyes and made them look unnaturally huge.

"I do wish you would have taken my advice and chosen the green satin," Charlotte told me. "Anyone who clothes herself as carelessly as you do, cannot possibly have the faintest notion of what colors are, or are not, flattering to the complexion."

"It makes little difference what I wear," I said shortly. "I will never be anything but plain."

With a groan of exasperation, she left me alone to sulk.

Given the lengthy period that had passed between his first and second call upon the squire, I half expected that Lord Blackwood would forget to come again until long after the London season had ended. Surprisingly, he wasted little time in returning.

Charlotte lay abed when he arrived. The blankets swaddled her restless body, and the steady drone of her sniffles were broken only by resounding sneezes. A few weeks back, she would have been glad of any excuse to avoid her betrothed's company; now, she peevishly complained that the fates had conspired to make her suffer, and she begged me to express her gratitude to his lordship for his gifts as she was unable. Since she had expressed no more fondness for him than she had ever felt, I could only suppose that she had hoped to use this opportunity to avail herself of his generosity once again.

I had neither seen nor spoken to him since his last words in my uncle's study, and I would gladly have traded my good health and both of my new dresses for Charlotte's fever. But when my aunt summoned me to the drawing room, I had no choice but to trudge downstairs and face his lordship.

He rose politely, as somber and as dark a figure as he had ever been, and I could not tell if his thoughts still dwelt on my inexcusable behavior. From his impassive expression, one might have assumed the incident in the study had never happened.

I curtsied and relayed Charlotte's message, disconsolately adding my own words of appreciation for the dresses I had been given.

Lord Blackwood's lips twitched at the corners, and with shrewd insight, he replied, "You may find the London seamstresses more to your liking."

Unreasonably, I resented his perceptiveness, and coldly replied that our seamstress was the best in the county—though, until that day, I had heard none but Miss Frederickson express that opinion, and it had been one I did not support.

"I am sure she is excellent," his lordship agreed politely, but his answer, instead of mollifying me, only served to irritate me further.

My sullenness agitated Aunt Emily, and she nervously tapped her wrist with her fan. "What is the matter with you, Redigan?" she demanded and advised his lordship, "She is turning into such a moody child."

"The sights of London will cheer her immeasurably."

"One can only hope that she displays more grace while she is there, or the entire trip will be for naught," my aunt replied, continuing to refer to me as though I had not been standing before her. At last, she bestowed her attentions on me. "Go and change into your riding habit," she commanded. "Lord Blackwood requires the squire's signature on some papers, but he is overseeing the work being done on the new irrigation system and unlikely to be home before nightfall. You are to conduct his lordship to the south fields." At that, she turned again to our guest. "My husband has been experimenting with some new methods which he hopes will cut costs and yet increase his harvest. You may find the process interesting." Before he could reply, she added, "Do hurry, Redigan. His lordship cannot be expected to wait on you forever."

I did not, as was my wont when given the opportunity to go riding, rush to my room, my fingers fumbling with the fastenings on my dress as I went. Instead, I dawdled, chattering to an uninterested Charlotte and defiantly prolonging each moment. At last, the maid tapped on our bedroom door and said that her mistress had sent her upstairs to see if I needed help.

"I am just finishing," I assured her, realizing my aunt would not stand for another second's delay.

Indeed, she looked most annoyed when I finally appeared, but his lordship, having no notion of the speed with which I usually dressed, did not seem disconcerted by his long wait. On our walk to the stables, it struck me that the last time we had both been there was the day that I had pretended to be the stableboy. The memory was not reassuring, and when I glanced at his lordship to see if the same thought had also occurred to him, he responded to my look with a broad grin.

Annoyed, I averted my eyes.

Henry had our mounts saddled and waiting. Lord Blackwood's horse was not the gelding I remembered, but a dappled mare whose tossing head and alert black eyes hinted at an unmanageable temper. I fancied that she eyed me with jealousy when she saw me at her master's side, then silently chided myself for being foolish. Assuredly, his lordship was not the sort of man who could win that intense a devotion from *any* creature.

Bessie, my lazy little pony, had died two years back, and since my uncle could not afford to replace her, he had reluctantly given me permission to ride Maribelle, James's mare. She had an uncertain temper, but had lost the friskiness of her youth. Thanks to those long runs we had taken along the cliffs, I had no difficulty in handling her, and my uncle's fears were quickly allayed.

Still, we were an oddly matched pair as we cantered down the lane. His lordship was dressed in the height of elegance, riding a spirited beast, the like of which was rarely seen in this area, save at his own stables. I felt sadly out of place, dressed in a riding habit that had originally belonged to Aunt Emily before she grew too stout and had the outfit made over for me. It was a cumbersome thing, with voluminous skirts that made riding far more difficult than it had been when I enjoyed the freedom and comfort of Peter's breeches. Half hidden beneath yards of heavy fabric, my mare thudded along complacently as though she were more closely related to a plow horse than a thoroughbred.

After a short silence, Lord Blackwood turned to me and said, "I fear I have deceived your aunt by suggesting that you accompany me this afternoon. I am quite familiar with the countryside hereabouts, but there was something I wished to discuss with you."

I listened with greater curiosity than I was willing to display.

He hesitated, showing the only signs of uneasiness that he had ever betrayed in all the time I had known him. Then he plunged on. "It occurs to me that, of all the Grenfels, you more than any are likely to be Charlotte's confidante. Has she shared with you her feelings about our betrothal?"

"We have spoken of it," I admitted, thinking he would know me for a liar if I said otherwise.

"Do you think she has come to accept me?"

"You have gone a long way in easing her doubts," I said, not entirely sure this was true.

"I fear that I am not the husband she envisioned."

"You are almost a stranger to her," I reminded him. "And. . . ."

"And this face of mine does not set maidenly hearts aflutter," he finished.

"I did not mean to be rude."

"Rather, let us say forthright."

"Then I did not mean to be forthright."

He lazily arched an eyebrow. "It has never concerned you before."

I blushed, for his remark was nothing less than the truth. "My aunt has warned me that young ladies who are forthright are seldom well liked."

He laughed again, a low chuckle that grew until it filled my ears with its deep resonance. I must say, I found the sound pleasant, as much for its warmth as for its rarity. And when he laughed, his eyes lost their wariness and crinkled at the corners.

He broke off and caught me studying him. I hastily averted my eyes, and to cover my embarrassment, I asked, "Would you like to race? First one to reach the end of the lane is the winner."

Without waiting for him to agree, I urged Maribelle into a furious run, and was several lengths ahead of him before he responded to my challenge. In a fair race, we were no match for his lordship and his feisty mount, but Maribelle had only my light weight to carry as well as the added advantage of a head start. I believed we could beat him. Suddenly, nothing else mattered but that I should defeat Lord Blackwood.

The stone hedges that edged the fields ran together in a blurred gray line. Mud splattered onto my riding habit, and my full skirts flapped wildly in the wind. Maribelle's legs relentlessly rose and fell in the jarring pace I knew so well.

Then I heard the rapid beat of the mare's hooves hammering nearby, and I glanced behind to see the gap between us had closed. His lordship pulled abreast of me with annoying ease.

The end of the lane lay fifty yards distant, too far away for me to stave off defeat. My mouth twisted with bitter disappointment, and I yelled at Maribelle to spur her on.

To my surprise, I gained an inch of the headway I had lost. Another inch followed, and we were a length ahead when the lane dropped away and we thudded across the grassy slopes along the cliff tops.

Our pace slowed, and he fell in beside me and offered his congratulations.

I looked at him suspiciously. His mare was not the least bit winded, while Maribelle's sides heaved. "For what?" I retorted. "Had you not pulled up at the end, you would surely have won."

He acknowledged the truth of my words with a grin. "Forgive me. But the race seemed important to you. I cannot say that, to me, the outcome much mattered."

"I am not a child who must be allowed to win," I said, sounding very much like a child indeed. But I disliked being patronized, and if I could not win fairly, there was no point in winning at all. "Besides," I added petulantly, "had I a better mount, I believe I would have won. But we have not a horse in our stables to compare with yours."

"Indeed, you do not," he agreed complacently. "I doubt there is a horse in all of Cornwall who could beat my Miranda in a fair race. You have an eye for good breeding. And I must say, your skill as a horsewoman impresses me greatly."

There was nothing in his expression to suggest that the compliment was mere flattery. Moreover, a marked look of approval shone from his eyes. Perhaps, I thought as I smiled back at him, Charlotte is less to be pitied than I imagined. And, in that moment, I ceased to think of him as ugly.

Chapter Four

THE COACH RATTLED and lurched along the narrow lane, swaying precariously as the huge wheels struggled to take each curve in the road and remain upright. Every jolt threatened to hurl me onto the floorboards or send me toppling against a white-faced Charlotte. Her battered bonnet and crumpled dress mutely reproached me for the abuse she had suffered. I supposed I looked no better, having more than once endured being knocked against the far wall, only to receive a second bruising when Charlotte promptly slid across the narrow seat and slammed into me. Across from us, Aunt Emily sat with her feet braced and volubly prayed for our safe deliverance.

Briarslea had long since disappeared behind the rolling hills and wooded copses. Tiny hamlets and neat farms, bordered by low stone hedges, their outlines smudged by drifts of fog, were captured briefly in the coach windows as we rolled past. Somewhere ahead lay Bodmin and the Bodmin-Launceston highway—or so our driver had assured us when we had paused at a wayside tavern to enjoy our breakfast.

The brief respite had failed to restore our spirits. The shepherd's pie we had hungrily devoured may have been hot and filling, but what the tavernkeeper had lacked in salt for seasoning his pies, he had more than made up for by liberally sprinkling the meat with pepper. Each mouthful had been hastily followed by gulps of icy well water, poured from the earthenware pitcher that sat at the end of our table.

The effects of such a meal should have been plain to all of us, and we had travelled but a short distance from the inn before we discovered the imprudence of stuffing ourselves with highly seasoned food. Aunt Emily's face was decidedly anxious, and every minute or two she cast doubtful looks at Charlotte, whose cheeks had now darkened to a motley green.

My own stomach rolled queasily, further aggravated by the scent of rose water and shaving soap which clung to the leather interior. The faint odor had lingered long after the men and women who had previously rode in the coach had arrived at their destination and disembarked. Upon first taking my seat, I had thought the scent delightful. Now I ached for a single breath of fresh air.

"I am going to be sick," Charlotte burst out with a sudden cry of dismay. Her hands flew to her mouth.

Aunt Emily rapped on the roof, but the horses continued their headlong rush with no sign of stopping. The driver, the sour set of his mouth displaying his resentment for the vagaries of all gentlewomen, had warned us to do our business before we had left the inn. Now, he stubbornly ignored our pleas.

To be fair, his indifference was not due entirely to unfair prejudice. Pools of water, a good six inches deep, spread across every low-lying stretch of lane and collected at the bottom of each dip and hollow. Having once braked, the coach would likely have settled into the mud up to its axles and remained there. Freeing the wheels would have required hiring a team of oxen, if one could be found, and wasted several hours of daylight.

"Aunt Emily," Charlotte cried again, her eyes filling with panic.

"Put your head out the window, child. There is nothing else for it."

The order came not a second too soon. After an interminable spell of loud retching, which did nothing to quiet the biliousness in my own stomach, she returned to her seat. Her face looked paler but immeasurably relieved. It was a relief Aunt Emily and I soon shared as first she, and then I, gave vent to our portions of the offensive shepherd's pie.

I could only be grateful that Lord Blackwood had seen fit to provide us with one of his own coaches, rather than letting us "be subjected to the rude travelling companions who fill the public conveyances," as were his exact words. To have behaved in this revolting fashion while being scrutinized by strangers would have been humiliating to the utmost degree.

As impressive as the coach had first seemed, with its green leather upholstery and the Blackwood coat of arms—three elms in black on a gold shield—emblazoned upon the door, when we tottered down from its seats at midday, I reviled it as an instrument of torture. Aunt Emily looked dazed and Charlotte near to tears. I took my sister's arm while the innkeeper helped our aunt into a chair near the blazing fire.

There seemed little point in ordering a luncheon that none of us could eat. I glowered with hatred for our driver and footman who gladly wolfed down a meat pasty and a mug of hot apple cider, and wondered if one could be hung for committing murder under such justifiable circumstances.

But upon reaching the turnpike road at Bodmin, the jouncing and rocking diminished, and our fears of being mired down in mud gave way to awe and appreciation for the great road that had been driven over the moors. Thenceforth, our driver continued at a moderate pace, showing greater caution and respect for our personages—or possibly for his own—and though it would be some days before our arrival, we lived in hope of reaching London alive and undamaged.

"I did not imagine it to be half so large," Charlotte exclaimed as she pulled her face back from the window. "Nor even a quarter." Her incredulous expression mirrored my own feelings, though I determinedly hid them behind an air of composure.

The city of London swelled around our small coach like the gaping mouth of the fish that had swallowed Jonah, and like Jonah I felt we had descended into the gloomy bowels of some monstrous creature.

Smoke poured into the air from the endless rows of chimneys poking from the rooftops and the grayness engulfed the city. Buildings, uniformly blackened with soot, squeezed between their neighbors as though space was too scant, too dear for them to be allowed to swell to their full width. Only the gaudy colors in the shop windows protested against the general dinginess.

The streets were congested with every manner of traffic. Carts, chaises, coaches, and wagons vied with pedestrians and the conglomeration of livestock being driven to market. Liveried drivers perched high on the seats of carriages. Farmers, damp patches spreading down the backs of their smocks and beneath the rolled arms of their sleeves, hunched over barrows of fruit and vegetables and untiringly inched forward through the teeming morass.

"I cannot recall ever seeing so many people in one place!" Charlotte exclaimed, having no memory of her early days in Calcutta.

Bootblacks, with grimy faces and tattered breeches, stood at every corner and accosted gentlemen in beaver hats, eagerly offering to rid their boots of the soot that had settled on them. Soldiers, in their regimentals of scarlet and blue, were everywhere.

"And it has been many years since I have heard such an unholy din," I added.

The steady clop of countless horseshoes melded into an unbroken stream of sound from which no one hoof-beat was discernible. Wheels ground against the cobblestones like a low roll of thunder, and mingled with the din of merchants hawking their wares, and the bleats, snorts, and lowing of the animals.

Worst of all was the smell that wafted into the coach, a stench of smoke and sulfur saturated with the odor of dung and unwashed bodies. My nose wrinkled with disgust.

Surely this cannot be London, I said to myself, for what a dreadful place. Never had I been so disappointed. Even Charlotte's excitement had waned and she stared in glum silence. Silently, I vowed that should I be lucky enough to receive an offer of marriage, I would not accept any man who chose to spend his days locked inside this gray prison of a city.

But my mood cheered considerably as we progressed into the West End. Here, the streets grew quieter as the markets dropped behind us. Being but midday, the hour was still too early for fashionable ladies and gentlemen to be about; but those men and women we passed in the street looked cleaner and more respectable, and they hastened about their business with a sense of destination and urgency that marked them as satisfactorily employed.

Lady Elizabeth Coudrey, nee Blackwood, lived in Mayfair, in a townhouse overlooking Grosvenor Square. Coudrey House was a stately brown brick building, set several steps back from the road, like a modest but elegant lady.

As the coach pulled abreast of the steps, our driver braked abruptly, dealing us one last jolt without which, I supposed, our journey could not have been deemed complete.

The footman promptly descended and mounted the steps where he lifted and let fall the heavy brass knocker. As the door swung open, he straightened and stiffly announced our presence.

"One would think he was announcing the Prince of Wales," I said, noting his pretentious manner with amused dismay. I smoothed my crushed skirts and glanced anxiously at my hands which were grimy with soot. None of us were at our best. But since the invitation to Coudrey House had been issued at her brother's request, I could only hope that Lady Elizabeth was predisposed to think well of us, despite our less than imposing appearance.

I had little time to devote to my doubts, for our footman quickly returned to help us down. Leaving him to tend to our luggage, we made our way up the steps.

Her ladyship's footman admitted us with an exaggerated bow, his face suffused with his own importance. His protuberant blue eyes flickered over us as he brushed a speck of lint from his spotlessly white gloves. His disdain for our party was undisguised, and I guessed that his opinion of us would be delivered in scathing tones in the servants' hall that evening. Even Charlotte's prettiness had suffered from the strain of these last few days: Her face had a peaked look and her eyes were puffy from restless nights.

But we did not have to suffer his scrutiny for long. From out of the shadows of the dimly lit entry hall came a woman. Until that moment, none of us had noticed her. She was a diminutive whisper of a woman, with neatly combed hair and quiet eyes the same shade as her dove-gray dress. Her delicate hands were clasped modestly before her.

"Lady Elizabeth," Aunt Emily said warmly. "It is most kind of you to invite us."

"Goodness, ma'am," the woman replied in a startled voice. "Lady Elizabeth is my mistress. I am Mrs. Garrett, the housekeeper. Her ladyship was called away yesterday morning to see to her daughter. She has been unwell. My mistress left instructions that you were to be made comfortable if you arrived before her return."

"Oh, to be sure. That was good of her," Aunt Emily said, flustered by her error and sounding faintly disappointed. I suspected that I was not the only one who had hoped this unassuming woman was our hostess.

"Harris will see to your luggage. If you would come this way, I will show you to your rooms."

A marble staircase, graced by a carved mahogany bannister, swept up to the first floor from the entry hall; gas lights, set in silver sconces, lit our way and cast faint circles of light across the patterned wallpaper and the portraits that hung in a somber line above our heads.

Mrs. Garrett hurried up the stairs with the agility of a child. We trailed after her, our muscles stiff from being cramped together in the coach. I would not be able to walk properly for a week and the thought of trying to ride a horse made me shudder.

"Lady Elizabeth thought the Rose Velvet suite would do nicely. It has two rooms that let out onto a sitting room, and the bay windows have a lovely view of the park. It means the young ladies will have to share a bed, but my mistress remembered the year she and her cousin came out. They enjoyed talking together after the balls so much."

"Her ladyship is quite right in her assumption," Aunt Emily assured her. "The girls have always shared a room before, and they are very close." Her voice rang with such sincerity that I wondered if she might not be telling the truth.

Mrs. Garrett smiled, giving my aunt the first look of approval we had seen since entering Coudrey House. "The maid will be up shortly with hot water. She can help you unpack your things. Shall I send up some tea and a few cakes as well?"

"Please do not put yourself to any trouble on our account. The girls and I can wait until dinner."

The look of approval promptly vanished from Mrs.

Garrett's quiet features, and I saw that she would have had greater respect for us if we had put her to some difficulty. If it is a troublesome temperament they demand, I mused, then long before this season's end, likely I shall have won their hearts. The thought was encouraging, but Mrs. Garrett left before I could put her to any tests, leaving us to relax and examine our surroundings.

The Rose Velvet suite was aptly named. The draperies, the velvet-upholstered settees, and the thick carpet with its heavily patterned design were preponderantly a muted shade of dusky rose, rich but not gaudy; and on the walls hung dozens of gilt-framed cameos and watercolors, idyllic pastoral scenes or still-lifes, each holding touches of the soft rose tones.

"The bedrooms have been done in the same fashion," Charlotte exclaimed with a rapturous smile. "Do come and look."

"Not until I have taken off my shoes," I said flatly, and collapsed on the settee with a groan of protest so that I could unbuckle them. "I cannot understand how feet can swell when they have not been walked upon for days."

"You are disgusting," Charlotte said. "And do pick up your shoes. Lady Elizabeth will think we were brought up in a pigsty."

"If she hears what her household has to say of us, she will think much worse. What a sorry lot we make. I cannot imagine what the beau monde will think of us, if we cannot even impress the servants."

"Pooh! Who cares about the opinion of an inflated butler or an ancient housekeeper?"

I glanced at her out of the corners of my eyes, trying to decide if she was sincere. Her face was innocent of pretense, and I reluctantly gave her credit for more self-assurance than I possessed. But Charlotte had been trained in the drawing room while I lay about the stables, and she had the distinction of being Lord Blackwood's betrothed. Why should the attitudes of two servants cause her distress?

But if she did not care for the opinion of Coudrey House's servants, Charlotte greatly desired to make an impression on its mistress. While Aunt Emily napped and I lolled on the window seat, rubbing my pinched toes and staring down curiously at the occupants of every carriage that rolled past, she washed herself and took down her hair, then carefully brushed out the tangles.

Her new day dress was consigned to the care of the maid, along with Aunt Emily's and my own, each to be pressed and returned. Hers, she donned the moment it was returned to her, then she sat down on the settee and prepared to wait for Lady Elizabeth to return home.

"You are a ninny," I told her. "She might not come back until late. Then what will you do?"

"I will undress and go to bed. But should she return while you still look like a chimney sweep, what will *you* do?"

I considered the question and saw her reasoning. Even Aunt Emily had taken the time to clean herself thoroughly and change into her best wrapper before she lay down. I had managed only a few swipes to remove the worst of the grime, then decided that nothing less than a hot bath would do the job properly and, having expressed that opinion, gave up entirely. Now, it looked as if I would be well-advised to make more of an effort.

As I lazily deliberated there was a tap on the door. Charlotte looked at me meaningfully.

"No doubt it is the maid," I said and crossly called out, "Come in."

The door swung open wide to reveal the startled face of a woman who could have been none other than Lady Elizabeth Coudrey. She was a milder version of

her fierce-looking brother. Silver curls threaded
through her short-cropped dark hair, and her eyes
were more hazel than green. But I saw in them the
same perceptive light that marked his, softened by a
look of purely feminine wisdom. But the prominent
cheekbones and finely carved mouth could have made
her his twin.

She was above average in height and slender, and
though she must have been nearly forty, her silhouette
was that of a much younger woman. Her muslin day
dress was so fine as to be almost transparent, and the
scooped neckline dropped almost to the tips of her
breasts. Her attire, and my own rudeness in admitting
her so brusquely, made me gasp.

"Is that the maid?" Aunt Emily asked, as she walked
out of the bedroom. "I wanted to ask—bless my soul.
Lady Elizabeth." This time she spoke with absolute assurance; confronted by her poise and dignity, it would
have been impossible to mistake her ladyship's identity.

Her ladyship smiled graciously. "Mrs. Garrett said
you had arrived. Welcome to Coudrey House." She
moved into the center of the room and gave Aunt
Emily a hug. "You must call me Elizabeth. There need
be no formality between us. I have looked forward to
making your acquaintances ever since Nicholas wrote
and told me of his intentions. It is high time he remar-
ried." She took my sister's hands and looked into her
eyes with an appraising look. "You would be Charlotte,
of course. I can see why you captivated him. You are
a beauty. I hope you will think of me as your sister from
this day forth."

"Oh, how kind you are," Charlotte said, throwing herself into her arms. "I was so afraid that you would not
like me."

"Nonsense, dear." Elizabeth seemed taken aback by
her candor and girlish impulsiveness. "I find you quite
delightful."

She gently disentangled herself and allowed her gaze to move to the window seat where I was curled up, in a magnificent state of disarray. Her eyes clouded with misgiving, and her dark brows drew a shade nearer together.

Rather than wait for her to think of some evasively polite remark I rose and announced, "I fear your brother has given you an impossible task. I have quite reconciled myself to the likelihood that I will return to Cornwall as unattached as the day I departed. You must not concern yourself overly much with me."

Her eyebrows arched. "On the contrary. I think I must concern myself with you more than ever. You seem determined to throw in your hand before the game has begun."

Nettled by this apt assessment, I retorted, "Suit yourself, then. But it is of little consequence to me—" My aunt gave a gasp of dismay which I ignored. "For I am not possessed of a temperament that is suited to marriage."

"Which of us is?" Elizabeth asked coolly. "Until men value themselves less and women more, marriage will be a chancy prospect at best. Why else would I have remained a widow for almost fifteen years? Still," she added, "if you think your temperament unsuited to marriage, then likely you would find yourself less suited to the life of a governess or a companion. And unless you are independently wealthy, which quite clearly you are not"—this she emphasized with a tartness that matched my own—"then your efforts must be directed to winning the interest of a wealthy man with precarious health. Then he can oblige you by dying forthwith and freeing you to live life as you choose."

I stared at her open-mouthed, finally at a loss for words, and tried to decide if her advice was merely the sarcastic set-down I deserved or if she truly believed that the life of a widow was preferable to that of a wife.

On the whole, I decided at last, it seemed a sensible attitude.

But Charlotte's face was aghast, and Aunt Emily looked as though she wanted to swoon and dared not lest our hostess take offense. Instead, she rounded on me, saying, "Redigan, his lordship's sister will think I have raised you entirely without manners. Not another word from you if you cannot be gracious." Her annoyance safely dispatched, she turned to our hostess and smiled weakly. "You must forgive my niece. The trip has left us in poor humor, and they are quite at sixes and sevens faced with the prospect of entering society."

Elizabeth's eyes narrowed speculatively, and I suspected she realized full well that my outburst was entirely in keeping with my usual behavior. But to my aunt, she said only, "I quite understand. The journey is dreadful in the best of weather. How long has it been since you dined?"

The first week of our stay at Coudrey House was devoted to establishing ourselves as ladies of fashion. This required an extensive and costly wardrobe. Elizabeth descended upon us early one morning and ruthlessly dismissed the dresses we had brought with us as "entirely unsuitable."

"But our day dresses are new and we have worn them only once," Charlotte protested, reluctant to see them tossed aside.

But she would not be budged from her decision. "It is a charming color, but a good four years out of style. You would be the laughingstock of all London were you to be seen in them. And Nicholas would never forgive me if I failed to keep my promise to see you properly turned out." She forestalled any more protests by adding severely, "You must think of Redigan, my dear. Your future is already secure, but she has yet to find a husband. Do you want her to become known as the sister of that 'delightfully pretty, but oh, so *provincial* Miss Grenfel?'" She delivered her pronouncement with a polite condescension that left us in no doubt as to the kind of verbal assault our attire would provoke.

Having handily dealt with our objections, she sent a message round to a woman who she said could be trusted to take our measurements and stitch up the essential garments without passing along gossip of an unflattering nature.

"Does that mean," I questioned, "that she can be trusted to pass along gossip of a *flattering* nature?"

Lady Elizabeth gave me a measured look. "That, you can leave to me." She pulled out the ribbons which tied back my hair and unraveled my braids. "Your hair is much too long. It will have to be cut."

I looked at her aghast. "There is little enough of beauty about me already. You shall not cut my hair."

"Long hair is unfashionable. Charlotte's, too, must be shortened."

"Charlotte may do as she pleases, but I will not cut off so much as an inch." My chin jutted out mulishly.

Elizabeth's lips set in a firm line as she studied my face. Then she shrugged. "Very well. I will send you my lady's maid to see what she can do. Perhaps the length of your hair will give you some distinction. She had better pluck your brows while she is about it. They are unruly and much too thick. One can barely appreciate the interesting color of your eyes."

The battle was not the last we fought, but it was the only one in which I got the better of her. Even Aunt Emily, who protested she had no need to impress the young bloods, was forced to give way beneath the woman's relentless determination to give us at least the appearance of sophistication.

Lord Blackwood reached London the following week and settled into the apartments he kept near Portman Square. He immediately sent round a message, telling us of his arrival, but it was not until the afternoon of the following day that he called upon his sister.

Having expected him to visit her with an eye to apprizing himself of our progress, Elizabeth had overseen our toilette that afternoon. As she looked on, her brow wrinkled and mouth pursed with dissatisfaction, we were twisted and turned, our hems checked for stray threads, our stays tightened, and our hairstyles poked and prodded until my head felt as though it had been punctured clear through.

"Is this what it is like to have a season?" I demanded, tiring of being treated like a prize bull, my mouth pursing petulantly.

"For goodness' sakes, smile. The prettiest dress cannot erase a disconsolate expression. I suppose you have no jewelry of any consequence?"

"None," I replied, exasperated by her utter disregard of my feelings and delighted to thwart her desires in any manner, no matter how small.

"I shall have to prevail upon Nicholas to find something suitable. Until then. . . ." She picked up three rosebuds of deep purplish pink and pinned them into my hair above my ear, yanking on a spot that was already tender as she did so. "Yes, that will do nicely. Charlotte, I think the violets would go nicely with your short curls. Then, if your aunt is willing, I believe we can make an appearance."

Aunt Emily immediately presented herself, for had she been unready she would not have dared to keep Elizabeth waiting. As we prepared to descend, I took a surreptitious peek at myself in the tall looking glass, too overcome by curiosity to sweep by and not deign to give it a single glance. To my amazement, I could not find my own reflection. Then I realized the tall, stately creature that peered back at me with startled eyes was myself, and I stared unashamedly.

Waves of hair had been drawn back from my face and fastened by a cluster of tiny rosebuds. The wide, square neckline of the muslin dress revealed a long neck and shapely shoulders; the satin ribbon tied beneath the bodice made my bosom look delicately appealing; and the clinging skirts emphasized the slenderness of my figure in a manner that seemed willowy and fragile.

I could barely credit the transformation. The carriage dress had only hinted at the possibilities that had flourished beneath Elizabeth's determined supervision. Now, she paused in the doorway and turned to me.

"Well?" she asked.

"I look quite . . . quite . . . presentable," I said at last.

She smiled. "You will never set men duelling, nor throw them in the depths of despair because you failed to bestow upon them a single glance, but there is every reason to hope you will make a good marriage."

I grinned. "With some gentleman of precarious health?"

"If not, doubtless his health will worsen drastically when he discovers what an impossible creature he has taken for a wife." She laughed warmly, and I knew she harbored no ill feelings for the trouble I had given her.

The drawing room lay directly off the entry hall and occupied a good quarter of Coudrey House's ground floor. It was decorated in shades of blue—Elizabeth seeming to prefer to keep her rooms predominantly one hue. The technique did give the room, with its high-vaulted ceilings, three-tiered chandelier, and silver-gilt sconces, an added touch of elegance; and the sense of clutter that was found in many a drawing room was absent—due, I supposed, to the gentle harmony of color.

Lord Blackwood rose from his chair as we entered and greeted his sister with an amused smile that suggested he knew full well how difficult the last week must have been for her.

"How good it is to see you back in London," she said, offering her cheek to be kissed. "Everyone has missed you. La! It has been nearly seven years, not since your mar—" She broke off with a quick glance at Charlotte. "Yes, well, it is good to have you back. I had almost forgotten what you looked like."

"But I have not forgotten how beautiful you are," he assured her. "If you were not my own sister, I believe I would fancy myself in love with you."

As he spoke, I absorbed him with my eyes. His dark hair curled becomingly over his starched collar, and the familiar scent of his cologne set my heart beating anxiously as I waited for him to mark the difference in my appearance. Suddenly, I cared wholeheartedly that Elizabeth's hard-wrung changes did not fall short of his expectations.

Unaware of the eagerness with which I awaited his approval, he bowed politely to my aunt and complimented her on looking more like a lady of fashion than women who came every year to London. Aunt Emily beamed and graciously thanked him for his generosity, her flow of praise ceasing only when he interrupted and begged her not to mention mere trifles.

Then Charlotte moved forward to greet him. Her tousled blonde curls gently brushed across her forehead, framing and exaggerating the sapphire blue shade of her eyes; the creamy tops of her full breasts rose discreetly above the low cut of the neckline. She dipped into a well-practiced curtsy that was spoiled only slightly when she glanced at his cheek and hastily averted her eyes.

He stiffened, but a look of admiration crossed his face as he gazed upon her, and a burst of jealousy flowed within me. If I had approached him first, he might have been suitably appreciative, but how could I compare with her loveliness? I wanted to dash from the room before being forced to see myself through his eyes and accept that nothing had changed.

"And here is Redigan," Elizabeth said, beckoning me to come forward. "What have you to say?"

Unwillingly, I did as I was bid and made a simple curtsy, knowing instinctively that trying to mimic Charlotte's gracefulness would only make me look awkward. Then slowly I raised my eyes to his, not daring to breathe until I had seen the look in his face.

To my dismay, his welcoming smile lacked even a glimmer of surprise. I might as well have been wearing my cousin's breeches, my face smeared with dirt, for nothing about his expression suggested he found me altered or improved.

Nor was there a difference, I told myself crossly. For while I might deceive myself, I was not likely to deceive anyone else. I lifted my chin defiantly as the tears threatened to flow.

Then he bowed to me. "I must compliment you on a job well done, dear sister," he said, his gaze lingering on me. "But, I admit, I expected nothing less. Redigan has always displayed a potential that has hitherto gone unnoticed."

"Except by you?" his sister asked, in the slightly mocking tone she often employed.

"It is a habit of mine to look beyond the surface. Could I not do so, I doubt that I could bring myself to look upon my own image."

"Then you must consider that scar a fortunate accident. Most men, I have found, are far too willing to admire themselves, and with far less reason."

He raised his gaze to hers. "Should I take that as a compliment?"

"It is as close to one as you shall receive from me, this day or any other."

"Then I will consider it fine flattery, indeed."

Their banter drifted over my head. I was beyond hearing, beyond thinking of anything save that he was pleased with me. I wondered if all the compliments that had been paid Charlotte were a tenth as sweet as the pleasure he had given me by merely *expecting* that I would make a creditable showing.

Chapter Five

My HAPPINESS kept me in a pleasant haze for the rest of that day. Twice Aunt Emily asked me if I was unwell, her concern provoked by my uncharacteristic silence. Long after we had retired to our suite, leaving Elizabeth to enjoy her brother's company undisturbed, my mind dwelt on that moment when his lordship had informed her that he had always been aware of my "potential."

It occurred to me then that my new self-esteem had been bought at great effort by Elizabeth, and my complacency gave way to agonies of shame for having treated her so rudely. Nothing could satisfy me but that I must immediately beg her forgiveness and promise to cause her no more aggravation in the future.

Aunt Emily, having become accustomed to early risings over the twenty-five years of her marriage, had already gone to bed; and Charlotte drowsed on the settee, a copy of *La Belle Assemblée* open on her lap. Whispering an excuse that failed to stir an answering murmur, I slipped from the room.

I had assumed that his lordship had already taken his leave, but as I approached the drawing room I heard them speaking, and their voices carried into the hallway.

"When will you announce your engagement?" Elizabeth was asking. "I thought to give a ball at the end of this month. If you have no objection, it would please me to have you state your intentions then."

"But I do object," he replied, a note of firmness in his voice. "I object most strenuously. I have decided to wait until the end of the season before disclosing my plans."

"You cannot be serious?" His sister's surprise echoed my own.

"I assure you, I am."

"Really, Nicholas. Since you have never been a fool, then I must accuse you of the utmost arrogance. The child is plainly a beauty, and you are not the kind of man who appeals to maidenly tastes. At the moment, she is awed by your title and grateful for your generosity. By the end of the season—"

"By the end of the season she will have won the hearts of any number of men, from families whose lineage is more impeccable than mine and whose unscathed countenances—"

"Whose unscathed countenances will not cause her to avert her eyes," Elizabeth said sharply and the cruelty of her words made me cringe. "Make your intentions towards Charlotte plain as soon as possible or, at best, she will fall in love with someone else and only marry you out of a sense of obligation and duty. Or if she has any spirit, she will spurn you and her uncle's wishes and elope."

"How kind of you to point out my limited appeal," her brother said dryly. "But remember, dear sister, I have failed at marriage once, and my freedom was gained at an unpleasant cost."

His words surprised me. It had not occurred to me that his first marriage might have been an unhappy one. The fault, I felt certain, must have lain with the woman he had married, for I could not imagine any woman being dissatisfied with Lord Blackwood—unless, perhaps, she was as silly as Charlotte.

But his lordship did not wait upon my reflection. "I

do not care to repeat the error," he continued. "Let her come to me at the end of the season, knowing that I am the man she wishes to marry. I will accept nothing less."

"And if she does not?"

"Surely you think enough of my virtues to believe I can win her love?"

"Are you sure she has the intelligence to appreciate those virtues. Charlotte is a sweet child, but you cannot claim that she possesses a discriminating mind. Had she her sister's intelligence—"

"My mind is made up," he said coldly, refusing to listen further. "The matter is settled."

I heard him rise and hurried to conceal myself in a nearby doorway. I flattened into the shadows as he strode from the room and walked off down the hallway to the front door.

After a long minute, I tapped softly on the drawing room door. Elizabeth stood at the windows, a worried frown creasing her brow as she watched her brother depart. She turned her head as I entered.

"Redigan," she exclaimed, with a note of surprise. "Is something the matter?"

"No, nothing. I came downstairs to thank you for everything you have done for me, and apologize for making your work more difficult than was necessary," I said awkwardly.

She looked at me and her eyes narrowed. "And, doubtless, overheard much of what passed between Nicholas and myself." She strode across the room and, with a savageness that startled me, said, "Men—all men—are fools beyond belief!"

Elizabeth rose later than usual the next day, not showing her face in the saloon until well after the rest of us had breakfasted, and the hollows of her cheeks seemed darker than usual. After scanning the platters on the laden sideboard, she poised over a dish of plump sausages and casually remarked, "Nicholas has decided to wait until the end of the season to announce his engagement to Charlotte. He would . . . would not like to inhibit her enjoyment of the festivities." She looked at Charlotte and smiled hopefully. "Unless, of course, you would prefer him to make his intentions clear from the beginning. It will give you a status the other young ladies lack, and I am certain he could be persuaded otherwise should *you* choose to ask him."

But Charlotte, I knew, had her hopes set on being considered the reigning belle of the season, a position she believed beyond her grasp solely because of her early betrothal. Her face alight with happiness, she replied, "But I am delighted with the arrangement. How like him to think of my pleasure."

Elizabeth's smile tightened but she said evenly, "Then I will let him know his decision has met with your approval."

Not if I have any say in this, I thought. And though I had privately resolved not to repeat a word of their conversation, I could certainly take Charlotte aside and denounce both his lordship's decision and her acceptance as shockingly inappropriate. It annoyed me that she could treat him so carelessly after all he had done for us.

The breakfast dishes had not yet been cleared away when the footman stepped briskly into the saloon, made a stiff bow, and announced Lord Blackwood's presence in the entry hall.

"Show him to the drawing room, Harris. We will join him there."

"As you wish, milady."

Lord Blackwood's face showed no sign that his sister's words had robbed him of his usual sleep. Good temper shone in his green eyes, and his lips curved with gentle humor. Bowing first to Charlotte, he remarked solemnly, "I believe you grow prettier with each day that passes." He raised her hand to his lips.

Charlotte glossed over the initial nervousness she always displayed on coming into his company by effusively thanking him for delaying an official announcement of their engagement. "I do not deserve such kindness," she exclaimed, oblivious to my own wholehearted agreement and the weary look in Elizabeth's eyes. But having told him of her agreement, Charlotte had unwittingly forestalled us from further meddling.

His lordship continued to hold her hand in his, and his benign smile remained fixed in place, although it had, I thought, a frozen quality. "I only pray that you do not give me too much cause for jealousy," he jested gallantly. "It has been many years since it was required of me to fight a duel, and I admit to being sorely out of practice."

Charlotte's eyes gleamed at the picture of two men risking their lives for love of her, but the image was quickly squashed by Elizabeth. "Do not let him deceive you, dear. He is both an excellent marksman and a master at swordplay. Those gentlemen whose abilities match his own possess too much discretion to provoke an argument."

Charlotte sighed with disappointment. "But duels are immensely romantic, do you not agree?"

Lord Blackwood smiled wryly. "Having acted as a second on several occasions and failed to staunch the flow of blood of two fine young men, I must confess the idea is more romantic than the actuality."

"La, Nicholas," his sister exclaimed. "Surely you do not need to treat us with vivid descriptions."

"Forgive me. Indeed, I came today with the hopes of entertaining you in a much more amusing fashion. I had in mind a carriage ride and a tour of London's historical sites."

My hopes for a day with Lord Blackwood rose, but Elizabeth dashed them by announcing she had plans for another fitting that afternoon. Something "elaborate" was necessary for our first ball. But after some discussion, it was agreed that she should take our measurements to the dressmaker herself; since neither our opinions or desires would be heeded, our presence was unnecessary. But it occurred to me that had Elizabeth not wanted Charlotte to spend as much time as possible in her brother's company, doubtless she would not have surrendered her charges so easily.

Our tour took us past the gates of St. James's Palace then on to St. Paul's Cathedral. We climbed up to the whispering galley and walked on to the leads of the Cupola from whence we looked out onto the rooftops of London.

Charlotte drew back, faint from the height, and Lord Blackwood was most solicitous, taking her arm and leading her away until she felt herself again. Guardedly, I watched them, hoping for his sake to see her affection for him grow. But I feared that, if anything, her hasty recovery was due to a wish to escape his attentions rather than because of them.

I scowled at her when we were once again seated in the carriage, but her only response was a puzzled look which was quickly erased from her face as we set off again, this time to Westminster Abbey, where almost all of England's kings since William the Conqueror had been crowned.

"I feel quite done in," Aunt Emily said as we returned to the carriage after this last tour, and assuring his lordship that neither Bedlam nor the Tower of London were suitable sights for her nieces, agreed to his suggestion that we stop at a coffeehouse.

But we had driven only a few blocks before my eyes were drawn to a gaudy shop front. Lettered with vivid red script, the sign above the door read Temple of Bengal, and on the window, painted in bright orange and black, was a tiger's head. At once, I was captivated.

"Do you think we might stop?" I pleaded. "Charlotte and I were born in Calcutta, and I would so enjoy seeing what this shop has to offer. My father had a collection of Indian knives that always intrigued me. And Uncle Arthur gave us some pin money when we left Briarslea. I have always wished I had a souvenir of India."

Aunt Emily peered at the establishment with a suspicious eye. "Really, Redigan. I cannot think that this shop is considered fit for young ladies. Who knows what sort of character lurks in these places. And while knives might be the sort of object suitable for men to collect and admire, I think you should turn your eye to something less bloodthirsty."

My heart dropped. I could hardly explain to Aunt Emily the attachment I felt for a dagger with an ebony handle set with emeralds. And though I vaguely recalled that Henry had sold the collection in order to pay for our passage to England, it was unreasonable to think I might find that same dagger in a tiny store in London. Or that I had enough money in my possession to purchase one, if I did. I sighed heavily.

"Come, there is no need for fuss," Lord Blackwood said. "I believe the shop is quite respectable, indeed a favorite of certain ladies who like to collect ornaments of teak and carved ivory. Stop here, driver. We will return in a few minutes."

Gratitude welled inside me. Surely, no one but he could have guessed how greatly I desired to go in. Words could not begin to express what I felt, but I murmured a fervent thank you into his ear as he lifted me down from the carriage.

He gave me a bemused look. "I could well believe you think more of this one excursion than of all the sights I have shown you today."

"That is unfair," I protested. "I appreciate all that you do for me. But any man might think to show us St. James's Palace or St. Paul's. I doubt there are many acute enough to appreciate that visiting this shop is more than a passing whim."

He laughed. "You do not strike me as someone who gives in to fancies."

He released me and, leaving me to wonder if he had paid me a compliment, gave his attention to helping Charlotte and Aunt Emily descend. After a moment's reflection I decided he had, and I smiled happily, a smile which accidentally fell on Charlotte who seemed more puzzled than ever by my erratic moods.

Having helped us out, Lord Blackwood opened the door, setting a string of brass bells tinkling madly and echoing the giddiness inside of me. As I stepped in, a cloud of incense wafted from the depths of the shop, enveloping me in its rich perfume. It recalled me sharply to a world of exotic color, where the fragrance of outlandish blossoms pressed against one's senses as heavily as the throngs of people pressed against one's person.

As his lordship had predicted, there was more than one lady of fashion admiring the teakwood chests and the shelves of carved ivory, although my aunt's first glimpse of the proprietor—a turbaned gentleman whose shrivelled face resembled a dried walnut—brought a slight gasp from her lips. But with his lordship to support her arm, she advanced into the shop with a grim look, her fingers clutching her reticule with a firmness that would have dismayed merchants and cut-purses alike.

We had not browsed long before the proprietor, who had been excitedly bargaining with an elderly gentleman, hit on a price that was acceptable to both parties and wrapped up his purchases. His gaze quickly travelled the room, and on noticing Lord Blackwood, he bypassed several, less expensively dressed customers and hurried to our side.

"Is there something you wished to see?" he asked eagerly. "A necklace for the ladies, or perhaps the gentleman would like an ivory snuffbox. I have several inlaid with mother-of-pearl and the price is most reasonable."

His lordship looked at me questioningly. "I believe we would like to have a look at knives."

"There I can help you. I have a goodly assortment. Of both silver and steel—all with scrollwork etched on the blade, beautifully detailed, with handles carved of ivory and horn. What did you have in mind?"

"Nothing in particular," I lied. "Perhaps, a dagger? About this long?" I held my hands six inches apart.

"Ah." He nodded sagely. "Something that would fit into a lady's reticule. Most wise. Although with as able an escort as this fine gentleman, there would be little need for such measures. Still, I think I have just what you are looking for. Very old and most exquisite. Please, come this way."

He turned and shuffled off into the gloom, brushing past moldering rugs and rows of carved Buddhas that smiled down at him from glass curio cabinets. With each step he raised a flurry of dust that swirled up from the floorboards, hung in the air for the space of several seconds, and then slowly settled.

Fearing to lose him amongst the clutter, we hastened to follow. The shop was narrow but deep, and he led us all the way to the back where there was a tall curio cabinet.

An elderly matron, her silver curls poking beneath a silk turban, was peering through a man's quizzing glass at the contents of the shelves. She glanced up as we approached, and casually glanced at our party as though thinking she should recognize us, but not recalling where we had met. Then she caught sight of Lord Blackwood's face and gasped. The small package she held slipped from her hands, and she swayed as though she was about to swoon. With great effort, she took hold of herself and, speaking sharply to her footman, hurried out of the shop.

"Goodness," Aunt Emily exclaimed. "Do you think she was taken ill?"

Lord Blackwood shook his head. "Perhaps the fragrance of the incense overpowered her."

The proprietor picked up the package she had dropped and shook his head with dismay. "Lady Edgmont forgot her purchases. When she remembers she will be most distraught."

"No doubt she will send someone for them later today," his lordship assured him. "If not, you can have them sent to Edgmont Manor. As I recall, it is in Kensington." He did not offer to deliver the package himself as I had expected him to do. I frowned. The oversight was unlike him. Then it occurred to me that if her ladyship had been frightened by his appearance, as it seemed clear to me that she had, he would only add to her fears by calling on her at home.

That horrible woman, I thought crossly. To make such a fuss over a silly scar. And how like his lordship to make excuses for her.

I tried to read the expression in his impassive eyes. There was not a shred of emotion in his face. But that only meant he had something to conceal—why else the mask? Doubtless he did not wish us to see how the woman's actions had embarrassed him. And though my anger deepened to think of him wounded in such a careless fashion, it pleased me to think I had come to some small understanding of him.

With a deep sigh for the foolishness of British gentry, the proprietor set the package down and proceeded to unlock the cabinet. "Here is the dagger I mentioned. There are others, but none as nice as this one."

It was, as he had promised, exquisite. Rubies and emeralds flashed from an ivory handle, and the silver blade gleamed with a light that seemed magical, for nowhere in the shop was there a lamp bright enough to create that sparkling reflection.

"It is not expensive," he assured me. "Not when you think of the hours that went into crafting this piece."

"It is loveliness itself," I assured him. "But not what I had in mind. Something simpler please. Perhaps with an ebony handle."

"I have such a dagger, but this is much nicer."

I shook my head.

"If you would allow me," Lord Blackwood offered, "I would be glad to purchase it for you as a gift."

"Absolutely not!" Aunt Emily said emphatically. "You have already done much more than is conscionable."

"But it would please me greatly."

"No," I agreed. "My aunt is right. I could not possibly accept your offer."

The proprietor's face lost its hopeful sheen. He returned the dagger to its leather sheath and pulled out another. But having showed us his finest piece, everything else looked lackluster by comparison. At last I decided to forget about the knives and settled on a three-inch-high elephant made of silver, and set with tiny emerald eyes. Even that demanded that I give up almost all of my ten guineas.

"You cannot seriously consider spending all your money on an ornamental elephant?" Aunt Emily exclaimed. "What possible use could you have for it?"

"None," I admitted. "I would just like to take it out and look at it sometimes."

"Really, Redigan. That is utter nonsense."

Lord Blackwood politely intervened. "If you will forgive me for contradicting you, I believe it is not an elephant she is buying, but a memory of her childhood. Sometimes that is of greater value than a few pastries or silk ribbons."

"Well, I admit that the thought had not occurred to me," Aunt Emily said, looking doubtful, but in the end she disliked to refuse me in the face of Lord Blackwood's support.

In the carriage I hugged my purchase to me, although I had some doubts as to whether I had bought a half-forgotten memory of my childhood in India, or whether the green-eyed elephant carried an entirely different significance. With such thoughts to consume me, it was some time before I thought again of Lady Edgmont.

Elizabeth did not understate her intentions when she said she planned "something dramatic" for our first ball. When it came time for our fittings, we found ourselves decked out like the moon and the sun, Charlotte in a silver tulle shot through with silver threads, and me as her counterpart in dark gold. Delicate silk rosebuds, white for Charlotte, pale yellow for me, caught up the hem.

By myself, I would have made a satisfactory impression, but I fancied that, together, we would draw more glances than either one of us alone. The evening of our first ball, after spending all day at our toilette, we sat in the coach and waited for the long line of chaises and carriages ahead of us to inch toward our destination and emit their occupants. Our impatience with the delay was aggravated by our dislike of being gawked at by the men and women who strolled along the street, and by the gusts of cool air that cared nothing for the flimsiness of ladies' evening wear.

But our suffering was soon rewarded when we entered the home of Mr. and Mrs. Gillingham, a middle-aged couple with three daughters of marriageable age, all of whom eyed Charlotte and me with great displeasure. The eldest, and the prettiest, found it in her heart to like me after making a few condescending remarks, but nothing could induce her to forgive Charlotte.

But there were other ladies, fairer and livelier, who seemed willing to admit my sister into their ranks, and they hesitantly included me by dint of association. Although by the doubtful looks on several of their faces, not all of them rated me as being a true fair.

Then the music started. His lordship had promised me the first two dances, and Charlotte the second two, since he had not wanted to give away his preference by dancing first with her. He collected me with a gentlemanly bow and led me away, leaving my detractors to murmur in astonishment.

"You are a proficient dancer," I told him after a few minutes of enjoying his skill.

"But too tall by half," he teased.

I blushed and fell silent, wondering if all my rude remarks would come back to haunt me, but when I dared to glance upwards, I found him studying me with a gentle smile that led me to think he did not hold a grudge.

When it had been seen that I was at ease on the dance floor, my card was soon filled with the names of pleasant young gentlemen, though more than one pestered me with questions about Charlotte. Finding that none of them truly aroused my interest, I could afford to answer generously, and my air of detached amiability won me compliments from partners who had hitherto reserved their flattery for the younger of the two Miss Grenfels.

During a lull in the dancing—and at Aunt Emily's insistence, although *I* was not at all averse to the suggestion—Charlotte and I went to sit with Lord Blackwood. He, after dancing twice with both of us, had withdrawn to a far corner where he stood, his scarred cheek averted from the main body of the room. A number of attractive ladies had tried to coax him back to the dance floor, twitting him for his neglect of them, but he politely, but firmly declined any further participation in the festivities. It struck me that all of his admirers were either married or widowed, and of an age much the same as his own; the younger women rarely, if ever, glanced in his direction and then it was with an air of great trepidation.

Eventually, he had been joined by a gentleman of my uncle's age, whose gingery side whiskers and full, florid cheeks gave him a leonine appearance. The two men sat talking companionably, both content to be overlooked and ignored. They rose and bowed to us as we joined them, and Lord Blackwood introduced his acquaintance to us as "Sir Frederick, a friend of Elizabeth's."

"Her closest friend," the portly man hastened to point out, and added that no doubt we would be seeing more of each other if we remained long at Coudrey House.

After a few pleasantries, he turned to his lordship, a wicked gleam in his eyes, and said, "Well, Blackwood. Which of these fine young ladies is it to be?"

"To be?"

"Your wife, man. Your intended."

"I am not aware that I have announced my engagement to either of the Misses Grenfel."

He snorted. "You cannot deceive me, you sly devil. The question is not whether you will wed one of these young ladies, but which of them you intend to have, eh? Mr. Montague is taking bets as we speak. Trust you to play the fox with us." He hooked a thumb in his waistcoat pocket, adding to the excessive strain already placed on its brass buttons, and stared at us both through his quizzing glass.

"I shall not offend either of you by admitting where I placed my sovereigns, but the decision was a deuced difficult one to make. For myself, I must admit I could be content with either of you, were I not already abjectly devoted to Lady Elizabeth. Blast the woman. I almost believe she intends to remain a widow for the rest of her days. Do say you will put a word in for me, Blackwood."

"I fear I would be no help whatsoever to your cause. Elizabeth manages her affairs superbly and has never found the need to take advice from anyone."

"As I very well know," he said with a sigh. "Admirable woman. Admirable. But quite without scruples. She has kept me dangling five years and thinks nothing of the suffering she causes me."

His lordship gave a short bark of laughter, and his eyes sparkled with merriment. "As long as you insist on dividing your hours between gambling, fox hunts, and fishing, she is likely to leave you dangling until the end of your days."

Sir Frederick squirmed in his chair. "That rebuke is entirely uncalled for. Why, just last month I escorted her to the theater, and I have troubled myself to put in an appearance today only to be snubbed. The problem is, women are never satisfied. It will serve her right if I were to offer for one of these young ladies."

Lord Blackwood's eyes narrowed. "Should you try, you will be handily refused, for both of them will receive better offers than yours."

"And one of those from you, eh?" He raised his quizzing glass again. "Hmmph. Yes, well, you may be right. And at my age a young wife might be the death of me. Delightful way to go, of course."

"Stick to fishing," Elizabeth advised tartly, coming up behind him and catching his last remark. "You will have more success with that rod than any other."

Sir Frederick's face suffused with color and his lordship frowned. "There are times, Elizabeth, when your tongue escapes you. Such remarks are unfit for young ears."

"Fiddlesticks. They will hear worse than that mingling with this company."

But our time for mingling had come to a close. Elizabeth drew us away from the festivities early, bustling us into the coach with a fierce protectiveness that impressed even Aunt Emily.

"But we are the first to leave," Charlotte protested as she settled back onto the leather seat. Her eyes sparkled with an unnatural light, and her cheeks looked decidedly pale.

"You are unused to late hours, and young ladies who

are tired do not look their best. Besides," she added
as she tucked a quilt around our legs, "your presence
will be missed more acutely and awaited more anxiously if the gentlemen see less of you than they would
like."

"And it gives them less occasion to become acquainted with my shortcomings," I said with a grin. In
all, I felt quite satisfied with the evening's outcome, and
the thought of my warm bed was more enticing than
dancing another reel with aching feet and tight shoes.

With a dreamy sigh, I let my head loll against the
cushions as I listened to the iron ring of horseshoes
against the cobblestones. Each step sounded to me like
the throb of music and the step of dancing feet, and
I remembered with pleasure the thought of strong arms
around me and a pair of teasing green eyes.

Chapter Six

"Do you think that we are being snubbed by certain members of the *ton?*" Charlotte asked me the next morning, between sips of hot chocolate. She lounged comfortably in bed, her blonde curls tousled across her forehead, the counterpane drawn up in a hump over her knees. I curled up on the pillow beside her, my wrapper draped carelessly over my nightgown and my bare toes wiggling luxuriously now they were free from the pinch of my new slippers.

"Snubbed?" I asked with surprise. "There was not a single slighting remark made to me all evening. If Lord Blackwood had not been known to be our benefactor, we might well have been ignored, but they can hardly look down their noses at us when we have his patronage."

"Perhaps you are right." Her voice sounded uncertain. "But several of my dance partners asked me whether or not we would be attending Lady Edgmont's soiree tomorrow evening, and though I vaguely recall the name, I cannot recall that Elizabeth ever mentioned the affair."

"Of course you have heard the name," I declared, staring at the elephant on the occasional table. "In the Temple of Bengal. Remember the woman who dropped her purchases."

"How silly of me. I had forgotten." She frowned as

she remembered the scene. "I wonder if—" she said and then hesitated. "I know his lordship thought otherwise but it struck me that Lady Edgmont took fright when she saw his face. Do you think her aversion to his disfigurement is the reason we have been overlooked?"

"If so, then she is more foolish than I thought."

Charlotte shrugged. "I suppose you are right, but surely you can understand her horror. Lord Blackwood may be a gentleman, but one would never know by looking at him. He looks as fierce as any rogue. I cannot bear to gaze upon him but briefly for fear that I shall swoon."

"Then you are more foolish than Lady Edgmont, for you know him too well to have such shameful misgivings. And I cannot understand either one of you. Lord Blackwood *is* a gentleman, and more handsome than any of the pretty boys who asked you to dance last night. His scar gives him"—I struggled for a fitting word to make Charlotte see him through more romantic eyes—"a *dashing* air."

"You used to think him ugly," she challenged. "I cannot see that he has changed."

I was saved the necessity of answering by a knock on the door. Elizabeth, still in her wrapper, her curls crushed beneath a lace cap, sailed into the room waving a fistful of cards.

"Just look at this. All for the captivating Misses Grenfel. I have made a success of both of you." She poured the cards onto the counterpane in a heap.

"Elizabeth," I demanded as Charlotte thumbed through the pile. "Who is Lady Edgmont?"

Charlotte paused in her perusal of the names to demand querulously, "And why are we not invited to her soiree?"

Our attack took Elizabeth aback, and a fleeting look of dismay flashed across her face. But quickly she composed herself and, shrugging as though the matter was of little account, she said, "I had hoped you would not hear of the soiree. I suppose that was foolish of me, but the matter is an awkward one and rather personal."

"If you feel uncomfortable discussing her with us, then you must say no more," Charlotte said dutifully, thereby irritating me on two counts. First, for showing better manners than I, and again for forestalling an explanation I dearly wished to hear. But seeing I had no choice, I grudgingly supported her.

Elizabeth shook her head. "No, better I explain before some bird-witted chatterbox fills your heads with a lot of nonsense. Lord and Lady Edgmont were the parents of Nicholas's first wife, Lydia. You know, I imagine, that she died in childbirth."

We nodded.

"Lydia was their youngest daughter and her father's favorite. He doted upon her, and her death was an unbearable loss for both of them. To this day they cannot bear to see Nicholas or invite him into their home. The memory is still a good deal too painful."

She glanced at me and I had the vague sense that she had skirted the truth and wanted to see if I doubted her tale. Her fear was needless. Whatever she had left untold I did not doubt that Lord Blackwood was blameless in any disagreement between himself and his late wife's parents. I would have said as much if we had been alone, but I did not want to put questions in Charlotte's mind if they did not already exist.

Apparently, they did not. "Was she beautiful?" Charlotte asked, her eyes curious.

"Not nearly as beautiful as you," Elizabeth assured her with a relieved smile.

Her vanity satisfied, Charlotte dismissed the Edgmonts and the soiree and gathered up the rest of the cards. With relish, she began reading out the names and the scribbled messages on their backs. A few callers, rather churlishly I thought, had singled her out for their attentions, but most of them were politely addressed to us both.

"But likely it is Charlotte they want to see," I said dolefully when she had finished.

"You underestimate yourself," Elizabeth admonished. "You made a creditable showing at the ball, and you dance beautifully. Besides, Charlotte cannot entertain a roomful of gentlemen. When her admirers seek you out for consolation, they will soon become acquainted with the charms of her elder sister."

"Then perhaps it is just as well his lordship delayed announcing their engagement. It seems I am to win a husband by default."

My prophecy was overly pessimistic.

That afternoon Lord Blackwood hired three horses and took us through Hyde Park. We followed one of the paths around the Serpentine, often a place of rendezvous for the beau monde, sometimes for the duels Charlotte thought romantic.

She usually disliked to ride, but Elizabeth had thought to have riding habits made up for us, and any invitation that gave Charlotte a chance to wear her new attire could not be refused. But, for once, I fancied her appearance came second to my own. She sat her horse poorly, and the masculine cut of the jackets, with the high-crowned hats and the silk cravats tied in a bow at our throats, suited me more than her.

As we cantered by the lake, holding to a pace that would not be unduly demanding on Charlotte, Lord Blackwood caught my eye. Something of my thoughts must have been betrayed in my expression or the tilt of my head, for he chuckled as if he shared in a private joke.

"It is a beautiful day for a ride, is it not?"

"It is," I agreed.

"I am convinced that there is no gentleman more fortunate than I this day. Not a rider has passed us who has not looked upon me with envy."

As if to prove him right, two riders pulled abreast of us, and cast their gazes in our direction. Both were young, of college age, and though the cut of their clothes showed them to be gentlemen, the fabric had a threadbare look.

The dark-haired young man nearest to me tipped his hat and cried, "Why, I declare. It is Lord Blackwood, I believe. We met last year at the faro tables, if you recall. Phillip Weston, at your service, sir."

"Good day, Mr. Weston. I do indeed remember you. The size of your losses impressed me greatly."

He made a small grimace, and looked hopefully from my face to Charlotte's as though waiting for an introduction. When he saw none was forthcoming, he prodded his lordship by saying, "May I introduce my companion, Mr. Edgar Carrington. He is at Cambridge with me."

Mr. Carrington lifted his hat politely, but his gaze slid from Lord Blackwood to me. I returned his look coolly enough but was struck by his handsome face—the curling sand-colored locks, strong jaw, and patrician nose—as well as the casual ease with which he handled his mount. His eyes perhaps, lay a shade too close to his nose, but that was easily overlooked when I marked the obvious appreciation for me that shone from them.

Since only outright rudeness would have permitted his lordship to ignore Mr. Weston's prodding, he politely replied, "Allow me to introduce my companions. Miss Redigan Grenfel—"

"You are Miss Grenfel," Mr. Carrington exclaimed, not allowing him to finish. "It is a pleasure to make your acquaintance. A friend of mine wearied my ear this morning with a litany of your charms. But, if memory does not mistake me, I believe he claimed the name was Charlotte."

"And Miss Charlotte Grenfel," his lordship said dryly, finishing his introductions.

Mr. Carrington did not seem the least nonplussed. "Now I see my mistake. You are both deserving of his rapturous praises. How fortunate that our hearts have not been captured by the same Miss Grenfel, for I am much in my friend's debt and would sorely regret vying with him for a young lady's favor. I hope you will give me permission to call on you."

"You may certainly call," I told him. "But whether or not you will be received is not for me to say. We are staying with his lordship's sister, at Coudrey House, and that decision must rest with her."

He smiled, pleased to receive this piece of information, and said, "I hope you can find it in your heart to persuade her to admit me. If not, I fear I shall do something rash, for now that you have stolen my heart, I will not rest until you have given me yours."

"I make no promises," I said, pretending a severity I did not feel. "But I will think on the matter."

"Then I will not bid you good-bye but merely say until we meet again."

Both men tipped their hats again and galloped off. I laughed, giddy with the joy of flirting, and looked to Lord Blackwood to see if he, too, had appreciated my success.

But he was staring after the two riders, and a dark scowl lay across his face.

"Redigan has made a conquest," Charlotte gaily announced to Elizabeth and Aunt Emily on our return.

She pulled off her hat and plopped down in the easy chair nearest the fire. The azure shades prevalent in the room—from the lighter hue of the damask draperies drawn back from the tall windows to the darker velvets and embroidered upholsteries of the sofas and settees—set off her delicate fairness, and she looked the epitome of feminine loveliness.

Elizabeth looked up at me with a question in her eyes.

"His name is Edgar Carrington," Charlotte continued, happily oblivious to her fiancé's silent disapproval.

After a hesitant glance at him, I ventured to add, "He asked if he might call."

"That is wonderful, dear." My aunt's voice sounded as amazed as it did relieved. "Did he seem a nice young man?"

"He was utterly charming," Charlotte told her. "And more romantic than the hero of any novel."

Elizabeth turned to her brother who had seated himself in the hard-backed chair and was staring at our little group as though he might watch actors performing in a play that did not meet with his liking. Her eyebrows arched. "You are very quiet, Nicholas."

"I dislike to disappoint you by volunteering my opinion."

"You are acquainted with him, then?"

"Let us say I am acquainted with his type. A coxcomb whose praises are as empty as his pockets. If he calls, I must advise you not to receive him."

"Perhaps the matter deserves a little study," she said evenly. "You say his name is Edgar Carrington. I believe I know his family. They are quite respectable and, unless I am mistaken, he stands to inherit a good living. Furthermore, if he admires Redigan's looks, he is likely to make an appreciative and attentive husband."

"It takes little intelligence to see she is attractive. Be warned, Elizabeth. I will not let you place so little value on her worth that you want to sell her to the first man who admires her face. I intend to have the best for her."

"A worthy aim, but I advise *you* not to place too high a price on her, or she will end the season with no husband at all. La, Nicholas. What is wrong with you? You are acting like a blindly devoted father." She laughed. "No, worse. A jealous suitor."

"With Squire Grenfel in Cornwall, I consider myself her guardian and will act as such," he said coldly. "Sir Frederick was right. You are the most damnable woman." With that statement, he rose and quit the room.

Her brother's feelings notwithstanding, Elizabeth delved discreetly into the background of "my" Mr. Carrington. When it was established that he would inherit an income of three thousand pounds a year from his grandfather on the day of his twenty-first birthday, four months hence, she left instructions that he was to be received should he happen to call when we were at home.

"For even if he lacks maturity—and that is the only one of Nicholas's litany of complaints that can be at all credited—his interest in you will excite the attentions of other young men who may well be more worthy. But do not"—she looked me squarely in the eye as though trying to instill in me, through force of will, her own good sense—"do not, I repeat, let my brother deter you from bestowing your affections upon this young man if that is your desire. I have heard nothing said of him that suggests he is deserving of either our censure or disapprobation, and there are many young ladies who would retire to their rooms with shrieks of horror at the thought of seeing such an attractive and amiable young man being turned from their door."

"But if his lordship forbids—"

"Please remember, Nicholas is not the master in Coudrey House. That position is wholly mine and I shall exercise my authority to admit or refuse visitors as it pleases me."

Her words were softened by her conspiratorial smile, and I knew that like her brother, she wanted to do her best for me. Only their opinions differed as to what that best might be.

"You are too kind by half!" I exclaimed. "And it would please me greatly to see the gentleman again."

Accordingly, she made plans for our first "at home."

It was a tumultuous affair, marked by lines of carriages and milling crowds passing through the house, after having first proffered their warmest regards to their hostesses. Conversation was impossible. There was hardly room to walk, much less play cards or dance.

Mr. Carrington appeared in the midst of this melee, stepping briskly up the stairs and making a low bow to Elizabeth on whom he pressed his compliments. Then, impatiently brushing his curling forelock from his eyes, he paid his addresses to me. "What a rout this is!" he said. "But I must attribute at least some of Lady Elizabeth's popularity to the Grenfel sisters. Upon my word, what a favor beautiful women do the world merely by gracing us with their presence. I can think of no feminine virtue more worthy of admiration."

"If you are including me in your praise," I said modestly, "then I must thank you, sir."

"I could do little else, confronted as I am with your perfection."

Mr. Carrington seemed quite prepared to elaborate on his statements, but he was quickly jostled deeper into the hall by the tide of people behind him, and when I looked up to search for him we were separated by a throng that Moses himself could not have parted.

I gave myself back to my duties, only to look up and find Lord Blackwood beside me. His gaze was directed to that same spot where my attentions had drifted, and he soon perceived the reason for my distraction. His jaw tightened and his scar drew a whitened line across his cheek.

"I see my sister delights in ignoring me," he said at last. "That, I suppose, was to be expected. But I had hoped you would have treated my wishes with greater regard."

The rebuke wounded me deeply, and defiantly, I retorted, "I hold you in the highest esteem, but that does not give you the right to dictate to me."

"No matter," he said arrogantly. "I fully expect the situation to resolve itself. I can only hope you do not meet with too great a disappointment when my advice proves sound."

There was little enough to concern his lordship. Mr. Carrington and I did not speak again, only nodded to each other briefly as he and his companion summoned their carriage and departed.

"What a lot of bother for nothing," I said with disgust when the last of our guests had gone. "It was impossible to exchange more than a few civilities."

"Yes," said Elizabeth, smiling complacently. "I believe our 'at home' was quite a success. Had I the stamina, I would begin immediately on planning another."

But it was not necessary to subject ourselves to another such affair for me to talk with Mr. Carrington. We met again at Lord Morton's ball, an elaborate affair that had been thrown with the intention of acquiring a husband for his eldest daughter, an accomplished young lady who had turned twenty-four and was whispered to be "well and truly on the shelf."

Lady Clara was not an unattractive woman, but shy and bookish, two traits which had earned her the dubious title of "bluestocking," and her father thought himself well-advised to display his wealth, and the power of his connections, to the gentlemen of the beau monde or find himself forever shouldered with the responsibility of an unwed daughter.

It was rumored that with this feat in mind, he had prudently invited two unattached men for every unattached young lady, and excluded any woman who was rumored to be exceedingly fair. Therefore, on receiving her invitation, Charlotte did not know whether to be pleased or offended, until we learned the reports of his scheming had been based not on fact, but on malicious gossip designed to poke fun at poor Lady Clara.

But upon our arrival, we saw that the rumors had been accurate as to the extent of Lord Morton's preparations. The ballroom was the most spacious of any I had yet seen. A circle of crystal chandeliers hung from the vaulted ceiling; the brilliant light suffused the room, highlighting the red and gold velvet wall hangings, sparkling off the gilt cornices, and reflecting from the polished surface of the parquet flooring.

"His lordship's ball will be the talk of the town," Elizabeth said to Aunt Emily as we admired the lavishness of the decorations. "I would wager there is not a single diamond left in any woman's jewel box this evening. I cannot recall when I last saw such a display."

Lord Blackwood and Sir Frederick had escorted us, and Sir Frederick had gone as far as to don an outfit that did not look as if it had been made before he had added several inches to his girth. But when I complimented him on the handsome figure he cut in his new attire, he said disconsolately, "I thought as much myself, but there seems to be little point in giving myself airs. Since his lordship makes up one of our party I will, perforce, look shorter and fatter than ever."

Although I promptly assured him he was mistaken, the surreptitious glances I cast in Lord Blackwood's direction told me that it was unfortunately true.

Since the "at home" our relationship had been strained. Both of us adamantly refused to admit we were wrong, and our exchanges of conversation were brief and excessively polite, a state of affairs that pained me deeply and embarrassed Aunt Emily.

It did not improve matters when Mr. Carrington promptly claimed me for the first two dances, and wrote his name on my card for the next two as well. I gave him my hand without deigning to look at his lordship, although from Aunt Emily's despairing face, I could well imagine his reaction.

The first set went well between us. Mr. Carrington showed himself to be an accomplished dancer, and I fancied we looked well together. His remarks to me remained flattering, then he drifted into lighthearted sallies directed at mutual acquaintances. When I professed an interest in his studies, he admitted he was a mediocre scholar.

"My father is threatening to cut off my allowance if I do not apply myself," he said with a careless toss of his sand-colored curls. "He has already reduced me to a sum that forces me to live a Spartan existence. But I confess, I have not the head for dull books."

I watched Lady Clara go down the dance with her partner, a middle-aged man with a distinguished air and a pleasing, if not handsome countenance.

"She dances well," I remarked idly. "And the gentleman seems pleased with her. Perhaps Lord Morton's money has been well spent."

"Ha! It will cost him a pretty penny to make some man forget that he is marrying a *learned* woman."

I looked at him in astonishment. "Surely you are not against educating women?"

"Not at all," he assured me in a benevolent tone. "An educated woman is a credit to her husband and a boon to society. But to be educated in the classics, the French language, taught an appreciation of music and art—that is one matter. For a woman to presume to study mathematics or the sciences, worse yet, to embroil herself in politics so that she is misled into thinking herself the intellectual equal of men—that is a sin against nature."

"What utter rubbish!" I exclaimed. "It is a sin to waste a mind, purely because that mind has been placed in a woman's body. I cannot help but wonder how many men would be so quick to condemn her if her accomplishments did not exceed their own."

He looked outraged. "Do you dare suggest that my reasoning is affected by vanity?"

"By your own account, *you* are not Lady Clara's equal."

"I cannot believe that you, of all people, are a blue-stocking. If you hold such modern views, why do you not crop your hair as other women do? It seems the fashion for them to try to look as much like men as they are able."

"As long as men tout opinions that should only be supported by fools and incompetents, I shall keep my hair the length you see."

"And as long as women persist in trying to dominate their superiors, I shall remain a bachelor."

With that announcement he dropped my hand and strode off, leaving me in the middle of the floor without a partner. By the look of the amused faces around me, our vocal discussion had been generally overheard.

Feigning indifference, I took out my dance card, scratched off his name, then strolled to the opposite side of the room. After several long minutes, during which I was the subject of much scrutiny and a few whispers, I was joined by Elizabeth.

"La! What is the matter with you, Redigan? There may be a few men who respect or possibly admire an intelligent woman, but even their appreciation wanes when that intelligence is used to make them look ridiculous."

"But he was spouting nonsense."

"It is a failing shared by many of his gender, I assure you. And unwed young ladies who seek husbands would be wise to overlook their shortcomings. At least until after they exchange their marriage vows. Besides, if women only wed men who were smarter than they, most of us would remain spinsters our entire lives. Upon my word"—she fanned herself briskly—"the human race would be at peril. For goodness' sakes, try to make yourself amiable."

With that word of admonishment, she wafted from

my side and drifted seductively back amongst the sparkling company that filled the ballroom.

I will not make myself amiable to idiots! I thought crossly, my irritation deepened by the knowledge that my embarrassment was due to my own quick temper and lack of tact.

"To the devil with all of them!" I muttered, and whirled off to the gardens where I could pout and stamp my foot to my complete satisfaction and no one would be the wiser.

Lord Morton's gardens had been as much decorated for the ball as the mansion's interior. Chinese lanterns hung from the lower branches of giant elms and threw a muted light across the sloping lawns. To add to the colorful pinks of the rhododendron blossoms and the soft blues of the azaleas, flowing streamers and bows had been wrapped around the columns of the portico and the base of the tree trunks, and the branches strung with fairy lights.

The breeze cut through the thin draperies of my dress, reminding me that strolls through the garden on an April evening should not be attempted without the accompaniment of some gentleman who would be able to offer the warmth of his person as well as the stimulation of his conversation. But if I had no beau to repel the chill, the heat of my anger made a handy substitute.

I had walked but a few yards when I heard footsteps coming after me, and I turned, half expecting to see Mr. Carrington. Instead, it was Lord Blackwood, the tails of his coat flapping at his legs as he hurried to catch up to me. Reluctantly, I waited until he had reached my side.

"Your young man has deserted you, has he?" he said with a complacency that made me question why I had ever liked him. "I expected as much. Otherwise I should have removed you from Coudrey House at the first signs of your forming an unsuitable alliance."

"You must be pleased, indeed, to see your hopes met with such immediate satisfaction," I said stiffly.

"Come now," he gently chided me. "I see no need to take on. I do not believe your feelings were much affected—only your vanity."

"You are entirely mistaken. I found his company pleasurable, his manners above reproach, his countenance and bearing noble and—"

"And his views on the proper conduct of women deplorable."

"We were not of the same mind," I allowed.

He laughed loudly. "That is just as well. For his mind has little to recommend itself to others, and your company would be tedious in the extreme should you share his pitiful lack of intelligence."

"I believe he thought my company tedious solely because of that intelligence which you extol. Had I been more prudent in expressing my opinions, I believe I should have met with greater success."

Lord Blackwood placed his arm about my shoulders and we strolled across the lawn together. "If you had continued long in his liking," he assured me as we walked, "it would have been at the expense of your self-esteem and my own good opinion of you. Trust me, if you care to curb your tongue and repress your mental faculties, there are many Edgar Carringtons in this world who will take you as their wife. The loss of one or two is meaningless."

"How can you say that? I am not like Charlotte, deluged by admirers."

"Nor," he said, "if you do not bend to the social pressures that are designed to keep women pliant and submissive, will you ever be. Your charm is not of a sort that attracts an endless line of admirers and dance partners, begging for the chance to make fervent declarations of love. It will take a man of spirit and intelligence to appreciate your virtues. I suggest you leave the foolish young men to ladies with vapid minds and affected manners. I will yet find you a husband who is worthy of you."

"More likely Elizabeth is right—your expectations will make finding me a husband impossible."

"Would you want a man whose mind and character you could not respect?"

"Elizabeth says men of worthy character do not exist, and I must learn to ignore their shortcomings if I am ever to wed."

"Elizabeth," he retorted, "married a man whose flaming stupidity was matched only by his utter arrogance. It has colored her opinion of the male of the species. I would not like to see you make the same mistake, for we are not all as venial as she describes."

"I believe she loves *you* dearly."

"I am her brother. Since we share the same parents, she is compelled to think well of me, though it pains her greatly to refrain from correcting my opinions and second-guessing my judgment. I fancy she believes only women are capable of insight and wisdom and that, left to my own discretion, I will hopelessly mismanage my affairs."

I grinned. "She is a most formidable woman."

"I respect her greatly," he assured me. "But I am not blind to her faults. I hope you will not allow your appreciation for her kindness and her uncommon perspicacity to mislead you into thinking her incapable of error."

"I promise to try to be a better judge of what is good advice and what is unfair prejudice," I vowed. "I only hope you will accept my apologies for ignoring your warnings. Your concern for my happiness is more than I deserve."

The light of the Chinese lanterns caught the flash of his grin. "You must attribute my attentions to purely selfish motives. For since we are to be related, whoever you take as a husband will, from time to time, be forced upon me. I do not suffer the company of fools well. Come, let us return to the others. We shall dance together and you can show everyone how little you care for Mr. Carrington's desertion."

His head bent solicitously over mine, and as I glanced up he brushed my brow with a soft kiss. I breathed a sigh at the tenderness of his touch and my mouth parted. He hesitated, and then his lips descended on mine, eagerly demanding what I so desperately wanted to give. There was a rush of warmth and the lights in the garden seemed to have penetrated my mind where they whirled around, circling faster and faster until I felt faint with dizziness.

I melted into him and, catching me up, he crushed me against his chest. I threw myself into the embrace, locking my arms about his neck and clinging to him with all my strength.

Then, with a dismayed cry, he broke away and his eyes sought mine in the darkness. "You must forgive me," he said hoarsely. "My behavior was inexcusable."

"It was the moment," I whispered. "Nothing more." But my trembling voice betrayed my inner tumult.

Willfully misunderstanding, he said stiffly, "We had better go inside. The cold air is making you shiver."

Silently, his back rigid, he led me back to the ballroom.

Chapter Seven

"SHALL WE DANCE?" his lordship asked carelessly as we re-entered the ballroom, and his nonchalance destroyed any romantic notions that may have still lingered in my mind.

I nodded, forcing myself to meet his light smile with one of my own.

He took my arm and we joined the line. There, he became the picture of a devoted admirer, his compliments and flattery confusing me further until I realized each remark was delivered in a voice calculated to carry beyond my ears. But if he had intended to reestablish my worth with the other gentlemen in the ballroom, his attentiveness seemed to have done more harm than good. Several of his friends assaulted us with their jests as we strolled off the floor and their good-natured complaints indicated that they thought their guineas had been carelessly wagered on Charlotte; while the faces of those young men whom I knew to be infatuated with her shone with hope that they, too, may have miscalculated when they had guessed that she was the object of his interest. Although it was clear from their expressions that they hardly dared to credit the possibility.

For once, Charlotte seemed oblivious to the increased fervor of their pursuit. Seeing me standing alone after Lord Blackwood had excused himself to partner Aunt Emily in a promised dance, she beckoned to me to join her. She stood near the windows, gracefully eluding repeated requests to dance while she talked to a fair-haired gentleman who hovered at her side.

The young man—Monsieur André—reluctantly withdrew his gaze from Charlotte's face for the few seconds it took for her to make the necessary introductions. From beneath heavy lids and golden lashes, he eyed me briefly, his initial look of expectation abruptly vanishing as he saw that in no way did Charlotte and I resemble each other.

For my part I was equally unenthused. He appeared to be about of an age with Mr. Carrington, possibly a year or two older, and he was dressed in a fashion that the most polite observer would have termed queer. Untidy, even dirty, would have been just as appropriate.

His shabby, loose-fitting suit appeared to have been made for a heavier gentleman, causing me to wonder if it had been borrowed or bought secondhand, or whether his thinness was due to the need for a good meal. The latter, I decided, was the most likely, for his gray eyes seemed too large for his gaunt face.

A faint layer of down smudged across his upper lip, but what was intended to be a moustache grew too sparsely to be looked upon as anything but affectation. Affectation, also, was his sweeping bow and the kiss he delivered to my hand, and I was none too sorry to reclaim my fingers. Had I been wearing rings, I would have promptly checked them to see that the stones remained in their settings.

"Monsieur is a painter," Charlotte gushed, oblivious to the wariness with which we regarded each other. "He wants to put our likeness to canvas."

"Mais, non, ma petite," he interjected, adding, in heavily accented English, "It is only you whom I wish to paint."

Charlotte looked up in surprise. "But you said yourself that a portrait of two sisters would be *très charmante.*"

"*Oui, oui.*" He shrugged. "But now that I have met your sister I can see it would be all wrong. You are too different." He turned to me and said apologetically, "You must see that the colors, the . . . the . . . emotion would not be . . . harmonious."

"Then we must be painted separately," Charlotte insisted, refusing to accept his utter lack of interest in me.

"Really, Charlotte," I exclaimed. "You know I do not have the patience to stand quietly long enough for a dress to be fitted. I refuse even to contemplate sitting in one position for hours on end."

Monsieur André seemed much relieved by my emphatic announcement, but Charlotte looked at me doubtfully. "Are you sure? His portraits are all the rage. The Gillingham sisters are having theirs done, and since I explained I have only the ten guineas Uncle Arthur gave me, Monsieur has promised to waive his usual fee."

"But how could I charge this lovely creature?" he asked, expressively lifting his palms. "Miss Grenfel I will paint because art demands that she be painted, and only André could do justice to those delicate curls, those exquisite eyes. I ask only the ten guineas to cover my own costs," he said with a deprecating shrug.

It struck me that Charlotte's ten guineas could buy enough paint and canvas to cover the stable wall at Briarslea, but I refrained from saying so. After all, my money had gone to purchase a silver elephant, and that was no more practical than Charlotte's wanting her portrait painted. And while painting her for ten guineas was not quite the generous offer he claimed it to be, I felt sure the Misses Gillingham were paying Monsieur André a great deal more.

Just then the musicians stopped playing and Lord Morton stood up on the dais and announced that supper was being served. "You must come to my garret,"

Monsieur André said, his eyes nervously flickering to the doors that let out on the garden where the crowd had already begun filtering towards the pink and blue striped tents which sheltered the banquet tables. "It is not in a fashionable part of town, but we *artistes* are notoriously underpaid," he said apologetically. "That will not dissuade you from coming, *non?*"

Charlotte profusely assured him that mere discomfort could not possibly prevent her from accepting his generous offer, although previously she had told me that nothing could induce her to ride through London's rougher districts, even with so formidable an escort as Lord Blackwood.

Either he was satisfied with her promises, or the lure of the banquet grew too great for him to resist. Monsieur André bowed once more and expressed his undying regard with great effusiveness, then hurried off to find a chair before those nearest the buffet were all taken.

Lord Blackwood and the others joined us and we proceeded at a more leisurely pace. Neither Charlotte nor I had much appetite. She was too filled with excitement at having been honored with Monsieur André's interest, while my stomach fluttered nervously whenever his lordship addressed a remark to me or glanced in my direction.

"Goodness, I do hope the child is not going to be ill," Aunt Emily whispered to Elizabeth. She cast a worried glance upon my untouched plate. "Quarrelling with Mr. Carrington must have been a severe disappointment to her. It was most unkind of him to treat her so poorly, but the fault is as much hers as his. If only she could learn not to act so impulsively."

I smiled ruefully. Thoughts of Mr. Carrington had left my mind with the same haste that had distinguished the departure of his personage; but, had she known the truth, Aunt Emily could still have regretted my impulsiveness and with very good reason.

*   *   *

To my surprise, neither Elizabeth nor Aunt Emily objected to Charlotte's wish to have her portrait painted. From the measured look in her eyes, I suspected that his lordship's sister thought that it would not hurt to have Charlotte's hours occupied in so harmless a fashion, while Aunt Emily exclaimed the portrait would make a lovely wedding gift and insisted on paying the ten guineas herself.

Charlotte was much delighted by this turn of events, finding that she was to have her portrait as well as keep her precious fortune. She danced into the bedroom we shared in the Rose Velvet suite, twirling madly around me as I struggled into the corset that Elizabeth insisted I wear, no matter how little it was required by my slender frame. Corsets had, I decided, an excellent future if ever the Inquisition returned.

"If you do not stop bobbing about me I shall use this to strangle you," I threatened.

She pouted. "Must you always be unpleasant. I only came to tell you I would share my ten guineas with you since Aunt Emily wishes to pay for the portrait."

"You had better keep your money," I advised, knowing that Charlotte would soon find something else she dearly wanted. "Besides, the end of the season is not too far off, and who knows what you may need to buy for your wedding."

A look of discomfort fleeted across her face, then she forced a smile. "It is hard to think of myself as engaged. Especially to . . . do you know, I believe that if Uncle Arthur had not accepted Lord Blackwood's offer, I could have made a marriage that was every bit as good. Perhaps better."

"Without his lordship's money there would have been no season in London," I pointed out acidly. "And therefore no chance for you to meet another gentleman of his rank. Besides, I daresay that without our connection to his lordship and Elizabeth's patronage you would not have been regarded as a serious marriage prospect by any of the young men who have sworn their undying devotion to you."

"You have no more sense of romance than Uncle Arthur," she said with a pout. "Marriage should be made for love, not security or position. And certainly not so that a piece of property can exchange hands."

"Pooh! What do you know about love anyway?"

"How can you ask me that?" Her voice blazed with outrage. "Why, I have fallen in love at least three times since we came to London. And yet each time I had to conceal my feelings and deny that love because I was secretly engaged. It quite broke my heart when I refused Mr. Weston a second dance so soon after the first. Only the thought that he could hardly support a wife on a student's allowance kept me from giving way to tears. But you—" She pointed a trembling finger at me. "You are the one who knows nothing of love. Why, you have not mentioned Mr. Carrington's name once since he spurned you. No, nor cried a single tear over his loss. I cannot believe you had a shred of real feeling for him. You are the one who knows nothing about love. Not I."

"I know that your silly flirtations have as much resemblance to love as Briarslea has to St. James's Palace," I shouted back and, losing the last vestiges of my temper, I stalked off before I gave way to my desire to pummel some sense into her.

My fury was all the greater for knowing her accusations were not entirely unjust. I had not loved Mr. Carrington. Nor, despite the balls and the lines of pleasant dance partners, had I found a single gentleman whose qualities could be measured against those of Lord Blackwood.

When the carriage was sent round the next afternoon to drive us to Monsieur André's garret, Charlotte and I had still not forgiven each other for the things we had said. I would have gladly stayed at Coudrey

House, but Aunt Emily insisted that I accompany them. "The visit may be educational," she said. "And I have half a mind to have a portrait done of you as well."

Had I thought she truly meant this, I would have quickly denounced the idea. But having seen the anxious manner in which she had pored over the calling cards left on the hall table, dismissing those directed to Miss Charlotte Grenfel and then grimly casting aside those more formally addressed to both of us with a doubtful shake of her head, I guessed that her real reason for including me was to remove me from society until my conduct at Lord Morton's ball had been forgotten. That suited me to a nicety.

My argument with Charlotte had not improved my temper one whit. She seemed more willing than I to put our differences aside, either because of her anticipation at having her portrait painted or because she saw our disagreement as going no deeper than our usual squabbles, but after receiving several grudging answers to her gay remarks, she addressed the rest of her comments to Aunt Emily. Their chatter broke off only when the cries of the market vendors grew too loud for them to talk without shouting.

Monsieur André lived above a fish shop on a narrow side street not far from Covent Garden. The first floor jutted out over the ground-floor shop and several petticoats had been draped over the windowsill above our heads to dry, although the white linen was already speckled with soot.

The garret lay at the top of two flights of wooden stairs, and each step creaked beneath the weight of our feet as we passed. The railing wobbled in our hands, and in several places it had come completely adrift from the wall where the water-stained plaster had crumbled around the brackets.

"I knew it would be like this." Charlotte gave a rapturous sigh. "There is something so romantic about a painter's garret."

"I wonder how romantic you would find a broken neck," I retorted, glancing dubiously at the steep drop behind me.

But Charlotte had come upon the landing at the top of the stairs and the dark oaken door with its small brass plate that read: Monsieur André. Portraits.

"Here we are!" she exclaimed and knocked with quick, light taps that must have betrayed her excitement to the garret's tenant.

But if her eagerness showed a childish lack of sophistication, Monsieur André was too enrapt in his own pleasure at seeing her again to notice. He drew us into his rooms with a warmth that was entirely un-Gallic and pulled the heavy draperies across an alcove to conceal the rumpled bed from which he appeared to have only recently risen.

"At last, you have come," he said, taking her hand and leading her to the tall windows at the end of the room. He tilted her face to catch the light and kissed his fingertips, making a loud smack that sounded faintly indecent. "I was right, was I not? You are the perfect subject for my talents. But the dress." He wrinkled his nose as though something worse than the stench from the fish market below had permeated the room. "It is all wrong. It must go."

"It most certainly will not," Aunt Emily snapped as Charlotte's cheeks turned a bright crimson.

Monsieur André turned to her with a look of amazement and contempt. "But madame, surely you see that her beauty needs no adornment. She is Venus. Aphrodite. Helen of Troy. These rags are not fit to cover her."

"Rags!" Purple blotches darkened Aunt Emily's throat and the wide expanse of bosom displayed above the bodice of her muslin dress. She gulped for air, making a strangled noise in her throat, then her back stiffened and she marched toward Monsieur André with a fierceness that made him release Charlotte's chin and step backwards until he was braced against the windows. From his pained expression, I could only assume that the latch had buried itself in a tender portion of his anatomy.

"Rags!" Aunt Emily exclaimed again, spitting the word out of her mouth. "That dress is pure silk, and likely cost more guineas than you see in a month. And if you think . . . If you *dare* to think for one second that my niece would consider disrobing—"

"Mais, non, madame. Non, non," he protested feverishly. "I mean to say . . . my English—" He threw up his hands. "I thought only to reveal the shoulders. What did you think? That I would consider something indecent? For this innocent? *Non!* A thousand times, *non!"* He gingerly eased himself away from the windows and back into my aunt's good graces.

Placing an arm around her shoulders, he led her to a row of canvases that stood against the wall and proceeded to show her his works in progress. Several did indeed display only the head and bare shoulders of his subjects, finishing in a preponderance of wildflowers after the briefest indication of décolletage. His work allowed viewers to assume that the ladies in question had, at the time of their posing, been properly and discreetly covered.

The painting of the Misses Gillingham was amongst the array, but each of them were fully clad. Not an unwise decision, I decided, thinking that the less they revealed of their persons and the more they showed of their father's ability to provide them with fine dresses, the better off they would be.

Still, the painting afforded me some understanding of Monsieur André's success. He had painted the ladies with little regard for the truth and a great deal of regard for the profit that was to be made if they left his garret satisfied. The features of the two youngest had softened, their noses and chins had shortened, and their eyes had lost the pink rabbity look which distinguished them. As for the eldest, she had turned into a beauty who rivalled Charlotte: Her light brown hair had become golden; her pale eyes took on an amethyst shade; and her gentle smile was suggestive of a good-natured disposition. I might have been deceived if I had not already discovered that her good nature depended entirely on being surrounded by those less favored than she.

Mollified by their obvious respectability—not to mention Monsieur's startling good sense when it came to artistic interpretation—Aunt Emily decided she had reacted too hastily. I, however, found myself wondering if the *petit malentendu* that Monsieur André now brushed away with a quick laugh had been more an error of judgment on his part than hers.

In the end it was agreed that Charlotte would pose, although her dress would remain on her shoulders, and Monsieur André admitted—albeit with a heavy sigh— that it was the exact shade of blue that was most flattering to her eyes.

"I have half a mind to insist he paint you, as well," Aunt Emily murmured to me softly as we sat on the frayed settee and watched him work. "I have never seen the Misses Gillingham look so well."

"Nor less like themselves," I pointed out unkindly. "However, the notion does not upset me as I thought it might. Given Monsieur's bent for invention, one need hardly make an appearance. Merely commission the portrait and we shall collect it when he has done."

"Really, child. Sometimes your sense of humor escapes me. I suggest you give my offer serious thought."

"I find the thought of being painted by Monsieur André most serious, indeed. The very possibility chills me to the marrow. For while it is unlikely he will be tempted to elaborate on Charlotte's natural beauty, I can only dread what he would do to me."

"I cannot see that a little enhancement would hurt you."

"It would hurt my pride severely," I countered. "I refuse to live out my days staring up at a portrait that shows me as I should have been instead of how I am."

"You take these things much too seriously. Still, if that is what you wish, I will not force you to sit for him. I meant only to do you a kindness."

"I know," I said, feeling a twinge of guilt. Impulsively, I gave her a kiss on the cheek, something I had rarely done in all of the thirteen years that I had lived with her.

Her full cheeks colored and she fluttered her fan nervously, more taken aback by my kiss than by my usual lack of graciousness. "Goodness, but it is close in here. I feel almost drowsy and the smell of fish quite overpowers one. I wonder how Monsieur can bear to live here."

Lulled by the heat and the boredom of watching the monotonous sweep of Monsieur's paintbrush, Aunt Emily soon drowsed upon the settee, her bosom rising and falling in an even rhythm. While Monsieur, upon finding that his movements and brief comments were no longer being supervised, relaxed and gave less thought to his work than to his charming subject.

"Is it true then, these rumors that I hear," he asked, as he paused to examine his canvas. "It is Lord Blackwood who is your guardian?"

"Since our uncle cannot leave Cornwall he has kindly agreed to act as such while we are in London," I replied, answering for Charlotte who was afraid to blink lest, by fluttering a single lash, she would forever destroy his muse and irrevocably damage her portrait.

But Monsieur seemed more interested in his lordship. "Kindness?" he demanded querulously. "But that is not a kindness. What man would not be willing to take on such a charming responsibility as Mademoiselle Charlotte. And yourself, *naturellement*."

"*Naturellement*," I said dryly.

He glanced at me doubtfully, but seeing that I did not seem offended by his clear preference for my sister, he continued, "Is it true also, that one of you has been promised to him?"

"Where did you hear that?" Charlotte asked coyly, finding herself unable to remain still a moment longer.

Monsieur André set down his brush and threw back the mop of blond hair that had fallen across his forehead. "But that is all I hear. 'Is it Miss Charlotte Grenfel he means to marry? Is it her elder sister? Surely he means to have one of them—but which?' Are you not aware of the curiosity your close relationship with his lordship has stirred?"

Charlotte clapped her hands and giggled with delight. "And which of us do *you* think he means to wed, monsieur?"

"So it is true then, *n'est-ce pas?*" He shook his head sadly. "I am *désolé*. For having seen the beauty of the young Mademoiselle Grenfel, I know there can be but one answer to that question and my heart weeps for you. *Ma pauvre petite.* What a fate will be yours. As an *artiste* I am capable of admiring feminine beauty for its own sake, without . . . without needing to possess a woman—to make her my own. That, you must know, is true romantic love. But as a man I know that others of my gender are not so, shall we say, chaste in their affections. It pains me to think that one so beautiful, so perfect in every feature, shall be wed to one so ugly as that madman."

"You have no right to say such a thing," I said hotly. "Lord Blackwood is neither ugly nor mad. And he is a better man than you will ever be."

"Oh, Redigan," Charlotte exclaimed. "Must you take on? One would almost believe that *you* were his betrothed, not I. And while his lordship may not be mad, you cannot possibly think him well-favored. That awful scar, his demeanor, the . . . the darkness that envelops him—"

"His kindness! His generosity! His genuine affection for you!"

"A certain grace of manners and goodness of heart cannot begin to erase the gloom and melancholic pall he casts simply with his presence," she protested. "Monsieur André has the heart and soul of an artist. He appreciates physical beauty in a way that other people cannot. An ill-favored countenance is an offense to the sensibilities of one such as he. Am I not right, monsieur?"

"Ah! You are, indeed, little one. The *artiste* in me must deplore what another gentleman might overlook. You are a creature of light and sunshine while he, he is born of the night and the shadows. In his rough hands the brightness of your spirit will surely falter and die for lack of nourishment. The match is a tragedy." He heaved a dramatic sigh that implied she was headed for certain death and nothing and no one could save her from her fate.

"You ridiculous little man!" I cried, stamping my foot with such force that the floor of the garret shook beneath us. I blindly ignored Charlotte's shocked face and Monsieur André's astonishment. "Their marriage will be the match of the season," I cried wildly. "Charlotte will be a lady and there are few men whose fortunes and estates compare favorably with his lordship's. There is nothing he could not offer her, nor would not do for her if she but asks. And it is far easier to accustom oneself to a ravaged face than to live with bigotry and smallness of mind. That is the true darkness of the soul."

Charlotte gasped with dismay. "Redigan! You do not mean to suggest that Monsieur André is guilty of—"

"If Monsieur André possessed half the talent he pretends to own, his hours would not be spent in flirting with silly young girls or feeding their vanity with paintings that are neither art nor reality, but overly sentimental and fanciful renditions that have been executed with an eye to the purse rather than to his intended subject."

Long before I completed this pronouncement, my voice had risen to the level of a shout that could be heard above the cries in the street beneath the windows. Aunt Emily, whose drowsy slumber had been shaken by the early portion of our quarrel, now came fully and completely awake.

"Redigan." Her face was aghast. "What on earth are you saying? You have insulted Monsieur André."

"I have done no worse than tell him the truth," I retorted, too angry to back down. "And if the truth insults him, then let *him* apologize for being a great deal less than he presents himself to be."

"Not another word!" Aunt Emily rose to her feet and stood before us, her ample figure trembling and her blue eyes dark with annoyance. "Apologize to Monsieur André immediately," she demanded.

"I will not."

Before my aunt could address this last piece of mutiny, Monsieur André rushed to intervene. In a tone that suggested he was not completely devoid of the knowledge of his own guilt in this little drama, he begged her not to distress herself on his account. "After all, dear lady, we cannot all of us view a painting with the same eye, the same opinion. Art is, at best, subjective—although my success in this field suggests that I, and not your niece, am better qualified to judge what is and is not art. Still, let it not be said that I am so egotistical, so vain of my abilities, that I cannot accept criticism—no matter how ineptly that criticism may be delivered."

Although his hands flew wildly about him as he talked, the more excited he became, the less distinct his accent grew. It occurred to me that the opposite should have been true, and I might have remarked on this oddity if what he was saying had not irritated me more than the manner in which it was being said.

Glancing quickly at me and catching my glare, Monsieur André hastened to add, "And after all, your niece

has unwittingly stumbled upon an unfortunate truth.
A painter cannot paint without oils or canvas, without
the paltry bread which sustains life. Indeed, I have on
occasion, sacrificed my talents to the needs of my
body. I am not too proud to admit my shame. For
shame it is. I can only promise you that with your
younger niece you need expect no artifice, no blurring
of the lines between what I see and feel and what I put
to canvas. For she, she has inspired me. With her, I shall
rise to the heights of my ability. But, now, you must let
me rest. I have done all that I can do today. I am not
a strong man and my emotions have been strained to
the utmost."

He took Charlotte's hand and pressed it to his lips
and hurried us to the door before there could be any
mention of the real reason for our argument.

We clattered down the wooden stairs, none of us
speaking although the tension stretched tautly between us. At the bottom of the first flight, Charlotte suddenly cried, "But Monsieur has forgotten to tell us
when to visit him again." She promptly turned and ran
back up to the landing, Aunt Emily's protests trailing
after her, and returned several long minutes later with
the relieved announcement that he would expect us
two days hence at the same hour as before.

"I have not been so humiliated since the day you bit
his lordship," Aunt Emily exclaimed to me as she settled her bulk onto the velvet-upholstered cushions of
the carriage. She pulled her handkerchief from her reticule and mopped the drift of moisture from her brow.
"Whatever possessed you to act in such a fashion?"

Charlotte's eyes implored me to say nothing of what
had passed between us before our aunt had awakened,
both of us knowing full well that she would not be allowed to return should it be known that Monsieur
André had been speaking harshly of our benefactor
and denigrating their engagement. That was not only
an insult to Lord Blackwood, but a criticism of Aunt

Emily and Uncle Arthur who had agreed to and whole-heartedly supported the union.

She had no need to worry. No matter how I would have liked to enlighten my aunt—and save myself the punishment that was certain to befall me—nothing could have induced me to let Charlotte's thoughtless behavior become known. The thought that Lord Black-wood might somehow learn of her faithlessness, and be deeply wounded by her cruel words, horrified me.

"It was just a silly quarrel," I muttered sullenly. "Monsieur André thought my opinions of the French masters childish and I took offense. You know how greatly I dislike to be mocked."

Charlotte breathed a sigh of relief but Aunt Emily's mouth settled into a grim line. "It would do you good to learn some humility," she said tightly. "I shall expect you to make your apologies when we see him again."

"I will not," I said emphatically, repeating my earlier refusal. "Nothing could induce me to apologize to that man. Nothing!"

Charlotte leaned forward and caught Aunt Emily by the arm. "Oh, but I am sure it will only upset Monsieur André if we refer to the matter," she said, anxious to see that I was not pressed into an admission she would regret. "He assured me he wished never to speak of it again."

"Very well. But do not suppose, Redigan"—she glow-ered at me—"that you will go unpunished. I had hoped that your temper had mellowed in the last few years but, once again, you have disappointed me. Since we have come to London for the sole purpose of finding you a husband—to which end his lordship has gone to no small expense—I cannot deny you the privilege of attending those functions at which your presence is required. However, there will be no more excursions undertaken solely for your pleasure. You may use your free hours to consider your contrariness. I only hope that Monsieur André is too much a gentleman to give an account of your behavior today. Goodness knows what that would do to your chances."

Elizabeth lifted her eyebrows in surprise as I stomped in the door, brushed past the footman, and darted up the stairs as though someone had set the hounds on me. "What on earth—" she began, quickly sweeping her trailing skirts out of my path before they were trodden beneath my feet.

"Do wait, Redigan, please," Charlotte called after me, and when I refused to turn my head or slow my pace, her light step pattered up the stairs after me.

I stormed into our suite, startling the maid who was dusting the curio cabinet, and disappeared into the bedroom, slamming the door behind me. It opened and shut again, this time more quietly, as Charlotte timidly entered.

"Please do not be angry with me," she pleaded. "I will soon convince Aunt Emily that the punishment is too harsh, and Monsieur André promised me that he will say nothing of your outburst, or of my engagement which was meant to be a secret."

"He is hardly likely to speak of my outburst since that would require him to admit something of his own behavior," I said tartly. "Although it is not his lack of manners but your own which truly offended me. How could you speak of his lordship in that fashion? And to a man whom you have met only twice. Have you no sense of propriety?"

"I know I was horribly wrong," she admitted, and tears quivered at the corner of her eyes, making them sparkle brightly. "But you do not know what a relief it is to me to talk to someone who understands. I can hardly confide in Elizabeth or Aunt Emily. They would be shocked. And whenever I tell you of my fears of Lord Blackwood, or mention the doubts I have about marrying him, you become cross and unpleasant. Monsieur André is the first person to appreciate what an unfortunate *mésalliance* I have made."

"Mésalliance? What effrontery." Her words restored my rage to a full-blown fury. "You flutter your lashes at Monsieur André. Pull at his sleeve and plead for his opinions. Tease and cajole him for compliments. Admire his work effusively. What did you expect him to say when you made your opinion of his lordship plain? You encouraged his insults and he willingly supported you in hopes of pleasing you."

The tears which had wavered at the edges of her eyelids rose in a rush and poured down her cheeks. "Now you are being nasty again," she said with a choked sob. "I believe you are jealous of the attention he paid me. Truly I do. You want him for yourself. Admit it. You are in love with him."

I laughed out loud. "You really are ridiculous. I neither admire nor like him. He is too full of himself. And, besides, there is something deceitful about the man."

"Now who is being ridiculous. And if you are not in love with him then why are you making such a fuss?" she demanded. Then she gasped and her rosebud mouth rounded into a delicate circle. "Surely you cannot be in love with Lord Blackwood?"

"Absolutely not!" I retorted, but my heart sank with a peculiar feeling.

Charlotte hesitated. "Well, perhaps not, for I am sure I do not see how anyone could be in love with him." She gazed at me doubtfully. "In truth, you do look peculiar, Redigan. Do you think you could be coming down with something?"

"It has been a tiresome day," I said, taking a tip from Monsieur André. "Would you be good enough to pull the curtains? I think I will lay down for a while."

Chapter Eight

CHARLOTTE did as I had asked and then softly tip-toed from the room, leaving me alone with my confused thoughts and the questions that whirled through my mind. Through it all I felt a blazing sense of outrage. How could I not have seen the truth?

Of course, it had been many weeks since I had told myself that I disliked his lordship. Without question I admired him and used him as a gauge to measure every man who was introduced to me—always to their discredit. I groaned. Surely, I should have seen that as a warning. But it had been blithely disregarded.

There had been the kiss in the garden. My cheeks grew warm at the memory. After the ball, I had dismissed the encounter as meaningless, as his lordship had done, perhaps to escape my own embarrassment. Now, I knew that whatever it may have been for Lord Blackwood, it had been anything but meaningless to me. Why else would I have suffered a loss of appetite and rounded on Charlotte whenever she dared to speak a word against him?

Feebly, I attempted to tell myself not to mistake loyalty and gratitude for something more compelling. But I needed only to feel the racing of my heart and the trembling of my hands to know that I was lying to myself. Somehow I had fallen madly, utterly, and completely in love with the very man I could not hope to marry.

I lay in the cool darkness; my pulse throbbed and my head ached. Across from me a shaft of light slipped through the draperies and fell across the silver elephant. His trunk glinted in the half light and his emerald eyes flashed with cool amusement at my predicament.

Perhaps, when you come to know men better, your tastes may change.

"Damn!" I exclaimed, daring to use profanity for the first time in my eighteen years and not caring who might overhear. "Damn! Damn! Damn!"

That said, I felt a great deal better. It amazed me how efficacious an oath could be and it struck me as entirely unfair that only men were allowed the use of them. It bespoke an unreasonable selfishness on their part, and I resolved in the future to allow myself more freedom—though not, perhaps, where Aunt Emily could hear me as I preferred not to distress her.

I found, as the days passed, that the recuperative powers of oaths were of short-lived duration, and tried to lose myself in activity. To that end, Charlotte was most helpful. As she had promised, she deftly dispensed with my punishment by insisting that it would soon become obvious that she was his lordship's betrothed if I ceased to accompany them on their outings. Yet I would have been happier if I had been refused the privilege of accompanying them, for Charlotte was unconscionably casual towards Lord Blackwood. She received each favor as one expected, each compliment was treated as no more than her due. And should we encounter a group of acquaintances, he was left to entertain himself as she gravitated to their company.

During one such defection, after Charlotte had waltzed away with a young fop who had sung her praises until I was almost grateful to see them depart, I turned to his lordship and said crossly, "I would think she would grow tired of hearing the same compliments repeated day after day, for none of the young men who court her appear to suffer from an excess of imagination."

His lordship, who had been thoughtfully contemplating the pair as they waltzed around the ballroom, complacently remarked, "I daresay she will settle down by the end of the season."

"By the end of the season, she will be a perfect little prig," I retorted. "She is growing more vain by the second. Charlotte was always immature, and all this attention has completely turned her head. And you are as much at fault as anyone."

His brows arched and he gave me a measured look. "I am to be her husband," he reminded me. A shadow seemed to pass behind his eyes, but whatever he was thinking, he merely said, "She has a right to expect my compliments."

"Not when she shows them no appreciation. It would serve her right if you turned your eye elsewhere," I said, sounding unreasonably hopeful.

He scowled. "I would not think of such a thing. I have given your uncle my word. Nor would it be kind of me to mislead some poor gentlewoman who believed me sincere in my attentions to her."

"That much is true. Well, then," I said generously. "If you like you may display an inordinate interest in me. I, at least, will know the truth."

I felt the heat of his eyes upon me; they glowed darkly, then his back straightened and the light in his eyes died, smothered from within. "My attentions towards you have already harmed your chances for marriage," he said stiffly. "May I suggest that you direct your attentions to finding someone to partner you in a dance."

He did not wait for my answer, but bowed politely and walked off.

*   *   *

I began to look forward to those hours which Charlotte spent posing for Monsieur André. Since she was usually accompanied by Aunt Emily, and Elizabeth and Lord Blackwood were forbidden to distract me with some more pleasurable excursion, my afternoons were my own. But whatever sense of peace or acceptance I gained during these hours promptly vanished upon their return. Then, Charlotte insisted I listen to a litany of Monsieur André's virtues and hear a repetition of each and every compliment he had paid her.

"But you would be proud of me," she insisted as she arranged a bouquet of roses—a gift from Lord Blackwood—in the tall rose-glass crystal vase that stood on the occasional table. "I have not once encouraged Monsieur to say another word against his lordship, nor told him again of my worries. Instead, I insisted that as our benefactor he is entitled to respect, and Monsieur must restrain himself in the future to remarking only upon my beauty. There! Was that not properly said? I assure you, he marvelled at my forbearance and told me I had a heart that was as fair and good as my person. Since then he has been wonderfully restrained and contrite. You would hardly recognize him."

"If he is as circumspect in his remarks as you suggest, then indeed I would not. Restraint and contrition are not qualities I would associate with him."

"You are hardly one to criticize," she pointed out in a hurt voice. "But you have never really come to know Monsieur. Not as I have done this past week. He is so dear, so passionate about beauty and love—"

"And why is he talking to you of love?" I demanded.

"He did not say anything untoward," she said hastily. "In truth, he could not. For Aunt Emily does not often drowse, although she cannot hear everything that we say. No, he talked of the *essence* of love, 'love that transcends mere legalities or social trivialities.' Those were his very words. Each time we meet I come away inspired." She dropped onto the sofa beside me and lowered her voice. "Do not be cross, but there is something I must tell you." She hesitated, then in a rush, said, "I believe he talks of love because that is what he feels for me, but dares not declare himself knowing that I am already engaged."

"Surely you would not welcome such a declaration?" I asked in horror.

"But I would," she wailed. "You were right when you accused me of mistaking silly flirtations for love. The others were as nothing compared to my feelings for Monsieur André. The hours spent in his garret are more precious to me than dresses or balls or meaningless flattery from young boys who have not one tenth of his sophistication. What am I to do? I cannot possibly marry Lord Blackwood when I love someone else. Surely he would not want me to become his wife knowing how I really feel?"

Remembering the conversation that had passed between his lordship and Elizabeth the evening I slipped downstairs, I imagined he would not. But nor had he contemplated Charlotte's breaking off their engagement, but assumed that by the end of the season she would have overcome her misgivings and gone to him willingly. To discover that she wanted to throw him over for someone as ridiculous as Monsieur André. . . . It was unthinkable!

"Do not think for one second that Aunt Emily would allow you to make such a marriage," I warned severely. "And Uncle Arthur has given Lord Blackwood his word as a gentleman."

"But if he married you he could keep his promise and Pendene's Wood. Monsieur André cares nothing for material possessions. And it would not be as bad for you to marry his lordship as it would be for me. You are not frightened by his appearance, nor are you in love with anybody. If you, too, loved another then I would not make such a suggestion. But since you have no strong feelings for anyone—"

"Nor has anyone strong feelings for me," I added, saying that which she had tactfully left unsaid. "I should no doubt leap at the opportunity to have a husband, even one you have so carelessly discarded."

"You do not have to put things in such a brutal fashion," she remonstrated. "But I do not see that your prospects are such that you can afford to belittle my offer."

Had she guessed my feelings for her fiancé, she would have understood my objections even less. But in all her plotting she had forgotten to consider his feelings. Lord Blackwood wanted Charlotte, not me, and I would not allow her to shunt him aside without a single qualm.

Her eyes pleaded with me for support, but the venom inside me must have shown in my expression for she drew back with a dismayed gasp. I struggled to control my features, but my hands twitched in my lap as though agitated by my murderous thoughts.

"It simply will not do," I said flatly. "You must make up your mind to marry him. He loves you and you will learn to love him. Have you forgotten already that you will be a lady, mistress of a great estate in Cornwall and able to come to London whenever you please?"

"No," she admitted. "It is the one matter that troubles me. Monsieur André can hardly afford to feed himself. Oh, why must love be so complicated!" she cried. "It is unfair that the means to support a wife and the desire to do so should not go hand in hand."

"There is a lot in life that is unfair," I said darkly.

Whatever pity Charlotte's unhappiness might have stirred in me was squashed by the knowledge that a mere mention of the financial difficulties was enough to resolve her to the impossibilities of the situation. In truth, my sympathies were entirely with Lord Blackwood. I was determined that should it be within my power, he would not suffer the pain of her indifference.

To see him hurt would have been harder to bear than my own disappointment.

But he could not have conducted his courtship more foolishly nor more carelessly. Had Monsieur André been well breeched, Charlotte might well have acted unwisely. But, given free rein, she would doubtless find another, more suitable man on whom to bestow her affections before the end of the season. I decided his lordship must be made to realize that if he was to win my sister's heart, he must impress upon her his own importance and standing—a position she would share as his wife—rather than trust her to come to an appreciation of his finer qualities.

I had, unfortunately, few chances to speak with him alone. Fate, propriety, and seemingly his own determination to talk with me only in the company of others, made a private conversation nearly impossible. But at last, he chanced to call upon his sister shortly after Charlotte and Aunt Emily had departed for the garret.

Their carriage had barely rolled down the street, the eddies of dust kicked up by the wheels and the horses' hooves not yet settled, before he appeared at the door and inquired after his sister. It was my good fortune that Sir Frederick had dined with us the evening before, determinedly ignoring his hostess's subtle mentions of the lateness of the hour and her pointed yawns, and remaining long after the rest of us had retired.

Elizabeth sent me down to the drawing room to sit with her brother until she could make an appearance, a duty which set my pulse racing and gave me a lightness of foot that had been absent for several days.

Lord Blackwood stood near the hearth, his elbow resting on the mantel as he perused a porcelain miniature that Sir Frederick had recently added to Elizabeth's collection. He turned as I entered, his dark curls set in motion by his abrupt movement, and a flash of pleasure crossed his face. Then, immediately, his expression darkened and he seemed to withdraw into himself.

"Good afternoon, milord," I said, seating myself in an armchair that was close enough for quiet conversation yet not so near that he might decide he had business elsewhere and could well return at a later hour. "Elizabeth will be down shortly," I hastened to add, forcing myself to meet his gaze with a composure that was entirely assumed. My voice sounded unnaturally hoarse, but I seemed to have lost the ability to relax in his company.

He regarded me seriously for a moment, then nodded stiffly. "I hope that my early arrival has not discomfited you in any fashion."

"Not at all."

After waiting for me to say more and finding I would not, he asked, "Am I to assume that your aunt and your sister are not at home?"

"Had you arrived a few minutes earlier you would not have missed them. They took the carriage and . . . went shopping," I said, not wanting to tell him where they had really gone, since the portrait was intended to be a surprise.

He regarded me narrowly as though recognizing me for a liar and suspecting me of concealing the real reason for their absence. "Your sister is well liked," and his words held the hint of an accusation.

"She is," I admitted casually, ignoring the undertones to his remark. But clearly he suspected her of keeping some tryst. It surprised me to think that he believed my aunt would be a complacent accomplice to such behavior—or had he noticed how easily Charlotte manipulated her without her knowing? Since, after a fashion, this was no less than the truth, I could not stop myself from blushing guiltily beneath his searching gaze.

His lips tightened with annoyance as he assumed the worst. I sat there miserably, not knowing how to right the impression I had given him when, after all, it was not entirely false. At last, I decided he must deal with his anger in his own manner. If nothing else, his presence and his suspicions gave me the opening I had long awaited.

"I have wanted to speak to you of Charlotte for some while," I began, and his gaze returned to me with marked interest.

"Go on."

"She is very young, even for her seventeen years, and I have often thought that the things which make this match so desirable are the very things you refuse to flaunt."

"And that would be?"

"Your standing, the obvious respect you command from your peers—"

"My title and my money," he said.

I flushed.

His dark lashes lowered, concealing his eyes and making it impossible for me to guess whether he was amused or offended by my words.

"I am sorry if—"

"If once again you are too forthright? It would seem that I am in need of some plain speaking. But I have never liked ostentation. It is the mark of poor breeding."

"And yet when one is young, they are more likely to be swayed by ostentation than by other, more admirable qualities."

"Are you suggesting that I buy her affections?" he demanded, his face dark with anger.

"I have never believed that affection can be bought," I said evenly.

"Then what are you suggesting?"

"That you are unlikely to win those affections unless you first win her attention. And while you patiently stand to one side waiting for her to appreciate your virtues, others, less scrupulous, are using every means at

their disposal to impress upon her their own importance."

With an exasperated cry, he rose and paced about
the room as though pursued by thoughts he would
rather not confront. At last he turned to me, his chin
arrogantly high, and demanded, "Do you suggest then
that I strut about like some dandy, jingling my purse
and spouting the names of my forebears? What a fool
you would have me look."

"And how foolish would you feel if your cautious
lovemaking gave some other gentleman the chance to
win Charlotte's heart?"

He frowned. "I cannot say that I like the advice you
are handing me. It seems that either way my dignity
is forfeit. I believe that Sir Frederick was right in saying
that women were put among us to teach us humility
and patience."

"If women could accomplish either of those tasks
then their place in heaven would be guaranteed," Elizabeth drawled as she entered the drawing room. "But
I daresay we must find other means, those doors being
barred, locked, and more strongly fortified than any
garrison. Be assured that I will deal harshly with him
when we speak next."

She collapsed on the settee and fanned herself with
her hand. Her silver-streaked curls escaped the scarf
that bound them in becoming disarray. "So you have
been talking to Sir Frederick," she said after a few languid sweeps. "Did he mention that he planted himself
in my drawing room last night, willfully disregarding
my attempts to retire, and kept me up all night until
he had scraped up the courage to propose to me yet
again? It is his sixth proposal to me this year and here
it is only the end of April. His company is becoming
quite tedious. I was already of a mind to refuse him,
but he looked so pathetic I permitted myself to say only
that I would give it some thought. Now I regret my kindness. When he calls next, I shall treat him to a resound-

ing *no*. Such insufferable impertinence should never be borne."

Lord Blackwood looked at her severely. "No doubt my unthinking remark has given you the excuse for which you anxiously searched."

She laughed. "La, Nicholas. If you were not my brother I would not put up with your presumptuous remarks."

"Were I not your brother, I would not dare to make them."

While Lord Blackwood had insisted he did not care for my advice, he must have thought it behooved him to listen. Having rented a box at Covent Garden Theatre, he arrived to collect us in a coach and four. The horses were perfectly matched dappled grays. White plumes had been attached to their bridles and waved gaily above their heads, and the driver was dressed in full livery.

Elizabeth was clearly taken aback by this unwonted display, but Charlotte gazed upon them rapturously. "Surely, we will see no finer carriage tonight," she exclaimed. "Everyone will be sick with envy."

By everyone, no doubt she meant the dozen or more foolish young ladies she considered her best and dearest friends, each of whom would have happily given up her favorite dress for the pleasure of oversetting any one of the others. On those occasions when they succeeded, they modestly claimed their victory "did not signify."

"I have never understood why you attempt to impress them if you deny yourself the right to gloat when you succeed," I remarked.

Charlotte gasped as if I had committed an obvious breach of good taste, and informed me, "That would be horribly impolite and beneath my dignity."

"No less polite or undignified than flouting your filled dance cards or pinched waistlines," I retorted.

Lord Blackwood chuckled and helped us into the carriage. The warmth of his hand and the secret smile he bestowed on me aroused a rush of confusion, and I was hard put to maintain my balance. Nor could I help but appreciate the care he had taken with his appearance that evening. Always dressed well, tonight his suit was obviously new, the brocade waistcoat glittered whitely beneath the glow of the street lamps, and the high pointed collar rose to stiff points that concealed the lower half of his scar.

"You look most distinguished, dear brother," Elizabeth remarked, cannily drawing Charlotte's attention to him. "I cannot say when I have seen you look so well."

Charlotte gave him a quick look but instead of letting her glance fleet away as she always did, her gaze fixed upon him as though she had never truly seen him before.

"Indeed, you cut quite the dashing figure, milord," I said, adding my praise to his sister's. "Do you not agree, Charlotte?"

"Yes. Why, yes I do," she stammered, her eyes blinking as she tried to recognize in him the same man whom she had seen almost every day for the past month and a half. Then her attention turned to his strong hands, and the massive gold and ruby ring which dominated them. "How lovely," she cried. "You have not worn that ring before."

"It is a family heirloom. The piece is very valuable, but overlarge and too ornate for my tastes," he confessed. "But there are other pieces that might interest you. My ancestors thought it prudent to invest a portion of their wealth in gold and precious stones. Land, while decidedly more useful, cannot be carried away under one's arm should the times demand a hasty departure, and even my father was not blind to the warnings of the French Revolution."

"Surely he did not think such a thing was possible

in England?" Charlotte asked, her eyes dark with horror and fascination.

"There were many who did. But this is a night for gaiety. We shall leave these somber subjects to those afternoons when our minds are devoted to more serious occupations. Besides," he exclaimed, his green eyes flashing with mischief, "I have something more interesting to show you."

Reaching into the inside pocket of his coat, he pulled out a rolled pouch and untied the ribbons which secured it. As Charlotte watched, her face alight with excitement and anticipation, he withdrew a sapphire necklace set in silver filigree.

A delighted gasp escaped her. There could be no question that the necklace was intended for her. The glittering blue of the stones matched the hue and sparkle of her eyes with such exactness that she might have been a porcelain doll whose eyes had been set with those selfsame stones. Impulsively, she reached out her hand, her quick movement stirring the scent of violets which she had discreetly applied to her wrist, her face a study in innocent greed.

"Charlotte," Aunt Emily reprimanded sharply, and Charlotte's hand fell back as quickly as it had been extended while a look of growing dismay replaced her pleased smile as she became aware of the presumptuousness of her actions.

"No, no," Lord Blackwood said calmly. "She is quite right. I have brought the necklace for her to wear this evening, for who else could do it justice. And it will not be long before the piece is hers by right. It is part of the collection that will belong to her when she becomes my wife."

"Collection?" Charlotte asked, pulling her gaze away from the lure of the gems to stare at him with even greater interest, a feat I would have deemed impossible.

"Certainly," he assured her. "My wife shall not want

for adornment, no matter how little that adornment
may be needed."

He lifted the necklace and bent forward so that he
might fasten it around her neck. The large square-cut
center stone nestled in her décolletage, and Charlotte
lifted her eyes to his with a look of gratitude touched
by wonder.

"I am afraid I shall have to ask you to return the piece
to me at the end of the evening for its safekeeping, but
when you are my wife, it is yours for the asking."

I sensed a faint edge of distaste in his voice, as
though the thought of bribing Charlotte for her affections still did not sit well with him. But he will not have
to do so for long, I told myself, as I had told him earlier,
and I brushed aside the veil of doubt and misgiving that
threatened to descend over my complacency.

His lordship now turned to me and his smile reflected none of the unease that it had hitherto shown.
"And I can hardly dress one Miss Grenfel in my family's
heirlooms and neglect the other, or our secret will be
a secret no longer." His green eyes twinkled as he
pulled a long rope of amethysts from his pouch. At the
very last, there emerged a pear-shaped pendant the
size of a small plum but dark lilac in color.

"Remarkable, is it not?" his lordship asked, lifting it
for us to admire.

Even a peremptory perusal was enough for one to
see that the strand was finer than the one he had
loaned my sister, and it surprised me that—if we were
not to be treated equally—he did not show a preference to Charlotte. But after remarking how well suited
I was to amethysts, Lord Blackwood slyly turned to her
and said, "This, too, will be yours after our wedding."

Her covetous gaze was ill concealed and it struck me
that had his lordship done as I had expected, Charlotte
might not have had such good reason to anticipate her
wedding day. I wryly surveyed his face, wondering

what thoughts and emotions played beneath that expressionless surface.

For one who disliked games, I noted, he played them exceedingly well.

Despite the obvious success of my machinations—or perhaps because of them—I was not sorry when we reached our destination. The Saloon to the Private Boxes at Covent Garden Theatre was impressively elegant and brilliantly lit. Dark pillars supported the vaulted ceiling, and statues lined the walls, presiding over the long room and the row of seats which had been set beneath them. The crowd of people who filed out of the boxes following the performance of *Macbeth* was unnaturally quiet. It was as if the spell Mrs. Siddons had cast with her performance still hung over them, and it was several minutes before they regained their cheerful volume.

Aunt Emily deserted us to greet an elderly woman she had known as a young girl, and Elizabeth paused to speak with a man and woman who were related to her daughter through marriage. For once, Charlotte seemed content to linger at his lordship's side and I, having nowhere else to go, remained with them.

Charlotte teased his lordship for his own thoughts of the play, seeking out his opinions as though she was consulting Monsieur André on the merits of a portrait she had chanced to view. I watched them disconsolately, feeling a sharp twinge of regret that my advice had met with such success, before forcing myself to direct my attention to those activities in the Saloon which did not cause me distress.

My gaze happened to fall upon a matronly woman, quizzing glass tightly gripped in her hand as she peered at the people she passed. It was some seconds before I recognized her as Lady Edgmont. Beside her walked an imposing gentleman with startlingly white hair and bushy whiskers. His blue eyes were hard and, set above a prominent nose, gave him a hawklike appearance. This was emphasized by a sharp chin and a thin mouth that was fixed in an unwavering line.

They had, apparently, but recently stepped from their own box and were making their way through the crowds of people who had not yet left the theater. We stood, unfortunately, directly in their path, and they could not help but see Lord Blackwood as they passed.

How awkward, I thought. For I could hardly tell his lordship that his first wife's parents were nearby without revealing a knowledge of his affairs that I had no business in knowing. But if I said nothing, they were almost certain to see him, and I did not like to think of the pain that moment would occasion all three of them.

But there seemed to be nothing I could do. It was quite ridiculous to think that with my small person I might shield his lordship from their view. I could only pray that they would turn aside to speak to someone and, in doing so, alert Lord Blackwood of their presence.

But Lord and Lady Edgmont continued their progress through throngs of animated theatergoers, her ladyship peering nearsightedly at the faces of each cluster of men and women they passed, his lordship growling out a brief "how do" or curtly nodding as he saw fit. As they drew nearer, his wife again lifted the quizzing glass to her eye, her attention no doubt caught by the rowdy group of young men jostling each other aside as they vainly tried to draw Charlotte's gaze away from Lord Blackwood.

With a loud gasp, Lady Edgmont stopped abruptly, dropping the glass which swayed wildly at the end of a long gold chain. Her husband, who had been but a half step behind her, collided with her back, almost knocking her down.

"Really, m'dear," he began as he took hold of her elbow to steady her. The reproach was broken off as he realized what had caused her agitation.

His head jerked up and he drew up the black walking stick he carried at his side until it pointed like a sword before him. "You, sir!" he cried in a loud voice, drawing all eyes in his direction.

Lord Blackwood turned slowly, as though having recognized the voice he saw no reason to respond in haste. "Lord Edgmont," he said mildly with a slight bow.

The man's face turned a mottled red, and his sharp features were bloated with fury. "How dare you, sir!" he exclaimed. "How dare you show your face in London after murdering my daughter!"

Chapter Nine

His cry sent a convulsive shudder through the gathering in the Saloon, and the faces around us shone with a keener interest than they had displayed at any point during the performance of *Macbeth*. Indeed, it was almost as though the play had not yet ended, there was something so melodramatic, even farcical, about Lord Edgmont's histrionics. I could not believe that a man of his stature would give credence to servants' gossip.

As the hero, confronted by his horrific accusation, Lord Blackwood looked suitably stunned, and his eyes glittered with the beginnings of outrage. But if Charlotte must, perforce, be cast in the role of the heroine, she did not play the role of the devoted and faithful lover with the same perfection. Already she had begun to draw back from his lordship, and her lips were white and trembling.

A portly man who had bid his lordship good day as we entered the theater cleared his throat and said, "I say, milord! Surely, you cannot credit that ridiculous rumor."

"Rumor! It is the God's truth, sir! And nothing less," Lord Edgmont cried and there was a touch of madness in his cold blue eyes.

Lord Blackwood stared at him as if measuring the effect of his words before he spoke. Then, in a quiet voice that carried from one end of the Saloon to the other, he said, "I had heard that you suspected foul play but did not for a minute think you capable of believing that I would have harmed Lydia in any way. I can only give you my profound assurances and my word as a gentleman that your daughter died in childbirth."

"Then why," he demanded, his face purpling, "did you not bother to inform us of her death until after the funeral?"

Lord Blackwood looked most offended. "Do you realize what meeting that demand would have entailed? Had I sent a messenger by horse to your summer home in Yorkshire and you returned posthaste, I could not have delayed her burial for nigh on two weeks. In all decency, I beg of you to end this nonsense."

There was a sudden snap in the tension, as though his calm words had returned the world to a normality that had unaccountably been ripped asunder, and a ripple of murmurs broke the silence that had weighed upon our shoulders.

The moment was short-lived. His lordship sidled past his wife and stepped forward until he was face to face with Lord Blackwood. The two men met each other's gazes with a hard look; their backs were as rigid and uncompromising as the marble statues poised against the walls.

"What kind of a fool do you take me for?" Lord Edgmont demanded in a voice that was as cold and sharp as shards of ice. "She wrote her mother weekly. Do you think she left us in ignorance as to the true nature of your marriage?" This last was said softly, as though his words were intended only for Lord Blackwood, but Charlotte and I could not help but overhear, although neither of us was the wiser for his disclosure. And Lord Edgmont did not seem inclined to elaborate.

It appeared that Lord Blackwood, at least, needed no enlightenment, for he blanched and a muscle in his face twitched, making the ragged scar twist upon his cheek. But his response was gentle and soothing, as though he was dealing with a spooked horse that needed careful handling. "Again, I swear to you," he avowed, "that I did everything within my power to make your daughter happy. And you have not only my word as to the nature of her death, but that of the doctor who attended her."

At this, Charlotte's cheeks grew a shade less pale. I heard myself sigh and realized I had been holding my breath. But if the mention of a person of so respectable a character as a doctor had satisfied Charlotte that his lordship's innocence had been proved, it did not assuage Lord Edgmont's doubts.

"Ha!" he exclaimed belligerently. "A certain Dr. Polharris was it not? I believe he signed the death certificate."

"He did." Lord Blackwood looked past him as if he had suddenly become aware of the audience their conversation had attracted. His gaze swept the Saloon with a look of distaste. "Surely, milord, this conversation would be better conducted elsewhere?" He raised his arm to take Lord Edgmont by the elbow and guide him into the privacy of one of the boxes, but his lordship yanked back his arm.

"Do not think you will silence me that easily, you damned blackguard. It may have taken me a few years, but I have found out a thing or two about your doctor that I fancy you never thought I would learn. He is a drunk and a gambler, and hardly fit to tend a sick dog, let alone a girl as delicate as Lydia. And there is a good deal more than that to arouse suspicion. Where is your Dr. Polharris now? Can you tell me that?"

"I believe he has since retired."

Lord Edgmont snorted derisively. "He has retired all right. Barely a week after my daughter's death, and on the money you paid him to conceal your foul deed.

Bribery, sirrah! Nothing less than bribery and do not bother to deny it!"

"I have no intention of answering such a slanderous charge," Lord Blackwood said, and his tone was frighteningly pleasant. "But if you were not twice my age I would demand that you meet me tomorrow morning and give me satisfaction."

"If I were your age, I would give you no choice but to face me! I am half of a mind to call you out despite my rheumatism. Nothing less than your death will give *me* satisfaction."

At this, Lady Edgmont did us the good turn of swooning and collapsing on the floor. Her skirts billowed around her as she sank, and she settled upon them like an air balloon that was being deflated.

Lord Edgmont turned and gave a soft cry of annoyance. He could hardly leave his wife lying on the carpet unattended although, clearly, he considered doing so. "Do get up, Sophie," he demanded impatiently, rousing only a slight moan. A young lady who stood nearby knelt over her ladyship and fanned her briskly while another woman patted her on the hand. At this, satisfied that he was not needed, Lord Edgmont turned back to us, but Lord Blackwood shook his head grimly.

"See to your wife, sir. I have given you my word that your daughter did not die through any act of mine. If that does not satisfy you, then you must address your concerns to a magistrate."

"Be assured that I have already done so. But as Dr. Polharris has gone abroad—and neither his ex-landlady nor his acquaintances seem to know precisely where—he can hardly be questioned as to the exact nature of the events that transpired that night. How fortunate for your lordship that he should make himself so difficult to find."

"You try my temper unduly, milord. Unless you can substantiate your accusations, I advise you to desist. Now, if you will excuse me, my carriage is waiting."

Whatever plans his lordship might have made for us after the theater were forgotten. Throughout the drive home we managed a stilted conversation, first one, then another of us complimenting the play, the performances of each actor in turn, Mrs. Siddons's uncanny portrayal of Lady Macbeth—each of us deliberately ignoring Lord Edgmont's wild accusations as though they had never occurred.

Had Aunt Emily and Charlotte not been present, I would have dared to announce, "What utter balderdash!" and commend Lord Blackwood on his sensible and moderate handling of the affair. But Aunt Emily would have been humiliated beyond endurance if I had dared to refer to any part of that awkward scene, and Charlotte's eyes had assumed the vacant look that forewarned a fit of hysteria. One ill-chosen word and she would give vent to loud wails and a veritable font of tears, and this was no frog that could be tucked behind one's back and disposed of later in the garden.

It was, I supposed, some proof of Charlotte's growing maturity that she was able to contain her outburst until after his lordship had bid us good night and we had retired. But barely had the door closed behind us, than she flung her outstretched body across the bed and buried her face in her pillow so that her howls could not be heard beyond our bedroom.

"A fine sight you will look tomorrow if you keep that up," I said crossly, wondering why God and my parents had decided to inflict her upon me. And when I considered that she would have had no reason to upset herself if she had had the slightest faith in his lordship— or even the good sense to realize the impossibility of someone of his character harming anyone—it rankled that I must give her fears the serious attention due a real problem.

"Do stop," I said at last when it appeared the sodden pillow had reached the extent of its absorbency and the mattress was threatened. "If you do not, Elizabeth will surely hear you."

When Charlotte's wails continued, even increased in vigor, I said sweetly, "If you cannot calm yourself, I shall have to add the strength of my pillow to yours and likely I shall smother you in the process."

Charlotte gave a last defiant hiccough, then warily raised her head. "I believe you will be pleased when I am dead," she said resentfully.

"Let us say only that I will not be much perturbed."

But, this time, my callousness, which was usually most effective in silencing her hysterics, had less effect than the pillow. Large drops rolled silently down her cheeks and her breasts heaved beneath the strain of containing her sobs. It seemed that she must run out of tears or the energy to express them, but they continued even as she mustered enough spite to say, "When I am dead, you will remember your words and your conscience will not let you rest."

"My conscience rarely troubles me," I pointed out complacently. "And since Lord Blackwood is a most unlikely murderer, I doubt that it will be disturbed over anything that I say to you tonight."

I pulled a handkerchief from my pocket, decided it was neither too soiled for her use nor too clean to be shared without regret, and told her to dry her eyes. This she did, wiping them with an air of despondency, as though she was fated to meet her end shortly and nothing truly mattered.

"You cannot seriously believe that his lordship would harm you," I said when she sat quietly, staring into the middle of the room, yet seeming to see nothing. "He has never shown you anything but kindness."

"No doubt he showed Lydia the same kindness, before he killed her." She turned her face to appeal to me. "Oh, Redigan. I know it is true. I feel it. I have always felt there was something forbidding about his lordship—more than just his scarred face. It is the darkness of his soul. Monsieur André felt it too. That was why he was so much comfort to me. Certainly, Uncle Arthur will not expect me to marry his lordship now. Not when he hears of this night."

"When he hears of this night he will think what I and everyone else in the Saloon thought—save you. That poor Lord Edgmont has been unbalanced by his daughter's death, and Lord Blackwood showed admirable restraint in his behavior."

Charlotte looked aghast as if the thought that no one would support her fears had not occurred to her. "Surely, he will not. He cannot," she said in a breathy whisper, and fear brightened her eyes.

"Do you think that Aunt Emily would let us remain in this house a moment longer if she truly believed there was an ounce of truth in Lord Edgmont's accusations?" I demanded hotly. "She would be packing our clothes this very second, and his lordship would have heard her opinion of him before we parted company."

Charlotte moaned like an animal caught in a snare, and her eyes darted wildly about the room as though she searched for an escape. "There is no help for me, then," she murmured. "Not here. None of you will believe until it is too late and then . . . and then. . . ." She sighed, a soft gentle sigh that might have been a cry of pleasure rather than dismay, and she fell back against the pillows and closed her eyes. Within minutes, her exhaustion had overtaken her and she had fallen asleep.

"His lordship is waiting," I said, giving Charlotte a cool stare as she lay back in bed. She was still wearing the dress she had not bothered to remove the night before; her fists firmly clenched the counterpane as though only the scissors would separate the two.

"You must tell him that I am indisposed," she said, and there was a look of determination about her eyes that I had never seen before.

I shrugged. "You cannot ask that of me. He is not a fool, Charlotte. He will know at once that you are afraid of him."

"Then let him know. One can hardly murder one's wife and then expect other young ladies to traipse happily to the altar with one."

"Never have I known you to be this stubborn," I said with a cry of exasperation. "Stay in bed then. I will tell his lordship that your face has broken out with pustules and your eyes have swollen shut!"

I paused to see if this announcement spurred her to her feet, but she merely glared at me and gripped the counterpane even tighter.

Seeing my threats were to no avail, I flounced out of the room, my temper flaring. It was bad enough that I had to endure her silliness, but now I would likely be forbidden a ride since Aunt Emily had not yet curtailed my punishment.

Lord Blackwood was sitting in the drawing room, his attention wandering from my aunt's chatter to the street outside where the groom waited with the horses he had hired. He glanced up expectantly as I entered, frowning when he saw that I was alone.

"Charlotte is un—" I broke off, remembering the last time I had said she was unwell and how quickly he had discerned the truth. "—unable to join us," I finished instead. "It was not until she dressed that she realized her riding habit was torn—she says it was carelessness, but I believe she has eaten too many pastries these last few weeks. More than one of her new dresses are uncomfortably tight. Either way, she insisted you were not to be disappointed, knowing how much you dislike to ride alone. She said we must go without her." This last was added with an eye to Aunt Emily. That shrewd woman saw immediately that I was attempting to circumvent her restrictions but was at a loss to decide how to regain the upper hand without appearing to disregard his lordship's feelings.

"Well, then. Shall we be off?" he said before she could think of an objection. "I believe Elizabeth's groom has more than he can handle." He bowed to Aunt Emily. "If you would be so good as to tell my sister when she returns from the millinery shop that she must expect me for supper tonight."

"Of course, milord," Aunt Emily replied, and taking that as meaning she was in agreement to our riding together, we quickly departed.

Leaving the groom to return the third mount to the stables from which she had been hired, we started off for Hyde Park. The horses' iron shoes rang out against the cobblestones as we trotted past the somber brick homes, but my mood was anything but sad. There was nowhere else I would have rather been than riding at Lord Blackwood's side, enjoying the manner in which the sunlight glanced across his dark face, throwing the hollows of his cheeks into shadow and darkening the line of his firm jaw.

Even the air smelled cleaner and fragrant with the flowery perfumes that drifted from the gardens. Either the breeze had swept away the smell of smoke and fumes, or I had become accustomed to the smells of London and they had ceased to annoy me.

Hyde Park was filled with riders, eagerly enjoying one of the milder, brighter days we had seen that spring. Our canter along the lake was punctuated by greetings from many of our new acquaintances. Were it not for that, I might have noticed sooner that his lordship had barely spoken since we had left Coudrey House.

He does not need to speak for me to be content, I thought idly, happy just to be in his presence, but even I could not remain oblivious to his mood as his silence continued. There was a stiffness in the way he held his shoulders, and his jaw was held with an arrogance that suggested he would not deign to comment on the thoughts which clouded his private world.

It is because of Charlotte, I thought petulantly. Her and her silly fancies. But my anger soon became guilt when I recalled how I had assisted her in avoiding our outing—however little I may have wanted to help. When I return I shall sit down with Aunt Emily and have a good talk with her, I determined. She will soon set Charlotte straight. The thought of our no-nonsense aunt verbally trampling upon her made me feel a great deal better and I laughed gaily as a flock of ducks scattered from our path and fled towards the lake.

My laughter drew Lord Blackwood's gaze and he regarded me solemnly for several seconds. I stared back into those green eyes and grinned impudently. "Shall we race?" I suggested. "Your horse is no better than mine today, and I believe you would be hard put to beat me."

"I believe I would," he agreed wearily. "I fear I must concede the race before it is begun."

"Well, then. If you will not race, you must talk," I teased. "You have been unconscionably quiet today."

"Forgive me if I have been rude. It was unintentional."

"Rude?" I laughed again. "You have said nothing, neither courteous or elsewise. I could almost believe you would have preferred to do without my company."

"Then you would be gravely mistaken," he said, his tone completely serious. "For if you had not accompanied me today, then I would have needed to single you out on another occasion so that we might discuss something that has been troubling me. It seems that lately you have become my closest and wisest confidante."

His remark encouraged me. Surely, he has realized that he cannot possibly marry Charlotte, I thought. And now he seeks my help in ending an engagement that should never have been. What else could he want from me? She has disappointed him yet again with her absence, and her mistrust has affected him as her silly flirtations did not.

Then a wild notion struck me and my heart quickened as I marked the approval in his eyes, the pleasant manner in which he addressed me. He had just indicated that he had become closer to me than anyone else. How could he help but know that the choice he had made when we were children had been a poor one? Even Charlotte had seen the wisdom of his marrying me instead of her. By doing so, he would have kept his promise to our aunt and uncle to marry one of their nieces, Pendene's Wood would be his, and Charlotte could marry as she chose.

My cheeks prickled with a pleasant warmth as I waited for him to speak. When he hesitated, I prompted him by saying, "It is about Charlotte, is it not?"

He nodded.

"Clearly, I did not deceive you with my stupid lie about the riding habit. I should have known I would not. Charlotte's behavior is unforgivable, but I was also wrong. I should not have lied to you."

"I imagine the truth would have been awkward for both of us. Especially if it were delivered in your aunt's presence."

My horse nickered and the leaves of a branch that stretched across the path scraped my arm. I barely noticed. He does not blame me, I thought, and a surge of happiness swelled up in my throat, making speech impossible.

His lordship gave me a sharp look. "I believe your aunt and my sister are unaware of her . . . hesitation?"

I nodded dumbly.

"I supposed as much. Elizabeth would not be slow to inform me, or to instruct me in the best manner in which to handle my difficulties. And likely your aunt would have taken a hairbrush to Charlotte before she permitted her to behave in any manner that could be construed as impolite."

"Aunt Emily has never used a hairbrush on either of us. With Charlotte, a look is enough to suffice, and something more sturdy is required to curb my unruliness."

"Doubtless." He grinned and fell silent again, as though measuring what he would say next before revealing what was uppermost on his mind. Does he think I would refuse him? I wondered. What nonsense. I could barely refrain from saying yes before he had managed to propose.

All around us the world shimmered and glistened. The rain had scrubbed the leaves, wiping off the dust and the mud that was kicked up from the riding path. Rays of sunlight splattered across the surface of the lake, leaving a blazing white trail, and bounced across the grass, splashing silver highlights across the jade-green leaves. Our horses slipped from sun to shade and back to the sun again, warming and cooling the outside of me as the heat of my emotions rose and fell within.

"Your sister is a sweet child," Lord Blackwood said abruptly, as if there had been no pause in our conversation. "But I fear she lacks your sense."

"Aunt Emily would not agree."

"There are all kinds of sense," he argued. "Charlotte may be pretty behaved, but she is frightened easily and inclined to be gullible."

I nodded, not caring that I was being disloyal. Besides, I told myself, it can hardly be disloyal to admit the truth. It is not as though he has accused Charlotte of slovenliness or thievery.

"It concerns me," his lordship continued, "that if she is easily frightened here—in London where there are no shadows or dark halls to unnerve her and you and your aunt are near at hand to provide her with some degree of comfort—that after our marriage she will be unable to cope with the doubts which upset her."

"Charlotte has always been timid." I strained to keep

my joy from showing in my voice and in my eyes, but it was hard not to shout aloud, or spur my horse into a mad run. Instead, I pointed out demurely, "And even the smallest of adjustments is difficult for her. The situation is most awkward."

"Most awkward, indeed." Then he smiled at me, a warm, tender smile that slowly spread from his lips to his eyes until I basked in its radiance. "If it were not for you—but I precede myself. To be precise, the situation is too awkward by half. In truth, it is quite impossible. But I believe I have found a solution to all of our difficulties."

"All?" Had he guessed how I felt?

"You have but to give your consent."

"You need not ask. It is yours already."

He looked surprised. "Then you will come to Blackwood Hall as Charlotte's companion after she and I are married?"

"Companion?" I stared at him in horror.

"Of course," he said in a puzzled tone. "What did you think I meant?"

"I . . . I thought you wanted me to speak with my aunt about releasing you from your promise to marry Charlotte." My tongue felt swollen and dry as I stared at his startled face. I could only be glad that his lordship did not realize the full extent of my fancies. At least, I was saved that humiliation.

"Release me?" he said coolly as if I had insulted him. "I have given my word, have you forgotten? There is no question but that this marriage will take place. I meant only to make matters easier for Charlotte. When we have been married a year, perhaps after she has had a child, she will forget this silliness and make me a good wife."

"And what difficulties plague me that I should also desire this arrangement?" I demanded querulously.

"I would have thought that obvious."

"You must forgive my failure to comprehend. I am not usually so buffel-headed. Please, enlighten me."

He cleared his throat, and addressing me as he would address a child, said, "It is beginning to be clear to me that you will not receive a proposal of marriage this season. The young men avoid you and those of an age to appreciate your virtues are either disinclined to marry or unwilling to offer for so headstrong a young woman. Nor can you live forever at Briarslea. Having five children to raise has stretched your uncle's finances to the utmost. It seems your only choice must be to take a post as a governess or companion, and if your temper continues unrestrained, it is unlikely you will survive long in either position."

"Unless I am employed by a member of my own family?"

"You would be well paid."

"And after Charlotte gains some semblance of composure," I said hotly. "Am I to be thrown to the wolves?"

"I do not believe in being cruel to animals," he retorted. "If you so choose, you may remain as a governess to our children. Otherwise, if a husband still cannot be found for you, I would arrange for you to receive a reasonable income, enough for you to live comfortably wherever you pleased."

"How dare you!" I cried, unable to contain myself a moment longer. "How dare you assume that I am incapable of attracting a husband. Had I listened to Elizabeth instead of you I would have had several beaux. Possibly a dozen or more. A little simpering and lash fluttering seems to go farther with your gender than either sense or honesty. And you are as bad as the rest of them. You are too blind to see—" I broke off, my mouth open. A wave of horror poured through me as I realized what I had nearly disclosed.

"To blind to see what?" he demanded, his face suffused with anger.

"Your sister was right. All men are fools!" I cried, and spurring my horse into a run, I raced off down the path without waiting for his reply.

Upon reaching Coudrey House, I scrambled down from my horse, paused long enough to press the reins into the hands of the startled groom, and ran inside. My habit was rumpled, my hat had blown off in the park, and the misery pent up in me pressed against my chest until my ribs ached. I burst into the foyer, my vision obscured by lengths of hair that had come unpinned and fallen across my eyes, and collided with a very solid and equally familiar back.

"Uncle Arthur," I cried.

He turned, his face wearing a look of mild surprise as he absorbed my disheveled condition, and asked, "Well now, lass. What bedevils thee?"

I immediately threw myself, sobbing, into his arms. Elizabeth and Aunt Emily, who had come to the hall to greet him, looked on in bewilderment.

"Now, now," he said calmly. "We can't have this. What's got into thee?"

"Nothing," I cried. "Except that his lordship asked me to be Charlotte's companion after her wedding because he thinks I will not be able to find a husband."

He squirmed awkwardly. "Well, that's as may be. But there's no need for thee to be rushing off into the world. Thy aunt can always use an extra pair of hands at Briarslea. And while I'm sure Lord Blackwood has his reasons, and doubtless good ones, a young newlywed won't be wanting her sister as a companion."

"But Charlotte refuses to marry his lordship. She is afraid of him. She thinks he murdered his first wife."

Aunt Emily gasped and even Elizabeth looked taken aback, but although his ruddy color deepened, Uncle Arthur managed a short laugh. "What kind of foolishness is this? Have thee been filling her head with your ghoulish tales?"

"I have not," I said, pulling out of his arms. "I have

done everything I could possibly do to make her see sense. She refuses to listen."

Elizabeth stepped forward and put her arm around my shoulder to comfort me. "Perhaps, I should explain," she said to the squire. "Last night Lord Edgmont accused Nicholas of murdering his daughter. The man is clearly unbalanced, but his raving must have disturbed Charlotte. I had no idea or I would have spoken to her, this morning. I am certain the matter can be easily set to rights."

Uncle Arthur nodded and he straightened his waistcoat. "Thee'd better go and fetch thy sister," he told me. " 'Tis clear enough we need to have a talk."

I wiped my sleeve across my nose and sniffed. "She is probably still in bed, but I will fetch her if I have to drag her by the hair."

I ran up the stairs, taking great pleasure in the knowledge that Charlotte, who had indirectly caused me so much pain, would soon be suffering Uncle Arthur's displeasure. It must, I thought, be somewhat awkward to discover that your niece suspected your benefactor of so dreadful a crime. Especially, when that discovery was made in front of the gentleman's sister.

By the time I reached our suite, my mouth curved up at the corners. But if my expression had the resemblance of a smile, it had none of the warmth and gaiety that should have accompanied the expression.

"Charlotte," I called out, and seeing she was not in the sitting room, I crossed to the bedroom and looked inside. The room was empty. Nor, I discovered a few moments later, had she gone into Aunt Emily's room. The Rose Velvet suite was mockingly silent.

On impulse, I checked the wardrobe and discovered that her pelisse and her favorite muslin dress were missing. A quick count revealed several empty hangers. The dress she had worn to the theater was tossed across the chair, a careless act so unlike Charlotte that

I knew she must have been in great distress. I had underestimated both her concern and her spirit.

Without wasting another second I hurried downstairs to the drawing room where the others waited.

"Where's thy sister?" Uncle Arthur demanded when he saw I was alone.

"Charlotte has gone," I said. "I believe she has run off."

Chapter Ten

WE HAD NO definite idea of when Charlotte had left, but certainly she gained valuable time while Uncle Arthur insisted that a methodical search of the house be made before we assumed the worst.

"Surely," I exclaimed impatiently, "she would not take several dresses with her if she intended only to sit in the drawing room."

"Don't be pert, girl. Could be she wanted to restitch some furbelow or ribbon. Ted'n no cause to think the worst." He loosened his cravat so that the blood that pulsed at his temples might be permitted to drain back to its usual place.

He had, I supposed, every reason to think that I had gravely overstated the situation. In her entire life Charlotte had never done anything to cause him doubt or concern, while not a day had passed that he had not shaken his head wearily over my escapades. If I had been the one who was missing, he would have known immediately that I had taken it in my head to run off, but for Charlotte to dash out into the streets of London, with no one to accompany her, was unthinkable.

The more I considered this, the more I became certain that she could not possibly have acted in such a fashion. Had she done so, she would have returned, trembling and in tears, before having walked beyond the sight of Coudrey House's tiled rooftop.

Which means, I thought shrewdly, that she must have had assistance. "Monsieur André!" I cried aloud, and my shout carried over the uproar of Aunt Emily's sobs, the banging of doors as the servants searched the rooms, and Uncle Arthur's thunderous questions, fired like cannon shot at regular intervals. They had continued since we first discovered Charlotte was missing, although no one was able to answer them.

"What's that thee say?" he demanded, turning to me. He was clearly happy that someone had finally spoken up, even though the answer I had given was singularly inappropriate to the question he had asked.

"She would not have left the house alone," I said. "And who else could she turn to but Monsieur André?"

This remark required more explanation, an explanation I would have preferred not to have given while Elizabeth was listening. But when I had finished, she was the only one who managed to retain her composure. Aunt Emily gave out a shriek and fled the drawing room while Uncle Arthur bristled with outrage that "some fop of a Frenchman" had stolen his niece's affections.

"We shall soon discover if there is any truth to your suspicions," Elizabeth said, her demeanor as placid and unruffled as the surface of a sheltered mountain lake. There was also, I noted, the same icy coolness to her tone and an impenetrable glaze to her countenance that made it impossible to guess what menace lay beneath the surface.

But whatever she thought of Charlotte's unconscionable behavior, she wasted no time in recriminations or emotional display. She rose and rang for the footman, a young lad with nervous eyes and a shock of drab blond hair that shivered across the top of his head, although the rest of him remained motionless. Elizabeth curtly inquired as to whether or not Charlotte had sent a message to anyone that day.

"Sent me off to Covent Garden, milady. With a letter

for that painter fellow." He licked his lips and in defense of his actions, claimed, "Told me she was 'spected elsewhere this afternoon and had to sit for him another day."

"By any chance, was there a reply?" she asked, ignoring his protestations.

"Yes, milady. Brought it straight back, just as I was told. The young lady wasn't half pleased to get it."

She dismissed him with a wave, and he bowed and hastily departed. The look of amazement on his face that he had somehow survived the interview and not been let go in the process would have been comical if his information had not confirmed my suspicions.

"I suppose there's no chance she meant t' break the appointment?" Uncle Arthur asked glumly.

Elizabeth shook her head firmly. "Just yesterday she told me the portrait was finished and was soon to be delivered. I am afraid we must assume that she turned to this man, and he promptly made himself available. Although how she left this house with no one knowing, I cannot fathom."

"That's neither here nor there," Uncle Arthur said. "If she's run off with him, then we must get her back. And the quicker done, the better. You say he keeps a garret near Covent Garden?"

The groom had not yet returned my mount to the stables, and Elizabeth had one of the carriage horses saddled and brought round for Uncle Arthur's use. Although Aunt Emily was reluctant to let me go, it was decided that I should accompany Uncle Arthur to show him the way. The less anyone else knew about Charlotte's disappearance, the better off she would be, for if word leaked out she would be ruined. Then, neither Lord Blackwood, nor any other man, would marry her if Monsieur André did not.

The streets had never seemed more crowded or so narrow. We squeezed our mounts past wagons and carts, coaches and carriages, often rousing a cry of "Oi, look out" or "Watch yerself"; some were a great deal ruder as Uncle Arthur seemed determined to ride over what he could not circumvent. I had no choice but to keep abreast of him or lose him entirely.

A poor guide I make, I thought miserably, forestalling Uncle Arthur from once again shooting ahead of me and taking the wrong turn. But surely some of the duty fell upon those who were to be led, a position that was poorly filled by someone who insisted in riding several lengths to the fore. It was, therefore, for a variety of reasons that I welcomed the sight of the dilapidated fish shop, with its overhanging second story and the line of washing—possibly the same line of undergarments that I had first seen, still gathering soot.

The rickety stairs shook dangerously beneath the weight and haste of my uncle's step. Only loyalty, and my own irritation with Charlotte, convinced me to ignore the threat to my life and hurry after him.

"What sort of gentleman would live here?" Uncle Arthur demanded as he pounded on Monsieur André's door with his fist.

What sort, indeed? I did not want to increase his fears by elaborating on my opinion of Monsieur André, and committed myself to saying only, "Painters do not often make a good living, I believe."

Uncle Arthur snorted derisively and pounded again. Both the door and the entire length of the wall trembled beneath the force of his fists. While he failed to draw a response from the garret's occupants, a woman, her dark hair unbrushed, a scowl drawn about her mouth, appeared on the second-floor landing and yelled, "Oi. Wot d' you think yer doin'?"

My uncle stared at her, his mouth pursed with distaste, and she hastily covered herself with the torn wrapper that had been carelessly draped about her shoulders. "Keep that up and you'll 'ave the flaming 'ouse down about our ears, won't you?" she said in a more conciliatory tone.

"Thee an't, I suppose, the owner of this establishment?" Uncle Arthur demanded.

"An' if I was, wot's it t' you?"

He made a noise in his throat that sounded like a cross between a growl and an oath. Then, pulling out his purse, he withdrew a few coins. The woman's eyes brightened and she darted up the stairs as though hurrying to greet a lover. She was older than I had first thought, and beneath her lavender scent, she reeked of fish.

"Why didn' you say you needed 'elp, then?" she asked, whipping the coins from his hand. "Ain't no need to break the door down. Lock's busted." She turned the knob and the door swung open.

A quick glance assured us the garret was empty. The covers of the bed appeared to have been tossed back in a hurry, and a dirty basin of soapy water sat on the water-stained shaving table.

"He ain't 'ere," the woman said unnecessarily, then helpfully added, "Hired a carriage an' went off at midday. Said he'd be gone fer a se'ennight."

"Did he give you any idea where he might be going?" I asked.

She gave us a leering grin, revealing a gap where one of her front teeth should have been. "Well, he didn' tell me 'is business, but he'd been 'alf daft over some young miss—There! That's 'er." She jerked her head at the portrait of Charlotte and then, plucking up the fabric of her wrapper as though it were the folds of a ballgown, she did a little dance around the garret.

"It would appear that they have eloped," said a voice from the doorway, and we all turned to see Lord Blackwood standing there. It was later that I learned he had returned to Coudrey House to ascertain that I had arrived safely, only to be promptly informed by Elizabeth of the event that had taken place. But I did not have to be told that he knew everything to see as much. One had only to look at the proudly stiff back, the arrogant tilt of his jaw, and the assumed, somewhat strained, carelessness of his pose.

"Lord Blackwood," my uncle said, a red flush washing up his neck and suffusing his face. "Thee dussn't know how ashamed I am by what my niece has done this day. Upon my word, sir, ted'n like her." He shook his head and looked down at his hands as if it were they who had failed him.

Lord Blackwood surveyed the room coolly, no doubt trying to gauge the character of the man who had stolen his fiancée's affections. The unmade bed, the tattered and worn furnishings, and the layer of grime that streaked the windows and the walls did little to recommend him. With one sweeping look, he absorbed the contents of the canvases and promptly dismissed them. By giving them not so much as a second glance, he had condemned the lot.

"I assume that this is where she has been spending her hours on those days when I could not account for her time," he said, strolling into the room after first checking the floor to see that he would not dirty his boots. "An unassuming establishment, is it not? Hardly the place where one might have expected love to blossom."

My uncle squirmed. "Ted'n love, milord. The child took a fright, an' bolted. Likely she'll have already seen her mistake and be wanting to come home. Charlotte's been spoiled, and she never did have much sense—I blame myself for not using a firmer hand. But she wasn't the one who always gave us trouble."

He glared crossly at me, seeming to blame me for his own oversight. Only the urgency of the situation prevented me from railing at this piece of injustice.

Lord Blackwood brushed the sleeves of his coat to remove some imaginary dirt that had sullied them. "I cannot help but wonder what kind of gentleman would risk her good name by supporting her fears and taking her away from the safety of her family. But if that is the kind of man she has chosen. . . ." He shrugged.

"What is the matter with both of you?" I demanded crossly. "You are acting like a pair of fools while Monsieur André absconds with Charlotte. If only we hurry we will probably catch up with them before nightfall."

Uncle Arthur was too much at a loss to reprimand me for my rudeness, but his lordship condescended to say, "And where do you suggest we hunt for them? I was not aware that they left some clue as to where they were going."

"Where else do lovers go when they's in a rush and things ain't as they should be?" the landlady said, making us all start. Her presence had been forgotten with the appearance of his lordship, and it was only now that we realized she had not slipped away.

Lord Blackwood gave the woman the same derisive glance he had given the paintings and dismissed her as quickly, hurrying her from the garret as though he and not she managed the building. Her mutters of outrage could be heard as she stomped down the stairs, and they climaxed with a loud bang as she slammed her door behind her.

"I do not like to think it of her," I said when silence was restored. "But Charlotte is not of age. Where else can they go but to Gretna Green?"

This announcement seemed to jar Uncle Arthur into action. But as he made to leave the garret, Lord Blackwood brought up an arm to stop him. "Charlotte is your niece, Squire, and you must do what you think best. But be aware, I consider that she has broken our engagement by her actions."

His lordship's words, more than his restraining grip, brought my uncle to an abrupt halt. "If we're quick, there'll be no harm done," he protested weakly. "Thee'll have thy bride as pure as the day she left Briarslea."

"And what of that? Do you think, sir, that this affair

is likely to remain a secret? Your niece has made a fool of me. I should be the laughingstock of all London if I announced my engagement to her after this trick she has played on me. And should I choose to swallow my pride, a notion which has little appeal for me, I could not bring myself to marry a woman who thinks me a murderer. As far as I am concerned, from this day forth, she is free to go where she will with whomsoever she pleases."

"But our agreement, milord."

"I do not feel that it was I who failed to keep my word. But no matter. It is easily fulfilled. There are few people who are certain which of your nieces I hoped to marry. I will have your eldest instead."

Uncle Arthur's mouth opened and his eyes bulged. "Redigan?" he managed, after several faltering attempts to speak. He turned to me questioningly.

But if his lordship's announcement had incapacitated Uncle Arthur, his highhandedness had infuriated me. How dare he substitute me for Charlotte without a second thought, nor with even a questioning look in my direction? "You most certainly will not!" I declared, spitting out the words at him. "Nothing could induce me to marry you."

For a brief moment, Lord Blackwood's icy composure wavered and a startled look flickered across his eyes. Then a veil was drawn down over them and in a sardonic voice, he asked, "And why not? You suffer from none of your sister's fancies, and your temper"— he paused meaningfully so that I could not miss the rebuke—"while lamentable, is preferable by half to her missishness."

"The sincerity of your love quite overwhelms me, milord," I replied, fanning myself with my hand as though I grew faint. "Indeed, you put me to the blush with the depth of your regard."

Uncle Arthur shifted his feet uneasily. "Now, Redigan. There's no call for that. I'm sure his lordship means you no disrespect. An' thee would be well-advised to think upon the matter before giving him thy answer."

"And why is that?" I demanded. "Am I such an inferior member of my species that I must accept any proposal that comes my way, lest I find myself on the shelf?"

Lord Blackwood regarded me much as he would have regarded a small dog who had dirtied his front step. "I do not see that by becoming my wife you are likely to suffer," he said coolly. "Indeed, you are hardly likely to do better."

"What a pity you cannot marry yourself," I said, my voice fairly dripping with awe. "You, at least, would show yourself the full admiration and high regard that you seem to expect. *You* could not hope to do better. I, however, have dreams of marrying a man who has come to appreciate *my* qualities, perhaps even near as well as his own."

"Thee won't find theeself a man who admires sarcasm and a quick temper," Uncle Arthur said sharply. "I daresay thee'll be lucky if his lordship dussn't withdraw his offer."

"Offer? I cannot recall being asked or even consulted in the matter. It was a decree. And whether or not his lordship revokes his decree means less than nothing to me, for I have absolutely no intention of marrying him."

"You forget—" Lord Blackwood's voice was dangerously soft. "I have been promised a wife, and I have gone to great expense to fulfill my half of our agreement."

"You were promised Charlotte," I retorted. "If you choose to let her run off with another man, that is no fault of mine. I can hardly be expected to suffer for her misdeeds as well as my own."

The late afternoon shadows had gathered around him, as if drawn to a darkness that matched their own.

When he spoke, his voice rumbled out of the gloom like the break of thunder. "I suggest you give your decision the thought your uncle advised. If you persist in refusing me, I will have no choice but to insist the squire recompense me for my troubles."

"The wood is your'n," my uncle said stoutly. " 'Twouldn't be right nor proper to think elsewise."

Lord Blackwood arched his eyebrows. "The value of the wood will scarcely cover my outlay for this season. There is also the matter of a small loan that must now be recalled."

Uncle Arthur's ruddy face blanched. "But milord—" he began.

His lordship raised his hand, cutting off the protest. "I am sorry to insist, Squire. But under the circumstances you can hardly continue to prevail upon my generosity."

Having made his intentions plain, Lord Blackwood wasted no further time in discussion. Whatever emotions he may have been feeling were concealed beneath a cloak of hauteur and a lofty manner, and he shrugged off our objections much as he shrugged off the dust and the smell of the garret. Outside the fish market he bid us a stiff good day and departed, leaving us to make our own way back to Coudrey House.

We watched him go, his head held erectly, his face turning neither to the left nor the right as he guided his mount through the wheelbarrows and carts that jammed the lane.

"Can hardly blame the man," Uncle Arthur mumbled. "Charlotte's treated him badly an' no doubt he was fair taken with her."

His words stung me more deeply than anything that had hitherto been said. I blinked hastily to rid myself of the film of tears which covered my eyes. Suddenly, I hated Charlotte. I hated Lord Blackwood. And most of all, I hated myself—my chestnut hair, my amber eyes, and my skinny body.

Beside me, Uncle Arthur muttered inaudibly; he seemed to be speaking more to himself than to me. The afternoon's events had shattered his composure: To his concern for Charlotte's safety and his dismay at her losing such a fortuitous marriage was added the confusion he had felt when Lord Blackwood had peremptorily announced that he would marry me instead. That I should refuse his offer, an offer that was so clearly beyond anything that I dared expect for myself, was incomprehensible. I tried hard not to think of the financial burden that my refusal had placed on him.

As my uncle struggled to understand how his neatly ordered plans had disintegrated in the handful of weeks that had passed since he had seen us last, he had neither the strength nor the desire to concern himself with Charlotte's whereabouts. When I jolted his memory by pointing out that while his lordship was not inclined to chase after her, certainly we could bring her back to London before she made the dreadful mistake of marrying Monsieur André, he gave me a bewildered look as if he had forgotten he had a younger niece.

"You cannot mean to leave her in his hands?" I demanded incredulously.

After a long pause, during which he deliberated the situation, he nodded sadly. "Ted'n no reason for her to come back now. His lordship's right. These sort of affairs come to light all too often—that's the way of them. If Lord Blackwood dussn't want her, an' clearly he dussn't. . . ." He shrugged, leaving me to assume that with her virtue in question, Charlotte was unlikely to find any other gentleman willing to marry her.

"But supposing Monsieur André does not—"

But that possibility was beyond my uncle's ability to comprehend. He shot me a sharp look, his eyes forbidding me to finish the question that I had begun, and kicked his horse into a quick trot as if he hoped to put distance between himself and the unspeakable notion that hovered in the air unsaid.

It was not difficult for me to understand his reaction. Uncle Arthur had doted upon Charlotte since she was a small child. That some man might want to elope with her when she was promised to another was understandable. But that any man might lure her away from her family and then fail to marry her was beyond his conception. I sighed and hoped that he had not placed too much faith in Charlotte's charm and beauty while underestimating the base character of a man like Monsieur André.

We fell into an uncomfortable silence; my unspoken question had risen like a wall between us, forestalling any attempts at further conversation. Uncle Arthur slumped above his horse. A light rain spattered around us, and tiny raindrops rolled off the brim of his hat and trickled down his back.

What a confoundedly miserable day it has been! I thought. And what a mess Charlotte has left behind her by running off like this. She really needs a good shaking.

And while my mind dwelled on her folly, I was able to make myself forget the irony of my own situation. For if I had been willing to overlook Lord Blackwood's arrogance, if I could have swallowed my pride and accepted marriage with him on any terms, I might shortly have become his wife.

We found Lady Elizabeth and Aunt Emily settled in the front parlor, murmuring their fears to one another across a pot of tea. Their cups were both filled to the brim, yet the contents appeared to have cooled, and both women clutched lacy handkerchiefs. The creamy brocade and gilt furnishings supplied a note of elegance to their pallid faces and distracted expressions, giving the scene the semblance of high tragedy.

"Have you found her?" Aunt Emily cried, looking up anxiously as we entered.

Uncle Arthur shook his head and she gave out a loud sob. "What can you think of me?" she asked, her eyes pleading with Elizabeth to understand and forgive her. "But it never occurred to me that the child had fallen in love with this man. Not when she had already made such an excellent match. I can only guess at the harsh feelings you must now harbor in your bosom for me."

"Do not think such a thing," Lady Elizabeth replied, patting her on the hand. "I daresay that Nicholas will discover their whereabouts and see that she is safely returned."

"I fear his lordship has no such intention," I said, and both women turned to me, amazed. When they learned of the shabby manner in which he had dismissed Charlotte to her fate and his casual decision to make me his wife in her stead, Aunt Emily abandoned herself to her despair.

Elizabeth was dazzling in her outrage. "Men!" she exclaimed, tossing aside her handkerchief and storming up and down the length of the room to release her agitation. "I had thought that they had ceased to surprise me with their foolish vanities and their highhanded assumption that the entire world should bend to their dictates. Though he is my own brother, I say he deserves neither of you."

The squire cleared his throat awkwardly. "I don't like to disagree with thee, your ladyship. But 'tis no fault of his'n that Charlotte runned off. A man's got his pride—"

"It was his pride that led to this ridiculous escapade. He should have announced their engagement at the onset of the season. If his pride now chokes him, he would be well-advised to loosen his cravat and swallow hard."

"At least I shall see one of my nieces married well," Aunt Emily said, wiping the corner of her eye. "Although I never thought it would be Redigan who would"—she gulped back another sob—"who would make such a catch."

"Nor shall I," I retorted. "I would not think of marrying the man."

Aunt Emily stared at me as if I, like Charlotte, had been struck by madness. "You cannot mean to say that you refused him?"

"I did."

Elizabeth's eyebrows arched, and she regarded me with great admiration. "I applaud your good sense. You could have given him no other answer."

"She could have said yes," Aunt Emily countered, daring to contradict her ladyship for the first time since our arrival at Coudrey House. "And if his lordship has not withdrawn his offer she will do so at the first opportunity."

"La! What a to-do," Elizabeth said, turning her palms to the ceiling. "And all for the sake of having a husband."

"A most respectable husband," Aunt Emily pointed out.

"It is my experience that no man is truly respectable. But some seem to conceal their shortcomings better than others. Perceived in that light, you might as well have Nicholas," she said to me. "At least he has a title and a fortune and can likely be prevailed upon to bring you up to London now and then. And regardless of his reasons for wanting to marry you, I cannot help but think you will make him a better wife than Charlotte."

My chin lifted mutinously. "And what kind of husband will he make me? Would you want me to marry a man who has, in anger and humiliation, chosen to substitute me for my sister?" I demanded with contempt. "We are not interchangeable, she and I."

"You most certainly are not!" Aunt Emily replied, her own temper rising now that she had Lady Elizabeth's support. "You have neither her sweet disposition nor her gentle nature. Although given her recent behavior, I can understand why her ladyship thinks you would make her brother a better wife." Her expression said clearly that she herself was not so easily misled. Then she burst into tears once more. "I cannot think what possessed Charlotte to flee from the very people who protected and loved her," she said between sobs. "But I do not doubt that you have somehow played a role. I dearly regret showing you such lenience as a child." Her gaze flickered about the room as though she were looking for a sturdy object that might be put to good use.

"Am I to be blamed for her stupidity?" I cried, deeply wounded by the unfairness of her accusation. I spun around and my eyes sought out my uncle who had retreated to a corner of the parlor, leaving the three of us to quarrel among ourselves until some kind of solution presented itself. "Would you wish me to marry Lord Blackwood after this afternoon's display of callousness?" I demanded. "You could not expect that of me."

He swallowed and his hands pulled nervously at his waistcoat. As he stood there, awkwardly searching for a way to answer me, I could not help but be aware of how greatly he seemed out of place in the elegant saloon. His clothes and manners were less grand than those of the footman, his speech rougher. He stood awkwardly, as if not daring to relax in the fine surroundings lest he smudge grime on the flocked wallpaper or knock over one of the delicate porcelain figurines that stood on the occasional tables. If, at Briarslea, he had seemed omnipotent, here he was only a country squire of humble means, hardly better off than a tenant farmer.

No wonder he is in awe of Lord Blackwood, I thought. He could not have been much more gratified if the Prince of Wales had proposed to marry one of his nieces. And how little gratitude either of us have shown him.

"You could not want for a finer man," Uncle Arthur

said at last, his eyes twitching as he glanced at Lady Elizabeth.

I had to admire his choice of words. If her ladyship had expressed a certain dissatisfaction with men, she was hardly likely to quarrel than her brother was as fine a man as any could be; and if the remark was repeated to his lordship, he had every reason to be flattered. Still, he had managed to avoid taking sides, either with or against me, although Aunt Emily promptly took the commendation as support for her cause.

"There!" she said. "That is the last to be said of the matter. When Lord Blackwood speaks to you again you will apologize and let him know you would be honored to marry him."

"I will not!" I shouted, bringing my fist down upon the nearby table and threatening one of the figurines that so unnerved my uncle. As the three of them gaped at me, I spun on my heel and ran from the parlor.

Without Charlotte, the Rose Velvet suite had grown too large for comfort or warmth. I sat on the bed we had shared, feeling miserably alone, and searched my memory for every oath that I had ever chanced upon. In the midst of this litany, there was a soft tap on the door.

"Come in," I said glumly. Knowing that Aunt Emily would have used greater force if she had knocked at all, I looked up expecting to see Elizabeth.

But it was not her, but my uncle. He entered hesitantly, but when he saw that I was neither crying nor flouncing about the room in a temper, his worried frown faded. Taking a seat beside me, he patted my shoulder with his callused hand.

" 'Tis been a tiresome day, an' none of us have kept our heads, I'd say," he said, after a minute of silence.

I grunted ungraciously, not having the faintest notion of how to grunt graciously and being unwilling to offer him any more encouragement than that brief noise.

"Yes, well," he replied as if he understood completely. "Thee know yer aunt means well fer thee. Allus has. She's a good woman, but a mite obstinate."

To this, I did not even bother to nod, but my uncle seemed too caught up in his own thoughts to notice. "But thee be my brother's daughter, an' I were close t' Dickie. I wouldn't want to let him down. 'Tis just that—" He coughed and gave me one last rough pat. "But thee must make up thy own mind. I'll tell Emily that I won't be hearing otherwise."

Giving me a last encouraging smile, he rose and left. But as he walked out I saw that his shoulders were slumped and there was a heaviness to his walk that was uncharacteristic.

It is Briarslea, I thought with dismay. He cannot possibly hope to repay Lord Blackwood and keep the farm. And yet he could not bring himself to tell me. If I had not happened to be in his study when they had talked, I would never have known until—

I stared glumly at my ringless fingers as my determination never to marry Lord Blackwood slipped away. And what, I supposed, did it matter if he did not love me. Nor did any other man. But the thought of living each day with someone who did not love me—while he aroused all my passions—struck me as the worst kind of torture. To have been able to look forward to being murdered, as Charlotte had done, would have seemed a kinder fate.

Chapter Eleven

LORD BLACKWOOD accepted my apologies gravely.
His searching eyes strove to break past my new-found
composure to the thoughts I had carefully concealed.
"I daresay that having suffered a severe blow to my
pride, my own less than creditable behavior was much
to blame for yesterday's unpleasantness," he admitted.

"Am I to assume," I asked, "that you regret the things
you said?"

He stepped back and turned away from me to study
the drizzling rain that streaked the drawing-room windows. The soft patter against the glass and the hiss and
crackle of the fire on the hearth were the only sounds
that dared to interrupt his contemplation. Elizabeth
and Aunt Emily had excused themselves and left us
alone to talk shortly after his arrival, Aunt Emily pausing only to give me a dire look before hurrying after
our hostess.

I had, as yet, satisfied only the first of her edicts and
made my apologies to his lordship. But my decision
had been made; it wanted only for him to repeat his
intentions to marry me.

I stared at the broad back, thinking how dearly I
would have cherished this moment if something other
than expedience and wounded vanity had persuaded
him to direct his attentions towards me. In my imagination, I could feel the roughness of his serge tail coat

against my cheek had I lain it against that powerful back; I wanted to rest my head in the hollow between his shoulder blades and feel the sheltering warmth of his love. Instead, I remained seated, garnering my warmth from the dancing flames in the fireplace as I struggled to ignore the chill that had sidled between us.

"My manner may have been brusque," Lord Blackwood said at last, talking to the rain and the bank of fog that pressed at the glass. "But I meant what I said. Nothing could induce me to marry Charlotte now that I know the depths of her aversion to me. The very notion is abhorrent."

The intensity with which he spoke sent a cold shiver through me. I felt a kind of pity for Charlotte, seeing how brutally he had cut away any feeling he had once had for her—although I knew she would not have appreciated the loss.

"But I did not come to talk about Charlotte," he continued. He deserted the window and strode across the room to stand above me. His eyes seemed more like emeralds than ever before, brilliant with some indescribable and compelling force as he stared down at me. "I fully intend to have you as my wife. I assume, from your apology, that you no longer intend to refuse me?"

I checked the angry words that started to flow. What did it matter that still he had not bothered to ask for my hand? This was no love match but a *mariage de covenance,* and I could not afford to risk ruining my uncle by objecting to his manner. "You are not mistaken, milord," I said quietly. "One thinks more clearly after a night's rest, and I am now able to see the advantages of being your wife." I managed a slight smile.

His eyes narrowed. "Besides which, I left you with no other choice. Do you think that I am so foolish and so unused to your stubbornness and your temper that

I would suppose your change of heart was due to a single night's sleep?"

I gave him a cool look. "And yet still you want to marry me?"

"I do."

"Then we understand each other."

"I strongly doubt that *you* understand *me,* at all. But there will be time enough for you to get to know me better after we are married."

I gasped. "You cannot mean to rush into this . . . arrangement? It is unseemly."

"I see no reason to delay. I fancy we have spent as much time together as most couples do before their marriage. Besides—" His voice grew angry again. "I have no intention of making the same mistake with you that I made with your sister. We will be married as soon as the arrangements can be made."

As soon as the arrangements could be made? I felt the blood drain from my face. I had presumed that there would be several months for me to come to accept my position. My stays pressed uncomfortably against my stomach, although I had not managed to eat a bite of food at breakfast.

Lord Blackwood tensed and his fingers tightened, curling into a fist then slowly relaxing. "You have, I imagine, no objection?" he asked. His deep tones dared me to disagree.

I swallowed and, in a voice that I did not recognize as my own, said, "None, milord."

I glanced at Nicholas, sitting beside me, perusing his newspaper as though the steady rocking motion of the coach did not affect him. Then, hurriedly, I looked away rather than risk having him raise his eyes and catch me staring at him. How strange to call him Nicholas, I thought. To be Lady Blackwood and driving away from London as a married woman. I had only the haziest image of our wedding and the haste with which our vows had been exchanged. It was almost as if it were a memory of something that had taken place in my childhood—a memory that returned to me in snatches and fragments that needed to be pieced together to make a complete picture.

But it was only yesterday that our wedding had taken place, amidst such haste and activity that I had had precious little time to dwell on where, and to whom, the fates had delivered me. Even our wedding night had been an anticlimax to the tumultuous scene that had been played out in the garret. Nicholas had advised me to spend the night at Coudrey House alone, as he had some business he wanted to attend to before we left for Cornwall. But I suspected that, his pride satisfied, he had no more desire to go to his wedding bed than I—albeit for different reasons. He could not have forgotten Charlotte so quickly.

My mood swung from gratitude to disappointment. Shortly before the wedding, Aunt Emily had curtly advised me to "lie still and try not to complain." To this, had been added Elizabeth's "encouraging" comment that, "After the first few weeks, few men bother their wives save on those occasions when all other entertainments have been exhausted."

Their attempts at kindness had provided me with little enlightenment and instilled a certain dread. By the end of the day, I had managed to assume a martyred stoicism over what was to follow, and it annoyed me greatly that my fortitude had gone unappreciated.

I peeked at Nicholas again and caught him studying me speculatively. My cheeks grew uncomfortably warm, my embarrassment increased by a sudden jolt of the coach that sent me tumbling against him. I caught a brief whiff of his shaving soap and a headier smell that could only have been the scent of his person before I could withdraw to my own side of the coach.

"Are you all right?" he asked politely, much as he

would have inquired after the well-being of any woman, no matter how brief their acquaintance.

"I am," I assured him. Inside, I was quivering with resentment that he could destroy my composure with but a brief touch, while easily maintaining his own.

Something of the emotions which troubled me must have shown on my face, for his brows arched and he asked, "Are you certain?"

"Quite," I returned.

He started to say something, then obviously thought better of it and picked up his newspaper. After flattening the pages that had been crumpled by my ungainly assault, he continued his reading.

The inn at which Nicholas had chosen to spend that first night had been rebuilt at the close of the last century. To me, it more closely resembled one of the smaller London hotels than the rustic country inns I was accustomed to seeing. Mounted on the pediment above the portico was a full-sized effigy of an eagle, and at either end of the lower porch, supported by wrought iron, there hung a great lamp, rather like those lamps that swung from the coaches that passed up and down the road between London and Exeter.

It was well after dark when we arrived, even though the days were lengthening into summer, and the lamps cast a ghostly glaze over the stately white pillars and the white-sashed windows.

Nicholas's face was pale in the silvery light. The blackness of his hair formed a stark contrast, making him seem paler still, and it seemed I ascended the steps with a creature devoid of both life and emotion. A sharp chill pierced my chest and I shivered, causing him to draw me closer and rush me up the remaining steps as though hurrying me to my doom.

My macabre fancies vanished as we entered the brightly lit foyer. After the cool of the night, the warmth of the inn was suffocating, and the voices and laughter emanating from the taproom chased away any vestiges of fear that had possessed me. If I am not careful I will become as ridiculous as Charlotte, I thought. Nicholas was the same person he had always been, and in that odd light I must have looked as ghostly to him as he had appeared to me.

Nicholas arranged for a suite, giving me a short-lived moment of relief that he intended to ignore me this night as he had the previous one. Then I realized the stupidity of my conclusion: It would not have occurred to him to accept anything less than a suite since he could afford the best accommodations. The knowledge filled me with an anticipatory dread.

After a brief wash in our rooms, we descended again to the dining room, with its vaulted ceilings and rows of linen-covered tables. Our supper, loin of veal followed by apricot tart, was deserving of more appreciation than either my mind or my stomach felt inclined to devote to it. I could not rid myself of the disquieting awareness I had of Nicholas, his knees brushing my own, his long silences emphasized by the chatter and raucous laughter of the other guests.

After our empty plates had been cleared from the table, Nicholas downed a glass of port, then suggested we retire. I stifled the murmur of protest that rose to my lips and nodded stiffly, silently hoping to recapture some of the stoicism I had used to brace myself the previous night. I might as well have saved myself the effort: It was not forthcoming.

The tread of Nicholas's boots behind me on the dark wood stairs sounded unnaturally loud, and goose bumps rose on my forearms and prickled down my spine. Already, his nearness unnerved me. The thought of the greater intimacy that awaited us made me tremble.

With each step my resentment grew. I was nothing to him. Not even his friend as I had once supposed, for who would use a friend as badly as he had used me?

Clearly, he placed a higher value on saving his vanity than upon our friendship.

Still, I might have forgiven him his pride, but I had other, darker doubts. Would he be thinking of Charlotte tonight? Would he be measuring my charms against hers? What a fool I would seem to him when he discovered that I was in love with him, for surely he would guess. I ached simply at the thought of his kiss. How could I hide the truth when his lips touched mine?

After the warm, brightly lit parlor, the dark corridor that ran down the length of the first floor was chilly and dark. Midway between the evenly spaced sconces, fingers of darkness stretched across the floor; they lurked there, as though waiting to reach out and grab the unwary, and Nicholas's presence at my back was more a threat than a comfort. When the door of our suite closed behind us with a slight bang, I jumped.

He regarded me with a look of mild surprise. "Is something the matter?"

"Of course not," I said shortly, irritated that I had betrayed my agitation. "The noise startled me, nothing more."

He frowned. "You do not usually suffer from nerves."

"These last two weeks have been a strain on me," I reminded him, not loath to point out that I had not entered this marriage either willingly or joyfully.

After an almost imperceptible hesitation, he said evenly, "Weddings are trying under the best of circumstances. I am glad that ours is behind us." He paused again, looking as though he wanted to say more, but unable to make himself say it. Instead, he stepped forward and cupped his hand under my chin, lifting my face to his.

I jerked back as though he had struck me. To cover my embarrassment, I said hastily, "Forgive me, but I am overtired." I pretended to stifle a yawn.

I thought I saw a flash of disappointment in his eyes, but it disappeared as quickly as it had come, leaving me wondering whether or not it had really been there. Then he said, "Forgive me, my dear. I forget that you are not used to travelling. By all means, get as much rest as you can. I have arranged to have the coach brought round at nine tomorrow, so there will be time for us to enjoy a good breakfast before we leave. We are not, after all, travelling on a public conveyance, and I see little reason to try to match their unholy schedules."

After adding a stiff good night, he excused himself. I, too, retired; and for the second night of my marriage, I slept alone, disturbed only by my regret at having refused his kiss.

Nicholas did not attempt to breach my defenses over the three nights that followed. I gladly professed to be exhausted each evening over supper, helping him maintain our pretense that it was the journey rather than some, more disquieting cause which was to blame for our having not yet shared a bed; and he murmured his understanding and departed to his own room, emerging the following morning, fully dressed and as eager to depart the inn as I.

But if I dreaded the awkward civility that marked our nights together, it was the long hours in the coach that placed the greatest demands on my self-control. Each bump in the road, each sharp curve threw us against each other as we sat, side by side on the leather seat. Through the layers of serge, velvet, and muslin that covered us, I could feel the hard muscles of his thigh brushing mine; I tensed whenever his hand brushed mine and steeled myself against the impulse to reach out and touch those supple fingers; more than once I felt the warmth of his breath caress my cheeks as he turned to speak to me. It was an exquisite torture. My anger and resentment paled next to my desire to be held in his arms and feel the pressure of those firm lips against mine.

But I refused to surrender to that final ignominy. He

had made me his wife against my will; he had substituted me for the woman he really loved. I would have rather died than allowed him to see how desperately I wanted him.

Blackwood Hall was a forbidding gray structure of granite and Cornish slate. It stood at the pinnacle of a rocky promontory, like a knight mounted high upon a stone war horse that plunged through the spray and the furious waves to claim a territory that rightfully belonged to the sea.

So alike were they in shade and substance, cliff and Hall blended together, as though the latter was merely a misshapen outgrowth of the former. Dark towers reached skyward, jutting into the drift of fog that crept off the water. Mists clung to the battlements and smudged their missing-tooth pattern into a single gray line.

We arrived in the early evening of the fifth day after winding through a forest of elms and oaks. They grew together in such density, I could not see more than ten feet beyond the first stand of trees. Thereafter, the branches and trunks and the shadows they cast ran together, creating a blackness that was as final as a burial tomb. In light of Nicholas's family name, it seemed peculiarly apt.

When I mentioned this to him, he agreed, saying, "It would not surprise me to learn that several hundred years ago my family name was an unprepossessing Wood, until some imaginative or puffed-up fool decided to enhance his self-importance with a more distinguished surname."

Possibly, I thought, studying him as he scowled out of the coach window as though condemning his ancestor for his weak character. But if Nicholas was a fair replica of his ancestors then it was also as likely that the name had been bestowed on them because of their black moods and dark countenances.

The Hall, which had been visible from the road, vanished as the coach was swallowed by the forest. It appeared once more as the trees gave way to sloping lawns and flower bushes—predominantly roses and rhododendrons. The bright pinks and purplish-red blossoms grew in garish defiance of their sober setting.

The coach halted in front of an arched doorway. I gave Nicholas my hand as I descended, trembling slightly as our fingers touched and our eyes met. Then I forced myself to look beyond him to the Hall.

A bolt rattled and the heavy oak door swung back, gliding open on well-oiled hinges. The bright light from the entry hall poured through the opening, silhouetting the dark figure of a woman. She was big, my height or taller, and easily twice my girth.

I could see nothing of her face until Nicholas hurried me out of the cool evening air. Then, beneath the glow of the three-tiered chandelier—lighting which no doubt flattered her—I was able to examine Blackwood Hall's formidable housekeeper.

Mrs. Ham wore a sensible black wool dress. The severity of her clothing was alleviated by a white collar and a crisp mobcap that sat neatly upon her steel-gray hair. She was not as heavy as I had first supposed, but big-boned and sturdily built. Her broad jawline and thick nose were not as unattractive as they might have been on a small face yet, still, her face was inutterably plain. In all, she seemed better suited for the role of prison matron than housekeeper to this wealthy household.

Her impression of me seemed equably unfavorable. She managed a deep, ungainly curtsy and a polite welcome in a gravelly voice, but I fancied there was disappointment in her expression. Then her features smoothed into quiet resignation, as if she had decided there was nothing else to do but make the best of the situation. Turning to Nicholas, she assured him that his rooms had been aired and the beds had been made up with fresh linens.

While they spoke I took a surreptitious glance around at my surroundings. They were impressive: The light from the chandelier bounced off marble walls and floors. Pennants, their colors darkened with age, hung from ornate, wrought-iron wall fixtures; the gleaming marble surfaces caught their reflections and their gentle swaying motion, and tossed them back until the entry seemed alive with the fluttering of darkly hued birds. There was something ominous in the effect and I shuddered.

It was then that I realized I was being watched. In the shadows of a corridor that led into the depths of the Hall, I saw a young man. As soon as he realized I had seen him, he limped forward into the light.

"I was certain I heard the coach," he said to Nicholas. "What a pity you decided to cut short your visit to Town. I have rather enjoyed being lord of the manor in your absence. But if you introduce me to your lovely bride, I will consider that fair compensation for my diminished status."

Nicholas looked reluctantly at me. There was a strange expression in his eyes that I could not read, but he said gravely, "Redigan, this is my brother Stephen."

The young man stepped forward, trying hard to disguise his limp, and bestowed a kiss on my cheek. I stared at him curiously.

He was, I decided, the most handsome man I had ever seen. In many ways, he looked like his brother. Like Nicholas, his hair was black and his skin olive, and his eyes were the same startling shade of green. But Stephen was more slightly built; his features were more sharply defined, and his movements had the fluid grace of a dancer—a gracefulness that was all the more pronounced for his obvious disability. Most importantly of course, he did not have the disfiguring slash across his cheek.

Charlotte would love him. The thought popped into my mind as if from nowhere, its irrelevance seeming all the greater when I considered that any woman would have fallen in love with Stephen—any woman who was not already in love with another man. Besides his grace and good looks, he had a look of sensitivity about his eyes; a look that suggested he was capable of great empathy and understanding, of deep love. That, more than his attractiveness, would have a devastating effect on ladies of all ages. His eyes seemed a trifle melancholic, but markedly absent was an air of smugness, an air that so often accompanies—and invariably ruins—a handsome face. And for all his good looks, he did not strike me as a womanizer.

I wondered idly if Nicholas resented his brother in the same way that I had resented Charlotte. Then I discarded the notion as ridiculous. Nicholas was the heir to the Blackwood title and fortunes, something that more than made up for any physical discrepancy between the two men. He also emanated a strength and masculinity that Stephen did not.

Then Nicholas cleared his throat and I realized how long and how intensely I had been staring. Realizing in what fashion both men must have interpreted my stares, I blushed. My response, though unavoidable, was damning. Now, it appeared certain to everyone that my interest had been motivated by more than mere curiosity.

Nicholas scowled at me. I felt a brief soaring hope that his irritation was due to jealousy; then I chided myself for my foolishness. Again, it was his vanity that suffered. I stared back crossly, although I was more upset with myself for my continual weakness where he was concerned.

Stephen noted the interchange with obvious interest. There was a speculative gleam in his eyes that suggested he had already surmised that all was not well with our marriage. Even Mrs. Ham, that stolid figure who could not possibly be possessed of either intuition or imagination, pursed her lips with disapproval.

Seeing the impression we had given, Nicholas's face grew darker. In an attempt to explain away my behavior, he said, "I daresay you are surprised, darling. I did not mention that my brother lives with me. I believe I spoke of him only once, that day in the drawing room at Briarslea."

I thought for a moment, wrestling with my memory. Then I remembered that he had indeed mentioned Stephen—the day I had asked him how he had come by the scar on his cheek. "Of course," I said triumphantly. "You were dueling with your brother when—"

Mrs. Ham stiffened and I broke off, suddenly regretting my words. The memory could not have been a pleasant one for either of them. Nicholas, too, appeared discomfited, but Stephen managed a chagrined smile.

"I believe he never thinks of me except in relation to that unfortunate incident. You will find you have married a most difficult man. Being so much in command of himself, he expects no less from others, and he forgives nothing."

As he could not forgive Charlotte, I thought. Better to marry me, her less attractive, less amiable sister. I looked at him reproachfully.

Unaware of the true direction of my thoughts, Nicholas said, "You must not let Stephen mislead you, my darling. He has yet to admit the deed was intentional. I can hardly forgive him when he has never truly apologized. Now, if you will excuse us, Redigan and I have had a long trip. We both need a hot bath and a good night's sleep."

"Yes," I agreed, very glad to end the tension-filled civilities. I turned to Stephen politely. "I look forward to becoming better acquainted with you at another time."

"And I with you." He bowed.

Nicholas instructed Mrs. Ham to have the maid bring

up hot water for our baths, after which she was to send up a hot meal which we would eat in our rooms. "Unless you would prefer the dining room," he said to me, almost as an afterthought.

I shook my head, as I knew I was expected to do: The remark had not been a question—more of a polite noise for the benefit of his brother and Mrs. Ham. In truth, the dining room, with Mrs. Ham stolidly serving up each course and Stephen seated firmly beside us, was preferable by far to the intimate arrangement Nicholas had suggested. This night, I knew, there would be no thwarting him when he came to my room. How gladly I would have postponed the inevitable.

"May I remind you that you are *my* wife," Nicholas said as soon as Mrs. Ham had excused herself and left us alone in our suite.

I pulled my gaze away from the lavishly decorated sitting room with its vaulted ceiling and gilt moldings. "I am not likely to forget the man who forced me into marriage," I retorted, keeping my tone as coldly civil as his had been. "And as for my interest in your brother, I was only remarking on the resemblance between the two of you."

"Resemblance?" Nicholas's laugh was harsh and unfriendly. "Do you consider this face of mine a match for his?"

"Your coloring is much the same, and his features, though not as prominent as yours, follow similar lines."

For a moment he digested what I had said. Then with a grim smile, he said, "Then you need not be disappointed that it is I and not he who will be sharing your bed."

"If that is a joke, the humor escapes me," I said tartly. My face grew warm at the thought of sleeping with Nicholas. To my chagrin, his eyes marked my heightened color and they flashed with anger. Clearly, he had read my embarrassment as a guilty desire for his brother. "You do not care much for him, do you?" I said.

"I despise him," he said harshly, then seeing my surprise asked, "Does that shock you?"

"I suppose that would depend on your reasons."

"My reason is that he is a coward. I can forgive much in a brave man, but I can find little worth praising in someone who is poor-spirited. It shames me to think that my brother would prefer to sacrifice his honor before putting himself at risk."

"You cannot judge him based on something that happened when you were children."

"Nor do I."

I waited for him to elaborate, but he did not.

"How did he come by his limp?" I asked at last.

Nicholas grimaced. "He was shot in the foot. By his own account, his pistol discharged accidentally while he was cleaning his gun. I am not convinced he did not commit the deed intentionally. His regiment was about to leave for France."

There was a tap on the door and the maid appeared, carrying water for our baths. Her presence put a welcome end to the exchange.

Supper was strained. Between bites of roast lamb, Nicholas glowered across the table at me. I pretended to be absorbed in my new surroundings. The drop-leaf table we shared was mahogany, as were most of the other furnishings, except for the elaborately carved Jacobean armchairs in which we sat. Those were of walnut, their mesh seats graced with tasseled and embroidered cushions.

The flowered pattern in the Persian carpet emphasized the same shade of plum that predominated throughout the room, picked up by the damask draperies and the upholstered settees. Even the delicately flowered wallpaper echoed the dark rich hues which distinguished the sitting room.

I barely picked at my meal. Thoughts of Nicholas and

the night ahead churned in my stomach and there was little room left for anything else. Too, the heat from the massive fireplace made me drowsy, as did the glass of mead that he had poured for me.

I glanced at him from across the rim of my glass; he chanced to look up and catch me watching him. He leaned back in his chair and took up his own glass. From across the amber liquid he regarded me, his eyes no longer hostile, a faint question arching his brows.

"You have barely touched your dinner," he pointed out. "Cook will be offended."

"I find I have no appetite."

"Would that I could say the same." He lay his serviette aside. "Perhaps you should attend to your toilette. I shall join you shortly."

Obediently, I rose and excused myself.

Chapter Twelve

THE BEDROOM that had belonged to the Hall's various mistresses boasted furnishings that were every bit as lavish as the sitting room. Only the colors were lighter, being mostly ivory brocades with floral patterns of pinks and greens.

I slipped out of my dress, laying it across the canopied four-poster bed while I donned the silk nightgown that had been a wedding gift from Elizabeth. Then, hurriedly, I pulled the pins from my hair. I glanced at myself in the tall looking glass that stood in the corner. In the glow of the oil lamp I appeared to be a waiflike figure, swathed in folds of white. My thin face was childishly innocent; only my stubbornly set pointed chin and the masses of unruly chestnut hair warned of the passions and temper that lay hidden.

Shrugging off the unsettling impression of threatened vulnerability that the looking glass had created, I sat down at the dressing table and began brushing the knots from my hair. Still, when I had done, I could not bring myself to slip between the sheets of the huge bed. Instead, I sat on the edge where I remained, playing with the folds of my nightgown until Nicholas should appear.

When his knock came, I was unprepared for the sudden pounding of my heart and the lump in my throat that prevented me from swallowing.

"Come in," I whispered, and just when I was certain he could not possibly have heard my feeble invitation, the door swung open.

Nicholas was still dressed, having removed only his tail coat and cravat, and the top buttons on his shirt front were unfastened. My heart skipped a beat as I stared at him. In the soft glow and his state of semiundress, he looked younger than his thirty-two years and less formidable. It was hard to envision him as the man who had stood across from me in the garret and coldly announced his intentions to marry me.

He paused there, outlined in the doorway, his broad shoulders and his dark curls brushing the wooden frame; then slowly he smiled, and his eyes were warm and gentle.

"I am not Charlotte," I pointed out defensively, regretting the words the moment they escaped me.

His smile wavered then grew steady, taking on a fixed look. "No," he agreed softly, a glint of pain in his eyes. Since the day I had agreed to marry him, he had not mentioned her name. Again, I wondered how much hurt was concealed beneath his anger, but doubtless, I was poor compensation.

"Do you intend to stand in the doorway all night?" I asked crossly.

Looking mildly surprised, he walked in and closed the door behind him. It was then I noticed the object he was holding. It was narrow, no longer than the length of his hand, and encased in a cloth bag tied with ribbons—much like the rolled pouch he had used to carry the necklaces Charlotte and I had worn to the theater.

Seeing the direction of my gaze, Nicholas said, "I brought you something. After all, I have not given you a wedding gift."

I frowned. That was untrue. For shortly after our wedding, he had presented me with the papers on which his solicitor had drawn up the terms of my uncle's loan. I had promptly torn them up, taking great delight in shredding them until none of the pieces were larger than my thumbnail. I only wished I could have disposed of his lordship with as much ease.

Did he now intend to buy my affections by decking me with the same jewels he had promised to Charlotte? I stared at him suspiciously. "I cannot imagine wanting anything more than that which you have already given me."

"The loan papers cannot be considered a gift," he said evenly. Let us merely regard them as a fair exchange for your compliance. This, however"—he lifted the silk pouch—"was chosen with my affection for you in mind. I waited only for the appropriate time to present it to you."

I took the pouch from his hand warily, as though it contained a poisonous snake. It was heavy and hard and all of a piece. I glanced into his eyes; they were warm and encouraging. After a slight hesitation, I undid the ribbons and slid out the pouch's contents.

There, in my palm, lay the dagger I had seen in the Temple of Bengal. Its blade flashed in the lamplight, the cold silver warmed into a pale gold by the amber glow; that same light made the rubies a smoldering glow and darkened the emeralds into an unfathomable sea green, the exact shade of Nicholas's eyes when he withdrew inside himself to a place no one could follow.

My initial surprise was tinged with pleasure that he had remembered how much I had wanted the dagger and gone to the trouble of procuring it for me. But my happiness was quickly routed by less settling thoughts. Whatever childhood memories I retained of India and my father had been supplanted by the recollection of drowsing in the hayloft on a sunny afternoon, the day Nicholas had first entered my life. The dagger also recalled to mind the cool night in Lord Morton's garden when the light from Chinese lanterns shimmered across a pair of green eyes, near as a heartbeat as they stared down at me.

Back, too, came the cluttered shop with its heavy fragrance, and Lady Edgmont's aghast expression. Were it not for the Edgmonts, it would be Charlotte standing here, not I. Somehow Nicholas's essence and all of my tangled emotions were captured forever in this exotic piece of silver and ivory; and the blade could not have set me in greater turmoil if it had been plunged into me, instead of merely dropped into my open hands.

I looked up. Nicholas's eyes were expectant, hopeful, as he waited for my response. I forced myself to recall the thought that had gone into his gift and struggled to think only of his well-meaning intentions and the effort he had expended in trying to please me. Viewed in that light, the knife was special indeed. How many men, I wondered, would have gone to the trouble of finding a gift that went beyond mere baubles or lacy doodads?

I stammered my thanks and my eyes grew moist.

Nicholas regarded me steadily. "I daresay some might consider a dagger an odd sort of wedding gift, even ill-omened. But I trusted to your good sense that you would not find anything amiss in my choice."

I shook my head, but I was unable to suppress a nervous laugh that promptly gave the lie to my denial.

His brows drew together. "If there is anything else you would prefer, you have only to ask."

"There is nothing," I assured him, managing to smooth the nervous edge from my voice. "Indeed, I am quite overcome by your thoughtfulness."

A tear, which had been hovering at the corner of my eye, spilled down my cheek. He lifted his forefinger and brushed the drop away. Startled by his tenderness, I looked up at him and found myself melting beneath the gaze of those impossibly green eyes. For a brief second it was as if someone had plucked us from our suite at Blackwood Hall and dropped us again in Lord Morton's garden. I saw the same gentleness, the same concern, and felt within myself the same desperate desire for him.

Then he bent over me and gently kissed my lips. One kiss followed the next, each more exquisite than before; my lips parted, giving way beneath the pressure of his tongue. He tasted of salt and thick, rich honey, a taste faintly like the mead I had drunk earlier. But this was the stronger flavor, and the effects were more potent. With each kiss I grew dizzier, until it seemed my mind was no longer my own.

My senses, too, deserted me. The pop and crackle of the fire, the crash of the waves against the cliff, the moan of the wind twisting around the turrets, all faded and died, drowned out by the soft hoarse rasp of his breath that swelled in my ears and was echoed by the quickened beat of my heart. The fragrance of his shaving soap rose like a cloud and swirled into my nostrils, making breathing impossible—but mere air could not have satisfied the craving inside me.

I might have been a leaf, tossed helplessly, mindlessly above a raging torrent of water: My will was not my own. Each second I remained in his arms I grew weaker, my limbs weighted down with his overpowering presence. Another moment and I would sink below the surface and lose myself in him forever. Something inside me railed against the injustice. The indignity of giving myself so completely to a man who did not love me, had never loved me, was more than I could bear. With a loud cry, I pulled out of his embrace, and sat trembling uncontrollably on the edge of my bed.

Nicholas stifled a groan, but he did not reach for me or try to force me back into his arms. A lock of black hair fell across his brow, and tiny beads of moisture dampened his upper lip. He regarded me steadily, saying nothing until his breathing grew more regular. Then in a quiet, controlled voice, he asked, "What ails you, Redigan?"

I barely contained a bitter laugh. What ailed me? Nothing that his love could not have cured. But I, too, had my pride. Nothing could have persuaded me to tell him how I really felt. Instead, I rose on unsteady legs and stood before him, angry and defiant. "You have got Pendene's Wood, and you may face your friends without fear of ridicule. But that is all you will have from me."

Calmly, Nicholas brushed back the hair from his brow. His gaze never wavered, but in his eyes I saw a haunted, troubled look—a look I had never seen before. Then he rose. Standing, he towered above me and I realized that should he choose, I should have little to say about what he would or would not have from me. I flinched, then steeled myself for whatever was to come.

His eyes noted the movement and they narrowed. "How little you think of me," he said harshly. "Still, you need not concern yourself on that score. Rape holds no appeal for me." Without waiting to see how his words affected me, he strode to the door. There he paused, and with a backward glance, remarked ironically, "It would seem that I have better luck with my mistresses than I do my wives."

Then he walked out, leaving me to puzzle over the meaning of his words.

To my astonishment, the next morning at breakfast Nicholas behaved as though the night had passed in a perfectly acceptable fashion. He served me himself, taking the buttered eggs and thick slices of ham from the platters and placing them on my plate which he then set before me. As he withdrew his hand, his fingers brushed across my arm, causing a warm shiver to course through me.

I glanced up quickly, but Nicholas merely smiled politely, and I could not be sure if he had touched me intentionally or accidentally. After he had filled his own plate, he sat opposite me, smiling again as he shook out his serviette. I eyed him doubtfully, wondering what new course this sudden graciousness heralded.

"Did you sleep well?" he asked, his face all solicitousness and concern.

I nodded but, in fact, I could barely stifle my yawns. It had been almost dawn before I fell asleep. "And you?" I asked, sincerely hoping he had been as miserable and uncomfortable as I.

"Extremely well, thank you. Indeed, I believe it is the first good night's sleep I have had since leaving Cornwall. There is nothing like one's own bed, do you not agree?"

"It is difficult to say since my bed remains at Briarslea."

He laughed as if I had said something amusing. "Never mind, you will soon become accustomed to your new home." He cocked his head and studied me with a critical eye. "And your new bed seems to have done you no harm. You look no less radiant this morning than you have always looked." This time he smiled with such complete sincerity that I found myself returning his smile—albeit unwillingly.

With no more ado, he picked up his fork and gave his attention to the meal in front of him. Between mouthfuls, he made casual remarks about the weather. Too damp for riding, unfortunately: He had wanted to show me the estate. About the Hall: I must have Mrs. Ham show me around this morning; he, again unfortunately, had paperwork that needed attention. And about the gardens: beautifully landscaped and well worth a tour, although not until the rain had stopped.

These observations were intermingled with compliments about my luxuriant hair, my wise choice of a simple gown which would allow me greater freedom to explore even the most remote corners of the Hall, and the fascinating shade of my eyes which never ap-

peared quite the same to him, fluctuating as they did
between pale gold and darkest amber.

At first, I was totally confused. Then I decided that
he had become as mad as his father before him, no
doubt being dislodged from sanity by my cruelty. The
notion appealed to me. But if Nicholas was mad, he
seemed comfortably oblivious to his misfortune. He
enjoyed his breakfast—and apparently my company—
with the relish of a man starved for both food and conversation. It would have been hard to say which he
heaped higher, his plate or the compliments that he
poured upon me.

It was the latter which was his undoing. After learning that my table manners were more graceful than
those of the young ladies who had been presented at
court, a piece of news which promptly caused me to
slosh tea from my cup into my saucer, I realized what
he was doing.

"Do you think to treat me like Charlotte?" I demanded, furious with myself for not having guessed his
motives earlier. "You cannot distract me with pretty
words or a few baubles."

He looked hurt. "It would not occur to me to try. I
thought only to make amends for my behavior, which
has been abominable of late." His face grew pensive.
"I lay awake for hours thinking about what you said to
me last night—"

"Then your sleep was not as comfortable as you
would have had me think?"

He looked chagrined. "I lied. I rested not at all. And
I could not blame you, as I would have liked to have
done, for our differences."

"How awkward for you."

"It was, indeed. It is always more comfortable to find
fault with others than with oneself."

"My own experience has taught me that," I said
lightly. "Since my early childhood, I have rarely blamed
myself for anything."

"Then you are luckier than I am, for I cannot help but blame myself. When I told your uncle I would have you in Charlotte's stead, I simply assumed without asking that you would find my decision acceptable. In truth—" His mouth twisted into a wry smile. "I believe if I had approached you first you would not have been so quick to refuse me."

So he had guessed how I felt about him. Certainly, he suspected. I said nothing and tried, instead, to assume a detached air, wanting him to believe that his opinions were merely that—opinions, not the facts I knew them to be.

If Nicholas was disappointed by my failure to comment, he kept his feelings hidden. After giving me only a brief moment to reply, he continued, "Still, my mind was made up. I told myself that when your temper cooled, you would come to your senses, and we would resume the comfortable friendship that once belonged to us."

Comfortable friendship? I was mistaken; he had not realized that I was in love with him. I struggled to determine if I was grateful or dismayed. In the end, I decided I was both and said crossly, "Amiability seems precious little upon which to base a marriage."

Nicholas shook his head. "It is more than enough. I do not expect to inspire love; I demand only respect—the same respect which I am willing to accord to you. And I assure you, it was not vanity, but fellow feeling which made me believe we could make a success of our marriage."

"And your feelings for Charlotte?" I demanded. "What of them?"

Nicholas deliberated some while before answering. Then slowly, as though carefully choosing his words, he said, "Your sister is a lovely child, but it has been plain to me for some time that she and I were not well suited. I hoped that the affection and attention I showed her would persuade her to overlook my appearance; her opinion of my character gave me graver doubts. But what choice did I have? I had given my word. I felt honor bound to go through with the marriage."

"And yet you were not at all pleased to learn that Charlotte had run off with Monsieur André," I pointed out.

"If my pride was offended by her elopement, it was quickly replaced by relief. The situation had promised to be difficult in the extreme."

I looked at him suspiciously, wondering if I dared believe what he was telling me. What man would not have wanted to marry Charlotte? But it was true enough they would have made a poor match, and Nicholas was not a stupid man. Grudgingly, I chose to believe him—at least for the moment. "Still, I cannot say that I forgive you for treating me so shabbily," I told him.

"Nor do I blame you. In my haste to marry you, I failed to court you as every woman deserves. Let us forget that we are man and wife. I shall expect nothing from you, except the chance to prove that I am worthy of being your husband."

"I will not be easily convinced."

"I can be most persuasive."

Of that, I had no doubt. Shortly thereafter, Nicholas excused himself, doing so with obvious reluctance and only after he had bestowed a kiss on my forehead. It was a gentle kiss, brotherly rather than passionate, but for a moment his eyes held me as though he yearned to do more.

Just as I felt myself responding, he said, "When you are ready, ring the bell for Mrs. Ham and she will show you the house. Or, if you prefer, tell her to show you into the library. Over the years, Blackwood Hall has acquired a wide selection of books, a fair number of which belong to that category which is considered unfit for either intelligent minds or feminine consumption."

With a teasing smile, he added, "I direct you to those books in particular."

Mrs. Ham was eager to usher me through her domain. I followed obediently, wandering through long, dimly lit hallways, or passing from room to room as each one entered onto another, all of them elaborately furnished and spotlessly clean. Our progress was punctuated by her monotonous, gravelly drone. The walnut armoire had once belonged to Louis XIV; a portrait hanging in the salon had been painted by Inigo Jones; the ruthlessly polished ebony pianoforte had been the prized possession of my predecessor.

On the south side of the house, her voice competed with the screech of gulls and gannets, the harsh pounding of water against rock, and driving rain that hammered the windowpanes. More than once she repeated herself when I had clearly failed to hear what she had been saying.

But it was not the groaning undertone of wind and water that had made hearing difficult. My mind was preoccupied with Nicholas and the conversation we had had at breakfast. He had not said that he loved me. Nor, I realized uneasily when I recalled our conversation, had he said that he had not loved—or did not still love—Charlotte. Only that they had not been suited for marriage, while he and I had a companionable friendship that would do admirably. It was little enough to satisfy the heart. But at least, I consoled myself, it was genuine regard that convinced him to marry me. And perhaps some day. . . . But I would not tease myself with fanciful romantic notions of things that might one day be.

It was several days before the clouds lifted, swept away by cool ocean breezes that were permeated with the fresh tang of salt and seaweed. During that time, Nicholas was in every way the devoted suitor he had promised to be. Little gifts turned up on my dressing table each evening: crystal bottles filled with rose water or violet scent; porcelain miniatures; and vases of wild-flowers and sprays of sweet-smelling heather. Each morning, he greeted me with a compliment; each night, he sent me to bed with a soft kiss, on the forehead, the cheek, or the tip of my nose. And, unless his business affairs kept him otherwise occupied, we spent our days in pleasant conversation, discussing art, literature, music, even politics and war, for he seemed to think no subject beyond my intelligence or comprehension.

I felt myself unfurling beneath his attention like a rosebud whose tightly closed petals relaxed and opened beneath the benign warmth of the sun. And as Nicholas had promised, the friendship that had begun that day on the cliffs near Briarslea and grown during our daily excursions in London was easily resumed. It was as though the period before and shortly following our marriage had never happened.

And so when I awoke to clear skies and brilliant sunshine I was disappointed to learn that Nicholas had duties to attend to in the small village that lay to the west of Blackwood Hall. As the local lord, he was also the magistrate, although his position rarely demanded that he do more than level a few fines for brawling or drunk and disorderly conduct.

"But you must not wait upon me to have a look at the estate," he advised. "Have the groom saddle a mount and bring it round to the front door for you."

Something about the flicker of pleasure in his eyes and the slight lift at the corners of his mouth convinced me that more than mere pride in his lands lay behind the suggestion. "There is nothing I would rather do," I assured him. "But are you sure you would not prefer that I wait until you can accompany me?"

"We shall ride out together another day." He pressed my hands tenderly between his palms. I found myself staring at the neatly manicured nails and his long, agile fingers, and anticipating the touch of those fingers on my throat, at the nape of my neck, feeling their languid strokes on my breasts.

I shivered and forced my mind away from those dangerous thoughts. Nicholas may have restored my liking for him, but I had yet to see the desire in his eyes that I yearned and waited to see. "I will miss your company," I told him truthfully, bringing a pleased smile to his face.

"And I will miss yours, my darling," he said, releasing me with an endearing reluctance.

After seeing that my instructions were relayed to the groom, I changed into my riding habit and pinned up my hair beneath the elegant high-crowned hat. Then I swept down the stairs as if descending for a ball. There was only the foreman to appreciate my elegance, but trusting to the inclination of household servants to gossip amongst themselves, I felt certain he would advise the other members of the staff that his lordship's new wife was, apparently, quite the lady, after all.

But my assumed airs vanished when I saw the mare that had been brought up from the stables. "She could be Miranda's twin!" I exclaimed with childish delight, remembering the name of the dappled gray that Nicholas had ridden on his visit to Briarslea.

" 'Es, mum." The young groom—he could not have been more than fifteen—allowed his serious face to relax and he grinned in shared appreciation of the horse's beauty. "This 'ere be one of Miranda's fillies. 'Is lordship says she be your'n."

I gasped with delight. Had he guessed that no other gift would mean as much to me? "What is her name?" I demanded as my gaze ran over her delicate legs and the glossy black mane and flowing tail.

"T 'tania, mum."

Titania was as light on her feet as the fairy queen for which she had been named. As her hooves danced down the gravel drive, her legs taking dainty, mincing steps, I half expected to look down and see that gossamer wings had sprouted from her shoulders. I spent a joyous hour reveling in her lightness of foot and her quick responses to the slightest touch on the reins. Then I began to look around and, for the first time, truly appreciate my surroundings.

I had taken the driveway that wound through the woods. Overhead, the branches had interlaced with each other, like gnarled brown fingers locked together in a clasp of undying friendship. The leafy coverage was too dense for the sunlight to penetrate, except where the woods drew back and left dark green pools of grass and moss.

Here and there, small paths led off into the heart of the woods, but though I yearned to urge Titania down one of them, I hesitated. My ignorance of the countryside, and the brooding darkness that swelled beneath the branches, warned me not to stray from the driveway. It would be too easy to lose my way, and I did not fancy the idea of spending a cold night, huddled under those forbidding trees.

But near the base of the hill, I came upon a winding lane, not as wide as the driveway, but still broad enough to admit a carriage. In fact, deep ruts cut by the wheels of some conveyance had dried and hardened, leaving tracks which could be followed as easily as a signpost.

Titania was as eager to explore as I was. She nickered with pleasure and her pace quickened. Here, at the base of the hill, sheltered from the sea breezes by trees, it was warmer. Wild irises bloomed at the sides of the lane, buttercups, daisies, and briar roses, scattered across the green velvet verdure like daubs of bright paint across a green canvas.

The thought of canvas and paint brought Charlotte to mind. We had heard nothing from her in the week before we had left London, and if she had since returned, likely it would have been too soon to have received a letter from Aunt Emily or Elizabeth, telling us of her whereabouts. I found myself thinking of her without rancor and realized how much my resentment of her elopement—and the predicament in which she had left me—had faded. Indeed, at this moment, I would have thanked her effusively for her foolishness and lack of foresight.

The lane curved sharply and suddenly the trees fell behind us. Ahead, sheltered by two massive elms and surrounded by lawns and flower beds, stood a two-story stone manor, much the size of Briarslea. From the lacy curtains in the windows and its general appearance of tidiness and good repair, I assumed at once that the house was inhabited.

But by whom? Nicholas had not mentioned a neighbor; and I seemed to recall his telling me when the coach had turned onto the gravel driveway that all of the lands around us were part of the Blackwood estates.

Seeing no reason why I should not introduce myself to the manor's occupants—after all, I was Lady Blackwood now—I rode through the gateposts and cantered up to the front door. It was set beneath a gabled and slated porch. A young man, who had been trimming the shrubs, dropped his shears and hurried to take Titania's reins as I dismounted. He looked at me through startled eyes, as though visitors rarely paid a call on the manor and he did not know what to make of someone who did.

Thanking him briefly, I mounted the steps and reached for the heavy brass door knocker. The grinning devil's face, intended to scare away evil spirits, leered wickedly at me as it fell, and the hollow clapping sound that rang out was like a mirthless laughter.

What a place this is to give one fancies. I might have hastened back to Titania and pretended I had never been here if my knock had not received an immediate answer.

The door opened, revealing a stout, middle-aged woman of small stature. She stared up at me with sleepy eyes and a dull-witted expression, as though trying to understand how I happened to be on her doorstep.

It did not help matters that I did not know on whom I was calling. But surely this creature was merely the maid or the housekeeper, I told myself. It wanted only that she should let slip her mistress's name and my awkwardness should be alleviated.

"I hope this is not an intrusion," I said civilly, "but I have come to call. I am Lady Blackwood."

Not moving or answering, she continued to gape stupidly.

"From Blackwood Hall?" I added, beginning to wonder if she had heard of anything or anyone who lived beyond her own gateposts.

" 'Es, mum. Won't 'ee come in," she said at last, bobbing her head. She ushered me into a large hall, nearly twenty feet square, that reached high above our heads to the curved roof timbers. Despite the summer warmth, the thick slate walls kept the house cool, and a fire burned in the large, open fireplace.

"Please, t' set down, mum." She indicated a Jacobean chair that was a match to the chairs in our private sitting room. "I'll just let Lady Matilda know she be havin' a caller."

Lady Matilda? Had Nicholas another sister? If she was as formidable as Elizabeth she would soon see through my grand manners. But, at least, I had learned her name. Just as I was congratulating myself for having met with even that little success, I heard a woman's high, quavering voice call, "Edith. Who was at the door?"

The voice had come from behind a wooden door set in the wall to my right. As I glanced in that direction, the maid looked at my face doubtfully and, without bothering to walk across the room, cried back, "She says she be Lady Blackwood, mum." The disbelief in her voice was not at all complimentary.

"Lydia?" the voice demanded querulously, her tone equally skeptical. "They told me she was dead." There was a long pause and then Lady Matilda demanded, "Well. Is she or is she not dead, Edith?"

"She don't appear t' be, milady."

"What a pity." After this exclamation, the woman's voice dropped to a more normal level, but her words carried clearly into the hall. She seemed to be deliberating with herself, and it was quite impossible not to overhear.

"One so rarely receives calls from ghosts," she said thoughtfully. "Even those ghosts from which one might reasonably expect a visitation. My own brother, for instance, has neglected me shamefully. Of course, when he was alive he was no better, so why should I have expected more from him dead. Now, why did they tell me Lydia was dead if that was untrue? How naughty of them." Her voice rose again. "Is she still there, Edith?"

" 'Es, milady."

"Well, stop dawdling and send her in."

" 'Es, mum."

Edith smiled at me politely, behaving as though I had not been able to hear a word of their odd exchange, and said, "Lady Matilda will see 'ee now. She be in drawing room."

Chapter Thirteen

"YOU ARE NOT LYDIA. You are nothing like her."

I stared in fascination at the sight before me. I stood in a small, private sitting room off the great hall. A Persian rug covered most of the flagstone floor, and above that was a jumble of chairs and tables, sofas and settees. Crocheted lace doilies had been scattered across table tops, chair and sofa backs, and armrests; vases of every shape and size had been set on any surface flat enough or sturdy enough to hold more than a thimble. These were filled with flowers: roses, rhododendrons, camellias, and azaleas.

In the midst of the clutter, lounging on one of the sofas, was a wrinkled, elderly woman—I gauged her age to be somewhere between seventy and a hundred plus—who stared back at me with as much interest as I showed her. Strands of pure white hair poked beneath her lace cap, and her eyes were an undiluted blue. An embroidered silk shawl, gaily colored in pinks and purples, draped her shoulders, and another, larger shawl, crocheted from wool, was wrapped around her legs. Despite the collection of wrinkles that creased her face, there was something childishly innocent and appealing about her—she might have been a four-year-old awaiting a promised surprise rather than an elderly woman.

"Did you think you could trick me?" she demanded

in a high-pitched voice, and then giggled triumphantly. "I knew Lydia too well to fall for your games."

"I am Redigan, the new Lady Blackwood," I explained. "Lydia died eight years ago."

"Oh!" Her face puckered with disappointment. "Then they were telling the truth. And all this time I wondered—But never mind about that. I suppose it is just as well. If you had been Lydia I would have had to be very cross with you for neglecting me all this time. Now, we can have a nice visit. Sit down, my dear. If you keep standing Edith will think I have forgotten my manners. She thinks I am getting senile but I could lose most of my wits and still put one over on her. Right, Edith?"

" 'Es, mum," the housekeeper answered dolefully.

"Goodness. Stop standing there dithering. Go and fetch us some tea," her mistress demanded. "And bring us some of those little cakes that are in the pantry. I know there are some left because I saw you eating one this morning."

" 'Es, mum." Edith hurried away, looking greatly offended by her mistress's accusation. By way of a protest, she banged the door shut behind her.

"And stop listening at the keyhole," Lady Matilda called after her. "I know your sly ways." She threw up a pair of ring-covered hands in mock exasperation. "Now, then. Did you say your name was Redigan?"

"Yes, ma'am," I said, feeling completely bewildered by this display. "Redigan Blackwood," I added, this time with slightly more composure. I took the upholstered armchair across from her, after brushing aside a few sprays of camellias that drooped across my path.

"You say you are the new Lady Blackwood—that would make you Lydia's replacement." She giggled again, amused by the notion. "You must have married Stephen—oh!" She clapped her hands over her mouth and stared at me in dismay. "No, of course not. How silly of me—you have to have married Nicholas. It *was*

Nicholas? I do get them confused." She laughed slyly.
"You must be careful, my dear, that *you* do not."

"I cannot imagine confusing the two," I assured her.

"Oh, it happens. Mark my words, it happens. But
never mind. Whether or not *you* confuse them remains
to be seen, does it not?" She smiled a pleased, little-girl
smile. "Oh, I do love secrets and I have so few of my
own. When you reach my age, nobody cares about
your secrets—they think you cannot possibly be up to
anything even remotely interesting once you pass
fifty."

"I am sure they are wrong."

"Well, not very," she admitted sadly. "There is the
vegetable gardener who comes down from the Hall
every Friday. A rather nice-looking man, but he could
hardly be called a gentleman. I have often thought I
would like to invite him in to tea, but Edith would have
to know and she would tell Nicholas. He can be so terribly stern when he thinks I am being wicked. He wants
me to act my age. How awful. Why would anybody
want to act my age, unless perhaps they were already
a good deal older? Then acting my age might be an improvement on acting their own. Did they tell you how
old I was?"

"They did not," I said, finding it hard to keep up with
her thoughts.

"Good! What did they tell you about me?"

I could not possibly admit that Nicholas had not yet
mentioned her; her feelings would have been hurt. But
I was most curious to know who she was and the exact
nature of her relationship with the Blackwoods. "Nicholas has been so busy since we returned, he has told me
very little about you," I explained and when her face
fell, hastily added, "I imagine he thought you would
enjoy telling me the particulars."

She brightened immediately. "The dear boy. He is
always so very thoughtful. Or is Stephen the thoughtful
one? Never mind. They are both my nephews. Great-

nephews, you know. Their grandfather was my elder brother. That makes you my great niece. You must call me Aunt Matilda. None of this great-aunt business—that is to remain between the two of us. Edith has no idea that I am a great-aunt. If she did, she would refuse to let me get out of bed in the mornings. Do you like to garden?"

The door to the sitting room banged open and Edith appeared, carrying a silver tray. Atop the tray sat a silver tea set and, beside that, two china cups, delicately painted in a pastel green, the rims and ornate handles trimmed in gold.

"How wonderful!" Lady Matilda exclaimed, her face now alight with joy. "You brought the good cups. I was so afraid you would forget. Edith hates to get out the best china cups for *my* tea," she confided in a loud whisper. "She insists I break them. I do believe she thinks I throw them at the wall when her back is turned."

Edith made a small derogatory noise under her breath, and I suspected that her ladyship's hearing was not as sharp as it could have been; otherwise Edith would not have dared to express herself in such a fashion. Lady Matilda struck me as the kind of mistress who would quickly squash any nonsense, imagined or otherwise.

As soon as her housekeeper had left the room—actually, been ordered to leave, since she insisted on hovering near her mistress's shoulder as though reluctant to trust her to either pour the tea, or hold her own cup—the old woman looked at me and said, "Now, what were we talking about? Oh, yes—gardening. Do you have a garden?"

"Blackwood Hall has extensive gardens," I reminded her. "Surely, you are familiar with them?"

"Oh, not a flower garden. I like flowers—" She waved airily at the surrounding profusion of blossoms. "But I will not bother to grow them. The gardener is quite good enough for that sort of thing. I mean an herb garden. They are so very useful for quite a number of things."

"I am not sure if there is an herb garden at Blackwood Hall," I admitted. "I have not stepped beyond the front door since the day I arrived."

"Well, the weather has been dreary, especially for the end of May. But you must not waste the sunshine. If you like I will send you home with some plants, today. Or perhaps the next time you come would be better. My joints are stiff, and I dislike to kneel in the damp earth when my rheumatism is bothering me. Goes straight to my knees," she confided.

She reached for one of the cakes which Edith had remembered to include with our tea. For a moment, her hand wavered over them as if she could not decide which one to take. Then she settled on the one farthest from her, and placed it on the edge of her saucer. "Have a cake, dear," she encouraged. When I helped myself to one of the others, she asked, "Does it have currants on the top? I have to watch Edith carefully, or she will pick them off and eat them."

There were two currants on the top of my cake. I gingerly took a bite, hoping that there had only been two when they were removed from the oven. Edith, I had noticed, did not keep her fingernails any cleaner than I kept mine. There were more currants inside, but the cake tasted dry and a little stale. I told myself I must bring some fruitcake the next time I came.

But despite the stale cakes, and tea which was only lukewarm, we enjoyed a pleasant hour. Aunt Matilda's mind hopped from one subject to another but, except for moments of confusion, she appeared quite lucid. When I left, I gave her my word I would call again the following week.

"Lydia used to come every day," she said wistfully. Abruptly, she clapped her hands over her mouth again. "Oh, dear. That was a secret. I promised not to tell. Do you think she will be cross with me? After all, it can hardly matter now, can it? Not if she really is dead." Her face puckered with doubt. I could not decide if she debated whether or not Lydia was truly dead, or if she felt uncertain about whether she was nevertheless expected to keep her promise. At last she demanded, "Promise me you will not tell anyone that I told you."

I assured her I would say nothing, though I could not help wondering why the visits had been a cause of consternation. Perhaps, I decided on the ride back to the Hall, Lydia had merely wanted to give Matilda a secret to keep since she obviously enjoyed them.

" 'Is lordship's in the study," the footman informed me as I entered the Hall.

I did not bother to change from my riding habit before I sought him out; not only did it suit me as well as any of the gowns in my wardrobe, I could not wait to thank Nicholas for his gift.

"Titania is absolutely lovely," I told him, bursting into his study without bothering to knock. "She is exactly the mount I would have chosen for myself."

Nicholas did not admonish me for interrupting him; he rose from behind the oak desk and came to greet me. In his study, he seemed more at home than in any other room in the Hall; the dark panelling, the massive Tudor furnishings with their dark-green velvet upholstery, suited his grave character as well as accommodating his great size. He belongs here, I thought suddenly, and with a happy thought realized that I did, too.

Nicholas bent over and kissed my forehead. I reached up and my arms encircled his neck. Uncertain, he hesitated. Then seeming to reach a decision, his lips tentatively descended upon mine. I allowed the warmth of his kiss to wash over me and felt with pleasure the firm pressure of his arms around my back. My fingers tangled in his hair, and I wished they might knot themselves among those thick strands so completely, they might never be freed.

When he released me, he said huskily, "I am glad you are pleased."

"I am more than pleased," I whispered, no longer talking about Titania. He smiled as if he had taken my meaning, and my cheeks grew warm. To cover my embarrassment, I teased, "But you have made a grave mistake in giving her to me. You will find her a rival for my affections."

"As long as she is my only rival, I will have no reason to be disappointed in you."

"Will you feel the same way when I spend every morning and afternoon in her company?"

"As long as you save the evenings and nights for me." He brushed back a strand of hair that had escaped my coronet and fallen across my cheek.

"I suppose I must," I murmured, wanting to spend every moment in his company and wishing that his desire for me matched mine for him. "Has your day been horribly dull without me?" I demanded jealously.

"Horribly," he agreed with a grin. "And yours?"

"I missed you," I admitted. "But I suppose I cannot say my morning was dull. I had tea with your Aunt Matilda. You never mentioned her to me."

Nicholas frowned, and his mood altered as swiftly as though a cloud had drawn across the sun. "It did not occur to me that you would call on anyone without first consulting me."

I looked at him in surprise. "I had not planned to make any calls when I left the Hall. But when I came upon the manor I was curious to discover who lived there."

"You must learn to curb your curiosity," he said sharply. "You are no longer the squire's wayward niece, but a lady and my wife."

His reference to my inferior background wounded me even more than the manner in which he spoke to me. "I do not see that politely calling on one's neighbors constitutes a social indiscretion," I replied haughtily. "And if my background embarrasses you, you should not have pressured me to marry you. I do not recall forcing *you* to the altar."

"Stop being childish. It is not your background but your behavior that bears criticism."

"I do not see that either needs to be rebuked."

Nicholas stiffened. He struggled to hold his tongue while his temper raged silently inside him. Then in a calmer voice, he said, "I suppose, *this time,* it is my fault for not having told you about Matilda or the dower house. My great-aunt has lived there ever since I was a child. I have always made certain she has everything she needs, and I will continue to do so. You are not to concern yourself with her."

Stunned, I stared at him. What possible reason could he have for denying me the right to call on his aunt? Was this why Lydia's visits had been kept a secret? It was a question I would have promptly voiced if I had not promised to keep Matilda's secret. Still, I did not feel the need to resort to deceit to talk to an old woman who clearly suffered from loneliness and boredom. "I enjoyed your aunt's company," I countered. "If it pleases you to continue to see to her needs, then by all means do so. But that is no reason for me to ignore her."

Nicholas's fist slammed on his desk. "I will not have you disobeying me whenever it pleases you. You are not to go there again, and that is final."

I gasped. "For what reason?"

"Because I have said so!"

"I am not a child, I am your wife. You have no right to dictate to me."

"As your husband, I have every right."

"My husband or my jailor?"

"Do you, or do you not intend to comply with my wishes?"

"I do not. I promised her before I left that I would go there again next week."

"Then you will write her a letter, sending her your regrets."

"I most assuredly will not."

"If you do not oblige me, then I will be forced to curtail your riding except on those occasions when I can accompany you."

This last piece of unfairness was more than I could stand; if Nicholas had had any hope of convincing me to give up my plans to see Matilda, his bullying had destroyed them. "How dare you order me around in this manner," I said, biting off my words. "First you forced me into this marriage. Now you think to dictate to me as though I am nothing more than a scullery maid. Well, you have chosen poorly if you think to make a mealy-mouthed, compliant wife out of me. I shall go *where* I like, *when* I like. And if you refuse me the use of my horse—since, clearly, Titania is only my horse on those days that it suits you—then I will go on foot. Or do you intend to lock me in my room?"

"If I did, it would be nothing less than you deserve," he said coldly.

"Then you had better chain me to the bed as well, for I am most adept at climbing out of windows." I stamped my foot for emphasis, then hurled myself out of his study. Taking my cue from Edith, I banged the door shut behind me. From behind the closed door came a violent oath.

I did not want to go up to my room, where Nicholas might easily find me and lecture me further. Instead, I made my way to a small alcove off the library where I could nurse my hurt feelings and allow my rage to cool. After firmly shutting the tall doors behind me so that my privacy would not be disturbed, I flung myself into the window seat, pulled the draperies around me, and burst into tears.

My weeping spell was violent but short-lived; the

fury with which my tears fell quickly exhausted the rage that Nicholas had aroused. All that remained was my misery and a growing chill for which even my heavy riding habit seemed to be no protection.

The library lay on the east side of the house; the sun's warmth had long since departed and the room was cool, even within the sheltering folds of the heavy velvet draperies. Outside, beyond the mullioned windows, the lawns were captured beneath the shadows of the Hall. The rich emerald had become jade, a jade so dark as to be almost black.

I shivered. It seemed that the sunshine rarely lingered around Blackwood Hall, preferring to flee inland to friendlier terrain. Even my prickly character needed more nourishment than was to be found here.

As if in answer to that need, a deep voice asked, "Are you all right?"

Nicholas! I hastily dried my face and yanked back the draperies. But it was Stephen who stood there.

Until then, it had escaped me how alike their voices were. We had seen little of Stephen since our arrival. Either he had discreetly remained in his rooms to give us the privacy most newlywed couples enjoyed, or he simply preferred to keep to himself. With Stephen, I could not be certain which was the most likely. Mingled with his obvious sensitivity was a touch of aloofness, an aloneness that seemed due to a melancholic disposition.

"Are you all right?" he asked again, his eyes shimmering with compassion.

"Yes, of course I am," I replied, wondering if he had overheard my loud sobs. "I am afraid I did not hear you come in."

"That is because I already was in," he explained gently. "You were much too distraught to notice me sitting in the corner, reading."

"Oh."

"Please forgive me. I know it would have been more

polite of me to have left you alone, but I thought you might like someone to talk to when you recovered."

His voice was warm and completely sincere. I realized that I very much wanted to talk to him. I managed a weak smile. "Did Lydia also confide in you when she and Nicholas argued?"

A shadow passed over his handsome face. "Lydia did not argue with Nicholas—she was terrified of my brother."

"Did he often lose his temper with her, as well?"

"No, I cannot say that he ever did. Nicholas seldom loses control of himself. Ever since we were children, he has tried most determinedly not to give in to his rages. He has always feared them as the forerunner of the madness that plagued our family."

I felt a reluctant twinge of compassion for Nicholas. What must it have been like for him, growing up in this gloomy, mist-draped setting, fearing that he might succumb to madness, never daring to give vent to his rages for fear they might erupt into something a great deal more horrifying than a childish tantrum? What a sad, somber child he must have been. "I cannot imagine Nicholas as a boy," I said aloud.

"That is hardly surprising." Absentmindedly, he stroked one high cheekbone with a slender finger. "I cannot say that my brother was ever a boy. A short adult, perhaps. But no, not a boy."

There was something sadly final about his pronouncement; something had been lost which could not be regained. "Were you also afraid of going mad?" I asked, suspecting that more personal fears lay behind his morose statement.

Quickly, his smile flashed. "I did not inherit the Blackwood temper."

He had not, precisely, answered my question, but it was all he seemed inclined to say, at least on this occasion. "I cannot fathom why my brother could be cross with you," he said, changing the subject. "You are both discerning and intelligent, and remarkably free of the nerves and vagaries that beset many young ladies. You must not let him bully you."

"I did not," I admitted. "Which is, in large part, the reason he lost his temper."

"Then I applaud your courage. Nicholas has always suffered from the notion that, as Lord Blackwood, he has the right to control the lives of everyone around him. I have never stood up to him, a weakness which has only made him worse. Perhaps, you will inspire me." He placed his hand over mine, a gesture that was not intended to arouse anything more than companionable feelings between us. Nor did it do so.

But it pleased me to think I had at least one friend at Blackwood Hall. Two, if I counted Matilda. Impulsively, I asked him, "I rode by the dower house today and met your Aunt Matilda."

His hand tightened over mine. Then it was quickly withdrawn. "Aunt Matilda?" he asked with studied casualness. "I have neglected her terribly of late. I hope you found her in good health."

"She is." His green eyes, more expressive than Nicholas's, were clearly troubled but, by what, I could not guess.

Seeing me watching him intently, Stephen added, "And is Edith still accusing her of throwing the crockery around again?"

"Yes," I admitted.

He laughed. "You must not believe her. One afternoon I caught Edith dropping a plate as she carried it from the kitchen. The woman is nothing short of a liar. She tries to blame Aunt Matilda for her clumsiness rather than risk getting her wages docked."

The image of dull, irritable Edith standing over shards of broken china, made both of us burst into laughter. Just then, the library door opened and Nicholas appeared in the doorway, his hand resting on the doorknob. He looked at the two of us, sitting in the window seat together, laughing like happy children, while the draperies partially concealed us from view.

Instead of the scowl and the rebuke I expected, his face whitened; his hand dropped to his side. Then, without a word, he stepped back into the corridor and closed the door behind him.

I stared at the closed door in disbelief. "Surely, he does not think—" Dismayed, I swivelled to face Stephen.

He, too, was staring at the closed door, eyes narrowed speculatively as he considered his brother's behavior. Given his sharp features, there was something almost foxlike about his expression. Then he looked across at me and caught me studying him. His features relaxed. "Do not upset yourself unduly," he advised me. "It is not as if he caught us in an embrace, and he can hardly deny me the pleasure of speaking with you. Still—" He rose and straightened his attire. "Perhaps I had better return to my reading. And you, my dear"— he gave me his hand to help me rise—"will want to change your dress for supper. Please, do not let me keep you."

Why, he is afraid, I thought. Was Nicholas's temper that impossibly wicked that his own brother needed to fear him? In London, he had been the perfect gentleman, until Charlotte had disappeared. Then, he had changed; but only for a short while—or so I had thought. After this afternoon . . . With a start, I realized that I knew nothing at all about my husband.

That night, after another strained supper, Nicholas tapped on my door, again—the same soft, but commanding rap I had come to recognize as his. I had not expected him to attempt to share my bed so quickly after his promise to court me—several days, after all, could not be considered an overlong courtship, even for the most impatient of lovers. From Nicholas, I expected, and intended to receive more. And our argument that afternoon had not made me feel well-disposed towards him. He had behaved more like a tyrant than a lover.

Despite my resolve, my stomach fluttered when I opened the door. Nicholas stood there; beneath his drawn face he appeared to be waging an inner war. Then, guiltily, his gaze slipped past me, into the room beyond. The stealthy look amazed me: Had he expected to find Stephen there? After a cursory glance that did not appear to satisfy the doubts which unsettled him, his attention returned to me.

"May I come in?" he asked stiffly. "There is a matter I must discuss with you."

"If you like," I said reluctantly, wondering whether he intended to harangue me further about Matilda, or if he was more concerned with the friendly scene he had stumbled upon in the library. Truly, I did not wish to discuss either incident; the day had exhausted my energies and my meager store of patience. But there was no point in refusing to listen to him; it would only make matters worse. I stepped aside so that he might enter.

His long limbs carried him to the center of the room in three strides. After closing the door, I followed more slowly and took a seat in the wing chair facing him; my hands clenched tightly in my lap.

Before saying a word, Nicholas gave me a measured look, and I became conscious of my state of dishabille—my unbraided hair draping my shoulders and flowing down my back, the loose flowered wrapper falling open to reveal a silky nightgown which clung to the curve of my bosom and slender hips, my unslippered toes peeking from beneath my hem. Uncomfortable, I pulled the wrapper across my breasts.

He swallowed, then glanced away, turning instead to stare at a watercolor which hung on the wall. It was one he must have seen many times before, but it held his attention for a lengthy period.

"I am not usually an unreasonable man," he said at last.

My agreement was halfhearted, but I said dutifully, "Not usually."

"And yet you seem to bring out the worst in me."

"Perhaps we are not as well suited as you supposed."

"More likely we are too well suited," he said, forgetting the watercolor, his gaze turning again to me. "Your temper is as hot as my own. But that is neither here nor there. I do not like behaving in an irrational fashion, whatever the provocation. Therefore, I have decided you may call upon my aunt whenever you wish." Before I could open my mouth to protest the highhanded manner in which this proclamation had been delivered, he said in a strained voice, "And I must ask you to forgive me for my behavior this afternoon. It was . . . unwarranted." The apology seemed to be forced from him and, without question, it had been difficult for him to make.

But it was, I decided, an apology. Clearly, he wanted to make amends. "Of course I forgive you," I said sweetly, then was unable to refrain from adding, "now that you have come to your senses."

His eyes flashed with anger, but it was quickly subdued. "Good. I am glad that is settled. Perhaps now we can be friends again."

"If you wish," I said coolly.

If my response was less than encouraging, it did not thwart him. With a determined stride, he crossed the room and lifted me from my chair. His arms encircled me, tightly drawing me against him until the air was pressed from my lungs; as I gasped, his mouth sought to capture mine.

It felt as if my body had turned to stone. Here was the reason for his apology: expedience. He had lost patience with courtship and was demanding a wife. Furious that I had been foolish enough to think him sincere,

I jerked my face aside. His lips brushed my lower cheek.

"Good heavens, Redigan," he said hoarsely. "You cannot mean me to wait forever."

I regarded him as coldly as I would have regarded a stranger who had broken into my home. "I mean you to wait until you learn to regard me as a human being, instead of the chattel for which you continually mistake me."

Chapter Fourteen

IT WAS ONLY after Nicholas had retreated from my room—in a fine rage, try though he might to conceal his temper—that it came to me why he had forgotten his promise to postpone taking his husbandly rights until after I had been properly courted. The stealthy visual search of my room, the apology he had forced himself to make, his unmanageable temper, and—most importantly—his failure to even mention the intimate tête-à-tête he had interrupted, all of these things suggested that he feared I was falling in love with Stephen.

How ridiculous, I thought. And how unlike him. He had allowed Charlotte complete freedom without ever considering the possibility that she might fall in love with another man. But one private talk with his brother—when I was already his wife—had Nicholas thinking the worst of both of us. His behavior was completely irrational. Unless, I considered, that by her elopement, Charlotte had undermined his self-esteem to a greater degree than I had realized.

It bothered me to think that I had not guessed the true extent of his love for her. Over the past week, I had allowed myself to believe that his good sense and his determination to make a success of our marriage had helped him to overcome any tender feelings that might have lingered for my sister. But clearly her elopement had wounded him deeply. It seemed that I was never to escape from Charlotte's shadow, no matter how much distance might lay between us.

I did not see Stephen the following day, and remembering his fear of his brother, it seemed probable that he had remained in his rooms rather than risk facing Nicholas's displeasure. It would not have surprised me if we had not met again for a week. But I was pleasantly mistaken: The next afternoon, as I strolled through the gardens, I glanced up to find him hurrying down the gravel path to meet me.

He smiled and waved when he saw I had noticed him. His face looked happier than usual, less guarded than it usually seemed, and I wondered what had happened to lighten his melancholy.

"You look well," he exclaimed cheerfully as he approached me. His fingers were still buttoning his greatcoat as though it had been grabbed as he rushed out the door, and the breeze blew his black hair across his face.

I laughed. "I was just thinking the same about you. Did you come out to show me around the garden?"

"If that is what you would like." He finished with his buttons and offered me his arm. "You had better take a grip on me," he warned. "The breezes from the cliff can knock you down, if you are not securely braced."

The gardens were lovely. Near the Hall, terraced flower beds had been laid out with roses, and beyond these had been planted camellias, carmine, and the rhododendrons I had seen when I first arrived. But to the west, the lower slopes were almost entirely covered by a huge maze, the clipped hedges curving one around the next in an intricate pattern.

Stephen insisted we stroll through the maze, announcing he would be my guide and gaily professing to know its winding path as well as he knew the corridors that meandered through Blackwood Hall. We had not gone far before he paused thoughtfully, as though struggling to remember his way. At last, when I rounded on him and told him that he was a shameless liar, he laughed and admitted to being hopelessly lost. It was only by accident that we stumbled into the center of the maze.

I was delighted by the scene that met my eyes. Water trickled into a small pond from a pitcher held by a cherubic stone boy. Nearby, a niche had been cut into the hedge and fitted with a marble bench. On top of pedestals at either end of the bench sat Grecian urns, both overflowing with azaleas. We collapsed onto the bench, exhausted. I noted that, although Stephen had tried to conceal his limp as we walked, he was as grateful as I for the opportunity to sit down.

"It is just as well the top of the hedges are well below the foundations of the Hall," he said, stretching his legs out comfortably before him. "If we do not appear for luncheon, Nicholas has only to look out the window to discover our whereabouts. Then, unless he decides to let us starve for our foolishness, we may be rescued."

I wondered if Nicholas would regard our friendly escapade as merely foolish. After Stephen's nervousness in the library, it surprised me that he viewed our situation in so light a manner. "I must apologize for misjudging you," I confessed. "Yesterday, I believed you to be avoiding me, so as not to upset Nicholas."

"I said you were a discerning woman, did I not?" He grinned, a deep puckish grin that was wicked yet disarmingly innocent. "You were quite right, of course. I have always been a coward."

"Then why the sudden bravado?"

He shrugged. "I warned you in the library that you might inspire me with your courage. Well, apparently, you have. If a mere slip of a girl can stand up to my brother and tell him off, then I can certainly manage the occasional act of defiance. I want us to be friends. If Nicholas objects then he may do his worst to me."

I wondered if Stephen truly understood the depths of Nicholas's suspicions. "I must warn you," I said

lightly, trying not to give credence to the notion by
treating it seriously. "My husband suspects we are falling in love."

"Does he?" Despite my levity, Stephen's face turned
solemn. "Then you must feel complimented. Lydia
might have entertained a slew of admirers, and he
would not have noticed or cared."

I was taken aback by his bluntness. Nicholas considered his first marriage a failure—he had said as much
to Elizabeth that first night he dined with us in London—but surely he had loved his wife. "You must be
mistaken," I said.

Stephen shook his head glumly; his face looked troubled. "My brother is not an easy man to know. He tries
to deny his own emotions, but he cannot hide them entirely. When you have known him as long as I have, you
will learn to read the nuances and subtleties of his expression. No one knows better than I how little he felt
for Lydia." He frowned. "You cannot imagine how
often I have wished that he had felt otherwise."

It seemed an odd remark to make. What difference
could it have made to Stephen whether or not Nicholas
had loved his wife? Or had he pitied Lydia? Had she
turned to him for solace? Fleetingly, I wondered if there
had been something more than friendship between
them, this handsome young man and Nicholas's neglected wife; then I discarded the notion as fancifully romantic, for if he had loved Lydia, Stephen would
certainly not have wished that Nicholas had also loved
her.

"Poor Lydia. She had so little happiness," Stephen
murmured, convincing me that it was pity he had felt—
indeed, still seemed to feel—for her.

"Will you tell me about her?" I asked, suddenly realizing that, beyond her untimely death, I knew nothing
about her. "Nicholas has never mentioned her, and I
cannot help but be curious."

"If you like." He tossed back his hair which had

blown across his eyes. He reminded me of a young
rajah I had once seen carried through the streets of Calcutta, seated high on the back of an elephant in a swaying howdah: There was the same grace and regality in
his movements, the same touch of remote pathos shad-
owing his face.

Stephen caught me studying him and smiled. "You
are not at all like her, you know. You are much too
thoughtful and observant. Lydia was highly strung,
flighty—and horribly spoiled, I suppose. Her father
doted on her. She was his youngest and his favorite,
I believe. I doubt that as a child she had ever had to
demand or fight for the things she wanted. She simply
accepted what was given, as though it was hers, by
right."

She sounded as bad as Charlotte. However much Stephen had pitied Lydia, I did not care for what he told
me of her. "And Nicholas?" I demanded. "Did she simply accept him, as well?"

He looked at me oddly. "In a manner of speaking,
yes. The marriage was arranged by her father, before
Nicholas or Lydia had met. Edgmont had had some financial dealings with my brother, and knew him to be
an honest and generous man. That, combined with the
Blackwood wealth and title, made the match especially
desirable. Lydia simply did not question her father's
decision. She had never had any reason to do so. He
had always given her the very best of everything."

"But what of Nicholas? Why would he agree to marry
a woman he had never met?"

"My brother has never been successful with young
ladies of matrimonial age. His appearance—" He
shrugged apologetically. "I suppose it pleased him to
have found a respectable wife with very little effort,
and the reports he had received of Lord Edgmont's
daughter spoke well of her manners and her beauty."

"She was beautiful?" I asked with dismay. Elizabeth

had led us to believe her looks were no more than average.

Stephen failed to see my disappointment. "She was lovely," he said. "With the fragile, transparent beauty of a butterfly." From the soft, distant look in his eyes and the gentle tone of his voice, I could not doubt his sincerity.

"And yet Nicholas did not love her?" I hoped Stephen did not hear the catch in my voice.

But he was too wrapped up in his memories of the past to be aware of the present. "I believe he tried," he admitted grudgingly. "Or shall I say, he intended to try. But when they met, Lydia discovered he was not—" His words hung in the air. Then awkwardly, he finished, "—what she expected. Still, the wedding was already arranged and, for once, her father would not listen to her when she begged him to let her break off their engagement."

"And Nicholas had given his word," I said, feeling strangely empty as I spoke.

He gave me an appraising look. "So you have already learned something of the man you married. Yes, Nicholas places honor above good sense."

"I am sure that is to be admired."

Stephen laughed shortly. "It is a failing. He prefers to adopt proud airs rather than admit his mistakes and correct them. His arrogance was costly. Lydia felt nothing for him except revulsion. It cannot have been pleasant, seeing himself through her eyes and knowing his own wife wanted nothing to do with him."

"Nothing," I echoed in a startled voice. Surely he did not mean that Lydia had refused to share her bed with Nicholas. But that was impossible. She had died in childbirth.

Stephen glanced at my distraught face and abruptly rose to his feet. "Forgive me, my mind wanders. Perhaps we should try to find our way back. The wind is picking up and I would not care to be caught here if those clouds drift inland."

After some confusion, we found our way out of the maze, but the laughter and the silliness that had marked our conversation as we had begun our walk was absent. Stephen's gloom had returned, and my attempts at conversation could not dispel his mood.

After receiving a few desultory replies to my remarks, I gave up and lapsed into silence, allowing my own nagging thoughts to occupy my mind. I would have preferred to ignore them, so dark were their content. Nicholas himself had said to me that he had better luck with his mistresses than his wives. At the time, I had puzzled over his meaning; now it seemed clear. Yet only a few weeks ago, he had sworn to Lord Edgmont that his daughter had died in childbirth. Unless I had mistaken the meaning of the remarks that had been made to me, that had been a falsehood. But why? How else might she have died?

I shuddered. The possibilities were beyond anything I wanted to believe. There was nothing for me to think but that somehow I had misunderstood.

As we emerged from the maze, I glanced up at the Hall; it loomed above us on the hillside, the mullioned windows, like many-faceted eyes, monitored our progress as we crossed the lawns. My hand was still securely wrapped around Stephen's arm. Until now, I had forgotten, but there was something vaguely disapproving and censorious in the gray stone face, and I could not free myself of the unsettling sensation of being watched. Not casually observed, but angrily studied.

My gaze drifted to the east wing, to the French doors which opened onto Nicholas's study. The sunlight glanced off the panes of glass, making it impossible to see into the darkened room. But as I stared, I thought I caught a flicker of movement, the swaying of curtains. Then it was gone.

With a guilty flinch, I pulled free of Stephen, startling him out of his reverie. "Are you all right?" he asked.

"Yes, of course," I replied, but I did not take his arm again, and I was glad when we had moved too near the Hall to be viewed from the east wing.

If Nicholas had been watching us from his study, he did not mention seeing us. The conversation over lunch was light and friendly, and once he went so far as to compliment his brother for his delicate handling of a disturbance amongst the servants during his absence. The praise startled Stephen, who seemed unused to garnering such compliments, and his "thank you" was delivered less graciously than it ought to have been. Save for that, all went smoothly, with only that single, indistinct movement and my own dark thoughts to ripple beneath the placid surface of the day.

The drawing room at Blackwood Hall being far too large and formal for my liking, I spent most of my hours in the library—which I sometimes shared with Stephen whose tastes leaned toward scholarly tomes—or in the morning parlor, a pleasant room that caught the early sunshine. It boasted an air of friendliness that was generally lacking in other rooms of the Hall. The furnishings were a mixed lot of pieces, most of the chairs and the long sofa well-stuffed and the tables large, sturdy, and equipped with a variety of drawers that could be put to good use. All of the decor had been chosen with an eye to comfort, rather than for any aspirations towards elegance, and I naturally gravitated to this room when I had no cause to be elsewhere.

Mrs. Ham no more approved of my choice of rooms than she approved of me. When her face appeared at the parlor door, her lips pinched tightly together, I did not assume that anything out of the ordinary had offended her.

She quickly set me to rights. "There's a young woman in the foyer, milady. She's been asking for you."

"A young woman?" I echoed, wondering who might be calling on me. "Did she give her name, Mrs. Ham?"

The housekeeper shook her head, but from her expression of distaste, I guessed the woman did not meet with her notion of "the right sort of person to be calling on Lord Blackwood's wife." I had not, as yet, become something more to the elderly woman than "his lordship's new wife." Of that, I felt certain. And I seemed to have sunk lower in her estimation by having brought this less-than-acceptable person, whoever she might be, to Blackwood Hall. Still, I could hardly refuse to see someone when I had no idea of who they were or what they might want.

"Show her into the parlor," I said, sighing heavily, for clearly turning this uninvited visitor away was exactly what Mrs. Ham felt I should do.

The lines etched around her lips deepened. "Yes, mum. If you are sure you do not want me to send her away."

"I am quite sure," I said sharply.

Face more aggrieved than ever, she withdrew.

Minutes later, she reappeared, followed by an obviously distraught young woman. The blonde curls poking from beneath her hood were tangled; her blue velvet pelisse was badly torn and its hem caked with mud. As she burst past the housekeeper into the room, her hood fell back to reveal her face.

"Charlotte!" I exclaimed in disbelief.

"Redigan," she cried, throwing herself into my arms with a sob. "I knew you would not turn me away."

I had almost failed to recognize her. Her eyes were puffy and ringed with red, and grimy streaks ran down her cheeks. As she sobbed in my arms, Mrs. Ham stared at us both, her face appalled by our obvious familiarity with each other. I could almost hear her gravelly voice, filled with outrage and disgust, denouncing my conduct in the servants' quarters.

"Bring us some tea, Mrs. Ham. And something to eat. Some of those little cakes." As a parting shot, I added, "And do not pick the currants off the top." The remark caused her to stiffen and gasp as though she had been struck. I cannot say that I felt a smidgen of remorse.

It was pointless trying to talk to Charlotte until she had calmed down. My questions received unintelligible replies, delivered between sobs and wails and self-recriminations. I had to be satisfied with removing her sodden pelisse and drawing her near the fire where she could warm herself. At last, after she had drunk several cups of tea, and ravenously devoured an entire plate of cakes, she grew quieter.

"Oh, Redigan. I have been such a fool," she said, giving one last violent shiver. "Whatever shall I do?"

"You might start by telling me what has happened," I said, being no clearer on the subject now, than I was when she first walked into the parlor.

Charlotte stared at her hands, running her thumb across her ragged nails while her face assumed a mournful air. "I have been deceived," she said, her voice no more than a whisper. "You were right about Monsieur André. Oh, Redigan, I am so ashamed. How could you see through him, when I could not?"

"Likely, because he reserved his flattery for you."

She started to cry again. "Oh do not torment me. I have borne enough. I can never show my face in public again. How my friends would laugh at me if they knew. *When* they know, for soon everyone will have heard of his infamy, if they have not already done so. It would not surprise me to learn that he has regaled every respectable drawing room in London with his infamous boasts."

"Do you mean he did not marry you?" I asked, suspecting the worst from her outburst.

"Marry me!" she cried aloud. "He had no intention

of marrying me. All his talk of love that surpasses the boundaries of mere convention. He meant only that he did not believe in marriage. He wanted me to live with him, as though I were nothing better than a ladybird. He said artists were not meant to have wives, they were already married to"—she gulped—"to their art."

"With Monsieur André it is a shaky match at best," I said dryly.

Immediately, I regretted my words because it drew another onslaught of sobs from Charlotte. When these, too, had subsided, she stared at me reproachfully. "Must you always make fun of him—and of me? He may have behaved unscrupulously, but I loved him. I will always love him. He is the only man who will ever mean anything to me. How could he do this to me?"

"Surely . . . surely, you did not . . . share his bed?" I faltered.

She gasped. *"Share his bed?* What do you take me for? I may have trusted him unwisely, but I am not so misguided that I would allow him to take liberties without—" She glared at me, her face red with outrage. "How dare you think that of me? I assure you, he has been allowed to do no more than kiss my hand, and that garnered him a rebuke when he grew too familiar with my fingers."

"Truly, you amaze me," I said, shaking my head. "It seems there is rather less harm done than your hysteria has led me to believe."

"Less harm?" She glared at me. "I am ruined! I, who had the most successful season of any debutante this year. I, who was to be Lady Blackwood and figure prominently in society. How can you say 'less harm'?"

There seemed no way to console her. Indeed, Charlotte seemed determined not to be consoled. And, privately, I had to admit that Monsieur André was likely to brag about having succeeded with her, no matter that his story would be cut from whole cloth. Certainly, he had never failed to boast of his artistic abilities, even in direct face of the evidence against him.

"We shall just have to wait and see what happens," I said. "Perhaps, Nicholas can be persuaded to write to the man and demand his silence." Or pay him to hold his tongue, I thought, but I did not want to cause another tearful outburst by admitting this to Charlotte. "Do Uncle Arthur and Aunt Emily know of your whereabouts?" I asked.

But even this seemingly casual remark was enough to upset her. "I cannot return to Briarslea," she said when she regained a modicum of self-control. "What must they think of me? I have not the nerve to face them."

"Then you must stay here," I said reluctantly, wishing there was some alternative. The thought of the pressures a distraught Charlotte would add to our already strained household did not please me. But I could no more send her out into the world to make her own way, than I could have turned a six-week-old kitten loose in a field to fend for itself. "I will write and let them know that you are unharmed."

"Unharmed?" she wailed. "My entire life has been destroyed and you say I am unharmed. Oh, Redigan. Truly you can be most insensitive, although you are my sister and I love you dearly."

"Be glad that I am sensitive enough to bother with you," I retorted. "Instead of telling you off as you deserve."

She pouted. "You should be thanking me. Except for my faith in the basic decency of all people, you should not now be Lady Blackwood. You have benefited through my lack of cynicism."

"Through your lack of sense, you mean. And I rather think it was your mistrust of Nicholas that led you astray. Not your faith in Monsieur André."

"Oh!" she exclaimed crossly. Thereafter, she refused

to talk to me, and I found her sulky silence a vast improvement on her sobs and bursts of outrage.

Charlotte's baggage had been left on the doorstep, apparently deposited there by the young man who had agreed to carry her in his donkey cart from the inn, where the coach had taken her. After directing Mrs. Ham to have the footman take her belongings upstairs to one of the guest rooms, and arranging for the hot water Charlotte needed to take a bath, I cornered Nicholas in his study.

I did not like to think of how my news must affect him, but simply asked, "Would you mind terribly if Charlotte stayed with us a while?"

He laid down the papers he had been perusing and leaned back in his chair. "Charlotte? Your sister is here?"

I nodded, wondering what emotions my words had stirred beneath his cool exterior. "She just arrived. If it is too awkward, then she must go on to Briarslea. My aunt and uncle are not monsters who will turn their backs on her."

"And nor are we," he said evenly. "Certainly, she may stay—if that is her wish. But what of Monsieur André? Are we to be honored with his company as well?"

I told him the whole story. Nicholas listened intently, saying nothing. As I talked, I could not help thinking that if he had but waited, Charlotte would have returned to him. I studied the grave face across from me. Was he sorry that he had acted impetuously? Or was he truly incapable of forgiving someone who had wronged him? How I wished my sister had gone home to Briarslea instead of coming to Blackwood Hall. When I had finished, I would not have blamed him if he had made a few smug remarks or smiled complacently, but he did not. He merely told me to make her as comfortable as was possible, given her circumstances. "It is," he said, "the least we can do."

*   *   *

By suppertime, Charlotte had regained most of her composure. A hot bath and a clean dress—a pale green creation, made of a sheer silk that merely drifted over her soft curves—had restored her normal appearance, except for a slight pinkness around the eyes. Her wan expression heightened rather than detracted from her beauty.

She gracefully took her place at the heavy oak table in the long dining room where we took our meals. Overhead, the chandelier cast patterns of light across the linen tablecloth and the highly polished silverware. The yellow-tinged candlelight accented the dusky gold of the draperies and the gilt-leafed moldings; the room, and Charlotte, seemed to be bathed in a golden glow.

"I only hope you can forgive me," she said upon greeting Nicholas. She rested a dainty hand on the tablecloth; the ragged fingernails had been scrubbed and neatly filed. "I can see, now, how badly I behaved. But, at seventeen, one is inclined to foolishness." This remark was followed up with a weary sigh that suggested she had aged twenty years since they had last met.

Nicholas smiled gravely, but amusement flickered in his eyes. "I am sorry to hear of your recent ordeal. Never, did I wish you harm."

"Naturally, you would not," she agreed. "You cannot know how much I regret running off and leaving you. But I am sure Redigan will make you a good wife in my stead." She looked at me doubtfully.

I smiled at her graciously—as graciously as I could manage when what I wanted to do was slap her. How dare she imply that I was poor compensation for the wife he might have had! Charlotte smiled back sadly, completely unaware that her remarks had given offense. Then, once more teetering on the edge of tears, she gazed up at Nicholas and said, "I will not impose on your hospitality for long. Merely until I can make other arrangements that are suitable, although what they might be I cannot help but wonder. The world is often cruel and unforgiving to foolish young ladies who have trusted to their hearts instead of their heads."

"You must not think of leaving," Nicholas assured her. "Redigan will be glad of your company. Now, she has only my brother to keep her amused while I am at work." He glanced at me briefly, his eyes hard, then casually added, "I think I shall make some inquiries into the recent conduct of Monsieur André. Perhaps he has shown more discretion than any of us would expect of him."

Charlotte waved her hand impatiently. "There is no hope of that. How could he resist boasting of his conquest? It is not as if I was nobody of consequence, or as ill-favored as one of the Misses Gillingham. Winning *their* love might be a matter for secrecy, but—"

"But deceiving a naive girl who gives herself the airs of a great lady *is* something to brag about?" I demanded.

Charlotte gasped and Nicholas regarded me sternly. "Redigan. You must not be so inconsiderate of your sister's feelings. Remember what she has suffered over these last few weeks."

"It is nothing to what she will suffer if she does not stop talking nonsense," I said crossly. "And you are just as bad to indulge her."

His protests were interrupted by Stephen, who slipped into his chair with an apology for being late. He caught sight of Charlotte and started with surprise. "Now, I must apologize again. I was unaware we had company."

I introduced them, fervently hoping that Stephen's handsome face would distract her from Nicholas, but for once, her behavior was uncharacteristic. After a single curious glance, one which displayed only a polite interest, she echoed his greeting and then fell back into conversation with Nicholas.

He gave her his full attention. His scarred cheek was

shadowed by the soft lighting, and they made an attractive picture: His dark coloring and strong physique emphasized her fairness and delicate bone structure. Even her movements were light and airy; her hands fluttered like butterflies, and her curls danced around her face whenever she lifted her head to speak to him.

I watched miserably, jealously marking each look he gave her, each smile that she brought to his lips. They had fallen back into the relationship they had once shared as though Nicholas was still her fiancé and our marriage had never taken place. Suddenly, I dearly regretted the arguments we had had—and my decision to refuse him his husbandly rights. If I had not . . . but what was the point in regretting what might have been.

"It is ironic, is it not?" I said to Nicholas, the very second the door to our suite had latched behind us.

"And what is that, my dear?" he asked politely.

"If you had only waited a few weeks, Charlotte would have come to her senses, and you might still have married her."

He looked at me with equanimity. "She does, indeed, seem to have recovered from the silly fears which plagued her. But that is hardly a reason to assume that I regret not waiting for her to return to me."

"Then you have not forgiven her," I said, stifling the sigh of relief which threatened to burst from me.

He seemed surprised by the question. "Naturally, I have forgiven her. I thought her apology most sincere. It would seem that she not only realizes that she was misled by this painter, but also is conscious of what she gave up by throwing me over. If I was of a vindictive turn of mind, I would be most pleased by the outcome."

"Which you are not?"

He looked chagrined. "I will admit to a certain satisfaction. Does that please you? I cannot say that smallness of mind, especially my own, brings me any gratification. I shall try to make up for the failing by doing what I can to repair the damage she has done to herself through this failed elopement."

My doubts were not wholly relieved by this apparently detached interest in Charlotte's welfare. "Are you certain you do not regret marrying me?" I asked, jealousy and suspicion firmly entrenched in every word of my question.

His eyebrows arched. "Really, my dear. What an extraordinary notion."

Taking my hands in his, he raised them to his lips and kissed each one in turn. "I give you my word, you have no need for jealousy," he said softly.

His assurance mollified me, but only for the moment. Later, when he did not tap on my door but left me to sleep alone for yet another night, I wondered yet again if he had spoken sincerely.

Long before I had come to any satisfactory conclusion, I fell asleep.

Chapter Fifteen

CHARLOTTE'S COMPANY quickly grew tedious. If she and I were alone, she fell into the depths of self-pity, bemoaning Monsieur André's perfidy and the contrariness of love, or remarking on the beauty of the estate and my own good fortune. This, she always managed to point out, was gained, unhappily, due to her foolhardy "elopement." On those occasions when we were joined by Nicholas, she managed to resummon her good spirits. She flirted and laughed, encouraged by his good-natured replies, and often reflected on the life they might have had together—a life that in her imagination, succeeded in surpassing his dull life with me in every aspect.

Nicholas was most tolerant of her lapses into these fantastic daydreams and advised me to be the same. "She clings to them because she thinks life no longer has anything to offer her," he pointed out. "It would not hurt you to indulge her."

I disagreed. I was becoming increasingly hurt, both by her insensitivity and by Nicholas's fatherly indulgence. And his repeated attempts to convince me that he had no interest in Charlotte failed to restore either my self-esteem or my good humor.

In Stephen, I had an ally. Charlotte, having scorned Nicholas once, did not mean to repeat her mistake. Stephen was treated in an offhand, dismissive manner, much as though there was another Monsieur André lurking beneath his handsome exterior. At those times when he offered to escort her to the table or show her the gardens, her coolness sunk to outright rudeness. Nicholas was the only man permitted to be her escort, or allowed to amuse her with his conversation.

After one entire morning spent listening to Charlotte's agonies of remorse, I flew into a temper, blamed her for a headache I had not yet acquired, and stormed out of the Hall. If I had lied, I consoled myself by pointing out that if I had remained in her company another ten minutes I would surely have felt as miserable as I had claimed. In truth, it had been more of a prediction than a lie, a prediction which saved me from the inevitable discomfort that was bound to follow. Mildly content, I strolled off across the lawns with the intention of not returning until suppertime.

After an hour's walk, I realized ruefully that unless I altered my plans, I would have to miss my luncheon. One way or the other, Charlotte succeeded in making my life miserable. Then, on reflecting how far I had already walked, I decided not to return but to carry on towards the dower house and Aunt Matilda. I had promised to visit her, after all, and there was always the hope of tea and cakes—with or without currants.

Edith admitted me with the same suspicion and doubt that she had shown on my first visit. " 'Ere again?" she asked. "With so much going back and forth 'tis no wonder a body can't get 'er work done."

"I am very glad to see you, too, Edith. Perhaps you would tell Lady Matilda that I am here."

"Didn't say I wouldn't, did I?" she muttered, wandering off to the back of the house and leaving me to stand with the dust that floated around the hall. Edith, it seemed, did not take her housekeeping duties as seriously as she would have had me believe. I wondered if she meant me to wait, or make my own way to the private sitting room. Uncertain, I decided to stay where I was, at least for a few minutes.

I did not have to languish with the dust for long. A door at the back of the house swung open and Aunt Matilda clomped out. She was wearing a man's great-coat over a heavy woolen dress. From beneath her hem poked two booted toes, and a floppy hat had been pinned to her white hair.

"The very person I wanted to see," she exclaimed, waving a small garden trowel at me. "Shall we go and pick out those herbs I promised to give you for your garden?"

"I am really not dressed for gardening," I protested. "I thought perhaps we could . . . have tea, again?" I finished hopefully.

"Tea. But I am not done. The damned plants are overrunning the place. They will be crawling in here the next thing you know and strangling me in my sleep." She looked at my disappointed face. "Oh, well. Never mind. I have lived long enough already. Edith! Bring us some tea."

We heard a distinct grumbling noise from the kitchen which Aunt Matilda chose to ignore. "Give me a moment to wash and get out of these wet things," she told me. "Edith will make a fuss if I am not properly dressed. She thinks I will catch pneumonia and then she will be out of a job. They would not put up with her at the Hall, let me tell you. Not for a minute. Go on," she waved briskly. "It is no good standing there. Have a seat in the parlor. Edith has the fire going."

Presuming she was referring to the sitting room, I meekly obeyed and seated myself in the armchair near Lady Matilda's sofa. Edith wandered in and out, first to make a hasty sweep of the table with a dust cloth, and then again to bring in the tea tray. She had barely left when Aunt Matilda hastened through the doorway. The greatcoat, boots, hat, and trowel had gone, although she still wore the wool dress which was stained with large damp spots at the knees.

"I expected to see you before now," she admonished. "At my age, it simply does not do to let a lot of time pass between calls. Delay too long and I could be dead. You will not get Edith to serve you tea, then."

"I meant to return before now," I said. "But my sister arrived unexpectedly, and I have had little time to myself since she arrived."

The old woman gave a loud harrumph. "You dislike her, I can see. Oh, you must not try to tell me otherwise. I may be nearsighted and getting deaf, but I know all about sisters. I had one of my own. Despised her. Nothing but a conniving little hussy. Should have strangled her in her crib the day she was born. She was younger, you know. By five years. I was quite strong enough to do it but, at five, I did not have the sense. Usually the way of things. Never mind—she is dead now. I have outlived her by a good ten years. Now that is one ghost I can do without seeing. Tell me, how long is she staying?"

"Who?" I asked, completely bewildered.

"Do pay attention, child. Who do you think I meant? Your sister—how long is she staying?"

"I do not really know," I admitted, struck by the sudden realization that Charlotte might linger at the Hall for years, clinging to Nicholas for comfort day in and day out. I choked on the bite of cake I had just swallowed.

"My dear life," Aunt Matilda exclaimed. "Bad as that, is she? Here, let me give you a handkerchief. You can have a good cry." She fumbled through her pockets. "Drat. Mine is gone. I swear Edith steals them when I am not looking. Have you one of your own?"

"I may have," I said, searching my own pockets to be certain. They were—as I should have expected— empty, save for a piece of string and a large horse driven away without being allowed to pay my respects, she grudgingly admitted me.

Aunt Matilda lay on the divan, perspiring beneath a thick layer of woolen quilts and shawls. Immediately she saw me, she sat up and threw them off. "There you are," she cried. "Edith swore you would forget. She thinks that young people cannot be trusted to remember dates or keep their promises, and she dearly loves to be a misery. I really ought to find her a hobby—might keep her mind occupied. And out of my business. If she had her way, I daresay she would have turned you away at the door, just for the pleasure of telling me 'I told you so.' Are you listening, Edith?" she called out to the closed door.

I did not admit how nearly she had done so. Edith, it seemed, got away with little enough—her disgruntled moods and a few surreptitiously stolen currants and broken dishes; I preferred to make allowances for her lapses rather than add to her trials. "I am sorry to hear that you are not feeling well," I said, feeling guilty. "I hope you did not overtax your strength in my behalf yesterday."

"Goodness, no, child." The old woman brushed off the possibility with a wave of her hand. "I had a *wonderful* time in the kitchen, digging out all my old pans, brewing up this and that. Stirring Edith into a fine temper." She giggled mischievously. "It has been ages since I have enjoyed myself so completely. You cannot imagine the smell in the kitchen when I was through. Takes weeks to completely disappear. Poor Edith will have to live with it. Oh, I do love to upset her. Mind you, it is a poor sport that can be had so easily. Are you hungry? It is almost time for luncheon. You are not to make me eat alone," she said, shaking her finger.

From the careless gaiety of Matilda's mood and the suspicious brightness of her eyes, I suspected that the cup of tea on her table had been liberally dosed with brandy or some similar intoxicant. Still, she seemed chestnut I had picked up during my walk through the wood. Neither was of much use to me now.

Aunt Matilda sighed. "No point in crying then. You will only make your face wet. She has her eye on Stephen, does she?"

She had confused them again. "Nicholas," I corrected. "It is Nicholas she wants."

"Nicholas? Are you in love with Nicholas? Dear me, I do wish I would stop getting them confused. You say your sister wants him, too?"

I nodded.

"And that upsets you?"

Her question astounded me. "Naturally, it upsets me. I love my husband."

"Really?" She looked surprised. "Silly of me. Of course you do. Good thing you told me. It would not do to make a mistake." She shook her head sorrowfully. "I find mistakes are so very easy to make, these days. But if Nicholas loves you, you have nothing to worry about."

"But I am not sure that he does love me," I cried, sounding a good deal too much like Charlotte to please me.

"Oh, dear." She frowned. "You do have a problem. Never mind. I am certain I can help."

I looked at her dubiously. "I doubt that there is much anyone can do."

"Of course there is," she said impatiently. "My dear life, there are potions for everything. Potions for falling in love; potions for falling out of love. Potions for making people go away, or bringing them back. Potions to improve the health . . . I must make one of those for myself, someday. That is not really done, you know. Potions should only be made to help somebody else. I could show you how to make a potion for someone with rheumatism but you would have to grow your own herbs, and by then. . . ." She shrugged. "What was I talking about?"

"About potions," I reminded her.

"Oh, of course. Now, what you need is *two* potions. One to make Nicholas fall in love with you, and another to make your sister go away. That would do nicely, I think." She sounded extremely pleased with herself. "No one has asked me to make a potion for years, not since . . . well, one should never talk about another person's problems, should one?"

Throughout the rest of our tea, Matilda hummed to herself like an excited child who had been given a new toy.

I stayed most of that afternoon. When I rose to leave, she insisted that I return the following day—that would provide her with enough time to brew the right herbs. After some hesitation, I agreed. Not that I had any intention of slipping either Nicholas or Charlotte a potion, although I doubted that an herbal mixture would hurt them. But the entire notion of herbs having a use other than medicinal or culinary seemed quite fanciful. Still, if it amused Matilda to make them, the least I could do was accept them gratefully.

I strolled down the lane, sidestepping patches of mud and dawdling beneath the shade of the elms. The smell of salt and seaweed that drifted across the gardens and clung to the Hall did not reach these sheltered glades. Here, there was only the fresh, moist scent of damp earth and moss, mingled with the faint scent of roses.

By the time I reached the driveway, it was growing late. The gravel crunched beneath my shoes, marking every step I took. Overhead, the branches blotted out the sun; I might have been wandering through dark, cool caverns—the driveway a winding river snaking through the shadowy underworld into which I had unwittingly fallen. Then, around a bend or at the crest of a hill, the branches would draw back and I would burst forth into the light of a golden red sunset, as though poured through a crevice and delivered back to the world that I had briefly deserted.

As the sun dropped near the ridge of hills to the west, the shadows darkened. Near the Hall, the breezes grew stronger. They tugged at my pelisse which flapped wildly and wrapped around my legs. Each step became a struggle as I wrestled with the heavy folds of velvet that encumbered me.

I grew increasingly uneasy. Perhaps it was the encroaching twilight; perhaps it was my inability to walk at a faster pace and leave the woods behind me. But no matter how I tried to rid myself of the feeling, I was possessed by the uncomfortable sensation of being watched.

Then I heard a noise, like a snap of twigs underfoot, and my gaze darted to the thicket of trees ahead of me. A shadow, darker than the rest, slid between the tree trunks and then melted into the blackness and was gone. A deer? It could not have been anything smaller. As I drew nearer to the spot where I had seen the movement, I thought I caught a whiff of pipe tobacco, but it barely teased my nostrils before being swept away by the breeze.

I had barely time to wonder if someone had been hiding there before I found myself out of the trees and standing on the lower lawns. Above me, Blackwood Hall clung tenaciously to the crest of the hillside; the windows were bright with the flickering light of candles and oil lamps. It occurred to me that if someone had been standing in the copse of trees, they must also have had a clear view of the Hall.

My fears did not survive the walk across the lawns. Having been freed from the shadow of the woods, my thoughts were once again preoccupied with Charlotte and Nicholas. It may have been that the afternoon spent with the old woman had some effect, for I felt less discouraged than I had when I had left the Hall. I was, after all, Nicholas's wife, and he had assured me that he was satisfied with the arrangement. Charlotte needed only to be warned to behave herself. Since I had told her off countless times in the past, it would not overtax my abilities to do so again.

Strains of a melody played on the pianoforte led me to the music room. Charlotte raised her fingers from the keys as I walked in, a dreamy smile hovered at her lips. I did not have long to wonder why her mood had improved. Nicholas was sprawled in the wing chair beside the hearth, his hand propped beneath his chin as he thoughtfully listened to her efforts. Immediately, he saw me, he rose, and after complimenting my sister on her light touch and inquiring as to whether or not I had had a pleasant walk, said, "I will leave the two of you to entertain each other while I return to my account books. I may yet get a couple of hours' work done."

Before he left the room, his lips brushed my forehead in a quick, absentminded kiss; but his expression was one of mild irritation. With whom was he irritated, I wondered—me, or Charlotte? One thing was clear: He did not wish to be detained. Before I could engage him in conversation, he strode from the room with a brisk, impatient step.

He had no sooner left than Charlotte's happy smile disappeared. "You have come back then," she said with an angry toss of her curls. "It was unkind of you to leave me alone when you know how poorly I have been feeling."

"If I had known you would disturb Nicholas, I certainly would have stayed," I retorted, choosing to believe that his irritation was due to an afternoon of enduring her company.

She glowered at me. "I did not disturb Nicholas. He asked if he might listen to me play."

"Then why did he rush off at the first opportunity?"

She lifted one shoulder in a careless shrug. "I suppose he left because you joined us. Until then, he was quite content to stay."

"He has work to do from which you, and an excess of good breeding, have detained him."

"Nonsense," she snapped. "He prefers spending his afternoon in my company to wading through account books. He said so himself."

I debated whether or not she was telling me the truth. Probably. It was not like Charlotte to invent compliments; she seldom had the need. But I felt certain that Nicholas had merely been being polite, and I dismissed the remark as meaningless.

But Charlotte's pride would not allow her to let the matter rest. "It was not so very long ago that Nicholas waited hours for me to glance in his direction. He would have been grateful for the kind of devoted attention I gave him today," she reminded me.

"It might just as well have been another lifetime," I scoffed. "Must I remind you that *I* am Lady Blackwood. You seem to think you are still his betrothed."

She gave an airy wave of her hand as though my marriage was irrelevant. "I would have been Lady Blackwood if Monsieur André had not led me astray with his lies. Besides, you cannot believe that Nicholas loves you. He only married you to save face. We are both deeply regretful of our mistakes."

My heart froze. "Nicholas said that?"

"Naturally, he would not speak his feelings aloud," Charlotte admitted. "It would be unkind and pointless. But I can read the truth in his eyes."

"You really are impossible!" I exclaimed, glaring at her.

She shrank back on the bench of the pianoforte as if she expected me to yank on her curls. But that would not have satisfied me; only by proving to Charlotte—and to myself—that Nicholas was no longer interested in her would I be content. I would accept nothing less.

I took great care with my attire that evening. The dress was one I had not worn before, an amethyst satin evening gown, the neckline low and cut square over my bosom. It was trimmed with frills of the same fabric, and its effect was to emphasize my height and modest curves while setting off the chestnut highlights in my hair. This was pulled up at the sides and tied with a velvet ribbon; long waves cascaded down the back of my neck and tumbled over my shoulders, falling below my waist.

Then, from my dressing table drawer, I removed the jewelry box that Nicholas had given me, the one that contained the heirlooms he had once promised to Charlotte. I had not worn any of the pieces before that night, telling myself that I disliked feeling their heavy weight about my neck. Now, I admitted that having never really become Nicholas's wife, I had felt awkward playing the role of "the new Lady Blackwood." But, tonight, I would play that part as none before me.

I hesitated over the amethyst pendant Nicholas had loaned me to wear to the theater, then set it aside. I did not want to stir up any unpleasant memories. Instead, I took a single rope of amethyst beads and two matching teardrop earrings. I had barely enough time to admire myself in the looking glass before Nicholas knocked on my door to ask if I was ready to go down to dinner.

"I am," I answered, sweeping open the door to the sitting room.

I was rewarded by the look of appreciation in Nicholas's eyes. "You look exquisite, my darling," he said in a deep, husky voice. "I am unfit to escort you to the table."

"You are always impeccably dressed," I assured him sincerely.

Covertly, I assessed him. His waistcoat, a gold and emerald-green striped satin, drew attention to his eyes, and the voluminous white silk cravat and high-pointed starched collar framed his aristocratic face. He looked, if anything, smarter and more elegant than usual. For Charlotte's sake? A twinge of jealousy stabbed at me.

Unaware of the thoughts which provoked me, Nicholas gravely offered me his arm, saying, "I shall feel quite the lord, this evening."

I bit my lip, choking back the jealous question that I had almost voiced: Tonight was not the night for doubts and unpleasantness. Instead, I managed a smile and said sweetly, "If I am to be the beneficiary of all of your compliments this evening, then I shall feel like a queen."

"Not all of my compliments, my darling. That would be rude. But all of those compliments that are sincerely meant."

He placed his hand over my own, and the warmth of his roughened skin against mine sent a thrill of excitement tingling down my spine. I leaned into him, pressing my body against his, enjoying the feel of those hard muscles beneath his smartly tailored coat.

Nicholas tensed. His eyelids drew down over his eyes like dark hoods, only partially concealing his smoldering gaze. "Really, my dear," he cautioned. "You must not provoke me or dinner will be sacrificed in favor of other appetites."

"I propose to satisfy all of my appetites, this night," I told him shamelessly, bringing a slightly startled but nonetheless pleased smile to his face.

"Am I to understand . . . ?"

"If you do not understand, Nicholas, then I confess, I am at a loss as to how to enlighten you. Surely, even a wife must maintain some sense of decorum, and I have displayed a forwardness that borders on wanton."

Nicholas brought my fingers to his lips and kissed them tenderly. "As your husband, you must let me be the judge of what should be considered overly forward. You will find I set broad limits."

I laughed gaily. Let Charlotte flirt with him, I thought joyously; she means nothing to him. I am the one who matters.

But while it was easy to convince myself of his devotion when we were alone in our rooms, in the ornate dining room, separated from Nicholas by both Stephen and Charlotte, I found myself surrendering again to my attacks of jealousy. As always, my sister unfailingly addressed her remarks to Nicholas, constantly seeking out his approval. The affair with Monsieur André had badly damaged her self-esteem which she appeared eager to regain at my expense.

Good manners forced me to direct most of my remarks to Stephen who sat on my right. Smiling and returning sensible responses to his lighthearted sallies became increasingly difficult when my mind was distracted by Charlotte's tinkling laughter. Nor did I hide my resentment well, for now and again, I caught a flash of sympathy in Stephen's expressive eyes; to spare me embarrassment, it was quickly concealed beneath a piece of wit that I had not the heart to appreciate.

A pair of heavy silver candlesticks stood in the middle of the table, obscuring my view of Nicholas. His head was bent toward Charlotte. Was his smile merely civil, or was it encouraging? I could not have said. But when he glanced up and caught me studying him, his smile deepened and there was a meaningful look in his eyes.

"You have chosen a delightful menu for this evening's supper, my dear," he said. "I believe with your good taste you have charmed even Mrs. Ham, and that is no small accomplishment."

Charlotte giggled and playfully swatted him with her fan, promptly recapturing his attention. "Your housekeeper is an ogre, Nicholas. Her face would curdle milk. I cannot imagine how Redigan dares to face her. I would be quite intimidated." She sighed. "But I was always more delicate than my sister. You must find us as different as chalk and cheese."

After making an apologetic shrug in my direction, Nicholas, once again, allowed her to monopolize him.

I marked each nod of his head, caught each smile, measured each somber glance. Was he merely being the gracious host? Or was the distraction pleasurable, indeed, welcome? The questions darted through my mind, as unsettling as a swarm of wasps buzzing around one's head.

My plates were returned to the kitchen as full as when they had been served to me. I did not recall whether we had eaten veal or lamb, if the pie had been apple or mince, or if Stephen had complimented me on my appearance or merely discussed the good weather we had been enjoying. When the meal ended, I rose from my chair with relief and hastened to Nicholas's side. "I thought we might retire early," I suggested. "After my long walk, I am rather more tired than usual."

"Oh, but I thought perhaps we might play a game of quadrille," Charlotte protested. "It is far too early to retire. Why if this were London—"

"This is not London," I said sharply.

Charlotte pouted and her eyes filled with tears. "You have no reason to be hateful. It is bad enough that I have been cruelly deceived in love. Here, in the bosom of my family, I should be treated with the kindness I deserve."

"I daresay," I agreed.

But, in the end Nicholas agreed we might play for an hour, an hour that dragged into two before Charlotte grudgingly agreed to retire to her room with a novel that he recommended she read. "But if there is even the hint of romance, then likely I shall have nightmares," she warned. "These days, I find I am brought to tears at the mere glimpse of dew on rosebuds, by bird song and butterflies. I suppose a heart, once broken, can never be truly mended."

Stephen—whose face usually remained a polite mask during her more ridiculous rhapsodies—started, and a shadow passed behind his eyes. Seeing he had drawn our attention to himself, he abruptly rose from his chair, almost knocking over his wine glass in his haste. "You must excuse me," he said with a feigned yawn. "I, too, am more tired than I realized."

After he had gone, Charlotte confided to Nicholas, "I believe he was touched by my suffering. Your brother has a sensitive heart."

Nicholas seemed too caught up in his own thoughts to reply, but I could not help but reflect on what I had seen. I thought it doubtful that Stephen had been overcome with pity for Charlotte; more likely he was suffering his own pangs of unrequited love—but for whom? Certainly not Charlotte. Could he have fallen in love with me? I had to be mistaken. But, I mused, Stephen rarely left the Hall and he was not the kind of man who would lose his heart to one of the scullery maids.

"I had begun to think we would never have a single moment to ourselves, this evening," I said to Nicholas when we were at last alone in our sitting room. "Must you encourage Charlotte as you do? It only makes her worse."

He frowned. "I thought her behavior vastly improved. She does not cry as often, or as wholeheartedly, and I believe she has recovered some of her good spirits."

"If she has, it is thanks to you," I said, sounding exceedingly ungrateful. Then I asked hopefully, "Have you learned anything of Monsieur André?" It would have pleased me immensely to have been able to pack Charlotte off to Elizabeth in London. There, she could flirt as much as she pleased, with whomever she pleased. As long as she left Nicholas alone.

But he shook his head. "It is rather soon to have received word. But I have sent a letter making inquiries. You must try to be patient."

"Patience is a virtue that has always escaped me," I admitted disconsolately.

"I believe there are many virtues that have escaped

you," he teased. "I particularly favor the lack of maidenly shyness you displayed before supper. Most becoming in a young bride." He grinned and held open his arms.

I stepped into them with a sigh of happiness and his arms tightened around me. "Oh, Nicholas," I murmured. "I had begun to think—"

He interrupted me with a severe look. "Surely, we have had enough conversation for one evening?"

"More than enough," I agreed, content to say nothing more. I lifted my mouth to be kissed.

Nicholas smiled. Gently, he bent over me, drawing me into the shelter of his body. I felt warm and safe there, captured in his embrace, sheltered by the long line of his body. As his mouth descended my eyes closed and, with a delicious shiver, I waited for the touch of his mouth on mine. Instead, his lips brushed each closed eyelid in turn, then he bestowed a soft kiss on the tip of my nose. My eyes fluttered open to gaze upon his face, so near to my own that I could clearly read the patience and the tenderness he exuded; in his eyes I saw a glimmer of relief, as though he, too, had worried that this moment might never come.

As it had never come with Lydia? I could not resist the troubling thought, although I tried hard not to let my suspicions sweep away the magical glow which had enveloped us.

Reaching up, I encircled his neck with my arms; my fingers curled around thick locks of his hair, and I gently tugged his face downwards, closing the last tiny gap which separated us. Then Nicholas's lips molded against mine, and I kissed him with a fierce hunger, demanding the love I had refused myself for so many days.

He groaned, and his hands slid down my back to my waist. His grip was no longer gentle but hard, insistent, as he struggled with the fastenings of my gown. Suddenly, I was no longer safe and protected: I was teetering above an abyss, a heartbeat away from an endless fall. Shivering, I clung more tightly to Nicholas, determined to plunge headlong into whatever fate awaited me.

But I was denied the opportunity; there was a sharp rap on the door. The abrupt invasion of our privacy shattered the fragile, mystical link we had forged between us. Nicholas pulled free of my embrace with an impatient cry. Straightening his waistcoat, he walked angrily to the door and pulled it ajar.

If that is Charlotte she will find herself on the next coach travelling towards Briarslea, I vowed.

But it was not my sister. Instead, the footman poised apologetically in the corridor, a white card in his hand. "There be a gentleman t' see 'ee, milord," he said, struggling to hold himself stiffly, although his knees were quaking badly. "Told'n 'ee had gone t' bed, but he wouldn' 'ave none of it. Said 'twas a matter of some note and that 'ee would be angered if he were sent away."

Nicholas took the proffered card. As he read the name inscribed, his expression changed from irritation to shock, and from shock to darkest rage.

"What is the matter?" I asked.

"Nothing for you to concern yourself about," he assured me, his voice as hard as tempered steel. "But it is a matter that I cannot ignore. You will have to excuse me, my dear."

"Oh, Nicholas," I cried. "You will not be too long, I hope?"

He glanced back at me, and the look in his eyes softened. "No longer than need be, I promise you."

Chapter Sixteen

NICHOLAS did not return. A half-hour went by; then another. I gazed longingly at the door, expecting that at any moment, it would swing open and he would be there. I began to grow concerned. The footman had said the matter was urgent. Had someone been hurt? But that would not explain Nicholas's smoldering rage when he read the name on the card. Admittedly, he had quickly mastered his anger, but not so quickly that either the footman or I had missed the card's effect on him.

Anxiously, I continued to wait. The fire grew low, the logs crumbling into charred embers and dropping from the grate to the hearth where they lay, glowing redly against the stones. In the wall sconces, the oil lamps flickered, sending flares of light up and down the flocked wallpaper. Outside the wind rose and fell, whipping the leaves against the windowpanes; they rustled and scratched like a cat clawing at the door to be let in.

At last, I jumped up, determined not to wait a second longer. If something was wrong, I wanted to know—and I felt certain that there *was* something wrong. Otherwise, by now, Nicholas would have returned.

Away from the sounds of the fire and the wind, the Hall was quiet: The servants had retired to their own quarters; Charlotte had no doubt fallen asleep over her novel; and Stephen had not reappeared after his sudden exit from the drawing room. I pattered down the corridor, hearing only the sounds of my own soft footfalls. At the top of the stairs, I paused and listened. Still hearing nothing, I quietly descended.

The pennants above the entry hall swayed gently, stirred by a draft that swept through the unlit rooms and darkened corridors; the cold air was as much a part of the Hall as the servants and the furnishings. I shivered, briefly regretting that my shawl lay forgotten upstairs on the Jacobean armchair. But my discomfort was quickly dismissed, overruled by my concern for Nicholas as I hurried towards his study.

It was here, at the entrance to the east wing, that I heard the first murmurs of conversation. This hall, too, lay in partial darkness, save for sparingly set wall sconces. At the far end of the corridor lay a crack of light, marking the bottom of the heavy oaken door that led into the study. The thickness of the wood and the stone walls should have made it impossible for me to hear the voices of the men within, but this was no typical conversation: Their words were angrily shouted and could be distinctly heard by anyone who chanced to be nearby.

One of the voices belonged to Nicholas, not a Nicholas I recognized but a furiously enraged man whose loud words had the dangerous sharpness of a drawn sword. I would not have cared to have stood on the other side of the door and faced his contempt. But the man who argued with him seemed heedless of his lordship's wrath. In deep guttural tones he persisted, pressing Nicholas as though he were certain he possessed the advantage.

I did not care for the sound of him. He spoke like an educated man, but his words were slurred, as though he had imbibed more than his share of port before daring to show his face at Blackwood Hall. That may have been the reason for his lack of caution. And if we had encountered one another in the drawing room—regardless of how fashionably he was attired or how nicely he spoke to me—I would have thought him out of place. Beneath the thin surface of gentility, I discerned a character both brusque and unpleasant, as though he were devoid of the moral sense and conscience that defined a civilized human being. Without ever having laid eyes on the man, I disliked him—intensely and absolutely.

It was hard, at first, to make sense out of what they said. The argument had clearly been prefaced by a long and, judging by Nicholas's emotional state, wearisome discussion. Clearly, money was involved—a loan, perhaps a debt—but the stranger continually harped on events which had been mentioned before I came downstairs.

"Since that incident, milord, my nerves have not been what they once were," the man protested, and there was an ugliness to his reference, the meaning of which escaped me.

"Your own habits are to blame for your nerves!" That from Nicholas. I silently applauded him.

They exchanged several more volleys, loud enough to make me glad the household was abed. I felt certain their remarks were not something Nicholas would have wanted overheard; nor did I care to be seen there, listening to things which were not meant for my ears. My suspicions were almost instantly confirmed.

"My mind is made up," Nicholas said. "I will not be blackmailed."

Blackmailed! My hands turned icy cold. Was that what had brought this vulgar stranger here? I felt a searing blaze of loyalty; Nicholas could not possibly be guilty of any crime.

But the stranger thought otherwise. "Do you expect me to live on nothing while you continue to expect my silence?" he demanded querulously.

"You have been well paid for your services."

"Yes, but it is the very nature of those services that provoke, no—*demand*—such interest." He spoke with an oily confidence that raised goose bumps on my forearms. I waited for Nicholas to deny the charge.

He did not. He said only, "May I remind you that it is *your* signature upon the death certificate. You cannot implicate me without also involving yourself."

I shuddered. Whose death? Were they talking of murder? It did not seem possible, but Nicholas had failed to deny any wrongdoing; that, in itself, was tantamount to an admission of guilt.

I was not the only one to have thought so. "Can you be certain that I will be blamed?" the man asked with a greedy confidence. "It was, after all, the only time I was called upon to attend someone at Blackwood Hall. I had no prior knowledge of my patient, a fact which made it easy for you to mislead me. Only time and much thought has brought me to the conclusion that something was amiss."

"Then, Dr. Polharris, you must take your suspicions to the magistrate and see what he will do for you," Nicholas answered.

I gasped. *A certain Dr. Polharris, was it not?* I cursed my foolish eavesdropping and my confounded memory—wishing suddenly that I was like Charlotte, able to forget a name the second it had been spoken. She would not have recalled the name of the doctor who had treated Lord Edgmont's daughter. Now, I could no longer tell myself there had been nothing awry in her early passing. If the name was not enough to convince me, it was apparent by the threat that had been inherent in Nicholas's slow and careful reply.

But Dr. Polharris was oblivious to the temperament of the man he faced. "Do not mock me," he replied with a sneer. "I am well aware that you are the local magistrate. You are better thought of in Cornwall than you warrant, I daresay. I do not mislead myself that my story will fall on sympathetic ears in this county. But, there is always an alternative." I heard the rustling of paper. "Since my return to Cornwall, I have received a letter from a Lord Edgmont. It seems he will pay very well to hear my account of that evening."

"Do as you must," Nicholas replied, his voice strangely flat. "But I vow you will not receive another penny from me."

"Are you mad, man?" the doctor cried. "There can be but one interpretation of your actions."

"It is time you were on your way. You have taken more than enough of my time."

A chair scraped, as though it was forcefully pushed back, and I darted to the nearest room. The door swung open as I touched the knob, and I saw that it had been left slightly ajar, something that had hitherto escaped my notice. I stepped inside, into a disused morning room that according to Mrs. Ham, had been popular with one of my predecessors. I did not allow the latch to catch, fearing that the noise would betray my presence.

Almost immediately, the door to the study banged open and there was the sound of footsteps, the whispering of Nicholas's slippers, soft but inexorably firm, and the angry impotent clap of the doctor's boots against the flagging. As they passed, I caught a brief, unsettlingly familiar whiff of pipe tobacco—the same tobacco I had smelled that afternoon as I had walked along the driveway. I shuddered afresh, my skin crawling as I was reminded of that skulking motion beneath the copse of trees. How nearly had I avoided a meeting with the unsavory Dr. Polharris? Then they were gone and I was alone.

Or so I had thought. The soft intake of breath from the middle of the morning room proved me wrong. I gasped but the noise had been commiserative, not threatening. Staring into the darkness, I discerned the vague outline of a man, sitting in the shadowed armchair across from me. I swung the door open wide and the light from the sconces fell across Stephen's face. He stared up at me, his eyes green pools of sympathy for what he knew I had heard. He, too, must have caught every word that had passed between his brother and the doctor. And he pitied me for what I had learned about the man I had married.

I did not wait for him to speak; I could not have endured hearing his sympathetic words. Nothing could console me for what I had learned this night. Already, tears filled my eyes. Spinning around before he could speak, I fled the room and hastened back down the corridor from whence I had come. As I reached the central hallway that divided the house from front to back, I paused to make certain that Nicholas and the doctor were not lingering in the entry.

I saw no one. Nicholas must have shown the man to the door and then promptly retired. Certainly, he had not returned to his study. I gathered my skirts about me and ran upstairs, taking the steps two at a time. I only hoped that Nicholas would believe me when I told him I had slipped down to the kitchen for a glass of milk.

But I quickly discovered that he had not reached our rooms before me. The fire had died and the oil in the lamps had burned low but there was light enough to see that our suite was empty. The lie I had prepared was unnecessary. Breathing a sigh of relief, I slipped into my bedroom.

It took but a few seconds to discard my dress and don the lacy nightgown that I had laid out before supper, happily intent on enchanting Nicholas. My hair went forgotten. Brushing it out would have taken precious minutes that could not be spared. Instead, I poured the pitcher of lukewarm water into the porcelain basin and quickly rinsed my face and hands. A quick wipe of the towel and I was as ready for bed as my nerves would allow. I lay there, swaddled by blankets, my heart thumping, waiting for Nicholas to appear.

My anxiety was for nothing. I could have dawdled over my toilette for several hours without need for concern. No one would have remarked on the lateness of the hour or my state of agitation. It was several hours before Nicholas returned; when he did, he went directly to his own room and shut the door after him.

The morning sun was well above the horizon before I awakened. The maid had already drawn back the curtains, letting in streams of golden light. They fell across the Persian carpet, splashing a lazy glow across the exotic woven blossoms and swirling vines. The heat thrown out by the glowing coals in the grate was an unnecessary extravagance. Yet even lying beneath the blankets and heavy velvet counterpane, I felt unnaturally cold.

I lay abed, silently contemplating the things I had learned. Lydia could not have died in childbirth as Nicholas had once claimed, but did that mean he had murdered her? Dr. Polharris, the physician who had been in attendance, thought that he had. As did Stephen. Hence the pity in his eyes when he saw I had learned the truth about his brother. But could I be certain it was the truth? Nicholas had not denied the charge, but nor had he given in to blackmail. If he had been guilty would he not have paid the man whatever he demanded?

I took a deep breath. That fact stood in his favor. Besides, the doctor was a drunkard. As for Stephen—I did not know if he had even been present when Lydia had died. The doctor's accusations may have misled him as well. I determined to ask him when next we met. Until then, I would not let myself convict Nicholas of a heinous crime when I had only innuendo, suspicion, and rumor to support the charge.

Warm again, I threw off the covers and rang for my breakfast. It looked a fine day for riding, and Nicholas had not yet kept his promise to accompany me. It would do us both good to get away from the Hall for a few hours.

It did not surprise me to learn he had already gone from his room. He was always an early riser, possessed of too much restless energy to find pleasure in idleness. I had often thought he would have been happier living life as a simple man, perhaps a sailor or fisherman, rather than having to endure the physical constraints suffered by men of his social class. His elegant clothes barely contained the athletic, broad-shouldered man they covered.

The image provoked a hunger that my breakfast could not satisfy. Nor did I care to eat alone, wondering why Nicholas had not returned to my arms once he had rid himself of the doctor's company. Doubtless, he had not been of a suitable temper. I drained my cup of hot chocolate and pushed aside the tray, leaving the buttered eggs and hot buns untouched. My thoughts and my desires filled me—together they left little room for food.

I donned my riding habit and carefully swept my hair up under the high-crowned felt hat. Except for the dark smudges beneath my eyes, marking my brief and troubled sleep, the woman who stared back at me from the looking glass appeared quite the elegant and stylish lady. If my sister had never shown her face at Blackwood Hall I would have been entirely content with my appearance. But now I wondered: Does *he* compare us as often?

I snorted derisively in an attempt to conceal my lack of self-esteem behind an air of bravado. Then, thoroughly disgusted with myself, I fled the room, dearly wishing that I could flee my doubts as easily.

Downstairs, I glimpsed Nicholas through the open door of the drawing room, ensconced on the plush, high-backed sofa. He appeared calm and completely comfortable; nothing about his expression or his appearance suggested that his night's rest had been drastically shortened, that his conscience was troubled, or his peace of mind threatened. His long legs lay before him in their usual sprawl; his white cravat was wrapped neatly around his throat; his arms carelessly draped across the back of the sofa. In all, he was the picture of complacence.

There was a soft murmur and Nicholas shook his head firmly. Until then, I had not realized that he was not alone. Then came the sound of quiet sobbing. Charlotte. I might have guessed she would have seized the opportunity to sit alone with Nicholas. Or had he rushed to her side this morning? I trembled and my hands grew cold.

But Nicholas was not displaying his usual patience. It cheered me considerably to see a flash of annoyance cross his face. "My dear, it must be done," he told her. "You have left me with no alternative."

"I know you would not make this suggestion otherwise, but I find the notion utterly . . . beyond . . . beyond . . . comprehension."

"Nonsense. You will find that nothing in life is beyond comprehension when you are left without other choices. I promise you the matter will be handled delicately. It is not my wish to cause you pain."

For once, my curiosity did not persuade me to remain silent and hidden: I had had enough of eavesdropping to last me a lifetime. Coughing softly, I stepped into the drawing room.

Nicholas and Charlotte looked up. Her head had been laying on his shoulder, and her curls were becomingly tousled. Catching my annoyed glare, she quickly straightened herself, and her gaze flickered guiltily to Nicholas.

He was not at all perturbed. With a smile, he rose and bid me good morning and insisted that I join them. "We were discussing—"

Charlotte gasped. "Oh, but—"

"—your sister's future," Nicholas finished, ignoring her interruption. Then he laid his hand atop hers. "Let us not keep secrets. Redigan, also, wishes only to see you happily settled."

"I do," I said fervently. "But what plans have you made?"

"I have had some letters from London. That was the matter which took me away from you last night," he said, lying with such competence and ease that if I had not known otherwise, I could not have helped but believe him.

I stared at him in astonishment. "You received word last night?"

"Yes. You must forgive me for getting caught up with making my replies, but I believe that Monsieur André can be prevailed upon to keep his misconduct a secret."

"That sounds most encouraging," I admitted, unable to really believe anything he told me. "But I can think of no way in which he could repair the damage he has done other than to marry Charlotte. And that would be unthinkable."

Charlotte immediately burst into tears.

Nicholas regarded her with a look of pity. "Indeed, it would. But some marriage must be arranged. And, as I have told your sister—with a little money and influence one finds oneself in the peculiar position of being able to overcome any obstacle."

"Anything?" I asked.

Nicholas nodded. "I think we may yet hope for a satisfactory resolution to our problems."

"I am sure we can depend on you to do your best for her," I said quietly, gazing at him. I supposed it was unreasonable of me to think he would wish to share his problems with me, but his complete lack of guilt or consternation disturbed me. I did not like to think of what it said of his character. Managing a tight smile, I told him, "If you have no objections, I think I will go riding this morning. For what is left of it," I added with a glance at the marble clock on the mantel.

"I see no reason for you to remain at the Hall on a day like this," he agreed easily. "Charlotte and I will manage admirably in your absence."

Neither of them suggested that they should accompany me, and—although the slight hurt me—I did not ask them to go. There had been enough lies told for one morning; I could not bear to listen to more.

As I waited for the groom to saddle Titania and bring her round to the front door, Nicholas's words echoed through my mind. *Charlotte and I will manage admirably in your absence. Manage admirably.* Clearly, he did not need me now that she had come; his thoughts were only of her. Would he truly relinquish her to another man, now that she had no wish to leave?

The dower house, with its sheltering elms and tidy rose beds, made a soothing picture. The twittering birds sang louder here, the trim stone house and spreading gardens being well protected from the cold breezes that whipped off the sea. Only gulls and gannets dared to glide high over the turrets of Blackwood Hall and make their nests on the rocky cliffs that supported the massive stone structure.

I, too, had come to see the dower house and Aunt Matilda as a haven, away from the tumultuous winds of conflict that swept through the dark corridors and shadowed, empty rooms of the Hall. Nicholas, Stephen, Charlotte, and I—all of us were caught up and swept along in their path, and I did not care to think where that path might lead.

Edith took great pleasure in informing me that her ladyship was not at her best. Despite her slightly bowed head and obsequious manner, she managed to infer that my visits were to blame for the old woman's ill health. "'Er drifts," she warned mysteriously. "'Er drifts." But after seeing that I had no intention of being

none the worse for its effects, and I was glad to remain anyplace where my company was welcome. "If it would not upset Edith unduly," I added with a grin.

"Bother Edith," she retorted.

But despite her good spirits, it soon became clear that Matilda was not herself. Inexplicably, she insisted that Edith set up the table for three people, not two, and her conversation was punctuated by repeated glances toward the door as though she was waiting for someone who had not yet appeared.

"Are you expecting someone else?" I asked, after she had broken off to stare out the windows while her fan tapped impatiently on the edge of the table.

Aunt Matilda turned to me, her eyes wide. "Me? But I thought you were expecting company. Will he not be coming?"

"He? Do you mean Nicholas?"

She frowned. "Nicholas? But you know this is not the day that Nicholas visits me. He comes the first of every month to check on me and pay Edith. Today is not the first as I recall." She looked bewildered. *"Is* it the first of the month already?"

"No," I assured her. "But who *are* you expecting?"

"I? I am not expecting anyone. Oh, dear. I am getting one of my headaches. What did you say your name was?"

"Redigan," I told her, growing seriously concerned. "Should I ring for Edith?"

"Did you want some more tea, dear?" she asked, the polite hostess once again.

"Thank you, no. My cup is still full. I was worried that you seemed confused."

"Oh!" She laughed happily. "Is that all. When one is eighty"—she broke off, then corrected herself— "seventy-four, one is entitled to be confused. Do you agree? Of course, you are Redigan. The one with the troublesome sister. I made a couple of my potions for you just last night. Would you like to see them?"

"Them? Are there more than one?" I asked, glad to see that she had collected her wits.

She shook her head over my foolishness. "What good would one do? If I gave you a potion to make your sister go away, what is to stop Nicholas from finding someone else?"

What, indeed? I thought. He seemed to have lost all interest in his wife.

But Matilda was too caught up in her own excitement to notice my chagrin. "I have made you two potions," she said gleefully. "One to make your sister go away, and the other for Nicholas. A love potion. It is by far the stronger of the two." Matilda beamed and her broad smile split her face.

I managed to smile back, trying to seem as happy with her news as she was. But while I had kept my promise to come by and collect the potions, I still had no intention of using them. On the way home, I would dispose of their contents. Later, if Nicholas had not lied about meaning to arrange a marriage for Charlotte, I could inform the old woman that her efforts had been a success. I sighed inwardly. If only my problems could have been dealt with as easily as she seemed to believe.

For the rest of our visit, Matilda chattered happily about her herb garden, Edith, and her childhood years at Blackwood Hall. At times, she might have been talking about events which happened yesterday, so vivid were her recollections, although it was quite obvious that a good seventy-five years had come and gone since those days. Her recent memories, those of Edith and her life at the dower house grew more vague, and she repeatedly confused names and people until I became quite bewildered in my attempts to follow her narration. Still, she spoke lucidly, addressing me by name, and I began to think that she had completely recovered from the odd attack which had assailed her.

But when Edith came to clear the table, Matilda

peered sadly over the top of her fan at the untouched place setting. She looked at me meaningfully and then at her housekeeper. When that irritable individual had stacked the dishes on a tray—none too gently—and stamped out of the sitting room, Matilda leaned forward and whispered, "I suppose it is too late for him to come now. What a disappointment for you, dear. But you must not be discouraged. Wherever he has gone, he will soon return. Then everything will be all right again. For now, let me give you the potion I promised you."

She stood up and walked unsteadily to a side table. Pulling out the drawer, she produced a green glass vial, filled with a brown liquid. She smiled, and then her eyes caught sight of something in the open drawer. Her hand rose to her hair and she nervously patted her white curls. "Oh, dear. There seem to be two. Did I mean to make two?" she asked, as confused as I had been when she had first mentioned them. She frowned then shrugged. "Never mind, you must have them both. If one fails to work, doubtless the other will. Mix them in a cup of tea." She pressed both vials into my hand. "You must not worry, dear. Nicholas will never know. I am quite good at keeping secrets. I have kept yours all this time, even when you did not visit me all these many years."

I thanked her profusely, wrapped the vials in my handkerchief, and then tucked them in my pocket. After covering Matilda up with the shawls and giving her a kiss on the cheek, I slipped away to find Edith.

"Her ladyship does not seem quite herself," I said. "Do you think I should arrange for a doctor."

"I warned 'ee. 'Er drifts," Edith said darkly. "Don't do no good fetchin' doctor. Reckon I can see to 'er, same as allus."

She muttered a few phrases under her breath, apparently about the thoughtlessness of callers who insisted on staying when good manners and good sense should have kept them away. I did not remain to catch the whole of her rebuke. If it did not please me to receive lectures as a child, I certainly did not mean to listen to them now that I was grown and a lady besides.

"I shall leave her ladyship to your good care, then," I said, and with a regal lift of my chin, I made my escape before Edith could give me the set-down I no doubt deserved.

Titania was glad to set off at a quick pace, having been forced to endure the relatively cramped stables that served the dower house. Compared to her usual quarters, they were musty and dark, although the stables at Briarslea had not been as grand. Nor did she like the young boy who curried her; idleness had made him careless and rough. If Nicholas had not been difficult about my visits to his aunt, I would have asked him to hire someone with greater skill and more patience.

As I cantered down the lane, the vials thumped gently against my thigh. I did not get rid of them immediately, not wanting my actions to be seen by Matilda or worse, Edith, who would promptly tell her mistress what I had done. But as Titania swerved off the lane and onto the driveway, I decided it was time to dismount and dispose of their contents. After all, I thought, it would not do to pour them out in the gardens near the Hall. I would not want to find myself having to explain my actions to Nicholas. He might be displeased to learn that his aunt and his wife were conspiring against him, no matter how innocent my intentions. Men, I had learned, could be most unreasonable.

There was a narrow path near the bottom of the driveway; it led beneath the trees and by riding only a few yards I would be completely hidden behind low-hanging branches and a thick cover of leaves. Should someone happen along at the wrong moment, they would pass right by me and never know I was there. It was an ideal location for what I had in mind.

I guided Titania away from the driveway and onto

the path. She seemed surprised at first by this unusual departure from our normal routine, and she tossed her mane and flicked her ears with a touch of annoyance, no doubt thinking of the supper that awaited her. But her displeasure was easily managed until we drew near the trees. Then she nickered uneasily, and when I tried to urge her forward, she danced sideways.

"What is the matter with you, Titania?" I demanded. "We will only be a few minutes and then we shall be off again."

The mare took another hesitant step, then shied again. I craned my head forward to peer into the darkness. Not far ahead lay a pile of broken twigs and leaves, a misshapen lump that stretched across the path. They could not have fallen naturally in that odd fashion, but had been scraped from beneath the trees and piled together.

"Surely, you are not afraid of a few leaves," I chided the mare.

She flicked her ears again as if she understood, but nothing I did or said would induce her to move forward.

"This is silly," I said, talking aloud to fend off the feelings of nervousness that had spread from Titania to me. With an impatient sigh, I jumped to the ground and strode forward to kick the leaves aside.

My boot hit the stack with a sickening thud; something lay beneath the surface, something too solid to be mere twigs and leaves, but too flaccid and yielding to be rocks. There was a quick, slithering motion, and a small patch of leaves fell aside. A man's hand and arm dropped limply in front of my feet. As I stared, unable to move, the sharp, strong aroma of tobacco rose from the disturbed pile; it swirled around my head.

I choked back my nausea. Dr. Polharris, it seemed, was no longer a threat to anyone's peace of mind. A strangled laugh escaped me. How easily Nicholas's problem had been solved.

Chapter Seventeen

WHATEVER MY SUSPICIONS, it was to Nicholas I hastened with my story, and within the hour we had returned to that self-same spot so that he could see the truth of my words. I waited with some anxiety while he studied the remains.

At last, Nicholas stood up and stepped back from the body. His jacket hung across the low-hanging branch of a squat oak; his rolled shirt sleeves bared strong forearms, the drift of fine black hairs caressing his olive skin. I yearned to slip into his embrace and remain there until my dreadful suspicions had been wrung from me. But his dark face was grim, forbidding intimacy or trespass. I could not detect a glimmer of satisfaction in his eyes or a tiny curve at the corners of his lips, but that should not have surprised me. When had I ever been able to read the thoughts beneath those hooded eyes?

The leaves and twigs that had covered Dr. Polharris had been brushed aside, rendering his bloated features and paunchy, sprawled body visible. He looked less like a man than a caricature, drawn by a satirist with an eye to mocking those who enjoyed dissolute habits. Only the blood that stained the front of his white shirt and seeped through the satin waistcoat was incongruous with the caustic levity of the scene.

"Do you know the man?" I asked innocently, carefully pretending that I knew nothing of the events that had transpired less than twenty-four hours ago.

Nicholas nodded. "His name is Dr. Polharris, but I cannot think how he came to be here. I believe that for the last six years, he has lived in Portugal." He glanced at me quickly but I, too, kept my features immobile.

Nicholas appeared satisfied by my pretense of impersonal concern and, emboldened, I added with a touch of dismay, "And who would have call to murder him?"

"Murder?" he returned sharply. "We have not yet ascertained that the doctor *has* been murdered."

"The man has been shot," I pointed out. "Surely that is, at the least, suggestive of some misdoing."

He laughed mirthlessly. "You disappoint me. I thought Charlotte was the one given to hysteria and fancies."

"I am perfectly calm. And I am certain that your Dr. Polharris will be thrilled to learn that I have only imagined the hole in his chest."

"You are behaving in an asinine fashion," he retorted. "Of course, the man is dead. But it is obvious enough—to those with cooler temperaments and more rational minds—" he added arrogantly "—that this was an accident. We are plagued with poachers in these woods. No doubt the doctor stepped off the driveway to relieve himself and was mistaken for a deer. Murder is seldom committed without a motive, and I am aware of no one in these parts who held a grudge against him."

No one except yourself, I thought. But to Nicholas, I said only, "I wonder what could have brought the man to Blackwood Hall?"

He shrugged. "He was once in my employ. Likely, he wished to inform me of his return from Portugal in the hope that he might again be of service."

His lies were told with such ease. I would have admired his talent for prevarication if he had been using those skills on someone other than myself—or had he applied them to matters less dreadful than murder. I sighed. Even if Nicholas had confessed that he and the doctor had spoken yesterday evening, I would have eagerly supported him when he lay the blame on the carelessness of poachers. It was his determination to conceal the truth from me that gave me reason for concern.

With consternation, I counted the number of hours I had lain awake, waiting for him to return to our suite. Had it been three or four? I recalled, too, his unaccountably calm demeanor in the drawing room this morning. Was it possible he had not been concealing his troubled thoughts or fears of recrimination? Had he already known the doctor could do him no harm?

"What of the poacher?" I said softly, knowing what his answer would be before he had spoken. "Surely, Nicholas, you do not mean to let this go unpunished?"

He frowned. "I daresay I will have little choice. Unless someone comes forward and confesses or gives us the name of the person involved—and I find either possibility most unlikely—then I doubt we will discover who was responsible for this night's work."

"Then unless they are troubled by a conscience," I mused sadly, "they need have no fear of reprisals."

"Does that upset you?" Nicholas asked, the first glimmering of amusement sparkling in his eyes. "I find you a most unlikely moralist. But you are quite right. It is unfortunate, even deplorable. Still, Dr. Polharris should have shown better sense. There is always some risk in wandering near these woods after the sun has gone down. It is something you should bear in mind since you insist on visiting Matilda."

I glanced at him sharply but he turned his face away, leaving me to decide if his warning had veiled a threat or if I had misinterpreted his meaning. At last, I decided on the latter. If Nicholas had wanted to be rid of me, he would not have taken the trouble to dissuade me from exercising Titania at unusual hours. But if my common sense had given me some meager reassurance, I was robbed of any cheer it might have provided by the question that promptly formed in my mind: Had Lydia fared as well at his hands?

"Come," Nicholas commanded, his voice breaking into my thoughts. He firmly removed his gaze from the doctor's prone form and raised his hand for me to take. "I am sorry that you came upon this sight. It must have been an unpleasant shock. Let us return to the house and I will send two men with a wagon to collect his body." His brows drew together again. "I advise you not to mention this to your sister. She is in no danger as she dislikes riding, and I see no reason to upset her."

Was he afraid that she would run away again? Leave him after he had finally managed to win her admiration. I knew my jealousy was childish, but suddenly I felt as resentful and intractable as a ten-year-old who watched from the window seat while her sister received a heavy dose of praise for doing nothing more than smiling prettily. Then it occurred to me that Nicholas might be less interested in continuing in Charlotte's good favor, as he was hopeful of discreetly ridding himself of the doctor. Sullenly, I asked, "What about Stephen? Is he, too, to be protected?"

His eyes flickered with surprise, but he said evenly, "I will tell Stephen myself. I would not like to see another accident."

I was not entirely pleased by his answer. It may have proved that Nicholas saw no need to keep the doctor's death a secret from those who were close to him—a good sign since his innocence remained in question—but it also meant that he genuinely desired to shield Charlotte. It was a terrible misfortune, I reflected, that we had grown too old for pig troughs.

Nicholas brushed the dirt from his hands and rolled down his shirt sleeves. Then, collecting his coat from the crotch of the oak, he slipped it on and fastened the buttons. Once again, he became the immaculately dressed gentleman—poised, reserved, and unquestionably honorable. I watched him, fascinated and yet horrified that he could appear completely normal at such a moment. Had he no conscience whatever?

Satisfied that he was properly attired, Nicholas reached for my elbow to help me back down the path. I flinched. His eyebrows rose, becoming two steep arches above a pair of intensely disturbed green eyes. His gaze probed my face, attempting to read my thoughts as I had so often tried to read his. The faint lines of doubt that creased his brow faded and he stared at me with growing conviction.

"I am sorry, Nicholas. You startled me," I said, hastily averting my eyes. "Finding the doctor's body has upset me more than I realized. My nerves are frayed."

"It is not like you to give in to nerves," he said, and there was an icy edge to his voice that chilled my heart.

He did not try to take my arm again or help me to mount when we reached our horses. As we trotted back up the driveway to the Hall, riding side by side, neither of us spoke a word. Nicholas was consumed by anger—the air between us almost crackled with his animosity—and I did not trust myself to keep my voice steady. The truth seemed all too clear to me. Dr. Polharris had suspected Nicholas of murder; it was his intent to expose him. Now, the doctor was dead, "accidentally" shot on Blackwood grounds. Would he not still be alive if Nicholas had been completely innocent of any wrongdoing?

I glanced across at him, at the high cheekbones, the dark hollows beneath them, the arch of his brows, the gentle curve of his lips. There was not a part of his face that was not familiar to me, that I had not loved and yearned to caress. And yet that face so beloved by me concealed a darkness, a cruelty of spirit, a touch of the insanity that he himself dreaded.

But now that we were beyond the shadow of the trees, now that the doctor's body did not stretch between us, those feelings flooded back to me. Why, I wondered, was I not revolted by the sight of him; why did the thought of his touch set me afire instead of making me shrink in fear? It seemed the heart recognized only desire; reason, sense, what role did they play when it came to love?

As the well-respected lord of Blackwood Hall and the local magistrate besides, Nicholas's opinion of the events leading to the doctor's death was accepted without question or hesitation. Those people who lived in the nearby village and remembered Dr. Polharris—and there were a good many who did—remembered him as a drunkard, a poor physician, and a man who could not be relied upon or trusted. It was clear there would be no one to regret or remark on the circumstances of his passing.

But several weeks went by before I accepted that no one was going to step forward and demand a proper investigation. Even Stephen, the one person other than myself who had reason to believe that his brother had not been entirely unbiased in his conclusions, appeared willing to say nothing that would provoke awkward questions. It may have been fear of his brother's temper that made him refrain from telling what he knew, or simply a willingness to let life and its problems drift over him or sweep him along in their wake, passive and unresisting.

I would have thought the matter entirely forgotten except for Nicholas's odd moods. He grew distant and uncommunicative, as if possessed by thoughts he could not share, and he began taking long rides alone across the estate, returning late or appearing suddenly in places he was not expected. Often, when I spoke to him, he failed to answer or would glance up after a minute or more had passed to give me a vague, distracted answer; then, almost immediately he would fall back into another of his long silences, a contemplative state from which he could not be easily aroused.

In the evenings, I was all but forgotten. He seldom retired until after I had fallen asleep, preferring to linger in the drawing room talking to Charlotte. And while we pretended that nothing had changed between us, he studiously avoided touching me, although this was accomplished in such a manner that no one who did not know him could have guessed it was done with intent.

At first, I was relieved: My mind and emotions warred inside me and I could not bring myself to give into my desires while still believing him guilty of murder. But as the days passed, I forgot the doctor's crumpled body and recalled only the touch of Nicholas's hand upon my cheek, and the intoxicating scent of his shaving soap.

Just as I had grown accustomed to our silent breakfasts, Nicholas looked up from his newspaper and asked, "Do you think, then, that the doctor was murdered?"

It was a strange question, coming from one who had emphatically denied the possibility, and it startled me. "I d-did," I stammered. "But I was not aware that we were troubled by poachers."

He nodded slowly. "True. Yet when I told you, you seemed unconvinced and I wondered—" He broke off and frowned thoughtfully.

"Yes, Nicholas."

"I wondered if you had reason to think someone wished him harm."

"I had never met the man," I reminded him.

His eyes narrowed speculatively. "And yet I seem to recall that you have always had a habit of hearing things that are not meant for your ears."

I blushed. "I do not know what you mean."

"Forgive me, my dear. It was merely a thought." He

disappeared behind his newspaper and nothing more was said.

But there was nothing more that needed to be said. He was aware that I knew his secret, and the knowledge appeared to trouble him as little as the doctor's abortive attempt at blackmail.

Nicholas did not seem to know that Stephen also had a knack for being where he should not be. I would have dearly liked to have seen his brother's face when he learned of Dr. Polharris's demise. Had he drawn the same conclusion as I, or did he credit the possibility that poachers had been at fault? It would have relieved me greatly to learn that his brother did not suspect Nicholas of any wrongdoing.

But Stephen seemed to have withdrawn from our society completely. Save for making brief appearances at meals, and agreeing to make up a fourth at cards whenever the occasion demanded, he retreated to his own rooms and stayed there. He did, when pressed by Charlotte, offer the excuse that his foot was troubling him and he could not concentrate for long periods.

I began to think that we would never get the chance to talk alone. Then, after almost three weeks had gone by, Stephen announced at luncheon that he was feeling "quite recovered."

"I believe I shall even wander around the maze, this afternoon," he added with a meaningful glance at me. Then he turned to Charlotte. "Perhaps you would care to join me. It is quite entertaining. Rumor has it that one of our insane ancestors used to lure young women to its heart and then brutally stab them to death."

Charlotte shuddered and her face paled. "No, thank you," she replied. "It sounds like a horrible place."

"Not at all," I countered, completely confident that nothing would sway her from her decision. "There is a lovely fountain, and I have been quite unable to find a single bloodstain though I have looked for hours."

"I think not. It was my intention to write Aunt Emily

this afternoon. She will be wanting to hear from me," she said virtuously.

Stephen nodded gravely. "I am sure you are right."

When I reached the center of the maze, he was sitting on the edge of the fountain, dangling his hands in the water that poured from the child's pitcher. It spilled over his fingers like liquid diamonds, sparkling and flashing in the sunlight. As I approached, he looked up and managed a sad smile.

"You sister is very predictable," he said. "I cannot think of two people less alike than yourselves."

"And for that I am eternally grateful," I retorted, plopping myself down on the thick carpet of grass and resting my back against the marble bench. Then I regarded him seriously. "We have had little chance to talk alone over these last few weeks. Have you already forgotten your promise to be my friend?"

His face grew solemn. "The habits of a lifetime are difficult to overcome. Do you know that even at the last minute, I nearly decided against coming here? I am convinced that our talking may be an irreparable mistake."

"Whatever do you mean?"

He strolled across the grass, his limp no more pronounced than when we had first met. Standing above me, his eyes nervously scanned the hillside that lay between us and the Hall. "Fears, doubts—both can be ignored, buried beneath the soothing reassurances of a reasonable mind," he murmured distractedly. "But give voice to them and, suddenly, they become real. One is propelled into action when it might otherwise have been avoided."

"Nonsense. The truth is the truth whether spoken aloud or kept to oneself," I retorted sharply, trying to dispel the shroud of gloom he had drawn around us.

He glanced at me with startled amusement. "Dear

Redigan. I wonder if Nicholas appreciates his good fortune in marrying you?"

I squirmed uneasily. Seeing that his question had discomfited me, he did not wait for me to reply but added hastily, "I believe that, were you my wife, you would be the making of me." He sat down on the grass beside me. "So be it. Let us talk. We shall plunge headlong into dangerous waters, and they may take us wheresoever they will."

But having made that announcement, he did not speak again but left it to me to begin. Despite my brave words, I found speaking my thoughts aloud harder than I would have imagined possible. At last, I asked only, "Have poachers been a great problem at Blackwood Hall?"

"Not that I am aware," he replied.

I shivered. "Then my misgivings are not unfounded. You, too, believe that Dr. Polharris was murdered."

Stephen shrugged, his face expressionless. "I would not have cared if he had been. The man was a complete blackguard, and fate dealt with him as he deserved. But his presence here convinces me that Lydia's death was no accident. And that, you have to admit, is an entirely different matter."

To my chagrin, I saw there *were* some things that, once said, could never be retracted. Too late, I realized that I had come here, not to share my suspicions of Nicholas's guilt, but hoping to be persuaded of his innocence. I stared at Stephen in dismay, seeing him now as an enemy to my happiness. Fervently, I wished I had bowed to his greater wisdom and returned to the Hall before a single word of this conversation had passed between us. Yet perhaps the damage could still be undone.

My voice faltering, I said slowly, "The doctor did not actually accuse him of murder. And even if we have not misunderstood his inferences, can we really rely upon his judgment? The man was obviously a drunk-ard."

Stephen released his breath in a long, drawn-out sigh. "And an incompetent doctor. If Nicholas had not wanted someone whose silence could be bought, he would never have admitted him into the Hall. Ever since learning that Dr. Polharris was summoned to attend her death, I have known something was not as it should have been. Now, I am convinced of the worst."

"Then why did you tell no one of your suspicions?" I demanded, feeling my temper rise. "You must have lacked confidence in them."

"I had no proof," he pointed out. "And you must understand, it is a hard thing to accuse your own brother of murder, harder still if you had known Lydia. She was so innocent and beautiful. I cannot imagine anyone harming her."

"What reason had he to kill her?" I demanded.

"Have you not already guessed?" he asked shrewdly.

I would not look at him.

"Their relationship was not . . . as it should have been," he said gently.

So I had been right. "That is no reason for murder," I said weakly.

"Not for a sane person," he agreed. "But perhaps he is a little mad. I have never forgotten the depth of his rage the day I slashed his cheek with my rapier. I believe he frightened himself as well," he mused, half to himself. "It was the last time he gave way to his anger without a masterful struggle for self-control. But, since then, I have never wholly trusted him."

"You have allowed your fear of him to mislead you," I said stubbornly.

He reached out and laid his hand across mine. "I have told myself repeatedly not to let that affect my judgment. I promise you, there is nothing I would like so much as to convince myself I am wrong. But there is only so much that one can excuse or explain away. I am afraid you must face the truth, as I have done."

I snatched my hand away. "Were you there that night?"

"I was not," he admitted. "I had left several days earlier to join the Hussars, and since I had told no one of my intentions, I did not hear of Lydia's death until several months later. I happened across a young lieutenant who had recently returned from Truro where he had become acquainted with my brother."

"Then if you were not here, we can never be certain of what occurred that night."

"Do you think not?" he asked wearily. "I wish I could agree. And of this much I am certain. Lydia did not die in childbirth."

Much as I would have liked to do so, I could not contest this last remark. Lord Edgmont himself had thought as much, claiming to have received letters from Lydia that indicated "the true nature" of their marriage. It seemed that Nicholas had trapped himself in a web of lies and omissions. I stared disconsolately at the grass, unable to reconcile myself to the things I had heard. It was as if my entire marriage was a maze, confusing, misleading me with its twists and turns; and now that I had come upon the secret at its heart, it was only to discover that there was no return.

Stephen seemed to understand. "The past is a strange thing," he said. "It is never truly gone from the present and it shapes our futures. You cannot know how often I dream of escape."

"From the past?"

"From the past, from this cursed Hall, and from the shadow of my ancestors."

So I had not been wrong in thinking that he, too, feared the madness that cursed the Blackwoods. "It may be impossible to escape the past," I said softly, reaching to take his hand. "But at least you are free to leave this place. Why do you stay when you can only torment yourself here?"

He smiled grimly. "For the longest time, I ceased to care. And when I finally had a reason to care, I also had a reason for staying."

"And what is that?"

"You," he said simply. "You are the reason I care. You have given me the strength to defy my brother, a reason to hope that I might put the past behind me and start afresh somewhere far away from here. Come away with me, Redigan." His eyes implored me. "I cannot leave you here unprotected. I have seen the way he looks at Charlotte, and the way she returns his admiration. What if—" He stopped and swallowed. "I could never forgive myself if something happened to you."

I stared at him, unable to answer. He could not mean what he was saying. But from the manner in which he looked at me, I knew he did mean every word. My head ached. "I have to think about this," I told him at last. "I cannot give you my answer now."

"Do not wait too long," he warned gently. Then he raised my hand and kissed the tip of my fingers. "But be assured that, in me, you have a protector. I will never let you down." His voice was hoarse and the *you* was faintly stressed.

If the notion of leaving Nicholas and running away with his brother struck me as fantastic while we sat alone in the maze, then in the Hall—with its stately elegance, myriad noises, maids bustling up and down the corridors or whisking their feather dusters across the polished table tops—the possibility was unthinkable. Here, nothing we had said seemed either likely or possible; it was preposterous, nothing but wild conjecture.

Admittedly, something was wrong. Lydia had not died in childbirth. But that was hardly reason enough to assume that a man as intelligent and honorable as Nicholas had harmed her. Even the doctor's demise, no matter how unlikely, could have been attributed to poachers, whatever Stephen believed. Nicholas had only denied speaking to the man. And what reasonable, decent man would upset his wife by informing her that he was being blackmailed. Especially a man like Nicholas. Both Lydia and Charlotte had been terrified of him for no better reason than his appearance and rumor. Had he any reason to expect more of me?

My heart needed little persuasion. I loved Nicholas; I wanted to believe in his innocence. Before the morning sun had risen above the purple line of trees and hills, I had managed to rid myself of the suspicions that plagued me. But as my turmoil faded there came a rush of loneliness. If Nicholas doubted my trust and loyalty, it was with good reason. When I had shown him the doctor's body, my fear of him had been obvious. Since then, he had avoided me.

I lay in bed, solemnly contemplating my awkward position. Sally, my lady's maid, unobtrusively folded my clean underthings and laid them piece by piece into the dresser drawer. The fragrance of fresh lavender wafted across the room as she slipped tiny sachets between the lacy, beribboned piles that rose beneath her busy fingers.

I took a sip of the hot chocolate she had brought me and toyed absentmindedly with the silver elephant that stood on my breakfast tray. The eyes glinted with a strange green amusement that put me in an exceedingly bad humor. It made me wonder what I had ever admired about the figure. Unwilling to stare another moment into those mocking emerald eyes, I pulled open the drawer of my bedside table and flung the elephant inside. It clanked against two green glass vials that lay on top of my lace handkerchief.

Bemused, I picked them up. Matilda's potions. After coming upon the doctor's body, I had forgotten all about them. "Sally," I asked, lifting them for her to see. "How did these come to be here?"

"They was in the pocket of your riding habit, mum. I set them there for safekeeping."

"Thank you, Sally." I stared at them idly. I was not superstitious; nor did I believe in magic. And, more importantly, I did not know which was which. It would hardly do to dose Nicholas with a potion that would send him away, and I had had enough of Charlotte's sisterly affections to last a lifetime.

I twisted them about in my hands. One of the vials had some scratches in black ink on the cork stopper. I peered more closely and read the letters. "LP." Love potion? What else could it mean? Aunt Matilda must have known her memory was not up to the demands of remembering the various purposes of her concoctions. She had labeled them and then forgotten; her eyesight, too poor for reading without spectacles, had made it impossible for her to see what she had done when she handed them to me. I smiled. What a pity it was that I did not believe in magic, for if I had . . . but, of course, I did not.

Over luncheon, I suggested to Nicholas that we take our supper in our rooms that evening, as we had been wont to do before Charlotte's arrival. "I am sure my sister understands our desire for a little privacy," I added. "And Stephen can be most entertaining when he chooses."

"Yes, of course," she said meekly, not raising her gaze from her plate. Her acquiescence, if out of character, was not at all surprising. Less than an hour ago, she had been warned that should she dare to raise a questioning brow, she would be bound and gagged and left in the maze overnight.

"Your sister is our guest," Nicholas protested mildly. "It would not be polite to desert her."

Charlotte glanced up with a start. "Really, I do not mind in the least." Her hand slipped below the table to rub her bruised shin.

Nicholas seemed perplexed, both by my suggestion and Charlotte's lack of protest. "Well, if you are quite certain," he said doubtfully.

She tucked her legs under her chair and nodded hastily.

I smiled sweetly and silently debated whether there was any value to be gained by pouring a love potion into a cup of tea instead of a glass of . . . say, port, for instance.

Chapter Eighteen

THAT MORNING, Nicholas had received a reply from
Uncle Arthur. It was in response to the letter he had
written them to say that Charlotte was safe and would
be staying at Blackwood Hall for "a few weeks, until her
life had become more settled."

He read the letter aloud to us after the plates and
silverware had been cleared from the table. After a few
lines in which Uncle Arthur wished that his letter found
Nicholas and me both well and satisfied with married
life, he had written a few stern paragraphs that addressed Charlotte's "wayward and incomprehensible
behavior." After gladly agreeing to bow to Nicholas's
judgment regarding her future, he finished by adding
pompously that "women, when left to themselves,
often confuse and complicate matters that were better
left to men."

"Indeed," I agreed. "Men confuse and complicate is-
sues with much greater skill and agility."

Nicholas frowned at me from atop the vellum sheets.
"Your aunt sends her best wishes to you both and says,
'Since your uncle has already addressed Charlotte's
thoughtless actions, I will not comment further. Suffice
it to say that she has deeply disappointed us both,
when all either of us ever wanted was her happiness.' "

Charlotte, unused to receiving rebukes from either
of them, promptly burst into tears. Through her sobs,

she managed to say, "Of course, they are right. I have ruined my life and yours as well. Oh, Nicholas. Can you ever forgive me?"

I glared at her, but Nicholas said mildly, "Surely, you exaggerate. Things are seldom as bad as they seem."

The rest of Aunt Emily's letter gave us news of Briarslea: The roses were in bloom and the blossoms were a deeper rose than ever before; the maid had left to get married and the new girl was "as lazy a piece as was ever their misfortune to hire"; and, now that "his girls" had gone, Henry, our groom, had retired and bought some property in Devon.

Nicholas folded the sheets and placed them back in their envelope. "I would say that your uncle seems content—no, happy—to leave matters for me to handle," he said complacently. "I shall feel free to make decisions in your behalf," he told Charlotte.

"Of course, Nicholas," she agreed, wiping her eyes with her handkerchief. "But there is little that you can do."

"You must have faith in me," he admonished gently. "I am confident that, given a few more weeks, I can bring you every happiness." She raised her eyes questioningly, but he said, "No. It is too soon to announce victory, and I would not like to see you disappointed again. You must refrain from asking questions, at least for a little longer."

"Yes, Nicholas." She sighed with resignation.

As Stephen had excused himself immediately after the meal, I suspected that he had realized the full portent of my desire to dine alone with Nicholas. But he was, I reflected, entitled to more of an answer than he had yet been given. When Nicholas excused himself, I had only to rid myself of Charlotte, and I was free to seek him out. This was more easily accomplished than I could have dared hope. Rising from the table, she announced her intentions to attempt a painting.

"I have a study of Blackwood Hall in mind. As a thank

you to Nicholas," she said. "Monsieur André taught me
a great deal about art while we were together and often
encouraged me to try my hand at a simple watercolor.
He could tell just by looking at me that I had talent. I
wonder now why Aunt Emily did not give me more encouragement. She did have those sketches I did of
Briarslea."

"I believe she felt music was a more worthwhile pursuit," I said, not mentioning that her efforts had gone
to line the cupboard drawers after being dutifully displayed for a painful week. But it would not do to dis-
courage Charlotte when she had promised to entertain
herself for a few hours.

I found Stephen sitting on the marble bench in the
maze, where I had known he would be. He was not in
a temper, but his face had grown sadder and his disappointment was palpable.

He rose when he saw me and walked forward to
greet me. The hollows of his face were etched by shadows, and his limp had grown more pronounced, as
though he no longer cared to make the effort to appear
graceful. Reaching my side, he held his hands out to
me and I took them hesitantly.

"I was not sure you would come," he said. "Am I correct in assuming you have made up your mind?"

"I have," I admitted.

"And?"

"I cannot leave Nicholas."

He nodded but his hands trembled. "Not even in the
face of the crime he has committed?" he asked.

I shook my head. "I cannot believe my heart could
be so completely deceived—that I could love a man
who was capable of such despicable and cowardly behavior."

He laughed softly. "My foolish darling. The heart is
nothing if not determinedly insensible to the faults of
those whom we love. I beg you to reconsider. It would

be impossible for me to leave Blackwood Hall while you remained. Not while I know the things I know."

I shook my head again, and my chin set stubbornly. "You must go, Stephen. You will never be happy if you stay. Do not fear on my account. I am convinced that Nicholas will not harm me."

Stephen's smile was unbearably sad, but he accepted my answer without rancor. "If I thought there was a point to my insisting, I would insist. But I can see that your mind is made up." He rested his hand on my shoulder. "I am truly sorry."

The straw-mesh backing of the Jacobean chair felt uncomfortably hard. I squirmed restlessly. Across from me, apparently not bothered by the same discomfort that plagued me, Nicholas silently chewed a mouthful of pigeon pie. As yet, the meal had not been the success I had hoped it would be. Save for remarking on the mildness of the weather or mouthing a few distant civilities, Nicholas had remained stiffly and determinedly formal. Despite his unresponsiveness, I forced myself to keep up a lively chatter, pretending to be unaware of the sparseness of his replies or the grim expression on his face.

I almost regretted insisting on this interminable torture, but eating in our suite gave me the opportunity to serve Nicholas myself. I could hardly have asked the butler to pour the potion into his lordship's glass along with the usual quantity of port. For a moment I imagined the butler's face, eyes bulging and lips quivering as he struggled to maintain his correct, emotionless expression after receiving such an unthinkable request from his mistress. I smothered my giggle with a spluttered cough.

"Are you all right?" Nicholas asked, looking faintly puzzled.

I lowered my eyes meekly. "Yes, Nicholas."

"I hope you are not catching a cold."

"It was nothing. A piece of pastry got caught in my throat."

"You must not eat so quickly. Food is to be savored, not inhaled. Life holds few enough pleasures."

I did not answer his pointed remark but resumed eating, slowly chewing each mouthful though each bite tasted the same as the one before—dry, bland, and unpalatable. I cannot recall when food had held less interest for me. When the last platter had been uncovered and suitably attended to, Nicholas lifted the silver bell beside him and rang for the maid to remove the plates.

I sprang up. My silverware scattered across the pristine linen tablecloth, leaving a trail of gravy spots behind them.

Nicholas frowned. "What is the matter with you tonight, Redigan?"

"I thought you might like me to pour you a glass of port."

"That is hardly a reason to behave like a hoyden," he remonstrated wearily. "Please be more careful."

"Yes, Nicholas."

With my back to him, I took the decanter of port from the side table and set the long-stemmed crystal glass before me. My heart pounded against my rib cage as I discreetly pulled the glass vial from my pocket. I eased out the cork and raised the vial to the glass.

My hand hovered there and I was struck by a sudden doubt. Was this what I wanted? If Nicholas drank the potion, I would never know if he had come to love me for myself or because of some ridiculous brew concocted by his great-aunt. Each time he looked in my eyes, whenever his hand brushed mine, every smile he bestowed on me, all would be received with uncertainty and a faint wistfulness.

Since early childhood, I had felt neglected and unappreciated. Was I willing to live out my life, never knowing if I was truly loved? The answer could not have been more obvious. I lowered my hand, replaced the cork, and then returned the vial to my pocket.

"Are you certain you are all right?" Nicholas asked, a note of genuine concern in his voice.

I nodded.

"Is anything bothering you?"

"No, Nicholas." I poured the port from the decanter and handed him the glass.

He took it, regarding me thoughtfully for a few seconds, before he drank. Inside my pocket, the glass vial lay heavily against my thigh.

Nicholas did not ask to come to my room that evening and, although I had intended as much, in the end I did not suggest that he did. As I lay in bed, thinking of him, I realized it would take more than a few moments of privacy to regain his trust, to reestablish the friendship we had once shared. True magic was like true love, I decided: more effective when developed over a longer period of time. If only I could be certain that Nicholas would give me those badly needed hours in which I might reinstall myself into his good graces.

It was still night when I awoke. The curtains were drawn and an owl hooted outside my window. Dawn lay some hours away, having not yet begun to paint its hazy golden lines around the edges of the draperies. Even as a child, I had been unafraid of the dark; I had lost my fear before leaving India since, having lost my parents, it seemed to me that the darkness could hold nothing more dreadful or tragic than what I had already endured and survived. But now, for some inexplicable reason, I felt deathly frightened.

I squinted into the room. At the foot of my bed, as on either side of me, I seemed to be surrounded by huddled figures, swathed in black, flowing robes that concealed their bodies. They poised there, immobile but menacing.

You are becoming as silly as Charlotte, I told myself caustically.

The insult, despite its magnitude, did not sting me into forced bravado. But as my eyes became accustomed to the blackness around me, the crouching, twisted figures that surrounded me meekly resumed their normal shapes, dissolving into tables, chairs, dressers, and the like, each standing in its usual place as quietly as though it had never wished to do otherwise.

What, then, had disturbed me? Not the owl. And I was as used to the rise and fall of the wind and the steady throb of the waves as I was my own heartbeat. I took a deep breath. The smells in the room were pleasant and familiar—a mixture of fresh lavender and rose water with a lingering hint of charred wood and smoke that drifted from the fireplace.

Then, from the sitting room, came the creak of a floorboard, followed immediately by that of another. It was not the comfortable groans often made by old houses as they settle more solidly onto their foundations, determined to entrench themselves still deeper. It was a stealthy, malevolent creeping only a few feet from my door.

"Nicholas?" I called, wondering—no—hoping that he had merely decided to claim the privileges due him as my husband. "Nicholas, is that you?"

The creaking stopped but no one spoke. If it was Nicholas, and he meant me no harm, he would certainly have answered, as would any person who had either reason or right to be there. I lay in bed, gripping the coverlets as a kind of shield.

A minute passed, then another. Everything was quiet. I allowed myself to draw a breath. Gradually, my heartbeat slowed. Just when I decided the sounds had been imagined, the floorboards squeaked out a loud complaint.

"Nicholas?" I demanded angrily, my temper no doubt provoked by my rising fear.

Again, there was no answer, save the definite sound

of footsteps crossing the sitting room. I heard the soft thump of a door closing and the footsteps, and the person who had made them, were gone.

I did not fall asleep again that night.

The next morning I had risen and dressed long before Sally brought my cup of hot chocolate. When she came, wearing a fresh apron, the frills of her mobcap crisply starched, she found the curtains drawn and the fire already crackling in the hearth. In answer to her wide eyes and dubious expression, I assured her she had not overslept, explaining that I had merely been restless and had preferred not to lie in bed chasing an elusive sleep.

"Do 'ee think, perhaps—" Her smile was hopeful. Then she shook her head. "Well, doubtless it be too soon t' say. But I'll bring up a cup of hot milk t'night. That should help 'ee get yer rest."

"Thank you, Sally." I did not try to correct her. To insist she was mistaken would only give rise to gossip in the servants' hall, and I did not like to think of them shaking their heads and clucking over our marital problems. Mrs. Ham already appeared to have formed too accurate an impression of the true nature of my relationship with Nicholas.

He, who always managed to rise and dress before my eyelids had flickered open, did not stir until after the clock chimed eight-thirty. Then he clattered into the morning parlor where Charlotte and I were taking our breakfast, looking decidedly irritable, his eyes puffy from lack of sleep.

"Did you not sleep well?" I asked politely, trying to keep any hint of accusation from my voice.

"I did not," he returned. "It would seem that I have rather more on my mind than usual."

"Monsieur André?" Charlotte asked, assuming that since her problems consumed her full attention, they must necessarily demand the full attention of everyone around her.

"Monsieur André," Nicholas agreed shortly, but his brief glance in my direction told me otherwise. Still, he appeared happy to let Charlotte provide an easy explanation for his sleeplessness.

"I am sorry to be the cause of so much trouble," she said, her eyes shining cheerfully.

"Do not distress yourself. Seeing you happily settled is of utmost importance to me," he assured her. "I am expecting to receive his reply, imminently. He has had ample opportunity to answer my letter."

"Perhaps, he will not," I said doubtfully. After all, he had already proven himself dishonorable. It was reasonable to suppose that he had already said more than he should, and no inducement would be able to repair the damage that had already been done.

But Nicholas's confidence was absolute. "On the contrary," he countered. "It is in his best interest to reply. I will be nothing, if not astounded, to learn that Monsieur's self-interest has failed him."

"You do not approve of him," Charlotte reproached him. Her lower lip protruded delicately.

"Not at all, my dear. I would think him a fool if he did not respond."

His answer mollified her but, in her place, I believe I would have been further insulted. Surely, it was better to admire a fool who was possessed of some moral character, than a shrewd man who thought only of himself. Still, when I reflected on what I knew of Monsieur André, I decided that Nicholas was no doubt correct in his assumption.

As we ate our breakfast, I studied him surreptitiously, trying to discern whether his eyes darkened with concern or a lack of sleep. It could only have been him in our sitting room, but why had he been prowling outside my room, with all the lights out?

When he caught me studying him, Nicholas did not avert his eyes, but returned look for look until I lowered my eyes. Whatever tension stretched between us

was broken by the appearance of Stephen. He strode
into the breakfast room, smartly attired, his limp indis-
cernible; there was a set to his jaw that I had not hitherto seen. Since we had come to Blackwood Hall,
Stephen had never made an appearance at the breakfast table. He often read well into the early hours of the
morning and slept late, rarely showing his face downstairs before luncheon was served.

"To what do we owe this unexpected pleasure," his
brother asked with obvious irony and a measured
glance at me, as if he thought that I was the cause of
his unwonted behavior.

Stephen either failed to notice Nicholas's suspicious
attitude or did not care. He heaped his plate with thick
slices of ham, several poached eggs, and added two
freshly baked rolls to the mountain of food. That, too,
was unlike him. He was a picky eater, and rarely bothered to help himself to more than a few forkfuls of food
from each dish.

We all watched him, our faces showing varying de-
grees of surprise. At last, he took his seat and looked
around the table at those of us seated there. "I have
come to a decision," he announced. "I am going to
leave Blackwood Hall."

"Leave?" Nicholas looked surprised, but not at all
displeased. "This is a rather sudden decision."

"Not at all," he countered evenly. "It has been on my
mind for quite some time."

Nicholas's look of disbelief made it obvious that he
did not think his brother capable of coming to either
a wise or considered decision. "No doubt you will want
my assistance," he said dryly. "I suppose I can make
some arrangements."

"I would not refuse your help," Stephen admitted.
"Perhaps a small allowance until I come upon some
means of supporting myself. A letter of introduction
might also be helpful. And the use of a coach?"

Nicholas smiled ruefully. "I see you have indeed considered this thoroughly. Is there nothing else I can do for you?"

"Nothing," Stephen replied calmly, then turned his attention to his meal.

Charlotte and I had kept quiet during this exchange. Now she demanded curiously, "Where will you go?"

Stephen chewed thoughtfully, then swallowed and said, "To London, perhaps. Elizabeth will certainly welcome me to Coudrey House for the little season, and it will give me a few months to become acquainted with those opportunities which might interest me."

His plans appeared sketchy to say the least, but I silently wished him well. I did not care to arouse Nicholas's irritation by showing a greater concern and interest in his brother's future than was seemly, and the conversation gradually turned to talk of London in general. This, aided by Charlotte, gradually degenerated into speculation as to whether or not she was sorely missed by the beau monde, and if Monsieur André had realized the impossibility of finding himself another model so peculiarly suited to his talents.

Here, Nicholas's chair scraped against the parquet flooring and he rose, politely excusing himself and wishing us all a pleasant morning. Soon after, Charlotte decided that she must finish her watercolor, upon which, she claimed, she had made an excellent start the day before.

"I will try to finish it before you leave," she advised Stephen. "With your refined tastes, you, even more than your brother, will appreciate what I have accomplished."

"I daresay," he agreed pleasantly.

"It is one of Nicholas's few failings," she said sadly. "He appears to have no feeling at all for artistic endeavors. The few times I have spoken to him of Monsieur André's paintings, he expressed no interest whatsoever and could not even comment intelligently on the

delicacy of his shading and interpretation—though I
believe he is familiar with his work."

I smothered my derision until she had gone from the
room. Then, sounding more like a barnyard animal
than a young lady, I firmly delivered my opinion.

Stephen grinned. "It is an interesting ability your sister possesses. She succeeds in viewing the world entirely through her own eyes, without being troubled by
an understanding of the thoughts and opinions of those
around her. I wish I could remain so solidly inured
from reality. At times, it would be a distinct comfort."

"Charlotte was never bright, and since her stay in
London she has become completely self-centered." I
shrugged uninterestedly. Talk of my sister often bored
me, likely because she found herself so interesting a
topic. It did not make sense to dwell on her when one
was free to discuss other matters. I regarded Stephen
seriously. "So you have made up your mind."

He nodded. "I have decided I must leave. I cannot
remain here, looking upon Nicholas's face each day,
knowing the things I know. And you?" he asked. "You
have not reconsidered?"

"I have not."

"We would not have to go to London. Rome is beautiful."

"I hope some day that Nicholas will take me there,"
I said gently.

He sighed heavily. "I should have known you would
not. It seems that you, too, are not wholly incapable
of closing your mind to the truth. Still, I had hoped.
Never mind. It is a fine day. Let us enjoy it since it will
probably be our last together."

"Our last?"

He nodded. "It is my intention to leave as soon as
I have packed. Tomorrow if possible."

"Charlotte will be devastated," I said dryly. "Her
painting is barely begun."

I did not try to change his mind, although I was sorry

to see him go. Without Stephen in the Hall there would be no one to call upon if . . . if I was wrong about Nicholas. Certainly, Charlotte would be of no use in an emergency. If only it had been she who was leaving instead of Stephen. Then Nicholas might be willing to spend his free hours with me.

It was thinking of Charlotte that reminded me of the second potion that lay in my drawer—the potion Aunt Matilda had given me to make her "go away." I could hardly object to the success of that concoction; it would merely allow Nicholas and me the privacy we needed to repair our marriage. And if he had not truly contacted Monsieur André as he professed, a second defection might convince him that she was too foolish to deserve his attentions.

"Shall we take a last turn in the garden?" Stephen asked, interrupting my thoughts. "Then I believe I will ride out to the cemetery and bid Lydia good-bye. I go there every week and put flowers on her grave," he explained. "Nicholas has never bothered—perhaps it stirs what is left of his conscience. But the sight of her neglected grave has always disturbed me."

Our walk through the gardens was a quiet one. We wandered slowly past tangled shrubs, beds of damask roses, pink and blue rhododendrons, and the honeysuckle-draped gazebo. July had come and the breeze from the water was warm and gentle, buffeting us with its caress and twitching my skirts merrily about me.

Stephen seemed caught up in his own thoughts—of London or Lydia, perhaps of Nicholas—I could not have said which. There was something sadly final in his eyes as he gazed around him, as if he were making his final farewells and did not expect to see Blackwood Hall again. I remarked on this, saying he must surely be back for a holiday if not for a longer stay, but he simply shrugged as though, either way, it did not much matter.

In all, I was not sorry when he decided to turn back

along the gravel paths towards the stables. He did not invite me to ride along with him to the cemetery, and I was content to leave him to make his pilgrimage alone, fearful that the sight of her final resting place would stir him into insisting more forcefully that I accompany him. Perhaps, too, I worried that when confronted by a headstone inscribed with her name, I might give in to the fears which lay at the borders of my consciousness, merely waiting for me to lower my guard before they assaulted me again.

It was an awkward parting, neither of us wanting to let the other leave, and yet both of us unable to retain the companionable feeling that had once existed between us.

I met Charlotte as I strolled across the back lawns, makeshift easel propped in front of her and one of Monsieur André's spattered smocks protecting her dress from the inevitable daubs of watercolor that flew wildly off the end of her brush. She had chosen to paint Blackwood Hall with the rugged line of cliffs at her back. It was a dreary picture—mostly grays and blues—but it failed to capture the brooding, melancholy air that always epitomized the Hall. Instead, she had tried to enliven her efforts by adding rose briars in full and opulent bloom. The effect was to bastardize the Hall into a kind of Briarslea with towers.

"I think Monsieur would be pleased with the results of his tutelage," Charlotte said, brushing a damp curl from her forehead and smearing her hair with blue paint.

"Yes," I agreed after a moment's thought. "I believe he would." If my first remark did not bewilder her, my next suggestion did.

"Do you mean you want me to join you?" she asked suspiciously.

Given the numerous occasions I had driven her away or fled her company in search of solitude, I supposed it was a fair question. "I thought you might like a cup of tea," I said innocently. "Surely, you have done enough for one day."

"Well, I *am* exhausted. I have always tired more easily than you."

"And sometimes it is better to reflect on what you have done before continuing," I pointed out.

She nodded. "That was what Monsieur André said, although I always supposed that it was his way of prolonging our sittings. Do you think I could have been mistaken?"

I shrugged. Privately, I expected she was right, since no amount of reflection could have improved the artist's efforts, but it did not serve my purposes to start an argument over his true merits or lack thereof.

"Perhaps we could have tea in my sitting room," I suggested. "Return your painting to your room and wash your face and I shall have Mrs. Ham bring up a tray."

"With fuggan cake?"

"If you like," I agreed.

She gave me an impulsive hug. For a brief moment I felt ashamed of myself for what I was about to do. Then I saw the blue smudges she had left on my favorite dress of white lawn and the brief rush of sisterly feeling promptly evaporated.

The tea tray arrived before Charlotte, as I had known it would. She rarely accomplished anything quickly, especially something as important as making herself presentable. Though how she managed to drag out her toilette, when she always looked delectable, I could not imagine. I supposed there was a certain satisfaction to be gained from staring at her reflection in the looking glass. Had I been similarly blessed, I might have happily indulged in the same pastime, but my looking glass had never given me the requisite encouragement.

Her tardiness gave me ample opportunity to produce the second vial Aunt Matilda had given me. It glistened seductively in my hand, and I carefully checked the cork to make certain I had not confused the two potions. It would be wiser, I decided, to dose Charlotte's cup and pour her tea before she appeared. That way there was no danger of being observed.

I sat down at the table and pulled the cork from the vial. The odor smelled inoffensively of mint, but not enough so that it would be detected when mixed with tea. With a vague uneasiness, I remembered my sister's tendency towards a delicate stomach; as a child I had always accused her of mollycoddling herself, but it was true she did not have my robust constitution. And Charlotte sick was infinitely more tiresome than Charlotte healthy.

While I deliberated on what I was about to do, hand poised above her cup, there was a loud commotion from below. Someone was banging furiously upon the door. I hastily stuffed the cork back into the vial, slipped it into my pocket, then rushed out of my suite and down the corridor to the head of the stairs.

By then, the banging had stopped. The footman had flung open the door and was restraining a fair-haired gentleman who appeared intent on hurling himself through the doorway. There was a fierce struggle, in which the young man was no match for Williams, our burly footman—a middle-aged man who had spent his youth in the tin mines. At last, the young man stepped back, gasping for breath, and though his face was cast in shadow, his identity was quite apparent when he spoke.

"I know that Mademoiselle Charlotte is here," he cried in a thick French accent. "Stand aside, monsieur, or I will be forced to cause you an injury."

Chapter Nineteen

I MARVELLED at the manner in which Williams maintained his dignity instead of giving way to outright laughter at the ridiculous threat. Luckily, the demands placed on his self-control by the artist's ridiculous posturing came to an abrupt end when Nicholas strode into the foyer.

Williams promptly fell back into his usual place and stood stiffly at attention. "The gen'lemun won't give 'is name or wait like he belongs t' do, milord," he said apologetically.

"What do you mean by this, sir?" Nicholas demanded. "Breaking into my home as though you were no better than a common thief."

Confronted by the master of the house, Monsieur André hastened to take several steps backwards and for a second he gasped impotently for words. He was saved from complete humiliation by Charlotte who must also have heard the tumult and rushed from her room.

"Monsieur André!" she cried, pausing on the landing only long enough to recognize the familiar face which now lifted to greet her. She flung herself past me and down the stairs.

Her flight was halted in mid-descent by Nicholas. "Charlotte, go back to your room," he commanded, his face black with anger. "And do not come down again until I have sent for you."

Even I would not have dared to disobey him when he was in this mood. Poor Charlotte, who could not have challenged Uncle Arthur in one of his more genial moods, spun about as though she had been struck and fled up the stairs faster than she had descended. Tears flooding from beneath her long lashes, she fled back down the corridor, her long skirts bunched in her fists to prevent her from tripping over them in her haste. Nor, during her flight, did she as much as glance back once over her shoulder. It was as though she feared that Nicholas would not have countenanced even the briefest hesitation from her.

But having dispatched her to her rooms, he had calmly returned his attention to the trembling man in his doorway. "Now, sir," he said, his words as smooth and icy cold as water drawn from a deep well. "I believe I am owed an explanation for your unruly conduct."

"I have come for Mademoiselle Charlotte," Monsieur André announced, trying hard to keep his hands and voice steady. "You have not the right to keep us apart."

I had to admire him for not turning tail and fleeing as Charlotte had done, but I would not have given ha'penny for his chances.

Nicholas regarded the painter much as he had regarded his work, briefly and contemptuously. "Since I am acting as her guardian in her uncle's behalf," he said, "it appears I have every right."

Monsieur André struggled to find an answer that would sway him from his implacable stance. For a second, he floundered, then, struck by inspiration, his face brightened. "You have no . . . *spiritual* right," he insisted. "We are the lovers. Our destinies are forever and . . . inextricably . . . entwined." With a majestic wave of his hands, he finished, "God alone can decide to keep us apart."

"Then it appears he has decided to do precisely that," Nicholas said dryly. "What a pity you did not bother to entwine yourself legally. I would then have had no choice but to deliver her into your hands. Since, however, you profess to be above the conventions of our bourgeois society, you must not be overly dismayed when those conventions fail to support you. You cannot have the girl—and the law, sir, is on my side. Not on the side of pretentious, would-be artists who devote themselves to making their fortune by flattering the vanity of foolish women."

I gripped the railing, waiting to hear the painter's answer. It occurred to me that he must love Charlotte, or he would not have travelled this far to face the displeasure of her relations. But surely Nicholas would not think of allowing Charlotte to marry someone of his ilk. Spinsterhood would be preferable.

Monsieur André's face whitened, but he stood his ground. Perhaps it was not bravery but an inability to move his limbs which appeared frozen with horror. "Monster," he said at last, his accent fading as it had done that first day in the garret. "You want Charlotte for yourself. Your only wish is to make her your mistress. Well, upon my word, you shall not have your way with her."

"Do not accuse me of your own base intentions," Nicholas thundered. "Unlike you, I will make an honest woman of her."

His words carried up the stairs to me as clearly as though Nicholas had turned around and addressed them to me himself. The blood pounded at my temples, and my legs wobbled beneath me; only my grip on the railing kept me from plummeting headlong down the stairs. How could I have been so stupid? Stephen was right; even Monsieur André could see the truth. He was in love with Charlotte and wanted to make her his wife. I was nothing more than an impediment to his desires—a mistake he clearly regretted. Now, I knew the reason he had hovered in the darkness outside my door. He meant to be rid of me, as he had rid himself of Lydia.

I did not remain to watch the painter's retreat—as no doubt would eventually be made when he grasped the futility of defying Lord Blackwood. I silently returned to my own rooms and closed the door behind me. Since there were no locks, I might just as well not have bothered: It gave a false sense of security at best. There was no protection to be had at Blackwood Hall. Not for Lydia; not for me.

It was some while before my senses rallied and I was able to consider my position calmly and rationally. My life was in danger as long as I remained under this roof. No doubt when Nicholas had stood outside my door last night, it was with the full intention of murdering me. What had stopped him? By awakening, had I robbed him of the opportunity of surprising me? Or had he, even then, been uncertain of what he wanted to do? Apparently, he had since come to a decision.

I breathed a prayer of thanks that Monsieur André had arrived before Stephen had managed to pack his belongings and set forth for London. I daresay I could thank him for my life. Now I had only to inform Stephen of my decision to leave with him, and we could be safely on our way before Nicholas realized that his plot had been discovered and thwarted.

But I could not leave Charlotte here by herself. Even if he loved her and wanted to marry her, it was unthinkable that she should be left in the hands of a murderer. To my dismay, I realized that including her in our escape presented us with a greater problem. She could not be relied upon not to betray us to Nicholas. At last I decided she must remain unaware of our intentions until the moment of our departure. Then we needed only to get her from her bedroom to the coach in silence. Even that, I reflected, would be no small accomplishment.

Having decided upon the necessary course of action, I gave myself a cursory glance in my looking glass. My face was paler than usual, but not obviously so. Save for that, I could see no sign either of strain or of the horrible disillusionment I had suffered. There was nothing about my appearance or expression to arouse Nicholas's suspicions. Satisfied, I forced a smile to my lips, then went in search of Stephen.

The foyer was deserted except for Mrs. Ham and the scrub woman who polished the marble parquet flooring. "Mrs. Ham," I asked, "where is his lordship?"

"In his study, milady," she said politely, keeping one eye on the scrub woman to see that she did not use this diversion to relax.

"And Mr. Stephen? Has he returned?"

She looked at me guardedly. "No, milady."

"Oh, dear," I exclaimed in dismay.

Had Nicholas been present, my disappointment would have most certainly alerted him as to my intentions. It was clear from Mrs. Ham's frosty air that she was convinced I was deceiving her master with his own brother. Under less serious circumstances I would have laughed outright. Instead, trying not to seem overly concerned, I asked, "Do you have any idea when he will be back?"

"No, milady."

"When he returns, please inform him that I would like to speak with him. I wish him to take a letter with him when he goes. It is most important that you do not forget."

"Certainly, milady," she said, looking completely unconvinced by my explanation.

"And please have another pot of tea sent up to my room," I said haughtily in an attempt to remind her that I was not one more maid under her command, but her mistress.

She agreed with a stiff, "Yes, milady." After giving the scrub woman a look that set her to scrubbing the marble squares twice as vigorously as before, she stalked off to the kitchens.

With Mrs. Ham gone, the scrub woman dared a glance upwards at me. "If he's visitin' *'er,* he won't be back 'til midnight gone," she whispered confidentially. "He allus stopt at t' inn them times."

I thanked her and she cheerfully returned to her work, no doubt convinced that she had assisted two crossed lovers. I had no choice but to return to my room and wait. I comforted myself with the conviction that Nicholas was unlikely to attempt to harm me while his brother remained at the Hall. Likely, he would wait until Stephen had left and there was no one of substantial character to be a witness against him—just as he had done with Lydia.

As the scrub woman had warned me, Stephen did not return that evening. Dinner came and went without his making an appearance. It was a quiet meal. A subdued Charlotte picked at the food on her plate, hardly daring to raise her eyes to Nicholas who presided over our moody gathering as calmly as though Monsieur André had never set foot in Blackwood Hall. I managed to make a few desultory remarks, barely enough to keep Nicholas from remarking on my unwonted silence.

Idly, I wondered what had happened to the young man, but I would not have dared to question Nicholas when he was in this mood. If I had, likely my impertinence would have been met with a sharp reprimand.

I glanced at Charlotte, her golden head still bent studiously over her plate, knowing full well that her thoughts wandered in the same direction as my own. Had Nicholas packed Monsieur André off on the first coach and warned him never to return? Perhaps he had threatened to expose him to those members of society who appreciated his talents. No doubt his intimidation was sufficient to dissuade the young man from returning, for there was a smug curve to his lips that convinced me the matter had been brought to a satisfactory conclusion—at least so far as he was concerned.

After finishing a meal that could have filled two men, and then downing a glass of port, Nicholas leaned back in his chair. His face lost its severity, and he inquired politely as to how we had spent our day. Charlotte's cheeks regained some of their usual pinkness and she scraped together a few lighthearted responses that brought a smile to his lips. Then, emboldened by his good temper, she asked, "And what has become of Monsieur André?"

If I had ever doubted her love for the man, that one daring question convinced me I had misjudged her, for it displayed an interest that far outweighed her timidity. Holding my breath, I looked at Nicholas to see what he would do.

He swirled the port around in his glass for several thoughtful seconds. Then, at last, he said, *"Monsieur André?* He has already set off for London. I suspect it is the last we will hear of him." Again, there was that curving, cryptic smile. That, combined with the finality in his tone, made the hairs on the back of my neck rise. I thought of Dr. Polharris and shuddered.

Without Stephen to make up a fourth we could not play quadrille that evening. It was just as well. I could not have kept my mind on the cards and, judging from Charlotte's expression, her game would have been still worse. After playing a few melancholy ballads on the pianoforte she complained of a headache and excused herself. I stayed up, slowly turning the pages of a book without once knowing what I was reading as I listened for the sound of Stephen's horse. Several times, Nicholas glanced at the clock and suggested that we, too, should retire, but I fobbed him off with varying excuses. At last, as the clock struck ten, he exclaimed impatiently, "Surely you can finish that book another evening."

His irritation startled me. "If you are tired, there is no need to wait up with me," I assured him.

He ignored this remark and demanded, "What are you reading that arouses such interest. It must be a thundering good novel."

Since I could not have told him without first looking at the cover of the book, I said, "It is not the book. I doubt that I shall see Stephen before he leaves in the morning, and I would like to say good-bye."

"Forgive me. I had assumed that you did that this morning in the garden." His eyes narrowed. "I daresay it was Charlotte."

"No," I admitted, knowing as well as he did that he was not likely to mistake her for me. "You were not wrong. But afterwards it occurred to me to send a letter to Elizabeth with him."

Even to my ears, the lie sounded feeble. Not for a second did Nicholas appear to be taken in. "Doubtless," he murmured, "it can be sent by post. It will get there almost as quickly and probably more reliably than if it is entrusted to my brother. Or"—he regarded me slyly—"if you prefer, you can give it to me, and I will see that he gets it. Undoubtedly, he will delay his departure until I have given him the letter of credit and the other of introduction that were promised to him."

"Do not trouble yourself," I said, feigning complete indifference although it fooled him not at all. "As you say, the post will do admirably." I closed my book and set it on the side table.

"Good night, my dear. I shall have Mrs. Ham send you up a cup of hot milk. I have a few matters to attend to and then I, too, shall retire."

Defeated and dismissed, I rose and left the room, wondering all the while if he had guessed my plans. If so, he had, for the moment, successfully forestalled me from carrying them out. But I did not intend to give up so easily.

I did not undress, but lay in bed fully clothed, the covers drawn up to my chin. It was uncomfortably warm but I intended to remain there only until Nicholas had fallen asleep. Then I would resume my vigil for Stephen.

I waited a long time. More than an hour passed and, lulled by the heat of the room and the added warmth of my clothing, I fell asleep. When I awoke I had no idea of the hour, or how long I had slept. But I was convinced that by now, Nicholas must have been safely abed.

A clatter in the sitting room followed by his muffled oath told me otherwise. There was no crack of light beneath the connecting door which undoubtedly accounted for the noise. But why was he stumbling around in the dark when a lamp stood near at hand, unless he hoped not to wake me? The thought was not one that reassured me.

I opened my mouth to call out as I had done the night before, then changed my mind, choosing to wait and see what he would do. My ears caught the sound of footsteps as they stealthily crossed the room. Directly outside the door, they halted. There, he remained. I could hear him breathing—inhaling and exhaling as rapidly as I.

My own breathing resumed its normal pattern well before his own. Then the doorknob rattled as a hand was laid upon it. Softly, I rose and pulled open the drawer of my bedside table and felt for the dagger which lay there. My fingers curled around the handle, and it struck me as ironic that I should be sitting here, preparing to defend myself with the single item I owned that reminded me most of my feelings for Nicholas.

I had barely pulled it from its sheath before the hinges creaked and the door swung open. A tall figure

stood in the open doorway, silhouetted by the moon-
light which fell through the undraped windows of the
sitting room. Instantly, I saw the shoulders were not
broad enough, and the body too slender to be Nicholas.

"Stephen!" I cried out with relief. I had forgotten how
much alike they sounded. Dropping the dagger, I lit the
small lamp by my bedside, and then thankfully turned
to him. My gaze fell on the pistol clutched in his shaking
hand and I gasped.

"There is no need for alarm," he said, his face dismayed. He stepped inside and closed the door. Then,
leaning his back against the wall for support, he took
a deep breath to calm himself. Beads of perspiration
shimmered across his forehead. "God help me," he
said at last in a ragged voice.

"What have you done?" I asked, fearing that he had
shot someone.

"Nothing . . . yet," he said, his voice still unsteady.
"But much can happen between now and sunrise."

"Surely you are not planning to shoot Nicholas," I
said in a frantic whisper, suddenly convinced he had
come here to do exactly that.

Stephen shook his head, his eyes as miserable as
those of a rabbit I had once seen caught in a snare. "It
is too late to kill Nicholas. I should have killed him as
a boy. I tried you know. Unfortunately, even with his
cheek slashed he was the better swordsman. What a
lot of trouble I would have saved myself and my poor
Lydia if I had done the job properly."

"Your Lydia?"

"I loved her, you know," he said softly, forgetting his
fear as his mind drifted to thoughts of her. "As Nicholas
could never have loved her. Would that he had. She
might still be alive." He caught the look of pity in my
eyes and said crossly, "Do not think for an instant that
I was merely a foolish young man, dreaming in vain

of my brother's wife. She returned my love in every way, I assure you."

I struggled to understand what he was saying. "Do you mean you were lovers?" I asked.

He nodded. "Does that shock you? We met at the dower house daily. Aunt Matilda made us very welcome. She adores secrets as you may have already learned. It gave her great pleasure to abet our romance."

No wonder the poor woman had been confused, thinking me to be in love with Stephen instead of Nicholas. Then another thought struck me, so hard that my legs wobbled beneath my own weight. "Lydia *could* have been with child," I cried.

Stephen's shoulders sagged. "I know for a fact that she was. She told me herself. Have you not guessed? That was the reason I left Blackwood Hall. Lydia wanted us to leave together. She told me to arrange for a coach and meet her at the dower house." An agonized groan escaped his lips. "I promised to meet her there, and then I ran away. What choice did I have? Nicholas would have followed us as soon as he learned we had gone, and I was no match for him. Nor had I the courage to stay and face him, knowing our secret was soon to be revealed."

It was not his pain and guilt that impressed me; or the realization that this was the reason that Matilda had expected someone to join us at lunch on our last visit. Instead, Stephen had provided me with an answer to a question which had troubled me for weeks. "Nicholas told the truth," I said, feeling a surge of happiness swell through me. "Lydia did die in childbirth."

He laughed bitterly. "Hardly, my dear. She had only just come to realize her condition. The baby was not due for another seven months." As my hopes crashed around me, he ran his long fingers through his hair. "I can only assume that, confronted with my desertion, she confessed to Nicholas what we had done. I daresay he gave into one of his rages and killed her, though he may since have regretted his actions. Still, he must be punished. Surely you understand," he said, as calmly as though he had just explained to me the need for a new suit.

I gasped. "You intend to shoot Nicholas?"

"That would not serve at all." His eyes glittered. "I wish him to suffer as I have suffered. Lydia was everything to me. With her gone, life is meaningless. That is what I want Nicholas to understand: What it is like to lose the woman you value above your own existence."

I gaped at him. "You cannot mean to harm Charlotte? I will not allow it."

"Charlotte?" His face was a study in bewilderment. "What reason have I to harm her? She means nothing to him." Then a glint of understanding broke through his confusion. "Do you think my brother is foolish enough to give his heart to that silly child?" he asked. "How little you understand your own husband. Likely he blessed the day she ran off with that painter fellow. No, my dear. It is you he loves."

He said this with such absolute conviction there was no question in my mind that he was telling the truth. My legs trembled; standing upright became an absolute impossibility. I sank onto the bed, overcome by the thoughts that assailed me. Nicholas loved me. He had killed Lydia, but he loved me. And whatever joy I might have experienced by learning I was the true object of his affections was tempered by the knowledge that having won his love, it would do me no good whatsoever. For it was I whom Stephen meant to shoot. Struck by the absurdity of the situation, I was possessed by a hysterical fit of giggling.

Like a true gentleman, Stephen waited until I had regained my self-control. Then he regarded me with a measure of pity. "Do you mean to tell me that you did not know?"

"Charlotte is very beautiful," I said falteringly.

"True," he agreed. "But a pretty face cannot compensate for an empty mind. Unless, perhaps, one's admirers are equally empty-headed. From what your sister has told me of Monsieur André I suspect the two of them would have been admirably suited."

"Nicholas told him he would make an honest woman of Charlotte," I murmured.

Stephen shrugged. "And no doubt he will. But not by marrying her himself, I assure you." Then his jaw clenched as if he had come to a decision, and a shudder ran through him. Hand shaking once again, he raised his pistol. "Now, let us have done with this," he said hoarsely. "Before I lose the small amount of courage I have washed down at the inn."

"As you lost your courage last night?" I asked gently.

He nodded, a look of shame in his eyes. "But tonight," he whispered, "I will not fail her."

"Have you also forgotten your promise to be my friend?" I demanded, calmly returning his gaze and praying to myself that his nerve would indeed fail him.

The pistol trembled violently. "Do not reproach me, I beg of you. After all, I am not entirely at fault. I asked—no, begged you to come away with me. Had you agreed, this would have been unnecessary. But, with or without your cooperation, I intend to rob him of your company." He pushed himself away from the wall and walked unsteadily towards me. "Please understand. I have never wished to harm you. You cannot know how hard this is for me."

"No harder than it is for me, I assure you," I retorted, feeling more like myself.

"Have pity on me."

"Have pity on *you?* Are you mad?"

He managed a sad laugh. "Perhaps a little. Not the madness of the Blackwoods, but a madness borne of guilt. I deserted my beloved Lydia when she needed me. I am as much to blame for her death as Nicholas."

"You will not escape your guilt by murdering me."

"You are right. But now I ask only for revenge. It is all that is left to me," he said helplessly.

His weakness gave me courage. My back stiffened and, in a quiet, unruffled manner, I said, "You may shoot me, but you will not escape. Someone is certain to hear the shot."

"The servants' quarters are too far for the sound to be heard above the noise of the wind and the waves. And doubtless Charlotte will merely bury her head beneath her pillow."

"Nicholas is not too far away, nor will he be frightened," I pointed out. "And likely he will regard a murdered wife as a more severe offense than a slashed cheek. Are you prepared to face him?"

"If he came, I would not care if he killed me. But I took the precaution of sending him a note from an anonymous person who wished to meet him this evening—a person who professed to have knowledge concerning the death of Dr. Polharris. It would not have done to have my plans upset before I carried them to fruition. I am afraid, my dear, that Nicholas is not here to help you."

"You are mistaken," said a strong voice from the doorway. "I am very much here."

Startled, we both turned to find the door ajar and Nicholas filling the doorway in a way that Stephen had not nor ever could have done. "Nicholas," I cried happily, knowing the moment I saw him that I could forgive him anything so long as he loved me.

He started forward, but Stephen raised his pistol and took aim at me. "Stand back, or I will shoot her," he cried.

"It would be a grave error," Nicholas said solemnly. "One that I know you would regret making."

"As you have regretted killing Lydia?" Stephen said harshly.

Nicholas shook his head. "I did not kill Lydia. You have my word."

"Why should I believe you?" his brother demanded.

"Do you think I was totally ignorant of your affair? Surely whatever you think of me, you do not take me for a fool? Had I been angered by your relationship, I would not have allowed it to continue for over a year."

The pistol in Stephen's hand lowered, then he jerked it upward again. "Why would you allow your wife to give to your brother what she denied to you?"

Nicholas grimaced. "It was clear from the onset our marriage was a tragic mistake. Does it surprise you that it pleased me to know that at least one of us had found some happiness?"

Stephen stared at him as though he did not believe anyone capable of such magnanimous behavior, but I had only to listen to his voice and see the gentle look in my husband's eyes to know he was telling the truth. My eyes brimmed with tears.

Stephen's arm dropped and the pistol hung limply at his side. "If you did not kill Lydia then who did?" he asked softly.

Nicholas addressed his brother as gently as he would have addressed a small child. "She killed herself," he said. "I returned to find her dying from the effects of some poison she had swallowed. I have no idea how it came to be in her possession. Until now, I was convinced you had bought it for her before you ran away. For six years I have despised you for that act of cowardice. I am glad to learn that I have misjudged you, although Redigan may never forgive me for what she has endured this night."

I had no chance to tell him it was already forgiven. Stephen's arm swung upward again and he leveled the pistol at me. "Now I know you for a liar," he cried, his anger renewed. "Lydia would never have killed herself. Do you think I never suggested it to her? It was the one way that we could have been free of you forever. But she was adamantly against suicide, and nothing I said made any difference. She told me she would rather forsake me and stay married to you her entire life than raise a hand to take her own life."

His statement stunned us both; neither of us doubted its veracity, for the light of righteous anger blazed from Stephen's face. Nicholas's brows drew together in a dark line. "I swear to you," he said, his voice puzzled. "I found a glass vial on her table near a half-empty cup of tea. It had to have been taken by her own hand for there was no attempt at concealment."

"Dear God," I exclaimed. Hand trembling, I pulled out the drawer of my bedside table and removed the two green vials which lay there. "Was the vial similar to these?" I asked.

Nicholas stared at them in horror. "Where did you get them?" he demanded.

"From Matilda," I said weakly. "She said they were magic potions—to be taken with tea."

"Potions for what?" Stephen demanded.

I blushed. "One was to make Charlotte go away."

"And the other?" Nicholas asked, his gaze holding mine.

"To make you love me." The tears which still brimmed in my eyes coursed down my cheeks.

His eyes rested upon me, never once flickering. "I think the answer we seek lies at the dower house," he said, his voice infinitely tender.

We could not descend upon the dower house at that unholy hour, but sleep was out of the question. Instead, I changed into my riding habit and joined Nicholas and Stephen in the parlor where a fire was blazing and a pot of hot tea waited on the deal table. Nicholas had already poured himself a cup and sat in the wing chair, sipping at the steaming brew and staring thoughtfully into the fire. Stephen had ignored the tea in favor of the decanter of port. As I entered, he was in the process of pouring himself another glass and, having already bolstered his spirits at the inn before returning to the Hall, he was well on the way to drunkenness.

Nicholas rose as I entered. Taking my hand, he led me to the settee. He left me there and returned with a cup of tea which I accepted gratefully. Then, fetching his own, he took a seat beside me.

"How did you come to be at the Hall?" I asked. "Did you realize the note was a trick?"

He smiled. "You are not the best of liars, my darling. When you refused to retire at your usual hour, making instead a feeble excuse about a letter for Elizabeth that you wished to send with Stephen, I grew suspicious. Having lost one wife to my brother's charming manners and handsome face, it occurred to me that you might be making plans to run away with Stephen. I gave the valet my greatcoat and told him to set off on my horse for the meeting place. Then I concealed myself in the sitting room and waited to see what would happen."

"It was my intention to go with him," I admitted. "After learning . . . believing that you planned to marry Charlotte."

"Marry Charlotte?" he said, astounded. "And how was I to manage that while I was wed to you?" When I could not meet his eyes, he murmured, "Good Lord."

Stephen raised his head and in a thick voice asked, "Then you meant to leave with me?"

"Not after seeing the pistol you were carrying," I retorted.

Nicholas shook his head. "What a pack of fools we have been."

Chapter Twenty

THE MIST had not lifted from the roof of the dower house when our horses turned up the gracefully curving driveway. The lawns and flower beds glittered with dew, sparkling beneath the first golden rays of sunlight that slanted across the elms and collected in the green hollow. Shadows still fell across the tiled roof and darkened the gray stone walls, and the draperies were still drawn across the windows. But while the house appeared to slumber, Edith must have already risen, for she was not long in answering our knock.

She was still in her wrapper, her hair pinned up in rags beneath her mobcap. In her hand she carried an oil lamp which cast a yellow halo of light through the gloomy hall. Her first cross words, spoken as she pulled open the door, died when she caught sight of Nicholas, his tall, commanding presence exacting a civility that I had not supposed she possessed. Bobbing a quick curtsy, she politely invited us to come in.

"Her ladyship's abed," she said apologetically. "Her don't like t' rise afore the 'ouse is warm."

"There is no need to wake her," Nicholas assured her. "I daresay you can provide us with the answers we need."

Edith glanced anxiously at our serious faces. " 'Er 'ealth be good. I does me job."

"I am sure you do. But that is not what we came to discuss. Is there somewhere we can talk in comfort?"

"There be a fire in drawing room," she said, the lines on her forehead deepening as she lifted her lamp to lead us through the unlit house.

Without Aunt Matilda to give the sitting room life, it appeared drab and cluttered. Yesterday's dead flowers had yet to be removed from their vases, and the fire had not had time to throw off the smell of must and age. Edith hastily drew back the curtains, but since the windows faced west, the light that filtered through the panes merely gave definite lines to the vague lumps of furniture and watered down the darkness to variegated shades of gray.

Stephen leaned against the mantel, as much for support as to be near the warmth of the flames. We took our seat on Matilda's plush sofa, and Nicholas directed Edith to sit across from us. She obeyed nervously and reluctantly, her eyes shifting from his face to mine and then to Stephen's, as though finding herself suddenly brought before the Inquisition and wondering where best to plead her innocence.

"Do you recall the first Lady Blackwood's last visit to the dower house?" Nicholas asked when her gaze had returned to him. "Usually she was accompanied by my brother, but I believe that day she came alone."

Edith nodded slowly. "Not a day I'd ferget. 'Twas a waste of good food, an' that's sartin sure. Cooked enough fer three, an' him, Mr. Stephen didn' come, an' her ladyship, Lady Blackwood, didn' touch 'er plate. Proper wasteful. That's what it was. An' Lady Blackwood makin' an awful fuss."

"Perhaps you also remember whether or not my aunt gave her a potion?"

"Couldn've stopped 'er. Went straight out t' 'er garden and comed back with 'andfuls of roots and leaves. Made a proper mess of me kitchen," she grumbled.

"An' Lady Blackwood wouldn' go on about 'er business 'til she'd done."

There seemed no doubt that the vial had come from Matilda. Stephen muffled a groan, and Nicholas tensed beside me. But whatever he was feeling, he did not betray his emotions. He paused but a second before asking with strained patience, "What was the reason for the potion?"

" 'Ow would I be knowin' that?" Edith asked, balking suddenly. Her hands trembled on her lap.

Nicholas's face darkened. "I pay you to look after my aunt," he said severely. "I would be most disappointed to learn that my trust had been misplaced."

Given Edith's habit of listening at keyholes, I felt certain there was little she did not know. I studied her face intently. Faced with the choice of displeasing Nicholas or admitting to a knowledge of matters which did not concern her, Edith struggled valiantly to decide which response would cause her the least grief. At last, after glancing again at Nicholas's stern expression, she capitulated. "I reckon 'twas t' make babby go away," she mumbled into her chest.

Nicholas nodded as though he had already guessed. "I rather think we had better have a look at Aunt Matilda's herb garden," he said.

The herb garden lay off the kitchen, surrounded by stone walls that separated it from the neatly tended vegetable plot. Edith had picked up a key that hung on a hook in the pantry. Now she used it to open the small wooden door which was always kept locked.

"She don't like anyone coming 'ere," she said as we entered. "She'll be vexed as fire if she 'ears 'ee been pokin' around."

Nicholas ignored the housekeeper as if she had not spoken. He strode into the garden, leaving Stephen and I to follow as we would. Edith scurried back to her kitchen as soon as she realized her presence was no longer required.

The garden was, as Matilda had said, overrun with plants. I supposed that years ago they had been planted in neat rows, but now they grew wherever they wished. It was impossible to find a bare patch of ground where one could safely place one's foot.

Nicholas knelt and ripped up a cluster of small plants from the soil. He examined them briefly, his jaw clenching as his gaze lifted to his brother's face. Stephen held out his hand for the plants, and his face paled as he saw what he had been given.

I looked to Nicholas questioningly.

"Nightshade," he said flatly. "The garden is overrun with nightshade."

I gasped in dismay. "Aunt Matilda could not possibly have known. Her eyesight is failing and her mind wanders."

"No," Nicholas agreed. "She could not have known. Nor must she ever know what damage her potions have done."

"What will you do about the garden?" I asked. "It cannot be left like this."

He shook his head. "When we return to the Hall I will send the gardener down to take care of everything. I will tell Matilda that she can no longer do the heavy work herself. I expect she will agree." He smiled sadly at me. "I can only be grateful that you placed so little faith in magic that you did not use the potions she gave you."

I swallowed, recalling how near I had come to giving the potions to first Nicholas, and then Charlotte. As it dawned on me that I had almost murdered them, my head spun and my legs wobbled beneath me. A pool of blackness came rushing up to greet me as I fell.

When I recovered, I found myself on the sofa in the sitting room. A cool cloth lay across my forehead, and

Nicholas was bending over me, his eyes glowing with tenderness and concern. "Are you all right?" he asked as my eyelids fluttered open.

I stared up at him, able to think of nothing save how handsome and strong he was, and how dearly grateful I was that both of us had survived to see this moment. "I have been a fool," I whispered at last. "I nearly killed you."

"And I have allowed my pride and vanity to mislead you into thinking I cared nothing for you," he said hoarsely. "Had I the courage I credited myself as having, I would have told you that I loved you on the day I married you, instead of waiting until I was certain my love would be returned."

He bent over me and gave me a soft kiss. Only our surroundings prevented us from exploring our feelings further. Edith must have been hovering in the corner, and Stephen could not have been far away.

"Where is Stephen?" I asked, looking around and realizing that he was not there.

Nicholas frowned. "I did not hear him leave. He must have already gone back to the Hall." He took my hand. "Come. If you can ride I think we must follow immediately."

We wasted little time in returning. After assuring himself that I could manage alone, Nicholas spurred on his horse. He reached the Hall several minutes before me and was already returning from his brother's room as I ran into the foyer.

Nicholas caught me up in his arms. "It is too late," he said, pressing his cheek against mine. "Stephen has swallowed one of the potions. He was already dead when I arrived."

"Dear Lord," I cried. Then I clung to Nicholas with all the strength I possessed.

Before he died, Stephen had scrawled a hasty note. It answered the last of my questions, for in it he admitted to having shot Dr. Polharris "rather than have his affair with Lydia come to light and see her honor besmirched. It was little enough to do for her," he wrote, "after betraying her faith in me." Sadly, he finished, "I find it ironic that I shall never know if this is my first act of bravery or my last act of cowardice. I shall leave it to you to pass judgment."

"To think that I suspected you of shooting the doctor," I said to Nicholas when I learned the truth. "I have never been more ashamed."

He took me into his arms, and his hand gently stroked the back of my neck. "It no longer matters," he said. "And, in truth, the fault was as much mine as yours. It did not occur to me that Stephen had shot the man. I was not aware he had overheard our conversation. Poachers seemed the only reasonable answer."

At the time, he had not been willing to tell me of his meeting with the doctor for fear of rousing the same doubts in me that Lord Edgmont's accusations had stirred in Charlotte. "The thought of estranging you was unbearable," he confessed. But the omission had not been to deceive me, but to protect our chance for happiness together, just as he had not deceived Lord Edgmont for any reason other than to protect his memories of his beloved daughter.

"It was not until I guessed that you had overheard my argument with the doctor that I saw how my deceit had worsened matters. You cannot know how it pained me to see you shrink from me that day beneath the trees. Afterwards, I did not dare to touch you lest you draw away from me again."

That night, I did not draw away when he touched me. Instead my body molded into his as though we were two sculptures, each perfectly fitted to receive the other. Catching up fistfuls of my hair, he drew my face to his, and his lips brushed lightly across my eyelids. I felt his breath on my cheeks like a soft summer breeze, gently teasing me with its warmth and promise.

Then, as his fingers entwined themselves ever tighter into my curls, his lips slid from the bridge of my nose to the tip, leaving a trail of gentle kisses in their wake.

Impertinently, I lifted my own lips to accept one of those gentle kisses. I waited several seconds but received nothing for my patience. Disappointed, I opened my eyes. Nicholas was smiling down at me, his eyes crinkling at the corners. I pouted in mock annoyance. With a pleased laugh, he bent down and covered my mouth with his.

There was a hesitance in his kiss, and a poignancy that made me ache with love and compassion for him. I gave myself up to him completely. Feeling my response, his kiss grew firmer, more demanding, as he too was swept away by the rush of passion that enveloped us. Around us, the air of our small drawing room had grown unaccountably warm until I realized the fire that raged with heat came from within and not without.

Then Nicholas lifted me in his arms and carried me to the canopied bed. "You must forgive me my impatience in not leaving you to disrobe," he murmured as he lowered me onto the lavender-scented sheets. "But this moment has been delayed beyond reason, and the last vestiges of my self-control have deserted me. Besides," he teased, "I have often found myself watching you, wishing to slide your dress off those perfect white shoulders so that I might discover what treasures hide below, and I find I am unable to deny myself the privilege any longer."

"Denying you would be to deny myself that which I most desire," I said huskily.

Expertly, he dealt with the fastenings of my dress, sweeping aside my attire as easily as he had swept aside the curtains that now cloaked our bed with shadowed privacy. As I lay there beneath his gaze, any doubts I felt as to the strength of my desirability vanished beneath his approving eyes.

Encouraged, I teased, "Methinks you are over-dressed for the occasion, milord."

He laughed. "Give me but a moment, milady, and that error shall be corrected."

Even in the dim half light his body glowed, and I reached for him as a child reaches for a long-wished-for prize, with an animal greediness that was tinged with awe and anticipation. His muscles were hard ridges beneath my fingers, and I pressed my face into the soft mat of hair that darkened his chest.

Nicholas groaned and his hands swept over me in long even strokes, touches of fire and ice that burned my flesh and yet made me shiver with delight. As I gasped with pleasure, his fingers slid between my legs, stroking and fondling until I grew damp with pleasure. Then he lowered himself onto me and, parting my legs with his own as he cradled me in his embrace, he entered me. There was a brief flash of pain and then there was only the pleasure of feeling Nicholas inside me, taking me, making me completely and utterly his.

Afterwards, he eased his weight off of me with a sigh of satisfaction.

"You have no regrets, then, that you married me and not Charlotte?" I asked timidly, at last admitting to my fears that I could never truly measure up to my sister in any man's eyes.

Nicholas looked at me, his expression one of mock severity. "Regrets? I have a few," he admitted playfully. "But that is not among them." He stroked my cheek with the back of his hand. "I regret that I allowed pride to rule me when good sense would have stood me in better stead," he admitted after a long pause. "I knew when you walked into the drawing room at Briarslea, the day of my second visit, that you possessed the character I desired in a wife. And a passion I dreamed of awakening. But honor forbade me from going to your uncle and admitting my mistake. I was well aware of their hopes for Charlotte, and of how my announcement would disappoint them. Instead, I told myself she was your sister, and likely possessed many of the same virtues. Only time and maturity was needed to bring them to the fore."

"You would have gone to your grave waiting for Charlotte to show even a modicum of good sense," I scoffed.

He laughed sheepishly. "Perhaps you are too critical of her. But, indeed, time only brought home to me my desire for you. You cannot know how it pleased me to learn you returned my affections the night we kissed— pleased *and* terrified me. I feared to remain too long alone in your company lest I lose the self-control I had cultivated and give way to my feelings. Even when I asked you to come to Blackwood Hall as Charlotte's companion I mistrusted my motives, although I told myself the arrangement was for your benefit and hers. When you supposed that I had wanted you to speak to your uncle about freeing me from my promise, I fear that my outrage was due to the guilty notion that you saw me better than I saw myself."

He laughed shortly. "You cannot know how rude a shock it was to learn that my struggles with my conscience had been for naught, that the woman for whom I had sacrificed true love had spurned me for another man, one who had neither title nor fortune to recommend him. It was a set-down I dearly deserved, and ever shall I bless your sister for freeing me to marry you."

"Then it was not pride that made you refuse to pursue them?"

He shook his head. "Had *you* run away with Stephen I would have stopped at nothing to retrieve you. Merely to see you in his company or to think of you at the dower house where he and Lydia had met drove me mad with jealousy."

"There would have been no need of jealousy if you had only told me the truth," I chided.

"That my first wife was an adulteress, impregnated by my own brother? That I believed he had given her poison with which she killed herself? That he had then fled rather than come to me and tell me of their love? I could not bring myself to tell you of their folly. Nor could I have respected myself had I tried."

I supposed I should have expected no less from him. He would not have been Nicholas if he had behaved otherwise.

Stephen's death was listed as accidental, and he was buried quietly the following week. Nicholas arranged for him to have the plot next to Lady Lydia Blackwood, and I cannot imagine his wanting any other resting place.

Several weeks later, we received an unexpected visitor. It was a contrite and much subdued young man who put me in mind of Monsieur André, both of them being fair-haired and slender and endowed with eyes of the same shade of pale gray. But this young man introduced himself not as a French *artiste,* but as the Honorable Andrew Sterling, the eldest son of a baronet and a Parisian lady who had left France shortly before the Revolution. Until recently, the Honorable Mr. Sterling and his father had been estranged due to the young man's intense desire to paint—an occupation that his father considered a complete waste of time, since he failed to see any merit whatsoever in his son's efforts, an opinion he did not fail to express loudly and repeatedly whenever the occasion presented itself.

The breach between them was resolved when the young man took it in his head to forget his artistic ambitions and go into the family business, that of buying and selling other men's masterpieces. It was hardly the noble profession he desired, but it allowed for a respectable income which, since the Honorable Andrew Sterling was of a mind to take a wife, had suddenly become of utmost importance. There was, it seemed, only one young lady whose companionship he desired. Since this young lady was of a mind to accept him, and neither her guardian nor her married sister were of a mind to object, the couple were shortly married and, forthwith, departed for London.

I was not sorry to watch them go. Neither Nicholas—who was wholly unastonished by this turn of events—nor I took much pleasure in their company, nor were we able to show them the appreciation they so obviously felt they deserved. But if we had disappointed them, they did not hold our lack of sensibility against us, for every Christmas, we received regular paintings from Charlotte—fanciful landscapes that were no worse than any that Monsieur André, in his heyday, could have created.

Penelope Thomas, who is the author of one previous book, also writes poetry. She lives in California.